YOK

Also by Tim Davys

YOK

TIM DAVYS

HARPER

An Imprint of HarperCollins*Publishers*
www.harpercollins.com

YOK. Copyright © 2012 by Tim Davys. All rights reserved. Printed in the United States of America. No part of this book may be used or reproduced in any manner whatsoever without written permission except in the case of brief quotations embodied in critical articles and reviews. For information, address HarperCollins Publishers, 10 East 53rd Street, New York, NY 10022.

HarperCollins books may be purchased for educational, business, or sales promotional use. For information, please write: Special Markets Department, HarperCollins Publishers, 10 East 53rd Street, New York, NY 10022.

FIRST EDITION

Translated by Paul Norlen

Library of Congress Cataloging-in-Publication Data has been applied for.

ISBN: 978-0-06-179747-7

12 13 14 15 16   OV/RRD   10 9 8 7 6 5 4 3 2 1

SORS

THE TASK

There was once a fox who was stricken by love. The fox's name was Antonio Ortega, and this love was of a rare variety, the kind you only experience once in your life. Her name was Beatrice Cockatoo, and the moment the fox saw her he knew it was her or no one.

Ortega was not a stuffed animal with much sense. Up to this point he had lived his life without direction, but the day he saw Cockatoo everything changed. From one moment to the next he was filled by a purpose that gave his life meaning.

Fox Antonio Ortega was one of the most beautiful stuffed animals that had ever been delivered to Mollisan Town. His intensely dark red fur glistened as if strewn with gold dust. His stuffing was so compact and hard that not the slightest unevenness could be found, his seams so discreet not even the rain could reveal them. His nose was made of onyx and his eyes were opals; his ears stood at strict attention and his tail, with a tip as white as sugar, was so majestic it caused other stuffed animals to turn around on the street and sigh with envy.

The day he went to ask for Beatrice Cockatoo's claw he

put on the finest clothes he had: a stylish, narrow-cut black suit in the latest pattern, a white shirt, and a dark red tie that reinforced the color of his own fur. Ortega the fox was as poor as everyone else in the neighborhood, but he had plenty of clothes. On his way toward saffron yellow Puerta de Alcalá he took the detour past Cle Torija, where he bought three long-stemmed, golden yellow roses at the Sors Rose Studio. A little farther down the same street he stopped at Sax's Fabrics and Notions and bought an exclusive polishing cloth for eyes, beak, and nose. The cloth had small embroidered roses on the edge, and he had it wrapped in a red silk ribbon that also cost a pretty penny. But, Fox Antonio Ortega reasoned, this was the first and last time he was going courting.

Beatrice Cockatoo lived on the top floor of La Cueva, a restaurant believed by many to be the foremost in all of Mollisan Town and run by her father, the frightful Dragon Aguado Molina. In his role as restaurateur and host at La Cueva, Dragon made an effort to appear jovial and a little silly. At the restaurant his physical appearance was more grandiose than unpleasant. He was not green, like many others of his sort, but dark and alarmingly violet. His sharp teeth glistened in his mouth, which was padded with a fiery red silk fabric, and from the farthest tip of his long tail, across his back and all the way up to the neck, he had triangular black patches of cloth standing straight up. His arms were short while the claws on his back feet were thick as bottlenecks.

Molina laughed loudly as he piloted the guests to their tables, he applauded his own jokes—though he knew how ridiculous that looked with his short arms—and he let his long tail sweep along the floor while pretending not to be aware of it. The guests loved it.

But Dragon Aguado Molina was only a fat, kindly, amusing restaurateur five evenings a week (La Cueva was closed Sundays and Mondays). When he had his henchmen smash the furnishings of a storekeeper who didn't pay his "insurance premiums," Aguado Molina no longer appeared silly. No

jovial laughter was heard as he mercilessly burned up squeal-
ers and forced the cubs of police officers to betray their parents. When he counted his protection money, he served up no
applause or good-hearted smiles.

For stuffed animals living in other parts of Mollisan Town,
Yok, the southeast part of the city, was one big source of in-
fection, an evil that could only be tolerated by being ignored.
For those of us who lived there, its four districts were distinct.

Mindie was Yok's northwest corner. Bordering Amberville
and Lanceheim, it was the entertainment district of that part
of the city. Stuffed animals went there at night and stayed
out until the wee hours. For the poor creatures who lived in
the midst of this melting pot of drug trade, prostitution, and
gambling, there was only one possible strategy: hose down the
sidewalks in the morning and go on with their laborious lives
without worrying about what happened outside their doors.

The area south of Mindie that bordered the forests south of
the city was called Pertiny. The cityscape in Pertiny differed
from the rest of Yok and was dominated by large, flat, and
similar industrial buildings, surrounded by expansive parking
lots and tall chimneys that day in and day out spewed forth
foul-smelling, gray-black smoke; anywhere you were in the
district there was a pungent, acid stench.

Corbod made up the southeast tip of Mollisan Town and
Yok. Corbod differed from the other districts in that trash col-
lection functioned, the bulbs in the streetlights were changed
when they burned out and the potholes in the asphalt were re-
paired instead of traffic being rerouted up onto the sidewalks.
The stuffed animals in Corbod got up in the morning, went to
work—some worked in other parts of the city—and returned
home again in the evening by way of food stores and day-care
pickups. They lived a life that made society function, and they
longed for nothing different and better.

Dragon Aguado Molina resided in the fourth district, called Sors, wedged in south of mint green East Avenue and east of deep blue Avinguda de Pedrables. In Sors were the official buildings and agencies that Mollisan Town had relocated to Yok for the sake of fairness and job opportunities, including the city's largest library; a large university campus; and a number of well-maintained stone buildings where the ministries of Environment, Finance, and Culture had been forced to house various less significant committees and departments. The area where Molina had ruled for more than thirty years was a bit south of the official buildings, and consisted of almost forty blocks where saffron yellow Puerta de Alcalá comprised the northern border and indigo blue Calle Gran Via its eastern boundary. Though Aguado Molina had controlled the neighborhood for so long, he took nothing for granted; internal power struggles, gang warfare, and maintaining official corruption were an ongoing process. For the past few months he had been provoked by an octopus who made repeated, irritating incursions from the north. Molina underestimated no one but did note that many of the octopus's sort had come and gone over the years.

The day when Fox was on his way with flowers and the polishing cloth to La Cueva had begun unhappily for the gangster boss. His breakfast was always served in the private dining room facing the courtyard, and this morning, before he had read the sports pages or wiped the egg yolk from the corner of his mouth, Luciano Hyena showed up with depressing news. In a pinstripe suit, Hyena stood at the threshold to the dark room like a little cub, voice shaking, and looked at the floor as he told what had happened. The morning liquor transport to Tourquai had been ambushed in one of Yok's thousands of narrow alleys, and now moonshine was running down the sidewalk instead of down the rich throats who paid generously for a beautiful label and a stylish bottle, regardless of the content.

Dragon threw down his napkin and hurried into the restaurant. He screamed his orders at Luciano: Everyone who had been in that truck should immediately appear at La Cueva and be held accountable. Just as the hyena was leaving to execute the order, Molina's personal bodyguard, Vasko Manatee, came running from the Little Bar, where he was having his morning coffee.

"Witnesses!" the dragon roared at Vasko. "There must be someone who saw what happened!"

The dragon placed himself at the headwaiter's station and dialed the number to the local police, while Vasko made his way to the streets in search of someone who would be forced to tell Aguado Molina what they had seen. The dragon listened to the phone ringing as he calculated in his head what he had lost on the transport, and how much he would be forced to raise prices to compensate for the reduction in income. But those details weren't the most essential. Most important was to set an example. No one was allowed to think you could challenge Dragon Aguado Molina and go unpunished.

It took a couple of hours, but then the unfortunates that Luciano Hyena and Vasko Manatee managed to get hold of appeared. Molina was sitting in one of the half-moon-shaped booths on a red velvet couch. On the round table in front of him was a small cup of espresso, which he sipped meditatively while Manatee brought up one stuffed animal after another who had to stand in the middle of the empty restaurant floor and tell what happened. Molina asked a question or two, but he wouldn't have needed to.

The stuffed animals who worked for the dragon and were responsible for the transport, like those who lived in the neighborhood and had seen, or thought they'd seen, what happened with the truck, stammered out their confessions. Shadows rested over the large dragon on the couch. He yawned at regular intervals, and at the sight of the sharp fangs in the massive red jaws, all the witnesses got talkative. It did not take long for him to understand what had happened.

Somehow Octopus Callemaro—these days it was almost always that confounded octopus!—and his crew had found out the route of the transport, constructed a barrier of scrap in the path of the vehicle, and overpowered the driver and guards when the truck was forced to stop. The load had been smashed, which was quicker than trying to carry away the thousands of bottles on the truck, and it was all over in a few minutes. Presumably Callemaro knew which wholesalers the liquor was headed for, and presumably today these wholesalers had to buy liquor from Callemaro instead.

Dragon Aguado Molina was listening with half an ear to the stuffed animals' confessions. In the middle of the day a restaurant can feel like one of civilization's most deserted places. The overly bright lighting above the bar, the chairs turned upside down on the tables, and the smell of cigarette butts and alcohol from last evening: a space created for life and enjoyment becomes frightening when exposed to daylight and emptied of stuffed animals. The coffee in his cup cooled before he could finish it. On the shelf above the bar on the other side of the room was his favorite wine, but he resisted the temptation.

When there were only a couple of stuffed animals left to question, Molina decided—one of each. That was always a sensible principle. He would punish one of his own, because someone must have told about the route, and one of the stuffed animals who lived in the neighborhood, because they hadn't told about the scrap barrier the octopus's crew had built ahead of time.

He could not bear listening to the final confessions. Instead he waved Vasko Manatee over to him, and randomly selected a vole and a nightingale that he thought were suitable to torture. Vasko dragged the wretches to the cellar below La Cueva, where they had to wait in the room next to the freezers, and where there was plenty of equipment to torment a stuffed animal with, artfully and at length.

Then Vasko sent the others home. The dragon sighed heavily,

yielded to temptation, and asked for a glass of the excellent red wine.

As Vasko poured, Molina muttered to himself, "We have to do something about that suckerfish."

Before Vasko could answer, the unexpected happened: Dragon and Manatee watched as a lone figure stepped unannounced into the restaurant through the doorway from the Little Bar. It was a fox. His fur shimmered like red spangles, his steps were light and determined at the same time.

"Dragon Aguado Molina?" the fox asked.

The dragon stared at the stranger. Vasko did the same.

"I have come to ask for your daughter's claw."

One might wonder about Fox Antonio Ortega's arrogance. How could he, how did he dare? But for one thing you must remember that Ortega was no intellectual giant, and it is unclear whether he truly understood the extent of his actions. Besides, Ortega was used to getting what he wanted, without having to ask. There were doors that beauty always opened, and the fox was used to being adored.

Would it be better, perhaps, to try to explain Antonio Ortega's hubris by telling it from a different perspective? I think immediately of Wolle Hare, and the evening Fox saw his beloved Beatrice for the first time.

Hare was a legend in the advertising industry, and had seen models come and go over the years. But he was the first to admit that Fox's pictures were sensational.

Hare leaned back, twirled around toward the window so that he was sitting with his back to the desk, holding up one of the photo sheets.

"Completely out-of-this-world amazing," he commented.

Cat Nikolaus sat on the other side of the desk in Hare's elegant corner office with adjoining conference room. The cat had on trendy short jeans, black patent-leather shoes, and a washed-out T-shirt, none of which was by chance. Now his mission was to agree with the boss in an intelligent way.

"Can't be said better," he said. "It's a brilliant piece of work. The composition. The tail that follows up the lines of the chair. And there's a forlornness in his eyes that's—"

"He's so damn good-looking"—Hare's voice was heard from the other side of the tall chair back.

"Yes . . . good-looking. But . . . it's not just that," Nikolaus agreed without losing integrity. "There's something in his eyes that makes stuffed animals—"

Wolle Hare twirled around and fixed his eyes on the cat, who only a week ago had been named vice president, executive creative concept director. Hare waved the pictures.

"Don't be so damn pretentious, Cat, or I'll take a few words out of your title. This has nothing to do with his eyes. This fox is just plain better looking than any other stuffed animal we've captured on film in the last decade."

Hare was the creative aspect of the duo Wolle & Wolle, Lanceheim's leading advertising agency. Together with the more financially talented Wolle Toad, the two Wolles had more than fifty years' experience in the industry, and the pictures the hare was holding were among the best he'd seen.

"And they said he could only do clothing," said Cat, pretending not to hear the reprimand.

Fox Antonio Ortega was nineteen years old at the time, and his first advertising campaign was pasted on large billboards all over Mollisan Town and shone through the night from the tops of buses. Fox Antonio Ortega had done what no one else could in Luigi Barcotta's tight-fitting suits; long cardigans; and narrow, colorful pants: He looked comfortable. The fashion industry realized at one stroke that anyone who got an exclusive contract with the model Ortega had gained an unbeatable head start.

But Wolle Hare was one step ahead, and in his paw he held his next challenge: He had decided to use Fox in a campaign for the new model of Volga Sport. There was infinitely more money to make in the car industry than in fashion and, besides, it was about linking Ortega to Wolle & Wolle, not to any brand or product. The pictures he was looking at depicted Fox behind the steering wheel.

"He's perfect here, too," Wolle asserted.

"Perfect," Cat agreed. "And if I may say—"

But he got no further than that; applause coming from the studio made him fall silent.

"What's going on?" Hare asked.

The cat was already on his way to the door to find out. He returned half a minute later.

"Speak of the devil," he said. "It's our new photo model."

"They're applauding him? Why are they applauding?"

"Don't know," said Cat. "Maybe they think it's thanks to him that Barcotta's campaign is a success?"

"Are you being ironic?" Wolle asked. "I hate irony."

"No, no," Cat Nikolaus quickly answered. "I mean it. They think Fox Ortega is a hero. And then they think he's beautiful. That's obviously worth some applause."

"Idiots," the hare muttered, getting up from the desk. "Go and bring Fox here before they gobble him up."

And Cat Nikolaus again ran out to the studio to do as he was told.

Less than an hour later, Fox Antonio Ortega was sitting with Wolle Hare in the backseat of a black limousine traveling south on sky blue South Avenue. The Evening Weather was on its way in over the city, the traffic heavy. On the ceiling of the car, a starry sky glistened in miniature and Fox could not tear his gaze from it. Hare poured a substantial whiskey for himself. He had not intended to drink this evening, but the crystal glasses in the car door's teak shelf clinked so delightfully that it was impossible to resist. Fox, on the other hand, had declined.

"That's wise, my friend," said Hare. "This evening is an important one."

"I've never had a drink," Fox Antonio Ortega explained.

"Of course you haven't," said Hare. Wolle Hare was fascinated. The young fox, from what Hare understood, had had a promising sports career ahead of him. He had gone to high school at some rinky-dink school down in south Yok, and thus remained "undiscovered" longer than what seemed possible. Three months ago Fox and his father—an unpleasant bear who reeked of alcohol—were up in Lanceheim to discuss a contract with the Lasers, the district cricket team. According to Fox, that was the first time he had set his paw outside the Yok city line.

Father and son had been on their way out of the club's office when one of Wolle & Wolle's talent scouts saw him. The rest, as they say, was history.

"Have you read the screenplay properly?" Wolle Hare asked, sipping the whiskey.

"I didn't understand that much," Fox admitted.

"No? I thought it was a thriller. Bang-bang, action, and car chases?"

"Well . . . it was mostly a lot of dialogue."

"You need that sort of thing when you're filming, I assume," said Wolle Hare.

"I know that."

"Do you know the lines by heart?"

"By heart? No. Was that the idea?"

"I'm sure it will be fine anyway," Hare answered, as he did not want to make Fox unnecessarily nervous.

The car moved slowly in the aggressive traffic. The seats smelled of old leather, there was gravel on the mats on the floor, and someone had stuffed a paper tissue in the ashtray in the door. Wolle Hare would tell his secretary to use a different car service next time. Back in the days when he needed to look powerful, he would call a limousine. Now he could use comfortable cars.

They were en route to La Cueva on saffron yellow Puerta

de Alcalà. Wolle Hare was proud of knowing the restaurateur of the six-star restaurant. There were many stories told about Dragon Aguado Molina; Hare had heard them all, but assumed Molina spread them himself. All advertising was good advertising. As far as Hare was concerned, anyone who prepared a béarnaise sauce with as much sensitivity as Dragon Aguado Molina could have whatever secret life he wanted.

"Do you think that was the idea?"

"What?"

Wolle was lost in thought.

"That I should learn it all by heart? I've never been good at memorizing."

"I'm sure it won't be a problem," Wolle Hare repeated.

The limo turned off of South Avenue and onto a narrow, raspberry-colored street that was typical Yok, with trash on the sidewalks and graffiti on the walls of the buildings. Wolle shook his head imperceptibly. He had still not made up his mind whether Fox was dumb or if it was simply a lack of experience that made him appear dim-witted.

La Cueva was located in a free-standing three-story building set off from the adjacent buildings on Puerta de Alcalà by two narrow alleys where yellow green tufts of grass struggled against clay and stone in hope of the sun's attention. Pink roses climbed across the facade up to the windows on the second floor; the outside door was completely surrounded by the blossoms and two old-fashioned gaslights stuck out from the dense foliage.

Wolle Hare was the first out of the limousine. He looked up at the sky.

"Well, at least we're not too early," he said, mostly to himself.

Fox Antonio Ortega got out on the other side.

"Has Father arrived, do you think?"

"I guess we'll have to go in and see," said Wolle.

Fox's father, José Bear, was waiting in the bar. Judging by

his gaze and unruly paws he had already consumed a couple of drinks, which did not surprise Wolle. Bear had put on a light blue shirt and his best suit: dark brown and double-breasted. In the dark restaurant he presumably thought no one saw the long tears in the lining or the mud on the seams of the trousers, and if he kept the jacket buttoned the oil stains on the shirt remained invisible.

"There you are!" José Bear cried out. "I've been waiting!"

La Cueva had been furnished at the beginning of time with heavy, red and brown furniture. Now the furniture was old and worn, which was part of the restaurant's charm. Outside the small, low-sitting windows in the Little Bar the daylight was gradually disappearing, and in another half hour the velvet curtains, motley rugs, and dark red leather couches would look truly elegant.

Against this shabby backdrop the food stood out as more spectacular.

"Where's the movie mogul?" Fox's father asked.

Wolle Hare raised one eyebrow.

"He hasn't arrived yet? Have you asked in the restaurant?"

Hare was right; while José Bear was drinking in the bar, Rex Pug had been sitting alone at a table set for four, waiting.

Pug got up when they appeared. He was a legend in his industry, and his smile was blinding white when he greeted them, each one just as fervently.

"Fox Antonio Ortega," said Pug with feeling, "you are even more handsome in real life."

"Now, now," José Bear retorted. "No homo fantasies, if I may. We're here to talk money."

Which was not Pug's understanding at all of why he had invited Ortega to dinner at La Cueva. But the film producer had as much experience as forbearance, and fired off another one of his perfect smiles and refrained from correcting the fox's father.

Dinner was consumed under unexpectedly congenial circumstances. Wolle Hare assumed the role of good-natured catalyst and observer. Fox Antonio Ortega focused on the food, and the few times he thought about saying something, his father was already talking.

Rex Pug was in a brilliant mood as always and he entertained with anecdotes from the world of film. Wolle had known the film producer for many years, but had never heard him sound so witty. Pug was behind many of the successes on the silver screen in the past two decades, and he not only knew everyone worth knowing in the film industry, he knew a lot of animals you really didn't need to know.

José Bear concentrated on one thing at a time. When there was food on the table he ate. When there was wine in his glass he drank. And when there was neither food nor wine he explained the principles of what he thought a business arrangement should look like. He talked about percentages here and percentages there, royalties on revenue from popcorn and ticket sales, salary floors and ceilings, fixed and variable bonuses, compensation for expenses and allowances for inconvenient work hours. Who knew where he got all this from. Maybe someone had given him advice in advance? Maybe he had stolen a book from the bookstore and browsed through the chapter headings?

When dessert was finished and José Bear had set forth all the demands he could think of, he got up on unsteady legs and explained that he had to hurry to another meeting. Without further apologies he left the restaurant quite unexpectedly.

"Your father is truly a colorful character," Pug ventured to say in the silence left behind by Bear's departure.

"Well," Fox Antonio Ortega answered meditatively, "it was probably just that light blue shirt against the brown jacket that made you think that."

With coffee Rex Pug could finally get down to business. When Pug had seen Fox Antonio Ortega gazing down from the advertising pillars in his Luigi Barcotta suits, it was clear that a new star had been born. By a quirk of fate, Pug had a screenplay sitting on his desk, and the hero role was seemingly tailor-made for Fox. He had sent over this screenplay, and now he was eager to hear what Fox thought.

"I haven't learned it by heart," Fox began, casting an anxious glance at Wolle Hare. "But I read it all."

"And?" Pug asked.

"Well, I don't know. He . . . Was he in love with her?"

Pug nodded. The hero in the screenplay was undeniably in love with the heroine.

"But," Fox replied, "why doesn't he say so?"

"I don't understand what you mean."

"Well," said Fox Antonio Ortega, becoming eager. "If he had told her right away that he was in love with her, he wouldn't have had to go through all that, right?"

"No, of course," said Pug. "But then there wouldn't be a movie."

"I see," Fox replied, looking sincerely surprised. "No, maybe not. Will you excuse me a moment? Wolle, do you know where the restroom . . . ?"

Wolle Hare pointed toward the restrooms, and Fox stood up. When he was out of hearing range Rex Pug leaned over the table and whispered, "Is he a little slow?"

Wolle shrugged his shoulders. "Maybe."

"Well, I've made stars out of idiots before," Pug reminded himself. "Many times. But this . . . Can he act?"

"No idea," said Wolle. "But judging by how he performs during photo shoots, I would have to say no."

"Can he even memorize lines?"

"Does he have to? Isn't someone standing there whispering from the side? Or else can't you add a voice afterward?"

"I understand that as yet another no," said Pug drily.

"I only promised to bring you two together," said Wolle Hare. "And I've done that."

Rex Pug sighed. "All that glitters is not gold."

———

To get to the restrooms at La Cueva guests had to pass a large, round window through which the restaurant kitchen could be seen. On his way there Fox had no time to stop and be impressed by the stoves and chefs, given the urgency of his errand, but on his way back he had more time. He stopped, stared, and way in the back, in the shadow of an exhaust hood—by the door to the pantry—he saw her.

Beatrice Cockatoo, according to Fox Antonio Ortega, was the most beautiful stuffed animal the factories had ever produced. She was white as a cloud in a blue sky. Her yellow comb stood up from her head like a plume on royalty. Her crooked black beak gave her face dignity, and the yellow spot on her cheek enticed him in a way he could not explain.

Ortega remained standing, enchanted, just staring through the glass. He did not notice at first when a waiter placed himself alongside and followed his gaze. He started, and blushed almost imperceptibly. The waiter smiled.

"That's Beatrice Cockatoo," he said. "She's the dragon's daughter. My advice? Forget you ever saw her."

But that was a piece of advice Fox could not follow. Overwhelmed by what he had seen, he did not care about the damper that had settled over the mood at the table when he returned. Furthermore, he did not notice that the previously so agreeable Rex Pug bid a hasty good-bye out on saffron yellow Puerta de Alcalá without a word about the future. In Fox Antonio Ortega's heart there was only room for the image of Beatrice, and as if in a trance he staggered home through the dangerous streets of Sors with an infatuated smile on his lips.

He returned to Puerta de Alcalá the following evening. This was not something he consciously decided, he just did it. He was drawn back, he explained to me. He stood in the shadows on the other side of the street for several hours, hoping to catch a glimpse of her in a window. When he felt the cool foreboding of the Evening Storm in his fur, he crossed the street and entered the restaurant, ordered a glass of milk in the bar, and ignored the bartender's look. He went to the restroom several times during the evening, and each time lingered outside the round window in the door to the kitchen, but she wasn't there. When he went home his disappointment was as great as his determination. He had to see her again.

For four evenings Fox Antonio Ortega repeated the procedure, but on the fifth evening he was turned away at the door. A hyena in a pinstriped suit stopped him on his way in.

"Unfortunately," said Luciano, "this evening we're only letting in dinner guests."

"Then I'll order something to eat," Fox replied.

"Dinner guests with a reservation," said Luciano, closing the door right in the fox's long nose.

Crestfallen, the beautiful Antonio Ortega remained standing outside the closed door. At last he shrugged his shoulders and was about to return to his place on the opposite sidewalk when a small package fell on his head.

"Ouch."

It hurt, and it was only when he bent down to pick up the package that he saw the lovely red silk ribbon. What he had thought was a stone appeared to be a small present. He looked up at the facade, but no windows were open. He picked up the package, taking in its aroma. It was feminine, subtle but enticing at the same time, and involuntarily Fox inhaled deeply. As he carefully unwrapped the paper he released even more perfume, and without being certain, he knew it was Beatrice Cockatoo who had thrown the package out to him.

Inside was a yellow piece of paper on which was written in neat handwriting: "Greenhouse. Gazebo." Even though Fox understood that the message was for him, he did not understand there was more to it than that. He was filled with the heady perfume, with the possibility that the piece of paper had been wrapped and thrown out the window by the beautiful

Beatrice, and as he walked home through the empty streets it was not with the feeling that he had missed something.

The next day Fox worked at a photo shoot, and he casually told one of the photographers about the note.

"Did you find the greenhouse?" the photographer asked.

"Find it?"

When it occurred to Fox Antonio Ortega that of course he ought to have looked for a greenhouse, he rushed out of the photo shoot and down to the bus. He rode to grass green Yiala's Arch, and ran three kilometers to Puerta de Alcalà.

Behind La Cueva there was a well-tended courtyard, and at the back was the lovely greenhouse the message had referred to. If Fox realized he was snooping around in a gangster boss's backyard, he might have been more careful. Now he went into the greenhouse and looked around. Pots of herbs stood on tables in long rows, and the aroma of basil and mint was so overwhelming he had a hard time thinking. He searched for a "gazebo," the other word on the piece of paper. As he did not know what sort of thing that was, he doubted he would find it. Not far from the herbs was a gooseberry bush, and Antonio Ortega took a berry. As he chewed—the berry was perfect, not sour or overripe—his glance fell on a slate standing on a dusty table next to a cracked mirror. Fox also saw that there was a piece of chalk next to the slate, and he could not refrain. He swallowed the gooseberry, went up to the slate, and drew a sun. With his paw he rubbed it out, and wrote "gazebo." It was just an impulse, and when a space opened in the ground under the table, he recoiled in fear. The dark hole led down to an underground tunnel. He thought he recognized the same marvelous perfume from the package wafting out of the hole, and that gave him courage. He climbed down a narrow ladder and began walking in the darkness, below the ground, in the direction back toward the house. The darkness was soon so dense he could not see his own paws, and for that reason he walked right into a door. Instinctively he fumbled ahead, found the handle, and opened it. On the other side was a modest room where the glow of a table lamp emitted enough light that he could see a worn armchair where, exhausted, he sank down.

At the next moment the door on the opposite side opened, and Beatrice Cockatoo made an entrance. She staggered, panting. "You came!" she exclaimed.

And the next moment the happiness that shone in her eyes changed to terror.

"You must never come here again. He'll rub you out. My dad can make bad things happen. Really bad things."

She ran over to the armchair, and he got up. She gave him a quick, fleeting hug, took a step back, and looked him in the eyes. Then she repeated her warning, and asked him to go.

"But . . . I have to see you again," he said.

"Of course," she answered.

"My name is Fox Antonio Ortega," he said. "You are the most beautiful stuffed animal I have ever seen."

She giggled. "You are the most beautiful stuffed animal *I've* ever seen," she answered. "Now leave."

"If I haven't heard from you by tomorrow evening, I'll come back," he said.

"Go now," she repeated with a smile.

Unwillingly he left her, going back the same way he'd come.

Beatrice Cockatoo is not the protagonist of this story, and her significance for me, and the story, only has to do with her significance for Fox Antonio Ortega. But because she was already the center of Fox's life, I want to devote some time to her.

By chance—which I will return to—I gained access to Cockatoo's diaries, and the best way to describe her character and the special circumstances under which she lived at one time is to quote directly from her diary. Here is an extract from a day a few months before she met Fox Antonio Ortega for the first time:

Dear Diary,

Daddy said I may never ever mention Stavros Panther again. I promised I will never ever do that. Daddy is furious, but he's still pretty nice to me. He says it's not my fault, it's all Panther's fault. I don't know if that's completely true, but of course that doesn't matter. In a couple of weeks Daddy will have forgotten everything, that's how it always is.

I LOVE my room. I have two big windows facing saffron yellow Puerta de Alcalà. My curtains are linen, they're yellow, too, but lighter than the street, and they hang on white curtain rods with big knobs. I can pull down the shades if I want it dark.

My room is on the third floor, so I look over the roof of the building across the street, I can see all the way over to the water tower by the old animals' home. I don't know how far that is, but it must be several miles.

I have wallpaper that is white with a pink pattern. I think of the pattern as branches, if you can imagine branches growing in circles. I have a big white bed with a canopy—like a small sky over my head—that always makes me feel safe. When the real sky turns black it frightens me with its endlessness and its small, distant stars.

Then I have a couch full of pillows. All of them are different, some have crocheted covers, some are linen. I have oblong and square pillows, a little pillow in the shape of a heart, and a big one that looks like a sun. But they are all shades of red and pink. They go with the wallpaper. The red heart pillow is the reddest of them all. On one of the armchairs is a woolly blanket, which I can't get anywhere near without sneezing.

My room is pretty big. My desk is in front of one of the windows. That's where I sit and write in my diary in the evening. In one of the secret compartments in the desk I have hidden an extra key to my bedroom door, which no one knows I have. Daddy sometimes has someone lock it from outside. I have never locked it from the inside. But I could, if I wanted to.

I'm not judging anyone. Diary entries are personal and not meant to be published. You should be able to write what you want in a diary without thinking about style or significance. I don't want to serve as some kind of filter either. I have chosen to publish Cockatoo's private thoughts and feelings because I think it explains something about her, and by extension about why she was so desirable to Fox Antonio Ortega. More from the same entry:

When I'm forced to sit locked up in the room, what I miss the most is not what I would guess that I would miss the most. There you see how little we know ourselves. You might think I ought to miss my girlfriends most of all. Going out into the city, sitting and talking at some café, each with a large latte that I would NEVER drink. Milk makes you fat. But it's NOT my girlfriends I miss the most.

I miss working in the kitchen.

That's totally sick.

Daddy lets me work in the kitchen in the evening. Not always, not every time I ask to, but pretty often. It usually turns out to be a few days a week. Usually I'm at the cold buffet. I like that the most. It's hard work, it's stressful, and Daddy tolerates no mistakes. Not by me, and not by the others. The restaurant is his pride, and only the best is good enough. But I think I'm good, and he thinks so, too.

That's what I always miss the most. Getting to chop cucumbers, whip cream, and sift powdered sugar over the chocolate cakes. That IS crazy.

Daddy always has them do the job the same way. Sometimes I tease him a little about that. Then he answers that only an idiot gets tired of things that work.

Mostly they hit the post offices, but sometimes the regular businesses, too. Never banks. If you hit a bank, you'll have the police on you.

Stavros Panther is the Second Driver. The First Driver waits outside the post office and drives off at a furious speed. This is the most critical stretch; here you have to be quick and capable. The Second Driver waits at a distance. They throw the money in his car, and while they continue with the First Driver, the Second Driver takes off with the loot. After at least fifteen but no more than thirty minutes he then turns it over to the Third Driver, who drives home to us.

Stavros was the Second Driver. He always said that he would soon be promoted to First Driver, but I don't know if he said that just to boast.

I don't know why he fell in love with me. It's the sort of thing that just happens, I guess. It started with a letter he stuck under my door early one morning. I shouldn't complain, a love letter is a love letter, even if it's poorly spelled. I didn't know who he was, he signed it simply "Stavros." It was page up and page down about my beak and my comb. I was his lovebird, he wrote. I couldn't keep from laughing at that. It sounded SO silly, especially when I didn't know who wrote it.

The next morning a new letter arrived. And then another. This went on for several weeks. Not every day, but maybe every other, every third day. For a while I thought my secret admirer was a doctor. He devoted so much time to describing my body parts—not in a vulgar way—that I thought he was more interested in anatomy than love.

Of course I could have waited by the door and opened it when the letter came through the chink, but I didn't want to know who my suitor was. It was more exciting this way.

Daddy isn't mean. I realize of course that he treats me like a little cub, and according to my girlfriends I'm living more or less completely CONFINED, which they think is a SCANDAL and TERRIBLE. But it's no scandal at all. For one thing I like being at home, in my beloved room. And when I go out Daddy always makes sure I have someone with me. That has to do with my SECURITY.

Daddy has never tried to lie about what he does. I know that La Cueva, his beloved restaurant, loses money. That's why it can afford to be so amazing. Yes, to be sure sometimes he robs a post office, but above all he takes care of security in Sors. The police aren't enough, not down here. So somebody has to take responsibility. And I know there are those who say that the payment Daddy rakes in for taking care of security is unreasonable, but I know just as many who think it's good that someone makes sure that society functions. Even in Yok, where society doesn't function.

For that reason Daddy has enemies. Trying to get at him through me is not an unnatural thought. I'm Daddy's jewel. I'm the finest thing he knows, the one he cares about most of all. Injuring me would hurt him frightfully. Everyone knows that. It's not strange that he sends a couple of bodyguards with me when I go out. It's not strange that I don't get to drive a car.

It's no wonder, even if my so-called girlfriends try to make it into something else.

Stavros Panther was waiting for me in the dry storage room—a big, windowless room at the back of the kitchen, and you go there to fetch flour, sugar, salt, spices, coffee; well, everything that needs to stay dry in a restaurant kitchen. I was going to get flour, and he almost scared the life out of me.

"Shh," he hissed. "It's me, Stavros Panther."

Because it was dark in the storeroom and the panther was completely black, I could see nothing but his eyes glistening in the pale light from the kitchen. The fear ran out of me. The bad speller, I thought.

"I'm taking a big risk," he said. "But it's worth it."

"And you're exposing me to great danger," I answered. "You're like all other males, only thinking about yourself."

Stavros became desperate.

"I promise," he swore solemnly, "that you, Beatrice Cockatoo, the darling of my heart, will never be disappointed in me again. If you want I will get out of your life from this moment, you only need to ask for it."

"Get out," I answered coldheartedly, but also to tease him.

I saw him blink in desperation, as if what I'd said was impossible, and he immediately broke the promise he had just made.

"But . . . you must give me a chance!"

Obviously I gave him a chance. I'm not mean. I can't keep from feeling a little sorry for all these pining males who are fascinated by me in one way or another. Is it my white feathers? Or is it the yellow comb on my head? Presumably it's neither-nor. Presumably it's because I'm unapproachable. That my daddy is dangerous and I'm his finest trophy. That makes me, in some eyes, exciting. I believe that was the case with Stavros Panther.

When I read this passage I could not keep from comparing it with Cockatoo's first encounter with Fox Antonio Ortega, and the similarities were striking. Obviously she had made it a habit to entice and seduce males, and whether her intent was only to tease, or if her naiveté was born from the same murky well of understanding from which Ortega had drunk, I will leave unsaid. This is how the story of Beatrice and Stavros Panther ended; this note was penned a few days later.

Stavros Panther got caught, of course. He wasn't the first, and won't be the last. The next time he was going to make his way into the dry storage room to meet me he hid in a barrel of flour and was secretly carried in there. If you're a panther, it's hard to shake off all the traces of flour when you're in a hurry. Stavros was in a hurry. And Daddy found him out. I don't even want to know what Daddy did with him. I said of course that I didn't know who Stavros Panther was, and Daddy believed me. Maybe. But maybe not. That's why he locks me in now in the evenings. In a few weeks Daddy will have forgotten Panther, and then I'll ask him if the door can't be unlocked again.

Beatrice Cockatoo really did make contact with Fox Antonio Ortega the day after he sneaked into La Cueva through the greenhouse. She called his cell phone right after the Breeze picked up in the morning, and they spoke for less than a minute. Then she hung up in midsentence, and called back a couple of hours later during the rain to apologize. It was hard for her to talk because her daddy didn't allow her to have her own phone in her room.

Whether this inaccessibility, this obstacle in the path of young love, contributed to making Ortega's longing even more intense shall remain unsaid. But during the weeks and months to come, every day became a struggle to outwit Dragon Aguado Molina, who kept his daughter under constant surveillance. The telephone calls were the loving couple's primary means of communication. Beatrice could talk on the phone for hours if she wasn't interrupted, and Fox could listen just as long. Neither of them cared what Beatrice said, love traveled freely through copper wires and radio waves and was greater than any single topic of conversation. On the few occasions they met in reality, they were struck mute by each other's beauty, and hardly talked at all. Fox was an old-fashioned gentleman and would never have thought of touching the beautiful Cockatoo. Beatrice was,

I assume, more experienced, but felt that it was not a female's place to take physical initiative. His waiting aroused her respect and curiosity. He was different, and this incited her.

I cannot refrain from quoting a section from Beatrice's diary that describes the effort the lovers put into stealing a few short minutes in each other's company during this period. It is not difficult to realize that the love they were experiencing grew and turned into something stronger and more powerful than any normal stuffed animal can understand.

Beatrice tells it like this:

> *It was Vasko Manatee who drove me. I knew it would be him because it's Thursday. We have a black Volga Deluxe with tinted bulletproof windows and lead doors that are so superheavy I can't open them myself. The interior was made especially for Daddy, with leather seats and a bar cabinet and a tinted glass window that can be raised between the backseat and the front so the driver doesn't hear what's being said.*
>
> *Grand Divino is on the other side of mint green East Avenue, up in Lanceheim. I'm not particularly well traveled, it's like there's no reason to bounce around in the city, I think. Most everything is in the vicinity of our saffron yellow Puerta de Alcalà, but Grand Divino is an exception. I confess that I love this department store. I love it much, much more than shopping. Sometimes I come home without buying anything, even though I've spent hours in all the departments. Above all, the ground floor, with the perfumes, is completely unbelievably awesome. What I really want to say is that I KNOW Grand Divino: every floor, every dressing room, every box room.*
>
> *Vasko Manatee drove into the parking garage. Daddy has a spot on the fifth floor, close to the elevators. Vasko opened my car door and then followed me*

to the elevators. I was used to that. I didn't think about it anymore; not even when I was looking at underwear and Vasko—or someone else—made everyone in the department feel uncomfortable.

I led Vasko through the store up to the third floor. I took it easy—not as easy as I usually do, but much easier than I really wanted. I went between different designers and picked up a garment here and there. Two dresses. A coat. A jumper. A pair of shoes. A hat. A pair of stockings. Two sweaters. And the whole time I was on my way to the fitting rooms that were almost at the rear of the department, between Missonno and lingerie. Without a glance at Vasko Manatee, even though I REALLY wanted to see whether he realized what I was up to, I vanished with my mountain of clothes behind the curtains, where males are not allowed. Vasko and I had been here many times before. He knew the rules. With a heavy sigh he sat down in the armchair placed outside the curtains, where he always waited.

I quickly went into the next cubicle and changed. New dress, new shoes, new coat, but above all: new hat. And it was this amazing hat that gave me the courage. I had seen it a few days before in an ad. It had a veil that completely covered my beak.

Without hesitating, I came out of the dressing room. I had practiced a style of walking that was different from my usual gait, with swaying hips, and I walked much more slowly than usual. And now the question was, would Vasko Manatee recognize me?

Of course I thought about what the punishment might be. IF Manatee exposed me. IF Daddy saw through me. IF I was caught red-handed. Of course that scared me. Daddy would never hurt me. I know that, I'm sure of it. But he usually locked the door to my room at night, and there was a room down in the cellar that . . . I didn't like.

I knew that he took stuffed animals down there some-times. I suspected what he did to them. He would never do anything to me, but he might make me SIT there. A pretty long time. Maybe.

So I was swaying my hips, and slowly I pulled the cur-tains to the side. I turned directly toward Vasko. I stared at him through my veil. I NEVER would have done that if I was me. Then I walked slowly away through the de-partment, without looking around. Was he following? So far it wouldn't matter; I could simply start picking out clothes and return to the fitting room.

When I came to the escalators I finally turned around. And when I discovered that there was no stupid manatee behind me, my heart started to race. Until now it had mostly been a game. Until now I could have changed my mind. But IF I got onto the escalator there was no way back.

I forced myself to stand completely still on the way up between the third and fourth floors, but when I got up to the fifth floor I more or less ran.

The tea salon L'Express was arranged like a train. I had never liked it: ceiling too low, colors too dark, too claustrophobic. Along the wall small compartments had been set up. With doors and curtains and everything. Just like on the train to Hillevie. And in the third com-partment counting from the headwaiter's station he sat, Fox Antonio Ortega, the most beautiful stuffed animal I've seen in my whole life.

Hearing what he said, thinking of something reasonable to say myself . . . was impossible. But I know that he said that he LOVED me. No one else has said that. Well, that is, not like that. Not like Fox Antonio Ortega said it. THAT I remember. I don't know how long we sat there, I was nervous the whole time. I could barely listen, I could barely talk, and at last I had to leave. I think I left in the middle of *a sentence. I don't know if it was one of his or one of mine.*

I ran through the fifth floor to the escalators. I had the hat on. I ran down the escalators. And then I walked in my pretend way over toward the fitting rooms. I have NEVER been so afraid in my whole life.

When I saw Vasko Manatee I almost started to laugh. The dumb cow was still in the chair, and when I got a little closer I saw that he had fallen asleep.

I sneaked in behind the curtain, into the fitting cubicle, and quickly changed, put on my own clothes. Only then did I realize what I had experienced.

True Love.

In brief, stolen moments the love between Fox Antonio Ortega and Beatrice Cockatoo grew to the bursting point, and I hereby intend to leave her and her diary in peace. The point was to show how well the cockatoo suited the beautiful but less intelligent fox, and I am certain this has now become clear.

Back to the moment when Fox was courting. The whole thing was absurd. Crazy. Picture it, and you can't help but smile. The dragon sitting with his wineglass after having judged an innocent nightingale and an equally innocent vole to indescribable pain, the bodyguard Vasko Manatee standing next to him with the wine bottle ready to refill, and before them the dumb Fox Antonio Ortega, asking for Beatrice's claw.

It was absurd to the point that Dragon Aguado Molina got distracted. If he had not just been drinking that good wine, and if Fox had not been so blindingly beautiful, Molina most likely would have asked Vasko to escort the hopeful suitor down to the cellar along with the others, and nailed him up against one of the walls intended for nailing up stuffed animals. There Fox would have been hanging alongside the nightingale and the vole, all while the criminal element of the kitchen personnel at La Cueva slowly burned them, hair by hair. Or else Aguado Molina himself would have retrieved the oil from the deep-fat fryer in the kitchen—in which the city's best deep-fried onions were prepared—mixed it with honey and then poured it over the suitor. In this way he had blinded others with eyes of plastic or glass so that they would never be able to cast their loathsome glances at Beatrice again.

But the situation caught Dragon Aguado Molina by surprise. "What the hell?" he exclaimed.

"I am Fox Antonio Ortega," Fox hastened to clarify, as he approached the booth where Dragon was sitting. "And I do not know your daughter. Yet I know that I am right for her, and that she is right for me."

Molina was speechless. He stared at the beautiful fox, who was now standing within reach, and turned toward Vasko Manatee, still holding the wine bottle in his forelimb.

Vasko shook his head slowly, but could not conceal an amused smile. And Molina could not keep from smiling himself. First carefully, tentatively—was this a joke?—but when he saw Ortega's surprised expression, he realized that this was not the case. This made the situation even funnier. He let out his restaurateur laugh, and Vasko joined in.

"Daddy, what's so funny?"

Suddenly she was standing there in the door to the kitchen, the beautiful Beatrice Cockatoo, and the laughter ceased. Dragon, fox, and manatee, all three of them, stared in surprise at the white apparition. Her father gathered his wits first.

"Beatrice, honey, have you seen this fox before?" he asked.

"Never," Beatrice lied.

"He has come here to ask for your claw," Dragon revealed, and could not hold back his laughter. "As if this was some damn fairy tale. Who the hell behaves like that nowadays?"

Beatrice did not reply. Fox Antonio Ortega had caught her gaze with his, and the suitor did not intend to let go.

"Listen, you joker," Dragon Aguado Molina chuckled, "you're not right in the head, are you?"

"My head has never been my strong suit," Ortega admitted without letting Beatrice out of his sight for a moment.

"No, no. No, you seem to be an honest, straightforward type. Of course you'll have her." Dragon Aguado Molina laughed.

Beatrice started and turned toward her father.

What was he saying? This couldn't be happening.

And the jubilant feeling of happiness that filled her in the next moment was stronger than anything she had experienced until now. During the weeks that followed she would return, again and again, to this feeling, confused and enchanted.

The fox, too, looked in surprise at Dragon Aguado Molina.

"You're a good stuffed animal," he said happily and contentedly. "I knew you would understand."

"Yes, yes, you will absolutely get to marry my daughter . . ." Molina continued cunningly. "But first you have to prove that you're the right animal for her. We don't know each other, do we?"

Fox nodded seriously. That sounded reasonable.

Vasko Manatee sensed what was coming and hid his smile behind his forelimb.

"You must give me three things," said Molina. "A feather. An arm. And a heart."

"A feather, an arm, and a heart?"

"We'll start with the feather," said Molina, getting up. "It won't be that hard. There's a prosecutor here in Sors. Hawk Schleizinger. It would be fun to joke around with him a little. He has lots of feathers. He'll give you one, won't he, Fox? Come back with the hawk's feather, then I'll tell you about the arm. You have ten days. If you don't have the feather by then, you can forget my beautiful Beatrice!"

THE FEATHER

Fox Antonio Ortega went to work without delay and without giving a thought to how strange the whole thing was. Why should he get to marry Dragon Aguado Molina's daughter by stealing a feather from Hawk Schleizinger's plumage? That didn't make sense. But Fox was so absorbed by his love for Beatrice Cockatoo that he did not care about logic or sense.

It was not hard to find out where Hawk Schleizinger lived. True, he wasn't in the phone book, but in Yok the phone book means nothing and contacts mean everything. Schleizinger was a known animal, and in the evening two days later Fox Antonio Ortega was standing on the sidewalk across from the hawk's house, peering in through one of the windows on the bottom floor. A warm light from the desk lamp illuminated a small library.

Hawk Schleizinger was sitting at his desk and looked up from his work. He rested his gaze on the long rows of leather-bound spines on the bookshelves. His nightclothes, blue-striped pajamas and a silk bathrobe, smelled of pipe tobacco and leather armchair. The silence was absolute.

The computer was not turned on. In the evening Schleizinger avoided modern technology. That was how he separated his work at home from the office. He could access all archives and files from home if he wanted, but in solitude at the polished desk, where piles of paper were arranged with a system as irreproachable as his arguments in court, buzzing electronics did not seem to fit in. With paper and pen in his claws, he forced the flood of associations into controlled reflection.

Above the liquor cabinet in the corner toward the terrace, four TV screens showed images from the surveillance cameras in the garden and out toward the street. At night they looked like blurry black-and-white photographs. Schleizinger lived in a stone building on fire red Mount Row in Amberville, and describing the neighborhood as tranquil was an understatement; nothing happened at night.

For that reason the hawk raised his eyes from time to time, and looked over at the screen image, where a fox on the other side of the street was moving in and out of camera range.

Schleizinger was an imposing bird, both by profession and by appearance. He always dressed in vest and suit, bow tie rather than necktie, and shoes polished so that the leather resembled varnish. Despite his curious gaze, Hawk Schleizinger always had a stern, cerebral air about him; heavy eyebrows; and a sharply curving beak. It was hard to imagine him in any other profession. He worked as chief public prosecutor at the court in the Sors District in Yok, and in the legal system in Mollisan Town there was probably no position more exposed. He had a reputation for being incorruptible; he had worked as a prosecutor in the district for more than twenty years, and had long ago given up on a political career. In other words, he was untouchable in a way that time and again made dragons, octopuses, and other animals of darkness plan attacks against him. Until now they had failed.

No stuffed animal in Mollisan Town was as well guarded as Hawk Schleizinger.

Schleizinger interrupted his writing and raised his eyes toward the surveillance monitors. Once again the fox passed the camera facing the street.

Irritated, the prosecutor threw aside the pen and paper, got up, and went over to the screens. He sat down in front of the control board, turned on the recording function, and rewound.

There.

There was no doubt. Fox was staring right through the windows into the library where Hawk sat working.

With his claw against the screen of the monitor Schleizinger drew a square around the fox's head, and in a few seconds enlargements were created. Schleizinger pushed "send," waited longer than was customary—perhaps the database was heavily used tonight—and then the information came up:

Fox Antonio Ortega. No criminal record, but school records, medical records, and a clippings file of sports achievements. A young animal with miserable grades in school, not registered as a gang member, but from experience Hawk knew that this was uncertain information because the gangs recruited aggressively among the young. What was odd in this context was that Ortega had an impressive record as far as accomplishments in youth sports was concerned.

Schleizinger continued reading, and it was only when he arrived at the family relationships that it started to make sense. The mother was Cat Bayas Delgado, the father a certain José Bear. In other words: the same bear who for the past four days had been sitting in jail in Sors waiting for trial.

Schleizinger could not keep from smiling at the fact that only an hour ago he had been sitting with the bear's papers before him on the desk.

He picked up the phone, the one in the middle of the control board, and without dialing he was connected to Smithson Yak.

"Is this about the fox out there?" Smithson asked before Hawk could even state his business.

"He has a motive," said the prosecutor.

"Then we'll bring him in," Smithson answered.

The hawk sat down again at the control panel. On the monitor he saw how Smithson's stuffed animals ran out onto the street. They were all armed, but none had yet drawn a weapon. They were hesitating, but then Hawk saw one of them point at something outside the range of the camera, and they all started running that way.

Poor fox, thought Hawk, smiling to himself.

The chief prosecutor decided to interrogate the young Antonio Ortega first thing the next day. It never hurt to let them sit overnight.

But in the car en route to court the following morning a surprise awaited. Hawk Schleizinger's personal security force had come up empty-handed the previous night. Smithson, who was behind the wheel and had an anonymous colleague in a dark suit and sunglasses beside him, was forced to admit the failure.

"I've never seen anyone run so fast," he said. "I mean it, never. Not in- or outside a stadium."

"I beg your pardon?" Hawk asked. "That sounds improbable. There were four of you and he was alone?"

"There could have been fifty-four of us," Smithson answered, while he gently and sensitively maneuvered the lead-reinforced car through the dense morning traffic. "If you can't catch them, numbers don't help. His father is José Bear?"

Smithson had access to the same database as the prosecutor.

"Small-timer," Schleizinger stated. "I'm not going to ask for more than three to six months. He seems to be the type who never climbs up to the next division. He was arrested for lottery fraud. Not much to make a fuss about."

"You've never run into Antonio Ortega before? There are no other connections?" Smithson asked.

"That remains to be found out," Schleizinger replied.

They turned off the busy avenue and continued south on deep blue Avinguda de Pedrables. Even though it was one of Yok's biggest throughways, it was noticeable how the pace of traffic decreased. In Mollisan Town's poorest district, car activity was sparse. Through its complicated structure, the many dead ends, the recurring pirate attacks, plus the fact that few stuffed animals in Yok could afford a car, bicycles, skateboards, and roller skates were more common sights on the streets.

The court in Sors was a gray, square concrete block of a building with long rows of square windows. It was on vanilla white Amiral Zee's street, and outside the entrance the police had created a so-called security zone to deter organized crime from rescue attempts. Personnel who worked at the court used the garage to enter the building, and this also applied to the prosecutor. The entry ramp was located a few blocks south, and underground you drove back north, parked, and took the armored elevator up to your floor.

With three cross streets left to the garage, Smithson Yak stopped at a light.

They saw him at the same time.

"Antonio Ortega!" Smithson Yak panted, pointing so his colleague could see.

"The audacity!" Hawk Schleizinger exclaimed.

On the sidewalk across from the court building, outside a small Springergaast, stood Fox Antonio Ortega. He was peering at the court's main entrance.

Even before the light turned green Smithson had given his orders. Via the internal radio he contacted the guards at the entrance to the court, and as the car with the prosecutor slowly passed Fox—who was on the left side—Yak could see police officers storming out of the building on the right.

"I want him in the interrogation room as soon as possible. Just call me; I'll come down," said Hawk.

"Understood, sir," Smithson replied.

He turned right onto the ramp to the garage and saw in the rearview mirror how Fox Antonio Ortega began running, with the police after him.

When no word had come by lunchtime, Hawk summoned Smithson. The shame-faced yak, after failing for the second time to capture the fox, had even sent animals to Ortega's latest known address, without success. Now he explained that he had not wanted to submit a report because he didn't consider the case over with.

"I'll continue to work on the fox this afternoon," the yak promised.

That his own guards had not managed to capture the fox last night was one thing, but that the police failed—with their cars, motorcycles, and communications equipment—was worrisome. Hawk Schleizinger was sincerely surprised.

During the afternoon the prosecutor managed to cross-examine a licorice troll indicted for having extorted money from his sister by threatening to expose her extramarital connections, plus make a final plea in the case of a drug-abusing locksmith, an argument that Hawk was personally satisfied with. It ended with the locksmith being sentenced to four years in King's Cross, a sentence that Schleizinger would not appeal. After a short visit to chambers to change shirt, vest, and bow tie, the prosecutor hurried off to the elevators just in time for the Evening Weather and rode down to the garage, where the car was waiting with the motor running. Behind the wheel sat one of the many security animals with a dark suit and strong jawline, whom Hawk could not tell apart.

He leaned back and closed his eyes while the car slowly rolled away toward the ramp. He did not need to say where he was going; his schedule had been confirmed and communicated for weeks. Twenty minutes' sleep in the backseat was just what he needed.

Once a month prosecutor Schleizinger had dinner with Manuela Hamster, the police chief in Sors. She was a professional administrator, an ambitious politician, but Schleizinger respected her anyway. She held her district in an iron grip, and her fight against corruption in the police force was genuine and reasonably successful. When the two did not meet at her office, they had dinner at Au Sultan. It was Schleizinger's favorite restaurant, mostly due to the pickled radishes that were served as an appetizer. Both the prosecutor's and the police chief's bodyguards felt comfortable with the place; it was simple to secure and guard.

Manuela Hamster was at the table when Hawk Schleizinger entered the restaurant. They had jointly decided that the table in the corner next to the bar was the best. They sat with their backs to the wall, with a view of the entrance and restrooms opposite. The bodyguards sat at the window tables, and from the other direction they were protected by the lead-reinforced bar.

"Congratulations," said Manuela, rising briefly as Hawk sat down. "I heard you had yet another brilliant performance today. Four years, was that it?"

"It wasn't me," Schleizinger answered modestly. "It was justice that triumphed. That happens sometimes. Extremely satisfying."

He was not a humorous stuffed animal. He picked up the menu from the table, but set it down again.

"I already know what I want," he said. "Have you decided?"

Hamster opened the menu. She liked variety, and tried to remember what she had had the last time.

"The salsicca, maybe?" she said.

Schleizinger immediately raised a claw and signaled to the headwaiter that they were ready to order. He was in a hurry; work was piling up at home and he didn't want to be too late.

It took less than an hour to finish the appetizer and entrée. Over coffee they discussed the intensifying struggle against the gang leaders in Sors, a program they had launched jointly six months earlier, and which had already borne fruit. The Ministry of Finance had placed expanded resources at their disposal, and Hamster maintained that she felt they were close to a breakthrough. But suddenly she interrupted herself, and nodded toward the window.

"That fox on the other side of the street, is that anyone you know?"

Schleizinger controlled himself. He refrained from twisting his head, and instead leaned directly toward the bodyguard sitting closest.

"Contact Smithson," he said. "Say that the fox is back. Outside Au Sultan. And before you start chasing him, I want him surrounded. He won't get away this time."

The bodyguard nodded, got up slowly, and went over to the kitchen to place the call. Schleizinger, meanwhile, let Hamster in on the situation, and together they continued conversing as they had their coffee, careful not to change body language or in some other way worry the fox, who was patiently hiding in the shadows on the sidewalk across from the restaurant.

Fifteen minutes after Police Chief Hamster noticed him, the fox was surrounded without his knowledge. There were animals inside the building where Fox was standing in the doorway. They had entered via the courtyard and waited for a signal. Farther up on the street stood twenty-two riot police hidden in a nameless, colorless alley never intended for anything other than drainage, and in the other direction two police vans showed up.

At Smithson's command the prosecutor's and the police chief's twelve bodyguards stood up inside Au Sultan and went as a group to the door. Antonio Ortega realized that he was exposed. He saw the police vans parked a block south as the door behind him opened.

He had no plan when he started running. Planning was not his strong suit. The street was blocked to the south by the police vans, so Fox ran north. There the riot squad appeared from the alley, and formed a wall with their shields.

"Now we've got him," said Schleizinger, who along with the police chief was standing in the window observing the drama.

As Fox Antonio Ortega continued running toward the riot police, neither the prosecutor nor the police suspected mischief. It was a desperate action in a tight situation, and even though they both witnessed what happened, they could hardly believe it.

Fox kept running; the riot squad got into formation, a single stuffed animal on his way toward a wall of heavily armed police officers. The situation was so peculiar that no one thought about the fox's speed. It was only afterward that someone said they had never seen a stuffed animal move so quickly. The riot police worriedly drew their weapons. When little more than five feet remained between the fox and the wall of police, some of the officers maintained afterward that they had seen the mattress abandoned by a garbage can. The next moment the fox used that same mattress as a launching pad and flew over the police wall with a good margin.

The jump was nine feet high and twenty-six feet long. The whole thing was over in a few overwhelming seconds, and the fox continued running along the street while the riot squad clumsily turned around and gave chase. Hawk Schleizinger knew only too well how this race would end.

"Unbelievable," said Manuela Hamster.

"Depressing." Schleizinger sighed.

"Fox Antonio Ortega, you said? No record? No criminal connection?"

"His father is in jail, accused of lottery fraud," Hawk replied. "But that's not much to go on."

"I want to recruit him," interrupted Hamster, who had not been listening.

In the car on the way home Hawk Schleizinger considered

his options. That Fox Antonio Ortega was after the chief prosecutor was obvious, as was the fact that the fox would not give up. But what did he want? Among the furious, embarrassed, and frustrated emotions that sojourned in Schleizinger's chest, he discovered a feeling of curiosity, which surprised him. For once it felt important to find out the fox's underlying motives. The prosecutor nodded to himself. That's how it was. The whole thing was so strange that he wasn't reacting reasonably. Which in a way was logical. And because he was a very logical animal, he felt satisfied with that conclusion.

Fox Antonio Ortega did not show up on the surveillance monitor until midnight that night. By then Hawk Schleizinger had already been waiting an hour. The chief prosecutor had put on his nightclothes, and stared intently at the screen as he grabbed the phone and gave Smithson the order.

"Don't do anything!"

Without waiting for the security chief's protests he hung up, tied the sash of the robe tighter around him, and left the house through the terrace door. He crossed the lawn on the back side, and used the low iron gate to make his way onto the street.

The fox was standing in the shadow of a tall maple tree that had grown up from under the asphalt of the sidewalk. Even though the prosecutor crossed the street with determined steps, the fox remained quiet and expectant.

Cars stood neatly parked along the sidewalk on the street in Amberville and the glow from the nearest streetlight made the prosecutor's beautiful silk robe glisten. Otherwise the night was completely still.

Schleizinger knew that Smithson and the security force were watching him in frustration from inside the house. When he had a few feet left to Ortega he stopped.

"I am Hawk Schleizinger," said the prosecutor.

"I know," Fox Antonio Ortega replied.

"I know you know," the prosecutor snapped. "I'm introducing myself to show a little common courtesy."

"Oh. Excuse me. My name is Fox Antonio Ortega," said Fox.

"I know that, too," the prosecutor said. "I'm the prosecutor in Sors in Yok. What do you think of me? I have more enemies than all my enemies have combined. Of course I've found out who you are. Why are you following me?"

"I want to talk with you. But I didn't know what to do."

"Talk with me? What kind of stupidity is this? You're lying. Schedule a meeting? Couldn't you just call, in that case?"

"But I have," Fox explained. "I've called your secretary dozens of times. But when I didn't want to reveal my business, she refused to let me speak with you. Or see you."

"But why didn't you knock on the door? Like an ordinary, civilized stuffed animal?"

Hawk indicated with one claw the hawk's house on the other side of the street. "I thought about that. But your guards came running as soon as I tried."

"That's natural, with the case against your father on its way up in the court."

Fox Antonio Ortega looked perplexed. "Dad? What has he done?"

"You didn't know?"

"No."

"He's accused of lottery fraud."

Fox considered this and found no reason to dispute it. Silence fell between them.

"So what is your business that you didn't want to tell my secretary?" Hawk Schleizinger asked at last. He was starting to get cold in his pajamas.

"I've been given a task," said Fox Antonio Ortega. "In order to marry the bird I love, I have to give her father one of your feathers."

"I beg your pardon?"

"I was wondering if I could have a feather?"

"Is this all about a childish bet?" Hawk roared.

"Not a bet. More of a test, I guess. And it's not childish. What I feel for Beatrice I have never felt for anyone else," Fox answered. "For her I would do dumber things than this."

The chief prosecutor stood silently and stared at the beautiful fox. Then without further ado he plucked a feather from his belly, gave it to the fox, and quickly returned to the house, where a warm bed awaited.

"How do we know this feather is Schleizinger's?" Vasko Manatee asked.

Instead of being happy about Ortega's feat, Dragon Aguado Molina and his bodyguard both seemed irritated.

"You have my word," a wronged Fox Antonio Ortega replied.

He was shocked by the suspicion. The thought of acquiring a white feather and pretending it was Hawk Schleizinger's had not even occurred to him. Fox was again standing before the dark violet dragon in the restaurant; the Weather was in the middle of the day but here it was dark. Beatrice Cockatoo was not to be seen. Molina yawned and showed his terrifying jaws, nodding at the same time. "It's Hawk's feather. It's all over town. Everyone knows he gave it to you yesterday."

Fox nodded. Vasko snorted.

"But the feather means nothing," Dragon Aguado Molina continued. "The next task is to get an arm. I want one of Octopus Callemaro's arms. He has eight of them, so he can surely spare one for you."

"Octopus Callemaro?" Fox repeated.

"Good luck," said Vasko Manatee.

Then he burst into laughter, and Molina joined in.

When Fox Antonio Ortega left, Molina looked contentedly at the feather. He was starting to get close to Chief Prosecutor Schleizinger, and with each passing day more time and money was required to keep him and the police away from business they had nothing to do with. The dragon was certain that the chief prosecutor's self-confidence was behind his growing successes. Schleizinger did not fail at anything, and the power that created was worrisome. Stuffed animals around him were starting to think he was invincible. Which in turn made them harder—and more expensive—to handle.

For that reason, that afternoon Aguado Molina burned half of the hawk's white feather and put it in an envelope that he addressed to Schleizinger's secretary, to be sure that the rumor about this letter and its threatening contents would be spread at the court and within the Sors police organization. It was not to frighten the prosecutor that the dragon sent the letter; it was to show that the chief prosecutor was also a stuffed animal—neither more nor less.

THE ARM

"You mutht put thith on," I said to Fox Antonio Ortega. "You do underthtand that? Ath a dithguith?"

My name is Gary. I am a dark beige vole with a gray belly and ears that are barely visible. I have lisped my entire life, I no longer consider it a handicap, but certain stuffed animals have a harder time hearing what I say than others, and Fox Antonio Ortega has always had problems understanding. That's not just because of my lisp.

"Mutht I?" Ortega repeated.

It was there and then I entered into the story in earnest. We were in a narrow alley that reeked of rotten cabbage and grease. On both sides red, sooty brick walls vanished up into the black sky; in the electric plant behind my back there had once been an assembly shop, before the auto industry moved to north Lanceheim. I had to speak loudly over the clatter from a restaurant kitchen farther away, but no one could hear us.

"Ath a dithguith," I repeated. "They would get you right away. Thinking you are alive. They will see you're not one of them. Put thith on now, and thith cap."

Fox shrugged his shoulders and squeezed into a gray, full-length coat with a worn-out lining. Someone had spilled a can of brown paint across the back. He tied it around himself with a simple belt because the buttons were missing. The cap I pressed onto his head was so large it not only concealed his ears, it also shadowed his beautifully shimmering eyes.

"Tie it like thith," I instructed, showing how the belt should sit. "No one careth if thomeone new thowth up. There are new oneth all the time. With the coat you'll look like one of uth."

"Of uth?" Antonio Ortega wondered, but obediently followed my advice and tied the big coat that concealed his lovely fur around him.

"Are you thure you want thith?" I asked nervously, as we walked toward the radio tower. "Octoputh can be . . . thurly thometimeth."

"Thurly?"

"I'll help you, of courth," I assured him. "I don't really know what you're up to, Ortega, but all the better."

"It's no secret," the fox answered. "I want one of Octopus's arms to give to Dragon Aguado Molina in exchange for his daughter."

I laughed. "I don't remember you as being tho funny," I said. Because I could not believe that Fox was speaking the truth, I was convinced he had something else in mind and was just joking.

Sometimes you may get the idea that we stuffed animals in Yok have made it a matter of honor to eradicate the traces of Mollisan Town's civilization in our part of the city, but that's not true. We were practical, and only destroyed the things we didn't need. Partly for that reason we let two of the original four radio towers remain standing. Two towers were enough, one in Sors and the other in Corbod, for cell phone and TV and radio signals to penetrate every wall.

Octopus Callemaro had located his headquarters at the top

of one of the towers, but he had been careful; he didn't want to be the one who made *Wheel of Fortune* stop spinning in the idiot boxes in the living rooms of Yok on Friday evenings. The reason he chose this unusual place was that in his teens he read stories from the Middle Ages, when Amberville, Lanceheim, Tourquai, and Yok were independent cities in constant war with one another, and learned the value of a high location for a headquarters so as not to be surprised or surrounded. There was no building in Sors higher than the radio tower.

Octopus Callemaro had expended both money and time on his house in the sky. The best way to picture the result was to imagine a lopped-off variation of the Savings Banks Bank headquarters in Lanceheim, or possibly a shrunken National History Museum, and then exchange brick and masonry for wood and cardboard. It was an impressive but lightweight building Octopus had erected at the top of his tower.

The furnishings were nonexistent in the outer rooms where stuffed animals of all sorts gathered and stood around, while in the inner rooms it was cozier. The innermost room, where Callemaro took his meals alone, was sumptuous, with wall-to-wall carpet, oak paneling, and a ceiling painting that told the story of the creation of the building. Once a month the octopus invited one of the crew who had particularly distinguished himself—the most brutal, the greediest, the worst—to have dinner with him in this innermost room. It was a gift that all coveted, but few got to experience.

The gangster boss otherwise had a simple attitude toward his followers: the more, the better. In the innermost circle Octopus counted two dozen loyalists, and beyond that there were just as many who would willingly take part if Dragon Aguado Molina went on the attack. Another couple dozen stuffed animals lived in the building. They hardly knew who Octopus was, even though they exploited his hospitality to avoid the chaos of Sors for a calm time in the sky. These parasites were Callemaro's best recruitment base.

Ortega and I came up to the radio tower at midnight, and began the long climb up the apparently fragile ladder.

"There are thix hundred thirty-thixth thtepth," I panted. "They thay it wath jutht to annoy me."

I knew that Fox Antonio Ortega could have run up the ladder without getting out of breath; he could have gone hand over hand if he wanted to. But he was a considerate animal, and so he rested when I was forced to rest.

"Do you think I'll get to meet him tonight?" he asked during one of the breaks.

"Perhapth," I speculated. "If he'th in a good mood. We'll make a try. Whatever it ith you want to thay to him, it'th jutht as well to get it thaid."

I was entrusted to the inner rooms. I had worked with Callemaro for more than a year, so when we entered the building I left Ortega to himself. It took a few hours before I was able to set up an audience with Octopus, and during that time the fox investigated the strange building.

Despite Fox Antonio Ortega's mental shortcomings he was fascinated, like anyone else who was up in the tower for the first time, by the view. The windows were not equipped with glass or mesh; the large, rectangular holes in the facade were cut directly out of the wall panels. From the top of the tower the labyrinthine street network and the colors of the streets in the illuminated night were silhouetted like a poetic, imaginative pattern in a kaleidoscope.

Everywhere in the outside rooms there were piles of trash and stuffed animals. The occasional armchair and mistreated sofa testified to a long-abandoned ambition to give the various rooms different functions. Since the stove had broken down, in the big kitchen—which was an extension to the other rooms—three portable butane stoves had been set out on a table. Once a week the pantry and refrigerators were refilled, usually on Monday. The food often ran out the same evening, so there were mostly empty packages on the shelves. From the three toilets there was a horrible stench because no one ever cleaned up after themselves.

Fox Antonio Ortega was not spoiled, but even he felt uneasy about how things were organized in this building.

When late that night Ortega was granted entry to the inner rooms, he was surprised at the difference. There were three living rooms in a row and a corridor bordered by bedrooms, where I lived among others, and things were very nice for us. Fifteen of us shared a well-equipped kitchen and two smaller bathrooms. Even if we were not meticulous, we kept our things in order. The octopus was careful not to soil the wall-to-wall carpets, made sure the oil paintings on the walls stayed free of burn marks, and ordered that we drink our liquor out of glasses. For Callemaro the image of success was important, and he associated it with a certain degree of manners and cleanliness.

Fox Antonio Ortega was led into the end living room, where Callemaro as usual was enthroned in his black leather armchair. I do not think the fox had any expectations, but like everyone who met Octopus for the first time, he must have wondered why the gangster was dressed in a tuxedo, why he wore all those clumsy—if glittering—ruby rings, and why he had a white silk scarf around his head. The answer was vanity. Octopus's most prominent attribute and most powerful motivating force was vanity. It had taken him all the way up the radio tower, and it would take him farther than that.

Around the boss on two leather couches sat, and stood, his closest stuffed animals: a tiger, an elephant, a toad, and a somewhat smaller koala. They were competing to see who could look the meanest, and it was impossible to name a winner. I was standing right behind Octopus's armchair. I nodded carefully to Ortega as he was led up to the gang leader, but we had agreed to pretend not to know each other. Amidst all the animals coming and going, I was the one who had wormed his way into the Octopus's inner room; for the moment I did not want to take more risks.

Ortega still had his big, ugly, foul-smelling coat on; the cap was pulled low down on his forehead so that no one could see his sparklingly beautiful eyes; and a dog who I only knew superficially led him forward. Fox stopped at a respectful distance, bowed shortly, cleared his throat and said, "Octopus Callemaro, I am a simple animal, and I come to you with a simple question."

"That's what they all say," Octopus rumbled, whereupon his crew laughed.

"In order to get the female my heart has chosen," the fox continued with no concern for the laughter, "Dragon Aguado Molina has decided that I must give him one of your arms."

It became dead silent in the room. No one moved, no one dared breathe. Had they heard correctly? Who was this idiot? Mentioning Molina's name here? Asking for one of Octopus's arms? There were furtive glances at the windows, because everyone was certain that the pitiful figure in the overly large coat would soon take that route back to the ground. I didn't dare breathe.

Callemaro had turned pale at first, but now his blackness returned, blacker than before.

"This female you're talking about, is it Dragon Aguado Molina's daughter?"

"That's right," Fox answered.

"Has he promised you his daughter?"

"In exchange for one of your arms," Fox confirmed.

Callemaro burst into loud laughter. It reminded Fox of Molina's hilarity a few days earlier. And just as the Dragon's henchman had chimed in with Dragon's laugh, Octopus's crew now joined in with Octopus's hoots. The stuffed animals on the black sofas laughed louder and meaner than those who were standing around the fox on the floor.

When the laughter subsided, Octopus began to speak.

"I see, it's the cursed Aguado Molina who sent you." Octopus chuckled. "We'll see what we can think of to answer him!"

And again salvos of laughter were heard in the room.

MY STORY

My whole body was shaking. I needed a drink, a pick-me-up—whether it was a lukewarm beer or vodka didn't matter. I was in a cold sweat under my heavy coat and the nausea was taking an elevator ride up and down my throat. I hadn't washed in more than a week, and even I could smell how I stank. The headache was pounding in my temples, it drowned out my thoughts, and every time a car engine accelerated nearby it was as if someone was pushing my skull into a pepper mill.

We were on the square at linen yellow Piazza di Bormio. Commerce was in full swing, in the stands the sellers were shouting out offers to outdo one another: bananas for a five-spot. Sunglasses for ten. Fried pineapples for fifteen bucks. Every time someone shouted I felt my forehead. Hurried stuffed animals passed us at a trot in all directions, and I wanted nothing more than to go lie down. First a pick-me-up, then lie down.

There were four of us, and at this time we had been together for several months. Days and nights followed each other, but our little group remained intact. Our leader was named Riccardo Spider, and he was the one who ordered us to the piazza. I didn't know then that Riccardo was working for Octopus Callemaro; I didn't even know who Callemaro was.

"Vole," said Riccardo. "I need a smoke."

I struggled to force back the vomit, and with the back of my paw I tried to dry the sweat from my forehead but was shaking so severely it must have looked like some kind of choreography.

"I don't have any," I said.

"Find some," said Riccardo.

With a gesture he indicated the asphalt on the square.

I looked at him perplexed, and there was a smile on his lips. He meant that I should crawl around on the square on all fours and hunt for butts. I knew just what he was up to. To maintain his absolute power, he was sometimes forced to degrade us so the hierarchy would not be disturbed. As we stood there on Piazza di Bormio we had been going for over twenty-four hours and had made two failed attempts to break into apartments; sold hash to teenagers who would be disappointed when they found out it was only resin; and, just that morning, had left a bar whose location I couldn't recall without paying the bill—but I do remember we drank up a couple of bottles of vodka before we split. I didn't have the energy to question Riccardo, and I didn't have the strength to argue. I got down on my knees and crawled slowly off toward a flower stand. After a minute or two I had forgotten why I was crawling around on the filthy square. The effort meant I wasn't able to hold back any longer, and I threw up behind a bucket of tulips. I got to my knees and wiped my mouth off with the sleeve of the coat, and at that moment I met his gaze.

My dad, Harry S. Bulldog, was standing six feet before me. Under his arm he held a package of gift-wrapped flowers that he must have just bought, and he stared. We had not seen each other for almost a year. I tried to say something, tried to explain why I was there on my knees, with vomit on my coat and my body shaking, but I could not make a sound. And before I could make another attempt, Dad's gaze glided past me and he went on.

That evening we fell asleep as we usually did in a garbage room somewhere in Sors. It was always possible to find unlocked trash rooms, and as long as you didn't stay two nights in a row there was seldom anyone who complained. You could sleep outdoors, and sometimes we did, but there were lots of rabble prowling around the streets at night, and you were always afraid of waking up without clothes and possessions. The trash rooms were safer, and we could lock ourselves in.

When my friends—even if I hesitate to call them "friends"—fell asleep and were snoring in their respective corners in the stinking, windowless room, I was lying there wide awake, staring into the darkness. The expression on my dad's face, the pain in his eyes, left me no peace. Every time I closed my eyes I was looking right into his eyes, and I saw disappointment. I imagined that I even saw his attempt to come up with an excuse, to smooth things over. Most agonizing was seeing how he forced himself to look away, to leave, because I knew he had done it for my sake. I knew that in his whole body he wanted to sink down on the square and embrace me and save me from a life that was unworthy and wasted. But he knew it wasn't possible, and for my sake he forced himself to pretend as if he hadn't seen, as if he didn't see.

I lay there the whole night, and the night after that and again the following night, staring into the darkness. Only when I drank myself blind drunk could I relax and fall asleep.

My dad lost his beloved peacock—and I lost my adored mom—when I was four. The notorious Chauffeurs, the ones who pick up stuffed animals who are worn out and used up and end their lives in Mollisan Town, will always strike me as capricious and merciless. Why did they take my mother when she was in her prime and had just gotten her longed-for son? No one can explain it, and I learned early on that life is cruel.

Dad became a single parent, and I assume that in the eyes of the world around him he was an improbable one. Six days a week he had breakfast down at the boxing club Fresco, which was at the far end of the east strip of mold green Rue d'Uzès. On Wednesdays he stayed away, because that day the club's youth sparred against a zebra named Carlos early in the morning. Carlos was one of the city's most promising, a featherweight boxer with a lightning-fast right hook. A few years earlier he and Dad had ended up in a conflict that neither of them could sort out, so Dad avoided Carlos.

When I was little, Dad had not boxed professionally for several decades, but he was far from the only veteran who continued to hang around the club even though he'd hung up his gloves. The familiar odors of fear, sweat, arrogance, and leather; and the mute, confident mutual understanding between the boxers were his survival strategy and a way to chase away the incomprehensible challenges of existence.

He left me at day care when the sky turned dark, and then took the bus two stops to Fresco, where he always sat at one of the small tables by the entrance. He always had before him a glass of orange juice, a hard cheese sandwich on a chipped plate, and a cup advertising car tires—that were no longer manufactured—of the steaming strong, bitter coffee that Dad could not live without. He took a bite of the sandwich and read the sports pages in the *Daily News*. At regular intervals he snorted out loud at the journalist's stupidity. He read the sports pages every day, so he knew that the whole lot of them were idiots.

At about the time the Morning Rain ceased Dad folded up the newspaper, got up from the table, and nodded to the crook-nosed sloth Charlie in reception. South Sors General Grammar School, where my dad, the fit and healthy bulldog, worked as a physical education instructor, was no more than five minutes from Fresco, and the first class started fifteen minutes after the rain. But he was in no hurry. No preparations were required before the lesson; he had already been working a long time when I was in day care.

The rector of the school took Harry S. Bulldog's situation into account. For that reason Dad could always pick me up at day care at the same time as the other cubs were picked up. We shopped for groceries on the way home, and we prepared meals together. Dad was not a painstaking or pretentious cook. He prepared staples, and it was our togetherness that was important, not the spices. This continued until I was fifteen. Preparing the food and then eating across from each other at the kitchen table, where there were two chairs, was something I thought all families did. We missed Mom, but while I soon made the loss into a part of my personality, it remained painful for Dad. He talked about her often, and thanks to him she was still part of my growing up.

The stuffed animals in and around Fresco became my family. Dad was quick to take an interest in young boxers, and when he accompanied them to other parts of the city for important matches in the evening, Charlie, the sloth, always took care of me. It was a quarter hour's quick walk to the boxing club from home. When I was eight or nine we went there a few evenings a week, and we always hung out there on the weekends. We seldom had any real reason to be there. It was more that we passed by, had a cup of coffee, chatted a little. Dad might help someone with technique or tactics, and then we went home again. For me it was as routine as the hours I spent at school.

If Dad's nearness and openness when I was really little had created a relationship between us that was closer than for most fathers and sons, the respect that everyone showed him at Fresco contributed to my growing admiration. A father doesn't need to do much to become his cub's idol, and in my case it was enough that a couple of times he showed what he could do with the punching bag or the jump rope. Dad himself was the first to admit that his talent had not extended very far in the ring, but when he said that everyone at the club objected, and soon even I believed that he really could have gone much further.

"Your dad," Charlie sometimes said, "is the nicest stuffed animal that has ever been produced."

And so he was, I could do nothing but agree. At school there were many who were afraid of him; he could be a strict teacher. But that he was the most considerate and loving dad you could imagine, I had always known.

When I was twelve I started training at Fresco. I'd wanted to start earlier, but Dad advised me to wait. He let me roam around in the big, light gym, jump rope if I wanted, or punch one of the sandbags until I was worn out; there were always so many active stuffed animals in there that no one minded. But he never encouraged me. It was too soon. It had to do with coordination and maturity, he would say. Boxing is like chess. If you're too little you should only play around, not play for real.

But when I started sixth grade he thought it might be time, and he set up a cautious training program. It included everything: diet and endurance, strength and flexibility; but above all it was arranged so I would not get tired. How many cubs had he seen come down to the club and burn their powder in one season? But my enthusiasm knew no bounds. To me being able to start boxing was a sign that I was big; I was no longer a little cub. It had never been about whether I would start or not, it had only been a question of when.

On Sundays Fresco ran a beginners' group for cubs who had turned thirteen, and after having struggled alone with

Dad for a whole year it was amazing to start training with those my own age. In my class in school no one boxed, and even if Dad was always around I realized, when I met Adam Llama in the Sunday group, that I really had been missing someone. For Adam boxing was only one activity of many. He played badminton on Saturdays and went to rhythmics on Wednesdays, because his mom forced him. For me there was suddenly someone to compare myself with, someone to complain with, and training became more fun.

Adam was strong, and that served as a spur. If we were doing pushups he managed fifty when I could do forty, he was always a couple of steps ahead of me when we did interval training, and I got tangled in the jump rope when he could always keep going a few more minutes. Dad seldom got involved when I trained with Adam; he realized that it was a different kind of training, and that the camaraderie was just as important as the training results. He liked my new friend, and often spoke of him in appreciative terms.

"Adam has tremendous explosiveness in his right arm," Dad might say, and somehow I felt proud then.

When we turned fourteen we got to go up in the ring and start boxing for real. We had various sorts of protection on, and if someone got angry and blew up, training was immediately stopped. It was hard to explain. The idea of the sport was to hit each other, and at the club everyone bragged about their knockouts, but at the same time they were afraid of conflict and extremely careful about the cubs and future prospects. I would go up with Adam because we knew each other so well. Usually I could only do one or two rounds before I was through. Dad said that was due to my footwork. I danced in the ring, while Adam was so agile he didn't need to jump around as much.

I never thought about what I am sure Dad had already seen. I was living in a dream world, absorbed by my training and my friendship with Adam. I was doing well in school, I was happy at Fresco, but the bubble burst one month after my fifteenth birthday when Adam unexpectedly reported that he was quitting boxing. It was his badminton coach who forced him to choose. He was promising in both sports, but to advance to the elite level he had to focus. And then, under his mom's influence, I contended, he chose the racket and shuttlecock.

I was devastated of course, and in Adam's absence I finally realized what everyone, including my father, already knew: I had fallen far behind the others in my age group; I was a mediocre athlete.

Just as in my young years I had been Dad's biggest supporter, he now proved to be mine. The insight about my limitations came as a shock, and I, who to this point had been spared the anxiety of puberty, had my first existential crisis. I lost the desire to train, I was truant from school, and I closed myself in and didn't help with cooking. It sounds a little ridiculous, but keep in mind that Dad and I had cooked together basically my whole life.

Dad left me alone. Afterward he said he understood that it was a grief process, and that each and every one of us has to do that sort of thing our own way. When I opened the door and came out of my room a week later, he was as wise as you might expect. He said that training was not about results, not at my age, it was about laying a foundation for the future. That boxing was not a sport but a way of life. At Fresco we had our family, and a healthy life had nothing to do with how many squats you could do.

Slowly he lured me back to the gym. Once again it was him and me, now that Adam was out of the picture. But I had changed forever and couldn't turn back time. From having listened to Dad, I now paid attention to myself in relation to all the others. And the comparison was not flattering. When I practiced footwork, stumbled, and lost my focus, Dad smiled in a way I had always perceived as encouraging. Now I saw that there was something else in his smile. When I practiced with the punching bag and wasn't able to hold my arms up after a couple of minutes, I felt something different in the consoling paw he placed on my back.

Disappointment.

"You're still developing, Gary," he might say when we had dinner together. "No one knows what your reflexes, your muscles, your coordination are going to look like in a few years. The important thing is not to be the best. The important thing is to exercise in a way that means you feel well."

I looked down at my plate. Why hadn't I heard the sorrow in his voice before?

During all of ninth grade I got up an hour earlier than I had to and did strength training. Stomach, back, and shoulders. I still hoped I could live up to his expectations. I would have done anything to avoid seeing the sorrow in his eyes when again and again I ran too slow, hit too slackly, or didn't move as fast as he hoped. I also started concealing my other interests from him, because I realized he would worry that they would encroach on training. I hid books under the bed, because even if he had nothing against me reading, he would have preferred seeing me improve my acceleration or explosiveness. He never said that, of course. He was extremely careful not to make demands on me. He repeated, in various ways and with many examples, that intent, not performance, was the important thing. And the better Dad concealed his disappointment, the more painful it became to see.

About the time I resumed training after Adam stopped boxing, there were four parallel fifth-grade classes at South Sors General Grammar School where my father taught, and during gym classes they were put together, two and two. But the males were not separated from the females. Now and then a parent protested the mixed classes, but the school resisted making any changes.

In Harry S. Bulldog's class almost fifty ten- and eleven-year-old stuffed animals ran into the gym and lined up in their places. Dad believed in discipline at school.

"Good morning, pupils!" Dad shouted.

"Good morning, Schoolmaster," the cubs responded.

With energy and enthusiasm Harry S. Bulldog then divided the pupils into four teams, and they made their way out to the schoolyard.

South Sors General Grammar School was the largest building along the street, the largest building in the area, and on the schoolyard there was a small patch of woods for the cubs to play in at recess. Across from the school some craftsmen had opened shops in recent years, and shoemakers, seamstresses, bakers, and cabinetmakers ensured that animals came and went on the sidewalks.

Dad's ambition was to divide his time evenly among the four teams, but when Rector Bergdorff showed up at the sprinting track, class was almost half over and Dad had only helped with the long-jump group.

The rector waved discreetly, and Dad excused himself and left the jumping group. The two adults placed themselves under an oak by the side of the cricket field, out of earshot but within view of everything going on in the yard.

"I'm sorry to disturb you like this, Harry, but I have promised to answer . . . a certain animal . . . before lunch. This is about the selection for the City Athletic Championship."

"Yes?"

Harry S. Bulldog knew exactly what this was about. He understood it as he turned in the lists of who would compete for South Sors General Grammar School last week. He had made his selections. This year he wanted to win.

"If I understand this correctly," the rector continued cautiously, "we are sending no more than ten cubs this year?"

"May be right," Bulldog said, shrugging his shoulders.

"And last year there were eighteen from our school?"

"May be right."

"And Leonard Louse is not one of the ten we're sending?"

"No, he's not."

"While Fox Antonio Ortega is registered in all events?"

Harry S. Bulldog again shrugged his shoulders.

"You realize, Harry," said Rector Bergdorff, "I've been on the phone all morning with Louse's father. He maintains that it's not just him, there are a number of parents who think this is outrageous. Fox Antonio Ortega is not . . . one of the school's stronger pupils. And his family is . . . well, I'll make no judgments on the cub's family, but many are upset that we are giving someone special treatment who . . . that is, why don't we give more cubs the chance to distinguish themselves during the championships?"

"Excuse me," said Harry S. Bulldog, "but you said 'distinguish themselves'?"

"Please, Bulldog, this is about eleven-year-olds," said Bergdorff. "They're in the fifth grade. There is time for them to win and lose many times before they leave school. Shouldn't we—"

"Look," Dad interrupted, pointing. "Look at him."

At the long-jump pit Fox Antonio Ortega had just started his run-up, and now he quickly picked up speed. Harry S. Bulldog could not keep from smiling. Never in his professional life, neither as a boxer nor as a gym teacher, had he seen anything like it. Fox Antonio Ortega was a physical miracle. It was not only the promise of great deeds in the way he moved, there was something so powerfully well-balanced about the fox's whole appearance that whatever sport he chose, he was meant to write sports history.

Fox Antonio Ortega was my absolute opposite.

Dad pointed, and Rector Bergdorff could see for himself. Fox's running gait was magnificent, aggressive but butterfly light at the same time. Even at the age of eleven he was a polished diamond. His sense of timing was complete; raw strength in combination with a focused desire to train would force every obstacle out of the way to medals and millions.

Harry S. Bulldog felt no envy on his own behalf; it was impossible to envy perfection, because it was unachievable. But unconsciously he must have compared the fox with me; it was unavoidable because I had been running around the same schoolyard a few years earlier. The gym teacher's son, who trained and trained but still wasn't able to achieve any results. Every time I stumbled, every time my energy gave out at the finish, every time the bar quivered and fell, it must have been like a knife that cut a little piece out of Dad's heart. He could not have helped feeling that way, nor could I.

Fox Antonio Ortega reached the plank and took off. He traveled through the air, and even from their spot under the oak they could see that the jump was a long one. Very long.

"If he were only twice as good as the others in any event," Dad explained, "I could make an exception. Then I would have set him to the side. But he is much better than that."

Bergdorff watched Fox get up in the long-jump pit and brush off the sand. The rector was obviously moved by what he saw.

"I see," he said. "Do as you wish. But make sure that Leonard Louse is one of the ten."

And with these words he left the gym teacher to his class.

Fox Antonio Ortega knew the jump was good, but also that he had jumped better. For that reason he didn't turn around to see where he had landed. No one else bothered either.

When he started school it had been different. Then his classmates were fascinated by what he could do. They begged and pleaded to see him hit a ball over the school roof; they kept time when he ran around the block and dragged him over to the ignorant cubs at Noah Whale Elementary to let him challenge them. Fox Antonio Ortega was their trophy.

But the grade school pupils became middle school pupils, and their interest flagged. When his classmates returned after summer vacation to the fourth grade, they were in search of new sensations. After the severe disappointment Fox experienced during the first few weeks, a deep satisfaction followed. In reality he was happier when he didn't have to be at the center, and he gladly assumed his more anonymous role in the social structure of the school class. Which did not mean, however, that his physical achievements were less astounding.

Now Fox Antonio Ortega walked back along the run-up and placed himself last in line to attempt another jump. The cubs who stood waiting were too little to notice how their classmate moved; how he walked, with his long, springy steps, his back straight and arms pleasingly swinging along his body. They did not see how the fox's sharp red fur glistened in the sun, as if it were gilded, and they did not see that his ears proudly stood up from his head, as if the wind were filling a pair of sails. For the coming years, and until Antonio Ortega finished high school, he continued to surprise Harry S. Bulldog, and remained a phenomenon.

The day Dad introduced me to Nick Rhinoceros, Charlie put up the posters in the reception area. He papered the whole wall toward the dressing rooms, and even put a few up outside the entry. The district boxing championship in Sors was only held every three years, for financial reasons, which made the competition even more prestigious. All the clubs in the district shared in hosting, and Fresco's logo was on the poster, too. That made us proud.

I had boxed a couple of matches "for real," but lost both, and Dad and I had jointly decided not to compete again for the time being, not until I was ready. When I saw the poster for the district championship and noticed the date, I realized it had to be then or never. There were fourteen months until the competition, and by then I would turn eighteen. All excuses that I wasn't fully developed so far were based on my being too young. After my eighteenth birthday it was no longer an argument.

"Nick, this is my son, Gary," Dad introduced me.

"Gary. Nice to meet you. I think I can help you," said Rhinoceros.

"That would be fantaththtic," I answered.

"Fantaththtic?" Rhinoceros wondered.

"He lisps a little," said Dad. "After a while you won't notice it."

"We're here to boxth, after all," I said.

"Boxth?" Rhinoceros wondered.

Nick Rhinoceros had been city welterweight champion in Mollisan Town. Dad had worked with Rhinoceros, and now the successful champion decided to repay the help.

Nick Rhinoceros was as stylistically pure as a boxer as he was miserable as an instructor. It took a few months for both of us to accept this. But when the rhinoceros finally stopped talking, and instead of listening I could concentrate on seeing what he did, how he moved, positioned himself, and hit, the training sessions went much better. Nick had a lot to teach, and he taught it to me in the ring.

Dad was fired up. He stood alongside, taking notes. Every movement, feint, and hit was noted, and then we went through the notes together in the evening. To say I regained my former self-confidence is not true, but our sessions went so well that I once again found delight in training.

I was done with school—no one I knew continued studying past high school. So Dad and I went to Fresco in the mornings. Charlie was at the reception desk with a greeting so disinterested you knew you had come home. Changing in the worn-out dressing room, locking the locker even though it wasn't necessary because everyone knew everyone at the club, and stepping out into the big workout room where the light flooded in through the broad windows in the day and where all kinds of animals and weight classes were training at the same time, in different corners and at different stations, conveyed a sense of security that is impossible to explain to anyone who has not experienced it himself. Slowly I again became one in the crowd, even if I was the only one training with a real champion. At first Nick had to sign autographs and tell stories from his glory days, but as the months passed, everyone got used to him and incorporated him into the community.

The reality that Dad primarily was training me for the district championship was not something we talked about, it was understood. When Nick showed up there was more than a year before the first match, and it would have been ridiculous to start talking tactics or speculate about opponents so soon. But time passed quickly, and however relaxed Dad tried to appear, I saw the expectations growing in his gestures and comments. In tempo with his restrained excitement, the pressure on me increased. I will not pretend that his enthusiasm was not contagious. I still carried the insight about my own mediocrity, but I was training with a master and I had a father who had always been able to separate the wheat from the chaff, and Dad said I was getting good. That did not leave me unaffected.

One evening when only a month or so remained until the match drawing and I had done a late training session, I remained sitting in the drying cabinet in the dressing room long after the cabinet had turned off. I sat in the darkness absorbed in my own thoughts. It was warm and pleasant and I don't think I was brooding about anything in particular when I was startled by a pair of familiar voices. It was Dad and Nick Rhinoceros who had entered the dressing room; they were talking loudly and I was just about to stand up and get out when something held me back. It was the sort of thing you can speculate about for a long time afterward, but presumably it was just their raised voices that made me hesitate.

"Frankly speaking, Harry, I don't give a damn," I heard Rhinoceros say through the closed drying cabinet door.

He sounded grumpy. He was no sunbeam normally; his tone was most often curt and neutral, but now he sounded irritated.

"You know you can trust me," Dad answered.

"I don't trust anyone," said Rhinoceros.

"I haven't been late a single time."

Rhinoceros did not comment on this, which is why I assumed that he agreed but didn't bother to acknowledge the point. I could hear how he sat down heavily on a wooden bench along the wall, and I assumed that Dad placed himself in front of him and started untying his gloves.

"I've had a little problem with the bank," said Dad.

Rhinoceros did not answer. I froze inside the drying cabinet. Not a single time during my growing up had I heard Dad talk about a bank. There had always been money at home, because Dad always had a steady job and no major expenses.

"I mortgaged the apartment, did I tell you that?" Dad continued. "And I sold Mama's rings. It was harder to get rid of the painting. I thought it was worth lots. But what do I know about art?"

Rhinoceros grunted. I knew exactly what painting Dad was talking about. It was a painting he'd inherited from Grandfather, which had hung over his bed all these years. I was seldom in Dad's bedroom, and so I had assumed it was still hanging there. It was our most valuable possession, Dad always said.

"Listen," said Rhinoceros when with a moan he pulled off his right glove. "I don't give a damn what you're up to. I'm not your mother. You give me the cash tomorrow, and I'll come back and train with the cub next week. No cash, no sparring. At least not with me."

"You'll get the money. That's not what I meant. It's just that . . . it's been a little tough . . ."

I remained sitting in the drying cabinet until I was certain they both had left Fresco, and I almost scared the life out of Charlie when I passed him at the desk; by then it was late in the evening, and he had been certain the gym was empty.

To say that I was shocked is an understatement. I was beside myself. I ought to have realized that Nick Rhinoceros was getting paid to train me, and in that case I blamed my own inexperience. But that Dad had pawned everything he owned was completely contrary to his whole character and all he stood for. I could only sense the moral sacrifice that was behind this. Even worse was that he had kept it secret. It gave me no peace, even if it took a week or two before I added this insight to the growing performance anxiety I felt prior to the district championship.

I was seeded against Conny Rooster in the first match. I didn't see the lists myself; it was Charlie who phoned and told me because he had posted them. I remember I was standing at home in the hall, staring at the wall.

It was over.

Until that moment I had tried to cheer myself up. I told myself that my combinations were instinctive at this point, and you couldn't complain about my footwork. What I lacked in weight and distinctiveness, maybe I could offset with my relative quickness? Winning one or two matches was not impossible. That's how I had been thinking, and the least I owed Dad after his sacrifices was a positive attitude. But Conny Rooster? I could have pretended but I wasn't an idiot. My championship ended even before it began.

I hung up and went back to my room and lay down on the

bed. That was where Dad found me later that afternoon. He instantly understood why I was lying there. He sat on the edge of the bed and placed his paw on my back.

"You got a tough draw, Gary," he said. "But it happens to everyone sometime."

"It'th over now."

"It's not at all."

"Roothter ith too good for me. He made it to the top five in the last championthhip. And he'th better now."

"No match is decided in advance," said Dad.

"Yeth," I said. "This one."

There were three weeks left, and even if the draw meant that I could give up on this championship, I continued training. I went out and ran every morning as the fog drew in over the city, and was at Fresco before the Morning Rain. I worked with the punching bag and the sandbag in the morning and sparred with Rhinoceros a few hours after lunch. I ended with strength training before I went home and made dinner with Dad.

"It'th not going to work," I said. "I'll be happy if I'm thtill thtanding after the third round."

"What counts is trying," Dad answered.

"Bullthit," I said. "What counth is winning."

"Not if you ask me," he answered.

I chopped a cucumber in silence. A vacuum was growing in my chest, and I still did not understand it, but with each day it got worse and worse. When I ran, I would stumble for no reason, and when I did strength training, my heart started racing. Never before had I had problems with my heart.

The following day, as I was sparring with Rhinoceros, I got so dizzy I was forced to sit down in the ring. Dad interrupted and took me to the dressing room, where he sat me on a bench and got me to hold my head between my knees.

"Competition nerves," he said. "I know how it feels. I was the same way. There's no danger. It's only a matter of not pressuring yourself. You're working too hard. Your body can't take it. Take the rest of the day and do something else. Don't think about boxing."

"But what if I can't do better, Dad?"

"Of course you can," he answered. "You and I both know that."

"I'll never be able to handle Roothter."

"You won't know that until you've tried."

That made me angry. I was suddenly tired of his clichés, of his tired excuses. He knew just as well as I did that it was pointless. I would never be the boxer he had dreamed of. And whose dream was it anyway? I got up. I was eighteen, and for the first time in my life I felt rebellion awakening.

"But I have tried, Dad! Thince I was twelve!"

"It's too much right now, Gary. I understand that."

But he did not understand at all. Why didn't he say the way it was? I screamed at him. I demanded that he look me in the eyes and admit that I had failed. I wanted to hear him say that all the expectations he'd had came to naught. But he didn't say anything.

I left him in the dressing room, and ran from Fresco. It was an eighteen-year-deep dam that broke, and it would prove to be hard to repair. Dad came home with food in the evening and thought we would prepare it together. But even then I realized that wrath was easier to give in to than forgiveness. I was still furious, and I let him know it. I ran in and out of the kitchen and screamed and shouted.

"You're making too big a deal out of this, Gary," he said.

"Too big a deal?" I screamed. "You pawned the whole apartment! You thold Grandpa'th painting!"

That hit home. Dad fell silent and stared at me. He was standing with a spatula in one paw and a saltshaker in the other.

"Yeth, I know!" I screamed in triumph.

"I only wanted to . . ." he said quietly, "give us every opportunity."

"*Uth?*" I exploded.

Then I screamed for almost a quarter of an hour without catching my breath. There were new and old injustices that were just as ridiculous as they were trivial. My dad had never done me harm, and I blush when I think about all I spewed out of myself. At last I ran into my room and closed the door. Not a single time that evening did Dad raise his voice or try to defend himself against all the invented accusations.

I never went to the tournament. The decision crowned my late, pathetic teenage revolt. I had calculated that this would hurt him the most. I stayed away from my first, and only, lottery-drawn match in the district boxing championship in Sors. I sat at a snack bar a few blocks away and felt the anger bubbling in my chest. I was feeling endlessly sorry for myself, I hated Dad for his dishonesty, and for the way he had manipulated me. To think that I hadn't seen it earlier! He used me to live out his own teenage dream. If he had seen me for who I really was, I reasoned, he would never have signed me up for the district championship. I had no talent at boxing but he refused to accept that. No, it would have to be this way. Dad stood waiting at Fresco in my ring corner, and the tough Conny Rooster won his match, not on a KO but on a WO, a Walk Over.

When I came home in the evening I expected a scolding. That was the least I deserved. But Dad was waiting in the kitchen with my favorite dish on the table, and even before I had hung up my jacket he said that he understood, that I had done the right thing. You should never go into the ring if it doesn't feel right. Boxing was not a sport you could fake, he said.

"I understand you, Gary, and I feel like a bad father for having driven you too hard. I hope you can forgive me."

I should forgive him? There he stood, with an apron over his belly, financially ruined after having paid Nick Rhinoceros to match his good-for-nothing son, who didn't even have spine enough to show up at his only match, even though I knew what it meant to him. And he was asking *me* for forgiveness?

It was suffocating. It was humiliating beyond the bounds of reasonableness. I could not handle the shame that overwhelmed me, and quickly I pulled on my jacket again and ran from home. The hatred I felt was so intense, so steely, that I could have cut apart any reality whatsoever with it. I had only myself to blame, and that made it even worse. I decided never to return home again, and then my life fell apart. I think of it as being like dominos that fell against each other, impossible to stop—and I'm still living in their rumbling echo.

> *Domino 1: I run away from home.*
> *Domino 2: I move in with Charlie.*
> *Domino 3: I get a job as a dishwasher at Zeke's, which turns my day upside down.*
> *Domino 4: I discover the nightlife that introduced me to stuffed animals who Dad would have warned me about.*
> *Domino 5: I move out from Charlie, who only nags about Dad, and move in with a horse who deals.*
> *Domino 6: I drink too much.*
> *Domino 7: To get money for liquor and to get away from the horse, who has fallen in love with me, I start hanging out with Riccardo and the others.*
> *Domino 8: I see Dad at Piazza di Bormio.*

I have described the nights in the darkness in the trash rooms, when I lay awake hour after hour without settling down. At last I realized how closely related hatred and love could be. Unfortunately it was too late.

When early one morning I left my sleeping companions and went home to Dad on mold green Rue d'Uzès, I was filled with my own fantasies about how we would fall into each other's arms, crying and laughing in turn. I could see it so clearly. I was sure that he would accept the apologies. He was perhaps the best stuffed animal who ever existed in Sors.

When I came home—it was late in the afternoon—the apartment was empty and quiet. I did not see the dust bunnies on the floor in the kitchen. I ran straight to Fresco, because I assumed Dad was there, and Charlie stared at me as if I were a ghost. I greeted him happily. It was as if the air in the reception area stopped moving. The stuffed animals stiffened and waited.

Charlie told me.

Two days earlier the Chauffeurs had unexpectedly come and fetched my dad, Harry S. Bulldog, in the middle of the day as he stood on the cricket field instructing his pupils at the school. Dad had not even turned sixty-five, and yet the red pickup came and took him, the way they make old and torn animals make way for new and young ones.

I loved my father. I was the greatest disappointment of his life. But I was also the greatest love of his life. He never had an opportunity to tell me that. And I never had an opportunity to say that he didn't need to say it; I knew it anyway.

THE ARM, *CONTINUED*

If I didn't want to see Fox Antonio Ortega burn up, be
thrown out the window, or cut into pieces and sent back to
Dragon Aguado Molina in a couple of crumpled envelopes, it
was time for me to intervene. I took a few rapid steps forward
to the gangster boss, bowed, and whispered in his ear.

"I know who he ith. The fathteth runner I've theen on the
track. Out of hith mind, but fatht. Pleath, let me have him.
Jutht a week? Pleath, pleath?"

Octopus Callemaro slowly twisted his head and looked me
in the eyes.

"Fast, you say?"

"The fathteth I've theen," I affirmed.

This made Octopus smile. Perhaps because he was amused
by my pronunciation of "fast," or else because he liked the
idea of letting Dragon's emissary work for us.

"Gary Vole thinks he can convert you," Octopus said to
Ortega. "What kind of animal are you under all those clothes?"

"My name is Fox Antonio Ortega," the fox replied.

"Vole thinks he can use you, Fox." Callemaro nodded.

"Vole, you have a few days. At the same time, the rest of us can think of other possibilities for our failed suitor."

Once again loud laughter came from the stuffed animals standing and sitting around the octopus, and I nudged the fox hard so that he understood he should leave while there was still time.

"You're theriouth?" I asked.

I had shoved Ortega to the outer rooms, and now we were sitting on the floor close together in front of one of the windows facing west. We spoke quietly, so that no one could hear. Mollisan Town was sparkling and glistening below us; the city seemed to continue all the way to the horizon. It was a view before which you could not tell a lie.

"Beatrice is the most beautiful stuffed animal I've ever seen," Fox answered, looking me deep in the eyes. "I must have her. Can you help me?"

"You're crazy," I said. "Did you think that Octoputh would give you an arm? Jutht like that?"

"I don't know what I thought," he admitted. "But if you don't ask, you'll never know."

I shook my head. His naiveté was so overwhelming I didn't know whether I should be furious or teary-eyed.

But I hadn't lied to Octopus, I knew that Ortega could be of use, and the next evening we took him out with us: me, the tuna, and the ape. The plan was not born until later in the week, but perhaps my subconscious was a step ahead? Competing for an invitation to Octopus's innermost room was part of our daily life, something we all strove for, just as obviously as we ate when we were hungry and slept when we were tired.

The tuna and the ape complained, of course. We were used to one another, and it was seldom fortunate to expand a trio to a quartet. At the same time I knew something they didn't.

We specialized in armored-car transports. The vehicles had alarms and guards, but in many places in Sors it was impossible to drive up to the depository. The streets were torn up, the alleys narrow, trash and car bodies were in the way. We attacked when the courier was on his way from the depot back to the vehicle on foot. We had our routine, and it wasn't particularly sophisticated. The tuna got down on the ground somewhere along the path of the guards, as if he were one of the many down-and-out homeless animals, while the ape and I sneaked up from behind. We shoved the guard, who turned toward us, giving the tuna free rein from the other direction. If we were able to overcome the guard, it was the ape's task to grab the loot and run away, as neither the tuna nor I was a runner. Three times out of four we failed, either because the security company used two or more guards on foot, which kept us from attacking, or else because the ape got caught when he tried to get away. Then the only thing to do was to let go of the loot and save yourself. But one out of four attempts was good enough to keep us alive and satisfy Callemaro.

With Fox Antonio Ortega on our team, the odds changed. I will always remember the first time the tuna and ape realized what the fox could do. Violet Calle Coleglada was long and winding, and went over high hills and down below intersecting streets. It was bordered by derelict apartment buildings from the sixties and seventies, with boarded-up windows and caved-in roofs, sitting side by side with stone buildings from the previous turn of the century, where far too many stuffed animals often lived in far too little space. We knew exactly where the ambush should take place, and we took our positions. Everything proceeded as usual; we overpowered the guard and tore the bag away from him.

Then we gave it to Ortega.

At the same moment all four of us—the tuna, the ape, and I, but also the overpowered guard—were transformed into an audience that could do nothing but be impressed and amazed by something we had never seen before. Fox Antonio Ortega's acceleration capacity exceeded our ability to understand.

The ape and tuna stared in bewilderment.

"I'm on his team," the tuna said at last.

I agreed. His was the only team you wanted to be on.

Fox's reputation grew quickly in Octopus's house in the radio tower, and after only a week or two he got to move in and sleep with us in the inner rooms. There was no vacant bed, but the wall-to-wall carpets were more comfortable and cleaner than the best mattresses out there.

By chance Fox chose a place by a window that overlooked South Sors General Grammar School. There he neatly folded up his sleeping blanket during the day, and spread it out over himself at night.

Every evening we stood looking out toward the grammar school we both had attended. I don't know what Fox was thinking, but for me it was a great experience to stand next to him by the window.

The last years I lived at home, Dad would talk for hours about Fox Antonio Ortega, the pupil who would crush all existing school records. I heard the love in Dad's voice, but I think there was also an undercurrent of concealed envy. A longing to have had such a talent himself, or at least see some of it in me.

Fox Antonio Ortega had been Dad's great joy during the last years of his life. If there was a heaven from which Harry S. Bulldog looked down at me, fate had given me a unique opportunity to restore some sort of respect.

After three weeks out on the streets with Fox and the others, I knew how I could help Ortega get his octopus arm. I was no strategist or psychologist, but Callemaro was no complicated personality either. I had already made sure from the start that Fox kept his big, ungainly coat on day and night, because I sensed that his appearance would be our trump card. The Octopus's vanity was legendary: He was obsessed by everything beautiful, and as long as Fox kept his cap pulled down over his face we had a surprise waiting.

And as I suspected, Fox Antonio Ortega was the one Callemaro invited to dinner in the innermost of the inner rooms in the month to come. No one could compare with the successes Ortega had had.

The evening before the dinner with Octopus Callemaro, I went through the plan with Fox Antonio Ortega. At first he thought no plan was needed. When I succeeded in convincing him of the opposite, it made him nervous. He asked over and over again about the slightest details, and I answered with endless patience. Fox Ortega had, as an attentive reader has already noticed, a limited learning capacity, but I was betting on the power of repetition.

During the appetizer and entrée, I instructed, he should simply listen. I knew what was expected, for even I had on a few occasions been given the honor of dining with Octopus. The ebony-colored gangster boss needed an audience, listeners, and he did not stop talking once he got going. The well-known vanity took various expressions, but the need for affirmation was constant and insatiable.

"Then it'th time," I said to Ortega. "Do ath we thaid, and you'll get your arm at latht."

Fox nodded. The most fascinating thing, I think in retrospect, is that he never, not once, questioned why I was helping him. He took my courage and my loyalty for granted, as if his love for Beatrice Cockatoo was everyone's concern.

Fox was shown into the innermost room and sat down to dinner as the Evening Storm picked up. The mood, Ortega thought, was magical—the stillness, the darkness. A table with a white cloth, heavy silverware, and candles whose flames danced dramatically in the ornate candleholders. Outside the window, high up in the black sky, the moon looked like a white, endless hole. Fox Antonio Ortega nervously placed his napkin on his lap. His filthy coat stood out as even filthier in contrast to the white linen. He kept his cap on, per my instructions.

The boss made his entry along with the appetizer. As usual, he had his elegant dinner jacket on and, in honor of the evening, wore a top hat.

"I've heard about you, you joker," Octopus began, occupying the chair so that it completely disappeared under his eight limbs. "You come up here, make fun of my arms, and I thought about killing you on the spot. But it was lucky I refrained. Nobody runs like you, they say. Nobody, except possibly me. I don't know if anyone has told you about when I ran from the giraffes? It must have been fifteen, twenty years ago. This is what happened . . ."

And then he was off.

Fox Antonio Ortega followed my advice and listened attentively to Octopus's bragging while the appetizer was served and taken away, while the entrée was served and taken away, and as the white wine with scallops was replaced by a thicker red wine with the beef filet. Fox did not drink anything, but raised his glass at regular intervals so that Octopus would not harbor suspicions. The gangster boss himself drank without reservation. Dessert was served, vanilla ice cream with warm chocolate sauce, and during one of Octopus's pauses for breath Ortega stood up unexpectedly.

"Excuse me," he said, "but it's extremely warm in here. May I take off my coat?"

Without waiting for an answer, Fox let the large, heavy coat fall to the floor at the same time as he took off the cap. Underneath he had on a white T-shirt and a pair of worn jeans from which his long, bushy tail stuck out. The Octopus fell silent for the first time during dinner. Mute, he stared at the exquisitely stunning fox, who had been hidden so long in his filthy coat. The gold-strewn fur, the eyes of onyx and the shimmering nose, the proud ears and the majestic tail; it was a surprise for which Octopus was unprepared.

"Unbelievable." Callemaro sighed, as he was filled with the envy that was unavoidable in a stuffed animal with the gangster's vanity.

Fox Antonio Ortega remained standing and let himself be observed. Without posing he turned to the left and the right, for it was essential that Octopus got to see him from all angles.

Then Fox sat down, fixing his eyes on Octopus.

"I have a proposal," he said. "I have the most beautiful tail in Mollisan Town. I'm not saying that out of vanity, it's a fact. I am prepared to exchange it for one of your arms."

Octopus Callemaro thought he had heard wrong.

"I have a splitter with me," Ortega continued, holding out a small case with sewing notions I had given him. "I have needle and thread. You have eight arms. Keep seven of them and get the most beautiful tail that has ever been produced."

"You're serious?"

"But only for this evening. Tomorrow I will have changed my mind," said Ortega, exactly as I had coached.

He stood up again and let his gorgeous tail sway back and forth. Octopus was bewildered. The wine he'd drunk, the shock of the fox's beauty, and now this crazy proposal.

"You mean you'll sacrifice your tail?"

"For love. But it's now or never."

An ordinary stuffed animal would never have said yes. An ordinary stuffed animal would have laughed and rejected Fox's proposal as idiotic. We were manufactured in a certain way for a certain reason. Simply because it was possible to tear up a seam and sew something else on was no reason to do it. But the fox's swaying, sparkling red, bushy tail was far too enticing for the black octopus.

"You get one chance," said Octopus Callemaro. "One chance. But if I don't like it, I take back the arm. And keep the tail."

Ortega nodded but did not answer.

I had been particularly clear about that: In no way could Callemaro perceive that Fox had won and gotten his way. Everything had to happen on Octopus's terms.

Now the fairly intoxicated stuffed animal instructed the fox in how he should proceed. Octopus was not cowardly, but tearing up a seam could hurt if the work was performed by someone who didn't know what he was doing. As long as you didn't get at the fabric but only the threads there was no danger, and Ortega reassured the gangster that he had done this sort of thing before.

"You can stay sitting on the chair," said Fox. "It will only take a moment."

"But sewing on . . ."

"You won't feel it. You have my word of honor," Ortega assured.

Fox bent down and quickly put on the coat he had thrown on the floor, then he rounded the dining room table and dove down on the floor behind Callemaro's back.

Ortega began ripping, and Octopus sighed; he felt the stitches being removed, but could not say that it hurt. Soon it was over. Callemaro had seven arms; the eighth one was in Fox's coat pocket.

"That was unpleasant," said Octopus. "I wonder if this was a good idea."

"It's going to feel better," Ortega promised.

"If it hurts when you sew your tail on we no longer have an agreement," Callemaro declared. "If it hurts I want no part of it."

Fox did not reply, but instead continued working in silence for a few minutes, and Octopus was forced to admit that he did not feel any pain; he hardly felt anything at all.

"There now," Fox Antonio Ortega said at last, getting up.

He went around the table again, holding up his coat to show his tailless behind.

"And me? How do I look?" Octopus asked. "I want a mirror!"

"You are very beautiful," Ortega replied.

"I want a mirror!"

Octopus picked up a golden bell that was on the dinner table and rang it. A moment later the waiter came into the room. Octopus ordered a large mirror, and the waiter disappeared for a minute or two, returning with an oblong full-length mirror, which he placed at an angle behind Octopus. Even though the mirror was dirty and the room was in darkness, Octopus could clearly see the fox's beautiful tail fastened between two of his own black arms.

"I don't know . . ." he said, turning to the waiter. "What do you think?"

"I think you're more handthome than ever," I answered, for I was the waiter that evening.

"Is that certain?"

"Thertain? You've lured the tail off of Fox and at the thame time kept theven arms. You're a geniuth, Octoputh!"

This pleased the gangster king, and he toasted with me and with Fox and took the opportunity to have a few more glasses between these toasts. Then he got very tired, which was his habit after these dinners, and fell asleep as usual on his chair with a pleased smile on his lips.

I removed the photograph of Fox's tail that I had fastened to the mirror, and together with Antonio Ortega, who still had his own beautiful tail stuffed into his pants, we slipped out. It was only as we were climbing down the radio tower that Fox happened to think about me.

"But," he said, "he's going to realize you were there and tricked him!"

"Thertainly," I said.

"But," said Fox, "isn't he going to be angry?"

"I have a plan."

THE HEART

Dragon Aguado Molina was counting money. He was in the office he had set up in a room directly above the restaurant kitchen. He loved the aromas from almonds baked in saffron and the garlic-rubbed spareribs as he carried out his administrative tasks. The furnishings were dull and heavy; dark red wallpaper, a brown swivel chair behind the large desk, a yellowish glow from the porcelain shade of the table lamp.

The dragon pretended to loathe bookkeeping. From Tuesday to Saturday he carelessly threw money into the center desk drawer, and on Sunday morning he sighed heavily.

"Now it's time to dirty yourself again," he would say. "You really ought to hire a bookkeeper to take care of this. But then wouldn't you lose half of it?"

Then he would laugh, but was careful to sound suitably resigned and went up the stairs with heavy steps.

If he was not interrupted—and he hated being interrupted—it took him about fifteen minutes to count and recount the amount. He then made a packet of bundles of cash and sent a courier to the bank's deposit slot. Even if the following morning he could see that the account had increased, the aching sense of uncertainty appeared: Would he be able to convince the bank that it was really his account? What did they do with the money? Were there large piles of bills sitting in a bank vault? Perhaps it was all a fraud and he was deceived?

It was only when he sat at the desk with his neat piles in front of him that he felt completely satisfied.

"Daddy?" said Beatrice, cracking open the door to the office.

Two thousand three hundred seventy-six, thought Aguado Molina.

"Daddy, am I disturbing you?"

She was dressed in a charming white dress with short puff sleeves and lacing in the belt, which emphasized her dainty midriff. In the rich plumage her figure was otherwise hard to see.

"Two thousand three hundred eighty-two," Dragon mumbled so that she would hear he was counting.

"May I come in?" she asked, opening the door.

"Two thousand three hundred ninety-five," Dragon answered.

Beatrice stepped into the office and closed the door. She went up to one of the dark brown leather armchairs in front of the desk and sat down.

"Two thousand four hundred," said Dragon.

With that, he had rescued the moment. The stack in front of him was complete, and he used a rubber band to secure the even amount.

"My beloved daughter," he said, slipping the bundle into the desk drawer and directing his concentration at Beatrice. "My sweet cockatoo. My only love."

He discreetly placed a couple of envelopes over the uncounted cash still on the desk.

"What's on your mind?"

She looked at him and tipped her head. She tried to imagine how terrifying those sharp teeth and that spiky tail were to his enemies, but it was impossible. He was her father.

"Daddy, I haven't heard a word, and now it's been almost a month."

"That's how they can behave, these suitors," Dragon teased.

"But, Daddy, I'm serious. Why hasn't he contacted us?"

"I don't know, honey," Dragon replied.

"I know that he loves me."

"Darling, there is not a stuffed animal in all of Sors who does not worship the ground you walk on."

"Stop it, Daddy," she asked. "He loves me. I know that I love him."

"You're still so young," Dragon replied, looking a little embarrassed. "You don't know what you're saying. Love is a . . . something else. You will probably live to experience it someday."

The noise from below in La Cueva interrupted him. It sounded like a stack of dishes falling to the ground, or perhaps a tray of silverware. And it continued. Rattling and crashing, followed by the sound of broken china. What was going on?

Dragon Aguado Molina stood halfway up, opened the right-hand desk drawer and took out a pistol. It was the heaviest caliber money could buy, a weapon as much to hit someone in the head with as to shoot.

Beatrice Cockatoo started panting.

"Daddy, what is that?"

But Dragon did not reply. Beatrice's question was rhetorical. She knew exactly what it was. Dragon Aguado Molina's daughter must be able to defend herself, and he had seen to it that she could. He had personally trained her when she was little, albeit with a smaller weapon.

He went around the desk with the pistol in his little hand. On the lower floor the noise had ceased, and it was silent. Much too silent.

"You stay here," he whispered to Beatrice.

But before she could answer, the door swung open. The dragon raised his weapon. Beatrice screamed.

Fox Antonio Ortega stood on the threshold.

"Fox!" Beatrice Cockatoo exclaimed, pushing her father aside and throwing herself right in the surprised Ortega's arms.

She pressed herself tight to him and threw her wings around him in a way that could not be misinterpreted. Without being directly brusque, Fox freed himself from the love of his heart. Cockatoo sighed contentedly, and took a step back to better enjoy the sight of him. Not even her most intense fantasies did him justice. She wanted to be his. Forever.

The fox was confused.

The reception had been contradictory, to say the least.

To make his way up to the second floor, he had been forced to fight with Dragon's henchmen all the way through the bar and up the stairs. Now here inside waited the love of his life and Dragon himself with a drawn weapon.

Fox Antonio Ortega did not know whether he should be overjoyed or scared to death.

"It's you," said Dragon, ignoring his hypersensitive daughter. "You're back. What do you want now?"

Dragon lowered his weapon just as Vasko Manatee and his brother, Luciano Hyena, showed up in the doorway behind Fox.

"Sorry, boss," panted Manatee, who had a tear on his chest out of which beige cotton was protruding. "We tried to stop him."

Dragon cast a worried glance at Beatrice, and silenced his shamefaced bodyguards with a wave.

"Almost as if you didn't want me here," said Fox Antonio Ortega.

"Nonsense," said Aguado Molina. "We have an agreement, after all."

He went back to the desk, sat down on his comfortable chair, and set the pistol on the envelopes that concealed the money.

"And what brings us this honor?" he asked.

Fox Antonio Ortega took a few quick steps up toward the multifanged imaginary animal, whereupon Manatee and Hyena crossed the threshold into the office. Dragon stopped them with another wave.

"Here it is," said Fox proudly.

From his inside pocket he pulled out a black arm and gave it to the astonished Dragon Aguado Molina.

"From Octopus Callemaro?"

"A vain stuffed animal," Fox replied.

"And he gave this to you?"

"For Beatrice's sake, I will succeed at anything whatsoever," Fox Antonio Ortega replied, turning his head and meeting the admiring gaze of the beautiful cockatoo.

Dragon nodded thoughtfully.

"Sit down," he asked.

Fox sat down on one of the armchairs in front of the desk. Beatrice Cockatoo immediately sat down in the armchair next to him, and in that way they sat like a married couple before the dragon. He looked from the one to the other.

"Two out of three," he stated. "That's not bad. Only the last challenge remains. Perhaps the easiest? I've got an octopus's arm. A hawk's feather. Now I want a heart. A fox's heart."

"A fox?" asked Fox.

"Fox Antonio Ortega's heart," said Dragon.

"My heart?"

Beatrice Cockatoo flew up from the chair. She fluttered her wings excitedly. The happiness she experienced knew no bounds.

"Oh, Daddy. Daddy! Thank you!"

She threw herself around the desk and gave him a hug. At the next moment she ran over to Fox—who, without understanding, remained seated—and bent down over him.

"Your heart, my darling, you've already given it to me!"

"That's true," answered Fox Antonio Ortega, who finally thought he understood the symbolism of what Molina had said. "My heart is yours forever, my darling."

Beatrice Cockatoo was beaming with happiness. Her yellow cheeks blushed, her black eyes sparkled.

"My child . . ." Dragon began, but did not know how he should continue, for he, too, was taken by the emotional intensity of the moment.

"Daddy, I never thought . . ." Beatrice began, and a single, lovely tear fell from her eye. "Sometimes I thought that . . ."

But she was not able to complete the sentence.

Fox had also stood up alongside his betrothed, and he, too, fumbled for words to thank Dragon Aguado Molina.

But then the dragon raised the pistol and aimed it right at Ortega's head.

"My children," he said quietly, "you misunderstand me. I meant that more literally than you understood. I want his heart, Beatrice. Literally."

With a curt nod from Dragon, Manatee and Hyena lined up behind Fox. Antonio Ortega made an effort to defend himself.

"Try," said Dragon with a muted voice. "Simply make an attempt, and I'll show you what this caliber can do with you and your fast legs."

Fox Antonio Ortega froze. And while the manatee and hyena bound Fox's feet and hands, Beatrice finally realized what was really about to happen.

"But . . ." she exclaimed.

Anxiety and terror tied a knot around her vocal cords.

The single tear of joy was now followed by a river of tears of sorrow.

"Daddy!" she screamed.

"Get her out of here," Dragon ordered. "Lock her up in her room."

Manatee shoved the bound fox so that he fell to the ground,

and then dragged him out of the room. After them followed Hyena, who gingerly pushed the uncontrollably sobbing Beatrice Cockatoo ahead of him.

Molina sat behind the desk and watched them disappear. Later, when the fox had suffered all the torments that Manatee and Hyena could think of down in the cellar, Dragon himself intended to go down and carve out the cursed fox heart. He would see to it that this Ortega never threatened the peace of his household again.

Dragon Aguado Molina removed the envelopes and looked down at the money. He opened the center desk drawer to continue his work, but became uncertain.

Was it two thousand four hundred or two thousand three hundred?

With a sigh he pulled off the rubber band from the piles on the table and started over from the beginning. A deep sense of satisfaction filled him.

THE END

The room stank of sweet perfume and the odor made me nauseated. It was the smell that made me realize this was Beatrice Cockatoo's room; I knew she lived on the top floor. I carefully placed my paw over her beak. With my other paw I turned on the lamp on her nightstand. She opened her eyes when she felt my paw, and stared in terror up into my eyes.

"I am Gary Vole," I whispered. "I am Fox Antonio Ortega'th friend. Where ith he?"

I waited until the words had penetrated her awareness and the fear disappeared from her eyes, and then I let her reply.

"In the cellar," she whispered. "We have to help him."

I nodded. You might ask how the cockatoo could be asleep on the top floor when her love was most likely being tortured a few floors down in the same building, but I didn't ask.

"You have to thow the way," I said.

"Thow?"

"Lead me down to the thellar," I clarified.

She nodded. She got up and tied a dressing gown around her that was as thin as her nightgown.

"But I'm afraid we're too late," she said. "Daddy has taken his heart."

I had counted on a lot, but finding my friend heartless had not been in my worst nightmares. I sat down heavily on the sofa next to the bed, and was almost swallowed up by its soft cushions and many pillows.

"What do we do?" she asked desperately.

And again fate stepped into my life. I had sat on something uncomfortable, and checked under me with my claw. It was yet another little pillow, and I tossed it aside. A moment later I saw: The pillow was shaped like a heart. A red heart.

"Quick," I said. "We have no time to lose."

The building was quiet and deserted. The last guests had left La Cueva hours before. We sneaked down the steps. The guards were outside, Cockatoo said. One on the roof, one in the alley on the back side, and one outside the front door. Having them stand outside kept them from falling asleep.

It would have been more dramatic if the stairs had creaked, if my heart had been in my throat, if I had heard a sound from the kitchen. But everything was quiet, and my worry about Fox Antonio Ortega overshadowed my fear of being discovered.

It appeared that the cellar door was behind a door in the wine storage room. This was a house with many secrets, I was realizing.

The cellar stairs were long and steep and you were forced to bend down where the ceiling was low. The smell got stronger the farther down you went. It was neither mold nor damp, just cold cellar.

Light was coming from below, and we stopped on the final stair to hear if anyone was there. But besides our own breathing it was silent, a silence so heavy I knew we were alone.

Fox Antonio Ortega was on a large baking table. The surface of the table was white laminate, the table legs were metal and bolted to the concrete floor. Fox's arms and legs were bound, tied to the back legs of the table, and his shirt was torn open. He was staring up at the ceiling, his eyes open, but he saw nothing; he was not conscious.

I took a few steps into the room.

Fox's chest was cut open. Cotton had been scooped out across his shirt. I took a few more staggering steps forward, and saw the hole where his heart had been.

Behind me Beatrice was sobbing. At the sight of her beloved's desecrated body her stomach turned in and out, and she threw up. This was no place for her.

"Run back upthtairth," I whispered. "Pack a thmall bag with ethentialth, and come back down here again."

In a daze she stared at me and nodded. Then she ran up the stairs.

I had ten minutes, maybe fifteen, that was what I assumed, but there was no promise. I was alive; that was what Callemaro had given me in exchange for the code: my life back.

After Fox took off from the radio tower with one of the octopus's arms stuffed into his coat I had considered disappearing. The night was young, and I could go far before Callemaro woke up the next morning. I could hide in one of Yok's other districts, and perhaps find a way to have an operation; transforming me into a hare or a mink was not impossible for a capable, criminal plastic surgeon, and there were plenty of those. But I thought again, and returned to my original plan.

I waited until morning, and it took no longer than until the Morning Rain before the furious Callemaro summoned me. I was prepared for the worst. He asked whether I had anything to say before I died, and I answered that I did.

"I can lead you into Dragon Aguado Molina'th houth, at night and without the guardth notithing anything," I answered. "I can help you thlay your enemy."

It had not been Fox Antonio Ortega's intention to tell about the greenhouse and the code word on the slate to give me something to exchange with Callemaro. Ortega had told me, because he was always talking about Beatrice Cockatoo.

It took an hour to convince Callemaro that what I said was true, and all he promised me in exchange was my life. Good enough.

I took out the pillow heart, and I admit that my paw was shaking. I took a few steps forward and carefully placed it in his open chest. I made room in the cotton and put back the stuffing that was on Fox's shirt and the baking table. From my inside pocket I took out the sewing kit I had brought along. I had counted on having to sew up the fox, even if I hadn't foreseen this exact situation.

Stitch by stitch I sewed, with a black thread that was almost invisible in his red fur. When I was finished I expected that something would happen, but nothing did.

I had a head start, but at this point Callemaro and his crew were surely on their way through the underground passage from the greenhouse.

"I'm ready," said Beatrice Cockatoo.

I jumped. I had completely forgotten about her, but now she was in the cellar again, with a small bag on her wing.

"Beatrice?"

On the baking table Fox Antonio Ortega turned his head, and looked at his beloved.

"Beatrice?"

"Quick," I said, "we must hurry."

With the cockatoo on one side and me on the other, we helped Fox up the steps and into the wine storage room. It was still quiet in the house. Beatrice opened the cash register in the bar and took a handful of bills. When we had made it halfway through the restaurant we heard the first shouts, and when we reached the outside door the battle was in full swing. Most of it seemed to be going on one floor up, and the door to Puerta de Alcalá was unguarded.

As we ran through the night toward deep blue Avinguda

de Pedrables, where the buses were, I thought about Dad and wondered whether my memory of when he saw me on the ground at Piazza di Bormio would disappear now. The dawn was not far off.

I remained standing on the sidewalk with the cockatoo's bag, in which she had packed her diary and a few other things, as the bus drove off. She won't need it anyway, I thought; she has to start over now. The last thing I saw through the back window of the bus was Fox Antonio Ortega leaning against his beloved Beatrice Cockatoo's wing. The night had been hard on them both.

PERTINY

This story begins with us getting a letter that changes everything, and if that sounds dramatic, it's because it is.

Some have it easier than others in Mollisan Town, which is due to circumstances you can't change. I'm not stupid, I don't think that everyone can be everything and I could be the mayor if I just believed in myself, but I'm basically a positive lizard (without having any good reason to be), and I still think you can influence your own situation, even if I have sense enough to keep quiet, because among the rats and voles and polecats down by the ovens at the brewery you would get a sound thrashing if you said what you thought—namely, that we all work there because we want to, and at the same time because we didn't get anything better.

This is not the first time the tabloid *Now!* has organized a program-host competition along with *Good Morning Mollisan Town*. On the contrary, it's the ninth year in a row, which shows how successful the competition is (and the TV show), and that a lot of stuffed animals want to be program hosts, appear on TV, and smile self-confidently and say what the next show is about, or read the news, or host a quiz show or whatever. I'm not a devoted TV watcher, because I always fall asleep a few minutes after I sit down on the couch and turn on the TV. It's not the first year either that my brothers, Leopold Leopard and Rasmus Panther, are applying for the competition. They've applied every year since the competitions began, which would certainly surprise almost anyone who has met Leopold or Rasmus in other connections, and there are neighbors and relatives who would laugh right in your face if they saw Rasmus's and Leopold's applications, because they are chock-full of lies about what they've done and what they can do. But my brothers wouldn't care. They would just look at whoever was laughing for a long, long time, with their eyes half-closed and their noses wrinkled in an ominous way, and then they would say something crushing about the animal's clothes or parents or job or something else that would make the animal in question run away with its tail between its legs, if the animal had a tail. Or else the animal in question would get such a beating that it wouldn't know whether it had a tail to put between its legs. My brothers are stronger and tougher than most, so it's probably wisest not to joke with them about the program-host competition. Personally I respect them because they're willing to apply, and they don't give up even though year after year they've sent in their pictures (photographs they've had taken in a real studio with a real photographer) and their completed forms without even getting an answer back. I mean, everyone has the right to their dreams, and it's the ones who don't dream you feel sorry for.

On TV the competition is called *New Mornings*, and the tryouts begin with thousands of hopeful stuffed animals sending in applications—a picture of themselves and a made-up news item—to the tabloid, which publishes the best (meaning the strangest) contributions every Friday. After that a more serious selection is made, and the newspaper calls several hundred stuffed animals to the tryouts in the TV building, where you get to read your made-up news item in front of a TV camera to do a voice test and also prove that you can memorize text and behave in front of the camera without being unnatural. After that you're called to the program itself, and this is where it starts for the TV viewers; we get to see fifty selected stuffed animals who are voted out on Friday evenings (of which certain ones get to test-read a news item or two on *Good Morning Mollisan Town* on Saturday morning), so that after a few months a winner can be chosen.

The chance of being included is like buying a lottery ticket, my brothers always say (but only to each other when no one's listening), and everyone buys lottery tickets. I don't know how many kinds of lotteries there are, but every year there's something new you scratch off or collect or just guess, and every week you hear about someone who becomes a millionaire and can move away. One time, even if it was many years ago, it happened to the cub of my aunt's coworker, she won thirty-two million, so I know it's possible, and she moved up to Lanceheim and no one saw her again, which is what I meant when I said you can't give up. I think it's possible to change your life, even for those of us who are delivered to Yok and work at Carlsweis breweries. If that cub hadn't bought a lottery ticket (which she wouldn't have if she believed that life was what it was and nothing could be done about it), she never would have gotten out of here. I'm not stupid, and I know that the lotteries profit most on all the wretches who buy lotteries with their last money down here in Yok (because around here, dreams are needed more than any other place in the city), and that the odds are like, one in a million, but the moment you win, well, then you're no longer a wretch, but an enviable stuffed animal, because then everything changes.

We live in a two-story house with a cellar on honey yellow Carrer de Carrera, which sounds like a privilege, and I would say that it is rather privileged because I know lots of folks who have worse places to live, and who would only get irritated if you complained about the cold at night and how hot it is during the day, if you mentioned that the stairs between the floors are so rotten that if you don't know exactly where to set your foot you'll be standing with one leg right down in the wood, or if you said that the water doesn't make it all the way up to the top floor even though that's where the toilets are. We live in a white wooden house with a balcony, where I've lived my whole life, and I have been proud of the house over the years, and my brothers have chased away lots of stuffed animals over the years who had the nerve to think they can live with us just because we happen to have a few extra rooms. It's not so strange, if you have something valuable there's always someone who wants it, and ever since that evening in the fall many years ago when Mom burned up (which is something I try not to think about), and a few months later when the police came and got Dad (which we don't talk about either), we've had to defend ourselves, my brothers and me, against the animals from social services or from the darker places in life who have heard about a house with three cubs alone that you could move into. But it wasn't just any three cubs, and we're still living here in our house without anyone taking it from us.

Nowadays I don't miss Mom and Dad. I don't think about them very often; it was horrible when it happened, and I know I cried at night, but I was little then. Now when I think that they lived here, it's like thinking about a movie or something: You can picture it, but it doesn't feel like you have personally been involved.

A letter arrives, and my whole life is changed even though the letter isn't even to me. I'm the one who takes care of the mail when we get any, which doesn't happen every day because no one except the authorities sends us letters; when the letter carriers don't think they have enough to bother delivering, they skip Carrer de Carrera for a while, and when they come back we get several letters and packages at the same time. I understand immediately that there's something special about this letter because it says *Now!* on the envelope, with the tabloid's familiar logo. I read the tabloids sometimes when stuffed animals leave them behind on the bus or on a bench, and I can see why some don't bother to take them home. There isn't much in them.

Finally it's happened; year after year my brothers have sent in applications without hearing a word, without getting an answer, but now the tabloid is in touch, and it's great. I feel how my whole body is tingling; this is not something I expected, but as I lean down and pick up the envelope from the floor in the hall I know that I've known, I've both expected and waited for this day.

The envelope is addressed to Rasmus Panther (and not Leopold Leopard), and so I know which of my brothers will finally be rewarded for his persistence and for having dared to resist the pressure from his surroundings which (perhaps) heckled him and called him foolish and vain. In the envelope, I assume, is a summons to a test filming at the TV building, because that's how it works, I know that and everyone else who follows the program, one of the biggest successes in modern TV history; and week after week we follow the voting, and then day after day at the end when it gets most exciting and only a few candidates remain, all of them smiling with their mouths full of white teeth and a hope in their eyes that always makes me thoughtful.

As I'm standing there, holding the envelope, and realize that my brother Rasmus Panther is one of those who will be competing to be on-screen, staring right into every single house in Mollisan Town, it feels unreal and amazing at the same time, and I'm certain that he can go far, if you compare him with previous years' finalists I think there's a chance he can go the whole way and win it all, but it's clear that I'm partial and . . . wait, now Leopold, our oldest brother, is coming, I have to run down and open the door.

"Hi, Leopold. I . . .

"Sorry.

"This came for Rasmus."

Leopard hits me across the neck and takes the envelope. He often hits me across the neck, he likes smacking me, or else it's just become a habit, and even though I know the slap is coming I can't fend it off but instead I fall forward down on the floor where I've learned to stay until Leopold has left (otherwise there's a risk he'll hit me again), but instead of going up to his room like he usually does, he remains standing and looks at the envelope that I gave him.

"What?

"No."

I remain lying on the floor as I answer him, and I don't look up.

"No, I think it's from the newspaper.

"I guess it must be . . . about the competition?"

The kick comes quite unexpectedly; his shoe hits me in the belly and I rise a few inches up in the air and land a little ways off, on our red-and-white-striped rag rug in the passageway out to the kitchen, and I don't dare say anything, don't dare move. Leopold remains standing a moment, I think he's still staring at the envelope. I imagine he's reading his little brother's name over and over, and then he screams that I don't have much time to get the chow ready, and that I'm going to get one hell of a beating if dinner isn't ready in time, because he has to go out this evening, probably before Rasmus comes home, poor Rasmus who in that case won't get to enjoy the moment and share the happiness with both of his brothers.

I get up and go out into the kitchen and boil water. We have a wood stove; most of the wood I carry home from the forest. The city limits aren't more than an hour from Carrer de Carrera but sometimes I have to search a long time to find anything burnable that can be carried home, and the problem is that I seldom start searching until twilight fills the sky and it starts getting dark (and if you don't find anything before it's dark you have to wait for the moon to come out to see at all, which means it's pretty late before you're back).

Just as I'm putting the noodles in the saucepan I hear the outside door open and close. It's Rasmus coming home. I hear him go up the stairs to the top floor, enter the bathroom, and then change clothes, and the whole time I'm waiting for that howl of joy that has to come when he realizes he has finally taken the first step toward the job as program host on TV, which is what he's been waiting half his adult life for. But when the noodles are drained and I hear the steps down the stairs and Rasmus still hasn't called out, I know that Leopold hasn't shown Rasmus the letter (there are certainly reasons for that), and my brothers sit down at the table at their usual places and I serve the noodles with a mushroom sauce that I made yesterday, and then I do my best to conceal my impatience, though it's hard and I'm about to explode.

"Yes.

"Sorry.

"I'll sit down here, over in the corner?"

But Leopold knows why I'm sneaking around like I am, and I'm feeling really lousy when at last he pulls the envelope out of his pants pocket—it's completely wrinkled, he just stuck it in without folding it—and throws it over to our brother, at him. Rasmus looks at the envelope, bewildered, and then at me (I'm still sitting on the floor in the corner next to the stove where they want me) because he knows I'm the one who takes care of the mail, and it's strange that Leopold, and not me, has a letter for him. But then when he looks at the envelope a second time and sees the tabloid's logo as addressee, he tears it open, sits quietly and reads what's there while Leopold and I stare at him, and at last he looks up and says that he's supposed to be at the TV building on Thursday in time for the Morning Weather.

Then he shouts, and I join in and Leopold, too, and it's a happy moment for us at home on Carrer de Carrera, and my big brothers decide to celebrate and leave the kitchen with their arms around each other, a black panther and a spotted leopard, they're beautiful and strong and successful. I do the dishes and feel happy.

Carlsweis, the place where I work, is located, along with three other breweries, in a stinking industrial area on dark brown Cle de Arenal, twenty minutes from our house. The building is located inside a fifteen-foot-high barbed-wire fence that runs four blocks in one direction and six blocks in the other. The area is not asphalted, but the ground is so hard-packed that the thousands of feet that trample it every morning and evening leave no tracks behind; we are all little cogs in a collective machinery that goes on without any individual effort being noticed or appreciated. The Morning and Afternoon Rains, however, carve out holes in the industrial area's expansive fields, holes that trucks must drive around when they pick up the cases of beer and mineral water at the loading docks. It's best not to go home before the ground has dried up, because the clay sticks to pants and penetrates socks and shoes, but today I'm forced to, because I have to leave a little early. I spoke with my foreman about it, he's a polecat and has always hated me, I really don't know why, we went to the same school but he's much older and at that time he didn't think about me, but from the day I started at the breweries he's been after me anytime he's had a chance.

We work in five teams at six different stations and the idea is that we will rotate monthly; it's a schedule that has been set with regard to ergonomics and the environment, they say, both social and physical. But I've been working down in the basement at the wood-fired ovens for almost two years now, which is prohibited according to the regulation that no one cares about, so I don't know how much the other regulations are followed either. Some of the rats (who have always scared me because they carry knives and are seldom completely sober, not even in the morning, and a few of them lack ears and tails and the stench from their street clothes in the dressing room is almost unbearable, even though we're working at a brewery) have even said they think I should be part of another team, but when the polecat comes and points and carries on, no one dares say a thing, least of all me. Because if I don't want the job there's always someone else standing in line, so I go down to my ovens in the underworld, usually so early in the morning that the sun hasn't even come up, and stay there the whole day apart from the time it takes to fetch the lunchbox I set in my locker in the dressing room when I arrive; the less daylight you see, the easier it is to be down in the darkness.

Today I'm leaving the brewery even before the Afternoon Rain, which I never would have gotten permission to do if I hadn't told the polecat what was going on, that it was my brother Rasmus Panther who needed help, and the polecat knows my brother (Rasmus was a year ahead of the polecat in school, which establishes their mutual relationship), and he doesn't dare say no, even though I see he's thinking of doing it anyway. The dressing room is empty as I take off my work clothes, the day shift won't be over for a few hours yet, the night shift doesn't come in before they have to, and I take the opportunity to clean my locker a little when I have the time and when the rats aren't looking over my shoulder in search of something worth eating or stealing. At home I sleep on the couch in the living room (Leopold and Rasmus have always lived in the large bedrooms on the top floor), without any place for more personal, or shall I say private, things (I make the bed with a bottom sheet and duvet cover and my pillows every night and fold up the bedding and place it on the shelf under the TV during the day), and for that reason I have a number of things in the locker in the dressing room that the rats would surely grab if they knew about it; for example, a silver snuffbox I inherited from my father (I found it under the loose plank in the bedroom when the police . . . when Dad left), a deck of cards with circus motifs that I won at poker once many years ago, and a cricket ball from the final match when the Yok Giants won after a seventh and decisive match against the Lanceheim Lancers; the ball is signed, even if I can't decipher the signature.

The Afternoon Breeze is sweeping across the gravel area outside the breweries as I cross it on my way to the bus stop, and I know that the black clouds that the chimneys force out of their tall necks stink, but the odor doesn't bother me, not even as I sit on the bus right behind the driver and know that the smell of my clothes marks me as one of the workers at the brewery, because I'm proud of my job, an honorable job in this dishonorable part of Mollisan Town, and I'm proud of being part of the structure of society . . . I'm proud of being a part.

I admit that at first I didn't understand why Rasmus wanted me to go along to the TV building, but I didn't care in the least, it was so long since I'd been out walking with my brothers that I felt swelling pride at simply being close to the handsome black panther on Carrer de Carrera's honey yellow sidewalk, walking over to bus number 17 that would take us up to Tourquai. Rasmus had put on the narrow-cut, light red suit I made for him last autumn, and the white shirt with a breast pocket that I finished last Monday, while the pink bow tie that was the crown of the work he had stolen himself last week in one of the stores on Glöckleinsgasse. What I am wearing is less interesting. I wasn't the one who would be test-filming as a program host, apart from the fact that I don't have the prerequisites to show off clothes the same way as my two brothers, which I'm secretly rather content with when I see the time and frustration that their vanity demands of them.

During the short walk—Rasmus was understandably nervous and walked faster than usual—to the bus stop on ash gray Carrer de la Marquesa, he rattled off the lines that I had written for him (and for Leopold) when they applied to the competition for the first time and were convinced that they would be called and selected immediately (and that the battle for first place would be between them). The first task, which you only see clips of in *New Mornings* because it's from the first round of judging, was to fabricate a news item of your own, write the copy, and read it in front of a TV camera. So many years later I thought it was a little embarrassing to hear Rasmus reciting, loudly and audibly so that everyone we met on the street could hear what I'd made up so long ago, words from my cubdom that came out of Rasmus's mouth as he walked a few steps ahead of me in his elegant suit; he had practiced the text year after year, a silly news item about a deluge that caused the Dondau to overflow and Lanceheim to be underwater, and normally he knew it all to the slightest detail, every emphasis and nuance, but now he stumbled along, stammering and forgetting and hesitating, and for his own sake I hoped he couldn't hear how he sounded, for that would have been devastating for his self-confidence, which according to the newspaper *Now!* should radiate from a contestant in order to succeed in the competition.

On the bus we sat at the very back, and as a sign of how nervous Rasmus was he didn't care that I was sitting next to him . . .

"Yes?

"I don't remember, but . . .

"Yes, now I know. A form! With name and address and a reason for why you are applying and why you qualify!

"Yes?

"But I don't really remember what I . . .

"No.

"Okay."

And I pretended to be absorbed in thoughts because I knew that was what Rasmus expected, this is how you looked when you reflected: wrinkles in your brow and your gaze directed far away, out through the windows of the bus where the powerlessness of Yok passed by, at the same time as I let a claw contemplatively scratch under my chin and pick lightly across my temples.

I'm ashamed to admit it but I'd forgotten what my brother remembered: that everyone called was supposed to fill out a form at the TV building; it was a kind of registration form, which was then weighed along with the camera test itself. When nine years ago the brothers applied the very first time, all three of us had thoroughly read the competition rules and I had written both of the news items for them, and two short essays besides—which they learned by heart—about why they were applying and why they were qualified as program hosts, which they could write on the form. For some reason Rasmus got cold feet during the week as far as the essay was concerned, and this morning he decided he ought to have something different, and I should write it, which was not that strange because Rasmus had always had poor self-confidence where writing was concerned, and that was the explanation for why I was here on the bus: I was along to fill out his registration form at the TV building.

"No, no, it's obvious that I . . .

"Maybe it's the next one?"

The TV building is a massive, white cubist stone building with lots of small, square windows, twenty rows across and six rows up. I'd seen the building lots of times because the stuffed animals on TV liked showing pictures of their workplace, and I assumed that this was an expression of the same kind of pride I felt when I saw one of the Carlsweis beer bottles in a store or on an advertising pole.

Rasmus and I got off the bus; the stop was right outside a glass atrium that was the main entrance to the building, and it struck me that the district council had located the bus stop at the entrance, not the other way around, which made me smile without anyone seeing it. Sometimes it feels as if TV decides everything, not only where you place bus stops; that black glass screen must be one of the most powerful drugs ever discovered in Mollisan Town; everyone wanted to be part of it and everyone wanted to watch.

The expansive entry level had a low ceiling in relation to the square footage, in the middle of the hall were two reception counters of frosted glass shaped like half-moons, they faced each other and together they formed a round whole around which moved a large number of apparently worried stuffed animals. They let questions and statements hail down on the four receptionists in dark blue uniforms who answered as best they could. Despite the diversity of types of stuffed animals in all the colors of the rainbow, despite the screaming framed advertising posters for successes of times past along the walls, despite the glimpse of famous faces running by on their way to or from programs I would surely be seeing in the week ahead, and despite the nervous atmosphere that hung like heavy condensation in the air around us, Rasmus Panther stood out in his light red suit. Dignified yet nonchalant, he strolled up to the reception counters; he moved as if he were already a star, and without hesitation or fear he asked in a loud voice where the tryouts for *New Mornings* were taking place. He was really a good actor.

We got our answer and directions. We found a long corridor at the far right corner of the entry level, a dark tunnel that led underground and where there was a faint odor of mold and nothing hanging on the walls, perhaps so as not to distract the big stars who must have walked here en route to acclaimed and sometimes classic appearances in one of the TV building's big studios from which concerts and events were broadcast live, and to which the general public could buy tickets and come and watch. (There were often ads for that on TV.)

I assume that the stuffed animals we met in the tunnel's shadows were there for the same purpose as we were, and that they were either going to or had just done the test for *New Mornings*, and I could not keep from trying to see who they were and fantasize about whether they were better or worse than Rasmus . . .

"Yes?

"No, there's no one . . .

"Of course I'll have time, I meant to stop by Monomart on the way home anyway."

The dark, silent corridor did nothing to prepare us for the activity going on in the room we entered, which was adjacent to the studio; we stepped right into an organized chaos, hundreds of stuffed animals running back and forth between the stations where the chosen applicants had to pass before it was time for the camera test; the registration, then the form that was my business to fill out, then makeup and costume (but when I saw the many racks of clothes and Rasmus's rivals who were trying on various garments in front of an oversized full-length mirror, I felt a cold shiver along my spine; what if they forced my brother to take off his light red jacket?), and then the final waiting on uncomfortable plastic chairs until a camel with a megaphone called out your number and it was time to go into the studio itself.

Rasmus forced his way up to the table where a pair of hardworking but disinterested officials were checking off the applicants, and my brother's attitude was still that everything had been arranged for his sake, he was the obvious winner and the *New Mornings* competition was only an excuse for TV and the tabloid to make use of Rasmus Panther's natural brilliance. I stayed in the background but admired him for his ability to seem relaxed when I knew how nervous he was, and the competition no longer looked harmless; there were several others like Rasmus in the room, who radiated the exact same sort of arrogance.

My brother and I went over to the table where the piles of registration forms were, and we each took a copy and sat down on the floor a short distance away from the clothes hangers to fill out the personal information and write our little essay. But to Rasmus's surprise, they had changed the questions—to be honest, we had not looked at this form in eight years. Instead of asking for a motivation for why we wanted to be program host, the survey consisted of alternative questions, the kind where you check off which TV program you prefer more than another, or what color of Volga you prefer, and to fill it out correctly Rasmus of course didn't need my help. He immediately told me to go to hell, which in this case meant he wanted me to leave, and he had already asked me to buy a bottle of gin on the way home, so after having wished him good luck I left, and the whole way to Monomart (I thought I would take the opportunity to shop for the whole week, since I had left work a little early anyway), I concentrated on thinking positive thoughts, for either that helped, or else it didn't help, but at the same time it couldn't hurt.

There is a space in the cellar in our house on Carrer de Carrera where my brothers sometimes lock me up; they attached a rubber shackle to the radiator and it's easy to slip onto my back foot and tighten, and then I'm not going anywhere (although I doubt that I would try to escape anyway, considering what a beating I would get when Rasmus and Leopold finally discovered I'd disappeared). The space is a little storeroom with no windows or ventilation, with just enough room for me if I pull in my tail and place it along my belly, and after a couple of hours it's hard to breathe because the air quickly gets bad when they close it up. There is a crack at the bottom of the door that I put my nose as close as possible to and then

I breathe as slowly as possible, which is a good exercise in many ways, not least because it's easier to remain calm when your breathing is slow and regular. They haven't forgotten me down there too often, which is because neither of my brothers knows his way around the kitchen, they don't know how to get the stove going (first you have to turn the handle under the counter to open the flue) and they don't know that the honey is in the pantry while the vegetables are in the fridge—they think it's the other way around—so when they start to get hungry they always remember to let me out. There have also been times (assuming I keep my breathing even and light in the dense darkness) that I've been lying in that storeroom and they believe they've locked me in, while I've actually gotten away. They think they've gotten rid of me, while in reality I'm the one who's gotten rid of them. In the storeroom I'm in my own universe, where I'm hidden and inaccessible, independent and without any requirements other than to breathe calmly and focus my thoughts on oxygen.

It strikes me, as I'm telling about the storeroom in the cellar, that it was long ago that I stopped obsessing about why I end up there; even when I was little I realized it was a punishment, but at that time I tried to put things I'd done or said in connection with their grabbing hold of me and dragging me down the stairs to the cellar, tried to figure out a reason, and sometimes I think I succeeded and then I was happy, almost overjoyed—not only because I'd understood something, but above all because a little spark of hope was lit about being able to avoid the storeroom the next time, if I just kept from doing what I'd done (or saying what I'd said). But that's not how it works, and to be honest I will say there were times during my teens when I thought I would go completely crazy; they dragged me down there without any reason at all, and I was lying in the darkness and going over the hours and days that had just passed and could not find a single miserable little reason to be punished, not a single little stain on their shirts after the laundry, not a single little scrap of food left on the plate after doing the dishes, not a single little sigh when I was scrubbing the toilet, not a single little crease when I made their beds; then I was about to go crazy, and it took several years before I stopped searching for reasons and accepted things for what they were; that's called maturity.

Four days after Rasmus and I had been in the TV building another envelope arrived from *Now!*, this time with Leopold Leopard's name on it, and I didn't know what to think, how was this possible? The letter, unassuming and a little dirty, was on the floor in the hall when I came home from work, and I crouched down and twisted and turned it and could hardly believe my eyes. Leopold Leopard! Not for a moment did I think that something had gone wrong or that the computers had made a mistake and sent one letter too many to us—my oldest brother had also been called to the program-host tryouts! After all these years I'd watched Rasmus and Leopold wait for a confirmation that never came, for evidence that they were special, that they were different from everyone else in the neighborhood and that they would actually get out of here, out of Yok and a life on the dark side; that there was a higher meaning—a purpose for Rasmus Panther's and Leopold Leopard's existence that fate and life had concealed for so long, not from them but from everyone else, and that it was finally revealed and their self-image was in alignment with what really happened. All these years of wearing a mask, of secrecy, of frustrated fury, and finally fate smiled its most beautiful smile, not only at Rasmus but also at Leopold!

It was amazing. At last I could use that word in the way it was meant—amazing. I ran into the living room and placed the letter on the coffee table. A few minutes later I removed the envelope, carried the paper upstairs and put it on Leopold's bed, but then I changed my mind again and took it back down to the kitchen and put it on the kitchen table. There I got worried that water or coffee or something else would spill on it, and so I ran with it into the hall again and put it on the third step of the stairs, so that it would be the first thing Leopold saw when he came home. I kept changing my mind like that back and forth for at least an hour until I realized how ridiculous I was making myself, and then I sank down into one of the armchairs in the living room and put the letter back on the coffee table where I had put it to start with. I spent the rest of the late afternoon trying to fix and caulk the molding around the windows in the kitchen, which isn't exactly easy. I'm not naturally good with tools; I saw and build and grind and paint but it takes twice as long for me as, for example, Leopold, who always hits the nail with the hammer, who always understands three-dimensional constructions, and who never puts too much paint on the brush; how that works, someone like me will never understand.

Rasmus Panther came home before Leopold. Late afternoon had turned to evening and the sun was on its leisurely way toward the horizon. Don't ask me where my brothers keep themselves during the day or what they do, I have no idea. I think they sleep until lunch, but they're not usually there when I get home from work in the afternoon. Then they show up for dinner and leave again when they're done, and the only thing that distinguishes weekend from weekday is that on the weekend I have no job to go to and I can take care of the odd jobs here at home that I haven't had time for during the week.

I was in the kitchen cooking beans when I heard Rasmus shout from the living room. He had caught sight of the letter with Leopold's name. Maybe he had been mistaken and thought it was for him, that it was the results of his tryout, and then, just before he tore it open with his sharp claw, he read the name on the envelope a second time and realized that it was for his big brother.

Rasmus has been bragging a good deal about how it went at the test. He said that in the studio, when he read my made-up news item, the camera loved him and the stuffed animals who were running the recording applauded him and said he was much better than all the others, so now all three of us—me, Leopold, and Rasmus, that is—are waiting for *Good Morning Mollisan Town* to call and say that Rasmus has been selected as one of the participants on *New Mornings*.

But now he swore, a long litany that was stronger than anything I could have imagined, and I pictured him throwing down the letter as if it had burned him. Then a few minutes went by when I don't know what happened, now I was frying sausages that my brothers had rejected and thrown out yesterday but which I'd rolled into balls and seasoned with rosemary today, which means they won't recognize them, and then suddenly the door to the kitchen opened and Rasmus stormed in.

"Hi, have you . . . ?"

But he didn't intend to talk with me. He took hold of my tail and yanked; I tumbled backward, struck my head on the stove, and must have fainted, because when I came back to life again we were already on our way down the cellar stairs and I knew that nothing I said or did would appease him, and I didn't ask myself why he opened the door to the little storeroom or why he threw me in and slipped the rubber shackle around my ankle. That was just the sort of thing he did.

I don't want to exaggerate because there is no reason to exaggerate. Melancholy is just a stop on the way to the burning anxiety in my heart, the flame that never dies down, that has burned a black hole in my soul. And out of that hole green slime gushes, which are the confessions that rotted long ago and decomposed and were transformed into a stinking pile of gooey truths that don't lead anywhere or to anything. I'm an ugly, disgusting little stuffed animal who never finished school, never fulfilled a single one of my intentions, and who therefore never needed to fail, never needed to challenge my self-image, and who could creep back down in my make-believe world where I was so wise and splendid and hardy and forgiving that it disgusted me, and where I live alone and bitter and scared to death. There are no excuses for not daring to look at yourself, there are no excuses for not daring to live, I deserve my burning anxiety, I deserve nothing but.

On the corner at ash gray Carrer de la Marquesa, barely fifty feet from the doorway to our house, is Sarah Mammoth's tobacco shop, and because my brothers smoke like chimneys I visited Sarah once or twice a day, which I had nothing against, it was really easy to feel comfortable in her cramped store. There was a stool in the corner with newspapers where I would sit and soak up the atmosphere of her smoking paradise: nicotine and caffeine, of course, but also the enticing odor of ink from the colorful magazines lining the walls, and the seductive aromas from the chocolate that seemed to bubble up out of the counter behind which Sarah sat in state, her hairy head sticking up behind the cash register in front of the coffee machine, always with a freshly filled pipe and always in a good mood.

No store gave as much credit as Sarah, and there was no one I was more faithful to than her, so as soon as I had money it went to pay off the debt for tobacco first (even if I sometimes had to work it off by helping her with inventory; doing tax forms; or cleaning the groaning, moaning, and at least hundred-pound stainless steel coffee machine with which she made the neighborhood's best espresso).

Sarah was on my side without making a big deal about it, she was on my side by letting me tell her things without asking, by letting me complain without feeling sorry for me, and by sympathizing without acting. I couldn't recall a time when I didn't feel an inexpressible coziness when I stepped into her little store (if there was another customer there I waited outside, it was that cramped), but unfortunately I could seldom stay longer than a couple of minutes, because then my brothers wondered where I'd gone, and they were right to, of course, as my chores were so many and so heavy that I didn't have time to sit and gossip with a friendly old mammoth.

I'm talking about Sarah because through her eyes I could see my brothers as they appeared in everyone else's eyes, how they had formed a team against the rest of the world, a team that maybe didn't win all its matches, but seldom lost. This image in turn had to do with the fact that most animals—if they were wise—kept a proper distance from Rasmus and Leopold, a distance that made them seem extremely alike, while I of course lived so close to them that I knew just how different they were.

One day the whole story about Leopold Leopard and Rasmus Panther will surely be written, and I probably won't even be mentioned. I don't play in their league, I'm the afterthought that came to the family when Leopold and Rasmus had already made history in our neighborhood by burning down Olson's garage after Olson stole their ball just because it happened to roll under his old wreck of a car that couldn't even be driven. But it also would be about how they looked and behaved, Leopold had hats when the other cubs were still wearing overalls, Rasmus used brass knuckles when his classmates were still playing with blocks, Dragon Aguado Molina sent his torpedoes to rip out Rasmus's and Leopold's seams before they even turned fifteen, and a few years later they had both served their first sentences at King's Cross, giving them experience in cruelty, credibility, and networks. In Yok in the area around Carrer de Carrera a few trips out to the prison were nothing to brag about, and believe me when I say there were many in school who worked to survive growing up by making themselves tough and hard (it was either that or lie low, which was more my own secret weapon, try to make myself invisible and not stick out, dress in black and gray and laugh when you were supposed to laugh and look away if you were supposed to look away), so what was it that caused Leopold and Rasmus to be different from the rest? For one thing there were two of them, they were no more than a year apart but they repeated so many grades I don't think anyone in school was clear which of them was really the older and which the younger, they were just two felines the same age who were brothers, dangerous and loyal to each other beyond the bounds of reason; you couldn't be the enemy of one of them. Then there was the fact that they were extremely well-dressed, always in colorful clothes that weren't suitable for our neighborhood, suits and shiny shoes, hats, and shawls. They worked hard at deviating from the masses, and with their sharpened claws and an endless growing arsenal of weapons in the attic, they created a myth around themselves: they were a black and a spotted mirror image of ruthlessness.

To me it has always been obvious that Leopold is our big brother, and that the responsibility for the family rests on his shoulders (which he has perhaps not always been comfortable with but which he still, I think, lives up to), something that in turn gives Rasmus the possibility to revolt against things that Leopold has decided. I know it's harder for Leopold than for Rasmus to understand everything that happens in Mollisan Town, it's not as easy for him to quickly find a solution to a problem like his younger brother. And I know that Rasmus reacts too quickly for his own good, that his spontaneity often means he ends up in strange situations and then he relies on his big brother's caution and thoughtfulness; in short, they're extremely different, Rasmus and Leopold. You see that if you're close to them, but they complement each other in a marvelous way, the one's weaknesses are the other's strengths, and vice versa.

———

I accompanied Leopold to the TV studio one morning, just as I had gone with Rasmus less than a week earlier. I called in sick; you can't do that more than a few times a year if you want to keep your job, but I relied on Leopold not taking any risks, all three of us (me and my brothers) lived on the money I earned at the brewery, and because Leopold also knew the polecat from school days I assumed he had assurances that it was okay for me to be absent.

Leopold had put on his light blue suit, perhaps because he knew that Rasmus had worn his red for his test, and while the suit made the similarities between them clear—giving a little free help, if it really had gone that well for Rasmus—it also underscored the differences; true, it was an identical suit (sewn by the same claw: yours truly), but a distinctly different color, and true, they were brothers, but one of them was older than the other. Basically during the whole bus ride Leopold talked about what clothes meant in these contexts.

"There are lots of clothes in the studio.

"No. No, I mean, clothes for the contestants. Many of the others . . .

"No. But I think there are lots of sizes?

"Yes."

And Leopold, who in contrast to Rasmus always likes explaining things to me (surely because he has a hard time understanding them himself and uses me to practice), explained that only amateurs used the clothes in the studio, it was a classic beginner's error, putting yourself in front of the camera in borrowed feathers, in a jacket too tight or too wide, in a color that didn't go with your fabric, in stripes when checks suited you or vice versa. Being properly clothed, said Leopold, meant more than if you knew anything about journalism, if you stammered, TV was a medium of surfaces, it was good of course to deliver some kind of content, but only if you looked good, in a not too intrusive manner. The light blue suit jacket (mild baby blue, almost latticed white in places) was an infinitely better choice than the light red jacket that Rasmus had on and that verged on pink, Leopold explained, simply because the color didn't compete with the news or the news anchor, at the same time as it was far from indifferent.

"But I would think that . . . ?

"I see.

"Well, you've thought of everything, Leopold."

We got off the bus outside the square entry to the TV building, and I felt experienced as I could show Leopold the way directly through the lobby over to the dark corridor, which led to the TV studio and the tryouts. I walked a few steps behind and whispered where he should go, and I knew him so well that I noticed how nervous he was, but I didn't say that.

"What?

"No, I didn't go in with him. I stayed here until . . .

"Sure.

"Over there.

"Okay. I'll wait."

Leopold entered the corridor, and I went and sat down on the bench I'd seen when I was here with Rasmus last week, the one all by itself next to the high glass walls toward the inner courtyard, the glass walls that admitted daylight into the middle of the wide, square building. The garden made me happy, perhaps because it was so well arranged, or else because it was so green and full of life, with the massive willow tree in the middle and the dense, low hedges right next to the windows, blue and purple flowers along straight, square gravel paths and lovely grapevines that fell down across the glass wall opposite. The only thing that was strange about the shady courtyard (which everyone who worked in the TV building could look down on, if your office faced the courtyard on any of the floors), was that I never saw doors; the gravel pathways and flowers were there to be observed, but not visited.

I sat down to wait, and I can't explain how special it is to experience time as I did right then, how amazing it is to wait, without demands or expectation, without fear or worry, just sitting and staring out over the flowers and the tree in the middle and not thinking about anything at all. I don't know how long Sparrow Dahl had been sitting beside me when I noticed her, but there was no doubt that she was staring at me, and I was startled because I felt found out, revealed in my total idleness. She was a cute stuffed animal with a light green plastic beak on which a pair of thick, round eyeglasses rested. She wore a green knit jumper with a tangled yarn that made you want to hug her, and a pair of ordinary jeans that my brothers would not have liked because they were hard worn; nothing in her exterior suggested that this was a bird with influence, a stuffed animal with whom many in the TV building were friends.

It's still hard to believe that what happened then really happened, but I can prove it wasn't my imagination.

"Excuse me?

"No, no . . . I'm just here with my brother.

"I see.

"Uh-huh.

"That sounds . . . exciting."

She fell silent and looked at me, studied me up and down, it felt unpleasant because I don't remember if anyone had looked at me that way before. I became aware of how I looked, with the long tail, my short back legs where a pair of gray shorts served as long pants, my narrow, long upper body that I've always had a hard time holding straight, I can't help that it sways to the right and left most of the time, to the short arms: thank goodness I'd put on a white shirt that was both clean and not torn.

"Excuse me?

"No, a gecko.

"Yes . . . sure . . . I don't know. I mean, I've never been anything else.

"You say?

"Yes, maybe it is? I don't know. Not particularly, I think."

Then she asked me to tell a little about myself, and she did it in such an encouraging way that I didn't get upset at all, which I usually do if someone wants me to get personal because I think my life has nothing to do with anyone other than myself, so instead of getting up and leaving I stayed and looked out over the purple and blue flowers and said something about myself that was neither true nor false, an art I've mastered.

"What?

"Me?

"Now?

"Yes, of course I can try . . ."

Rasmus and Leopold had practiced my news items for many years, they had learned every pause and nuance, sat in front of mirrors that they pretended were cameras and carefully studied their own facial expressions as they furrowed their handsome brows deeply to emphasize the seriousness behind the invented news items, and even if I was often forced to listen to these rehearsals, and even though I'd written the pieces myself, I quickly decided not to try to recall those clever, precocious formulations, but improvise instead, inspired by the beautiful garden that was unreachable a few feet in front of the bench, and now afterward I don't know exactly what I said, but it must have been something along these lines:

"Tonight a fire broke out in south Pertiny, probably caused by a spark from an idea that Laskoo Cow had long harbored, and the destruction may have far-reaching consequences for city planning in the area, because Cow is the nephew of Professor Ghandi, the long-time chairman of the Ministry of Finance's committee for alternative energy, and thereby an influential animal, even where park administration in the district is concerned. In brief tonight, Cow's idea burned down the abandoned valve factory that for years has stood deserted in the corner of Carrer de Carrera and Los Estiz, so that a flower meadow could be created there. We hope to return later in the afternoon with pictures of this meadow."

I fell silent, astonished, because I never would have believed that I could, well, think of so much, the words just came out, I didn't stop to think, just let them tumble out of my mouth, and perhaps it was a little strange, the part about an idea that starts burning, but the kind sparrow seemed to think I'd done something good, because she looked flabbergasted, in a positive way, and what she said took me completely by surprise.

I thought I'd heard wrong, but when I was about to ask if it was really true Leopold came out of the dark corridor, and I stood up, almost at attention, I was so excited, and—still without answering the sparrow—started going to meet my brother, because he expected me to escort him out to the bus. The sparrow called after me, repeating what she had already said, that she would hold a place for me at the tryouts on Monday, that she believed I had a good chance to be included on *New Mornings*, the program my brothers fought over to win with a longing greater than life itself . . .

"What? No, it must have been to someone else."

This excuse of a life that I live, this masochism that I expose myself to daily, cuts into my soul, it may seem I accept it without thinking, as if I enjoy being bullied and held down, but inside I'm burning up, as if someone were vomiting into my open mouth, and I swallow and want more and more, and it's inconceivable, of course, that every day I choose to continue and act as though I have no choice. Life is mysterious, and not a second goes by that I don't despise myself for this self-imposed punishment that no one sees and no one promotes; however hard I work, however complete my humiliation is, I still can't free myself from the tormenting awareness of my own spinelessness. I'm not just a wretch, I'm worse than that,

I betray myself, and when you've betrayed yourself you can never, ever regain any dignity, and you can never look another stuffed animal in the eyes.

Life doesn't always turn out like you expect, and I'm not the type who likes surprises. I resist when I notice that things are about to change, and I'm not ashamed of it. I'm not ashamed of wanting security; I don't think I'm different from most, we are all creatures of habit even if some want to present themselves as more adventurous, we're used to dreaming about something other than what we are and used to not daring to live that dream.

On the bus to work the next morning the encounter in the TV building with the sweet Sparrow Dahl was already removed to the stockpile of memories I save in the hindmost parts of my brain, where dreams and hopes remain. In part because the encounter had been so unreal: the garden in the courtyard, the sparrow's proposal and my own behavior, but also because I didn't want to admit what had actually happened and the proposal she shouted after me. I could imagine that my brothers would one day be sitting on TV reading the news, that was how it should be, but that I . . . no, I couldn't even formulate the thought, it was so absurd, and the question of whether I would or would not go to the sparrow's program-host test was not only hypothetical, it was worded wrong: I had nothing to do at that kind of test.

Together with hundreds of anonymous workers, I walked across the open fields of the industrial area on my way to the brewery, and the sky was dark as it usually was and the first raindrops struck against the barred windows as I stood in the dressing room and pulled on my work overalls in ten minutes, then I set my lunchbox in the locker and shut the metal door with a bang and quickly twisted the padlock so that none of the rats saw what I was doing or figured out the combination.

And with steps that were neither especially heavy nor especially light I went out into the factory where the odors and sounds of the brewery surrounded me and protected me from the world outside. I passed the first of four cisterns and went down the steps between the foreman's office and the spice room, and all during that time I did not think about anything at all. Last year's austerity package meant that all the light-bulbs in the lower level were exchanged for a lower wattage, and the light down there was barely more than a night-light nowadays, which the union complained about, of course, to no avail. And I went over the trampled dirt floor (that rested in dark shadows) over to my oven, the fourth counting from the stairway, and when I got there no one turned around, no one welcomed me or took particular notice, and I took my place in the team and spent the day feeding the oven with chips at a pace that was as stingy as possible, but without risking that the heat went down.

The quarrel that started later that morning was nothing unusual, it was a couple of rats who started squabbling, most likely it was over money (the rats at the ovens made bets and wagered on everything they saw, so it was usually about gambling debts), and I kept at a distance as normal. There were hard words, swearwords being thrown in different directions, there seemed to be three of them who were mad at one another this time, and soon they started scuffling with their small, hard claws. It wasn't long before the fistfight was in full swing. The foremen most often let the rats be, as there was no point in intervening, the internal pecking order was impossible for an outsider to figure out, and we workers who had nothing to do with the matter were forced to concentrate on the ovens because now a number of animals (the ones who were fighting and the ones who were watching) were neglecting to shovel chips into the openings.

What happened next happened frighteningly fast, but when I think about it, it feels like it went on for an eternity, I had only seen it at close range once before and it must have been ten years ago; I'd forgotten how repulsive it was.

The rats fought, and without thinking about it they rolled over to the ovens where I was standing. The circle of observers moved with the fighters, and the audience was so absorbed by the struggle (they yelled and hooted for their favorites) that they didn't realize how close they were to danger. And the spark that flew away—we were working in protective clothing, the overalls were specially treated, on all the pillars in the cellar there were foam extinguishers, and there was an automatic sprinkler system along the low ceiling, no one underestimated the risks of fire or neglected trying to foresee them—landed on the shoulder of one of the rats watching the fight.

I was the one standing closest, I saw the spark fly out of the oven and I heard the terrified rat's desperate scream. Loud and anxiety-ridden, it cut through the noise from the fight. I took a few steps toward him out of pure reflex, and then I backed up again in terror: He was in flames before I even realized what was happening. I ran over to the nearest fire extinguisher, no more than five or six steps from where I stood, but by the time I'd grabbed it down from the wall and pulled out the safety pin the rat was already past saving. I sprayed foam over him—over what remained of him—but I knew that it was no use, and I didn't even notice that the fight had stopped and that everyone stood looking at me and the pile of cotton and fabric that was still burning on the floor in front of me, only now with smaller flames.

Together we all stood awhile and stared, then I dropped the extinguisher on the dirt floor, turned around, and went quickly through the dark underworld over to the stairway and then up into the brewery to the dressing room, where I sat down on the bench in front of my locker and just stared vacantly into the air in front of me. I don't know how many fire drills we've had since I started at the brewery, I don't know how many warnings I've gotten from older workers, and I can't count all the times sparks landed on the ground next to my fireproof boots; small, dangerous, yellow flames that died in a few seconds and left a final puff of smoke behind them, a last breath, visible as a gray veil against the black dirt, and every time it had been possible to be wiped out within the course of a few seconds.

At last I got up, without anyone having come up after me from the cellar (I'm sure they were occupied with compensating for the reduced heat in the ovens during the fight), tore off my overalls, changed, and left the factory. I had to see the sky, had to breathe fresh air, had to be alone with my thoughts, and I let them run free in any direction they wanted; they surprised me by not being occupied with fear of death or existential questions. On the contrary I knew there and then, and with an astonishing certainty, that I would do as the sparrow asked me, I would return to the TV building on Monday, but this time for my own sake. I would go through the tryout and be tested for *New Mornings*. It was obvious. Why had I been so hesitant?

I think about her often, but not as often as I thought about her before, she's starting to fade in my memory, the outlines are fuzzy, it's unforgivable, I don't recall her voice any longer even if I recall her screams the night that formed me into who I am—this loathsome little stuffed animal who's me and who is never even going to find a punishment harsh enough to atone for my crime. I was six years old that autumn, I'd started school, I had a mom and a dad to come home to in the afternoons, and even if she had often had too much wine, even if she often smelled bad (I thought it was the smell that made her ridiculous, pushy, and hard to understand), she was there and she was my mom. She smoked too much and I know we were in the living room together that evening, I don't know where Dad was, I don't know where Leopold was, I don't know where Rasmus was, it was her and me and she was going to light a cigarette with a match and her paw was shaking like it always did when she'd been drinking, and I imagine that I can see it before me, the shaking paw with the lit match, but that's probably something I've thought up afterward. How she raises the match to the cigarette she's holding between her lips, but how the flame flutters and lights her whiskers, and it's then that she starts to scream. Get water, get water, put out the fire, put out the fire, I've never heard her sound that way before. I'm only six years old and don't understand that it's distilled terror I'm hearing, fear of death. Frightened, I leap off the couch and run out to the kitchen and search in the cupboards for something to put water in. At last I find a large saucepan, I put it in the sink and turn the tap, and while the water runs into the saucepan I hear the screams from the living room, ghastly screams, I start screaming myself, I don't know why but it's my instinct to drown out Mom, and at last the saucepan is almost full. I lift it up, almost drop it because it's far too heavy, and drag it out to the living room, where the screams have fallen silent, and when I see her on the couch there's nothing left of her. I drop the water on the floor and then Leopold comes running, I don't know where he's coming from, but he sees that the couch is about to ignite, and he throws a blanket over the fire and suffocates it and screams at me to get more water, and this time I don't fill the saucepan as much as before . . . if I'd realized that the first time . . . if I'd known about the blanket . . . if it had been someone other than me sitting across from her that evening . . . I killed her by sitting by . . . I let her die, and I have to live with that.

I can tell you how you rot from inside; you consistently refuse to show courage, you piss on yourself, swallow your own desires so many times that at last you suffocate and gasp for air, but the air is polluted by your own stinking resignation and so it's not enough, there's no oxygen left.

A vicious circle, and I've lived in it my whole life, it leads nowhere, not up and not down, not forward and not backward. It's an eternal wandering in the shadow of a life that never became more than a promise, the bitterness tastes like a sour belch and I swallow and swallow but can never be rid of it. I'm a lowlife—the worst kind, because I have enough imagination to visualize a different life, I can't even blame stupidity or narrow-mindedness, it's simply cowardice that paralyzes me, it's simply a need for security so overwhelming that it condemns me to live in degradation, rather than risk experiencing something that I don't know in advance what it will be.

And the circle closes when self-contempt paralyzes and pacifies me and makes me even more afraid than I was before, which disgusts me so much that for a few dizzying moments I think the energy generated by the disgust will be enough to break the pattern, but in some inconceivable manner it doesn't work that way. I know I have to stop cowering under this life, that I have to stop letting myself be exploited by my brothers; but when I think that nothing happens, my dishonesty becomes even clearer and I shake with anxiety before the pitiful wretch that's me, Erik Gecko.

Today was Tuesday, so I only had five days left (two of them on the weekend, so the opportunity to prepare before Monday was limited because my chores at home were particularly numerous and difficult on the weekend), so in reality I was very short of time. Instead of going back into the factory I went out onto the street, waited for the bus, and went home to Carrer de Carrera, where I got off, passed our doorway, and went to Sarah Mammoth . . .

"Hi.

"Yeah, I know. But . . . today it's not like that.

"No, not today.

"May I look at your magazines a little?

"Yes, maybe you could say that.

"If you don't want to, then I can . . .

"Okay."

Sometimes humor and irony are difficult and as usual I misunderstood the mammoth, who liked to joke. Actually, she had nothing at all against me browsing in the magazines, so I went about my work systematically, starting in the upper left-hand corner of the shelves, and five hours later (true, I got up every time a customer came in, waited on the sidewalk, and then resumed browsing where I'd been interrupted), I was done. By then I'd read about cars and houses, about rugs and yarn, about handbags and dogs, about celebrities and actors, and food and flowers but perhaps above all, I'd read a great deal about politics and business, I browsed through loads of theater magazines and literary journals and architectural magazines, and now my plan was to let all this information sink in during the evening and night, so that I could extract selected portions from my memory tomorrow and make a really, really good news item to read for Sparrow Dahl on Monday. Best of all was that I didn't get home later than usual and so I had time to clean my brothers' room and make their beds before it was time to start dinner. I had read the newspapers in the tobacco shop at the expense of my job, and I also decided to call in sick on Monday, which would be the fourth day in three weeks (because I had taken a "day off" with both Rasmus and Leopold), and to be honest I knew what was waiting, because no one is gone for four days in three weeks and gets to keep their job, least of all someone the polecat doesn't even like to start with; with all due respect to Rasmus and Leopold, there were limits even to what they could accomplish and I assumed my job was lost.

I realize, as I'm writing this, that this sounds irresponsible, sacrificing a permanent job in this way, but that's not true. I have no talent for melancholy or thoughtlessness, I'm a realist, I'm pragmatic, and while I was airing Rasmus's blanket out the window of the top floor, I again realized the obvious: I'm going to lose my job, I'll be forced to look for something new, and the only thing that worries me are my brothers, who are going to wonder and be worried and perhaps be mean to me, but at the same time they are going to be more worried about me being unemployed than about what I've done. And with my work ethic and seriousness and their ability to convince employers about my work ethic and seriousness, it will work out (because even if there aren't many job openings in Yok, there aren't many stuffed animals looking for jobs in Yok).

During dinner the brothers asked how my day went. They almost always ask that, and I told them that a rat burned up at my feet, and they laughed so that the tears ran and I did nothing to get them to understand that the event had been so unpleasant that I had made a life-changing decision afterward, in a way that was not at all typical for me.

The strangeness continued, because I can't describe it any other way and when I look back on those days I don't understand how I dared (because in most cases I don't dare anything) or where I got the energy from (because after work and then with everything that has to be done at home in most cases I don't have energy for anything), but down in the cellar, next to the storeroom where my brothers sometimes locked me in, was our linen closet of heavily patched and mended sheets, pillowcases, and towels, and on the way to the brewery the next morning I went past the linen closet and took one of my bottom sheets and one of my pillowcases, the blue-and-white-striped one, that I decided to turn into a jacket. That was what Leopold had said, and Rasmus, too, without saying it: If you wanted to be in the game and compete for a place on *New Mornings*, you had to dress for it, and I could sew, that was no problem, I had made almost all my brothers' clothes.

When I got to work I changed as usual (being in the brewery without overalls was a sign that something was off), but I didn't go down to the cellar because it was too dark to sew straight seams down there, and besides the odor of burning wood chips was so strong that the fabric would get all smoky. No, instead I sneaked into the large drying cabinet in the dressing room, which complied with a union demand that there should be a drying cabinet that size for the workers. I don't know why, maybe working hours were different before?

The cabinet was so large that there was a ceiling lamp inside and a bench to sit on, and like all drying cabinets it was well-insulated, which meant that after I'd climbed in and closed it no one could see or hear me unless they opened the door. I remained in the drying cabinet all day Thursday and Friday instead of going down to my place by the oven, and because the time clock is in the dressing room I clocked in and clocked out and changed, so I admit that a hope was born that I might still be able to keep the job, because the question was whether anyone actually missed me on the team. At least, I had never felt that I was more than yet another shovel, yet another pair of arms among a number of shovels and arms.

The jacket turned out elegant, if I may say so myself, with the sheet as lining and the blue-striped pillowcase transverse in the sleeves and lapel, which gave a striking but not pretentious impression. For buttons I used bottle caps, which I realize sounds cheap, but at the brewery there was a whole room of bottle caps and by no means were all of them used on the bottles Carlsweis currently produced. It wasn't hard to find a pair of small, white, nice-looking caps for the sleeves and another pair, blue and a little bigger, for buttoning.

Over the weekend there were several times I thought I would give myself away in front of my brothers and reveal my secret, but I can thank alcohol that it didn't happen: On Friday and Saturday Rasmus and Leopold got drunk and disappeared out in the city to find females to hug, and on Saturday and Sunday the hangover made them sluggish and irritable so they didn't want to have anything to do with me. My life continued on the surface exactly as usual: I scrubbed floors, did laundry, and prepared food. I took the opportunity to scrape and paint the window moldings on the top floor—which I should have done years ago—and I filled out and sent in all the forms, for myself as well as for Rasmus and Leopold, that the social service authorities required every month. But the whole time I was rehearsing the invented news items in my head, so that even if physically I was doing what I should, I was absent in every thought and moment and if either of my brothers had spoken to me, I probably would have started to ramble on about how a church is being built in postmodern style in north Tourquai, or that a (made-up) hostage drama was playing out at the Concert House on Pfaffendorfer Tor in Lanceheim.

I swear that when I went to bed on Sunday evening I was empty inside, exhausted from the mental overdrive I'd been in since Friday, and at the same time on tenterhooks from nervousness about the next day. Although I was so tired I felt ill, I didn't fall asleep until it was basically time to wake up again, so you may question whether I gave myself the best possible chance before the test that awaited me.

I betray myself, again and again, daily and hourly, I hate myself, I despise myself, I loathe myself, and all these feelings make my steps so heavy I don't have any oomph left. I'm finished. I'm nobody. What does integrity look like? Is it about standing by your thoughts, or standing by your actions, or standing up for yourself, and is it possible to distinguish one from the other: Shouldn't my thoughts lead to actions that add up to who I am? Can I call an insight that remains an intellectual seed an insight, even if it never develops into anything more than a fantasy, a stupid and childish and irresponsible and romantic idea that hovers freely by itself and has nothing to do with my identity? The sum of my fantasies is not me, the sum of my dreams is a taunt that makes me doubt, and only cynicism can raise me up from my anxiety, while the sum of my actions is just as pathetic as the spineless stuffed animal who every day is stuck in deadlock that inhibits and holds him back, and that must be the way I want it to be, on a deeply unconscious level, but this is impossible to understand rationally, because I am ashamed to my stuffing about my helplessness, and all the beatings I get from my brothers are exactly what I'm worth, all the work they force me to do is only a small repayment that has to happen daily so that I can put up with the quivering, evasive stuffed animal that is me. Integrity, I ask myself again: What does it look like? It strikes me that this very question is one that someone like me can never answer, because if I could, I never would have needed to ask it.

They ask me to begin, but it's as if the voice is coming from nowhere, that I'm hearing it through a filter that makes it impossible to place, the same fog that keeps the world at a distance, that makes reality diffuse. I look down at my short claws on the table before me and I think that it's not my toes they're attached to, not my toes that are moving, even though I've chosen to move them. It's as if I've taken some kind of drug that isolates me from experiences, from feelings—physical as well as mental—and they are asking me to begin. At first I don't feel my tongue moving in my mouth and after a while it feels much too tangible, it's moving out of sync with the words.

Just a few minutes ago I was quivering with nervousness;

every movement, every sound made me jump, on tenterhooks, the slightest vibration transmitted through the floor and up into the chair I was sitting in, waiting for my name to be called, the smells from the stuffed animals sitting alongside, the colors of their clothes, I registered everything with an acuity that I'd never experienced before, and no matter how much water I drank my mouth and throat dried up again the next moment. I didn't rehearse my speech because I was much too nervous to remember so many sentences in a row, and then they called out my name and I got up and went straight into this fog.

They ask me to start, and I start, I let the words run out of my mouth without understanding what I'm saying, I hardly hear my voice, I stare right in front of me because there somewhere I think I see a camera lens staring back, but I'm still unsure, I stare and talk and talk and stare and nothing seems to happen, no one reacts to anything I'm saying, and deep down in my closed-off brain panic is sneaking around looking for a door. What if what I'm saying isn't coherent, what if it's just nonsense, what if I'm not looking into the camera, and once my brain has started to formulate these questions there are more and more: What if my jacket split, what if I have milk on my chin, what if I stutter?

They ask me to start, and I don't know how or why I know that I'm finished, but when I'm finished I get up right when the words come to an end and leave the room. I run out of there, and when I feel someone take hold of my shoulder I tear myself loose, a button in my jacket comes unfastened, and when I get home several hours later I discover it's gone, the button must have fallen off.

Back home on Monday afternoon on my honey yellow Carrer de Carrera, I can't say I regret it, for even if the experience of having lost all control feels horrible, deep inside the discomfort a little kernel of joy is hiding. It's strange how it works, and I can't explain it better than that, even though it was horrible and I landed in a black hole of terror and performance anxiety, I'm longing to go back, and I know that I take with me a memory, a blurred memory, of a great moment in life.

It's almost as if I'm not afraid when I step into the hall and carefully call to my brothers who aren't home, thank goodness, and I go to make dinner as usual and wonder what the polecat will say tomorrow at work and whether it's over now, if I'll be forced to look for something new.

On the bus on Tuesday nothing has happened yet, even though I woke up and thought that now something has to happen, something else, now the brothers have uncovered me, now the polecat has uncovered me, I've been talking in my sleep. I ought to throw away the jacket, to remove evidence, and my plan was to slip it into a half-full Dumpster that I've seen on my way from the bus stop to the brewery, and which day after day is filled with trash and rubbish from stuffed animals who come during the night and (probably just like me) dump some kind of evidence. But I can't do it; there's too much care and struggle behind every seam in my blue-striped jacket, it carries the memory of My Great Experience, so even if it does sound a little pathetic I've hidden it in the storeroom in the cellar, wadded it up so it looks like all the other worn-out linens we have down there.

I go into the dressing room, clock in, pull on my overalls, fiddle with the padlock, go out into the brewery, down into the cellar, and shovel chips. At lunch I go up and get my lunchbox, then back down to the cellar again where I eat two liversausage sandwiches (just like I always do, but today I forgot the cucumber, which is a trifle but completely exposes my inner chaos), and as I'm sitting on the bus on the way home—I have to stop and buy groceries and then this evening go out into the forest to hunt for wood—I'm still the only one who notices that I'm no longer the same.

But these days Rasmus isn't really Rasmus and Leopold isn't really Leopold, because all three of us are filled up with ourselves in a way that makes us even less attentive to each other than usual, which in my case is a blessing. For the first time in their lives my brothers are also fixated on the postal service and the letter carrier, a moose whose massive horns make the little postal service cap even sillier, and I am no longer entrusted with picking up the junk mail we usually get.

When I came home after my experience in the TV studio, Leopold—or Rasmus—had already thrown the day's mail (a wrinkled advertising flyer from Monomart) on the living room table and, probably in a fury, left the house, and today when I open the door both brothers are at home, which is un- usual. I feel the atmosphere strike me in the hallway, dark and threatening, and I hear by the way my brothers are impatiently moving in the living room that I have to lie low, that this is serious now. I sneak up the stairs without the third, sixth, or twelfth step betraying me; it's a matter of millimeters, but if you know where to place your foot you can remain silent.

I hide on the top floor for half an hour, but then I have to go down and start making dinner, and I make myself as light as I can and go down again, without them hearing me even though the sixth step creaks faintly, and sneak into the kitchen. The letter carrier hasn't arrived; he isn't coming at all today, it's the sort of thing I know because I'm used to taking care of the mail, and I can only fantasize about my brothers' reaction when they realize they've been waiting for no reason. In the usual arrangement I prepare myself for them to take their anger out on me, we all need outlets and the least I can do is to help out. In return my brothers see to it that the house stays ours, because I don't know if I could live without the house on Carrer de Carrera.

After more than fifteen minutes, as the kitchen fills with the aroma of boiling cabbage heads and I've set the table as nicely as I'm able, a tremendous crash is heard from out in the living room, and I look down into the kettle and hope that it appears as if the cabbages aren't going to cook completely if I don't watch over them carefully. The next moment the door to the kitchen is thrown open, and Rasmus comes in, sees that I've set the table, takes hold of the tablecloth I've laid down and pulls it out, whereupon plates and glasses and the vase with a tulip falls to the floor, the sound of porcelain breaking against stone jangles in my ears, and he screams at me to pick it up.

But nothing else happens, and only a minute or two later both Leopold and Rasmus have left me alone in the house with the broken dishes and, as it turns out, a smashed coffee table out in the living room. I assume they're on the hunt for liquor, they intend to drink away the disappointment and frustration at still not having heard anything from *Now!* or *Good Morning Mollisan Town.*

I gather up the shards of porcelain from the floor, get the smallest pieces with the vacuum cleaner, fail to glue the vase together again (it was already glued together twice), and take the bedclothes out of the TV stand—sheets and pillowcase that are always going to remind me of my own great experience of *New Mornings* because the jacket in the cellar means that now I only have one pillow—and make the bed on the sofa; it's crucial to be asleep before my brothers are back. The smashed coffee table has helped me: It will serve as wood for two, three days, and so I don't need to go out to the forest this evening.

Wednesday passes and Thursday passes and I become myself again, it's impossible to retain the feeling that everything is different when nothing is changed, when neither the rats nor the polecat ask a single question; I didn't clock in last Monday and I didn't clock out and I have no explanations, but no one asks why; I don't see a glimpse of the polecat during these days so I don't know who would comment on my absence.

Going to work, changing, and shoveling chips and at the end of the month having money put into the bank account is a system that works. I've never felt that I should question it, but who actually judges that what I do, I do better than anyone else? Sometimes months go by without me seeing the polecat, and when I think about it I realize that it's that way now, it's been months since I saw him, maybe he's not even still working here.

At home it's the same thing, everything goes on as usual with the exception of my brothers' fixation on the mail and the letter carrier, the poor moose who I believe got a visit last night when my brothers' frustration was uncontrollable and they had to talk with him (if I understand it right, they got him to promise to come by every day whether or not he has any mail for us).

It's impossible to feel different when the memory of what happened becomes vague, so distant and unclear that I remember details from my cubdom with greater clarity; I recall dreams better, and the memory of my beloved mom (whom I almost hardly saw and whom I idolize in my dreams so that I'm almost ashamed when I wake up) is more real than those moments before the TV camera. And I think that in only a week, in a few weeks, the program-host tryouts will be yet another piece of evidence that fatalism is my inheritance and my salvation, and that dreams and fantasies are not only vain, they're dangerous, because when they are crushed the life that remains is a little bit less valuable. Don't ask me why this is so, but it is.

On Friday there was more going on than on Wednesday and Thursday, but, you might say, nothing that hadn't happened before. At work I was pulled into a card game, it's during lunch and against my will, but the rats down by the ovens take hold of me and force me to sit with them, one of them is sick to his stomach and they're missing one player and they know that I can, so . . .

"I don't have any cash.

"But I'm not going to . . .

"A little while, then?"

I don't win. You can call me lots of things, but I'm not stupid—not like that, sitting with the rats during lunch and winning a card game would be stupid—so I play carelessly, just good enough, so that no one gets angry or happy and I can get up and leave when the lunch hour is over without anyone recalling that I was even there. But I'm afraid the whole time, though I'm usually not, I feel the heat from the ovens and I'm aware of the fire burning in there, and the memory of the rat that burned up last week haunts me. I carry that image with me in my daydreams, and it takes the whole afternoon for my pulse to calm down.

When I come home my brothers are there, I've already gotten used to that, but something is different today and when I close the door I know what it is: I'm missing the sauntering steps, the loud, agitated voices, all I hear instead is silence. I remain standing a few moments with my coat on and just listen toward the living room, but I don't think anyone is there, and I take a few steps into the hall and try to listen upward. Even though it's completely silent I'm sure my brothers are up in their rooms, and I think that maybe the mail has arrived earlier today, maybe their expectation has already turned to dejection, because Rasmus and Leopold are hanging their heads now, they are resigned, it's worse than during all the years when we never heard a word from *New Mornings*, because then my brothers thought they had been unjustly screened out; now they've shown what they can do, and there's nothing to blame.

But there I'm wrong when I think about it, because I'm here, Erik Gecko, who wrote the news items that caused them to fail, so they can blame it on me. They're going to blame me anyway, and when I go into the living room I see an envelope with the familiar *Now!* logo lying wadded up and thrown on the floor in front of the stove, and I realize it's their results, for either both or one of them, because the silence doesn't suggest there's celebrating going on in this house, so I go over to pick up the envelope but just as I'm leaning down I hear steps on the stairs, and I turn around and see my big brother Leopold coming into the living room, and lightning bolts are shooting out of his eyes. I don't have time to say or do anything, I get a blow across the ear that immediately sends me to the floor, and he takes hold of my long tail and drags me toward the cellar stairs, and I can't say I'm surprised. He more or less heaves me down the stairs, and in order not to be kicked I voluntarily crawl into the storeroom so he only needs to slam the door, but I don't sense that it's going to be different this time. After hours long as years I fall into unconsciousness and I don't come out of it for a long, long time.

When at last the door is opened and I am pulled out, I hardly notice it, a weak tugging on my legs, I feel the steps against my body as I'm being dragged up from the cellar, my head striking the threshold into the kitchen, and they set me with my back against the wall and ask me to drink, but I don't have strength enough to hold a glass or to put it to my mouth. So they help me, and then they help me eat, Leopold holds me while Rasmus forces bread in between my lips, it's unbearable but I realize I have to, it's an instinct that makes me chew and swallow, reflexes that have nothing to do with reason.

Slowly I come around, and my brothers are . . . I wouldn't describe them as remorseful, but never ever have they taken care of me the way they're doing right now, I have no emotional memory that anyone has held me like Leopold is holding me and I can see in their eyes that they want to revive me, they want me to live.

At last all three of us are rewarded as my strength returns, slowly I'm filled with life, literally, but the fatigue that comes over me is numbing, and when it's clear that my brothers expect me to leave for work I almost start to cry, I can't help it, I don't see how I'll manage. But I pull myself together and thanks to Leopold I get on my feet, even if I stagger and sway even more than usual and it takes me almost five minutes to go from the kitchen out to the hall. Then when I'm sitting on the bus I'm so groggy I have a hard time sorting out my thoughts: recently in the storeroom, now on the bus, recently barely alive, soon at work, and every time the bus turns it makes me almost fall off my seat, every stop means that I have to parry with my hands, but at last I arrive, get off, and drag myself across the industrial area over to Carlsweis brewery, where a surprise awaits.

In the dressing room the polecat is standing to meet me. He's in bad shape, his short arm is hanging in a sling and he's missing one of his ears, which seems to have been recently torn off, you can see the stuffing in the hole, but I pretend not to see either him or the hole but instead hurry over and open my locker as usual. He follows, places himself really close and speaks in a low voice, so that no one else can hear because we're not alone in the dressing room . . .

"Yes?

"I understand.

"Tuesday? Is it Tuesday? But . . .

"I don't know anything about that.

"I understand.

"No, this was the last time.

"Yes, I'll pass that on.

"I understand, but what do you mean this is Tuesday?"

He goes away, he's furious and wants nothing better than to take it out on me, but he doesn't dare, it's Rasmus or Leopold or both of them who tore off his ear, who tore off his arm—even if the doctors have already sewn it back on—and the polecat can't fire me or bawl me out, because then something even worse would happen to him. But he lets it be known to my brothers that the next time he'll turn the matter over to his boss, and then he can't save my job again.

I don't care about any of that, the only thing I hear is that it's Tuesday today, and while I'm changing it grinds in my head, that Leopold locked me in the storeroom on Friday, which means that I was locked up for at least three days (which has never happened before), but the thought I can't get rid of is a different one: Today is a Tuesday, but in what week?

It's during dinner that my brothers make a joint decision, I'm standing over in my corner by the stove stirring a leek stew so it will stay hot without burning at the bottom, and they are sitting at the table talking with each other and assuming I hear everything they say (the way it works is that if Leopold thinks there's not enough salt in the stew, he tells Rasmus, but expects that I'll come running with the saltshaker, and if Rasmus says to Leopold that he thinks the radiator on the top floor smells disgusting, he expects me to fix it as soon as I've done the dishes).

Now they're saying that *New Mornings* is a goddamned worthless program, and that only jerks are program hosts on TV, cowardly, unsuccessful idiots who sit there and smile ingratiatingly and read some bullshit that the weather is going to change when everyone knows that's bullshit, and the only ones who look at *Good Morning Mollisan Town* are retirees who stare at the TV day and night; damned good luck that no one knows they sent in applications to *Now!* every year, and what were they really thinking, did their drinking kill too many brain cells?

Then they laugh out loud at their own stupidity and explain that they will never, ever look at *New Mornings* or *Good Morning Mollisan Town* again, that in this house those TV programs are banned, and I realize that this applies to me, too, that I won't be watching anymore either, and I know that during the time I was in the storeroom in the cellar they both must have been turned down by the tryouts, even if I only saw one of the envelopes . . .

Of course.

I run over and put more stew on the plates, I fill their water glasses and I know that never again will I hear about the tryouts or what happened to my brothers in the TV studio. This chapter of our lives is now history, and it will be mentioned here in the house on Carrer de Carrera as seldom as we mention our parents.

My brothers make it an early evening; they go to bed after sitting a couple of hours in front of the TV watching cricket, I don't know who's playing, the game has never interested me, there are too many rules and the rules are too complicated and it seems like the Yok Giants always lose, which makes my brothers irritable and for that reason it's best for me to stay in the kitchen until they go upstairs. This is the condition for my life, and perhaps I'm going to think about it as before and after *New Mornings*, perhaps I'm going to think about it as before and after my week in the cellar, or else I'm not going to think about it at all.

Sarah Mammoth has something on her mind. We've exchanged our usual greetings, I bought a couple packs of cigarettes for my brothers and got a small cappuccino from Sarah, but she continues looking at me in a peculiar way, and the only conclusion I can draw is that she wants to say something but isn't sure if she should. She is in her usual place in front of the shiny, steaming coffee machine behind her large chocolate counter, and I've already put a hand on the door handle to go out. I have no curiosity left in my body, curiosity was something I got rid of long ago, as it only leads to melancholy, so I don't ask Sarah if she has something on her mind.

"Yes?

"Shut the door? Yes?

"Who was asking?"

Sarah doesn't know, but she seems embarrassed by the question because she doesn't think it has anything to do with it, what happened is sensationally strange regardless of who called; that she picks up the receiver in the tobacco shop and a voice is heard that she has never heard before, asking about a lizard . . .

"No, it sounds strange.

"No, I have no idea.

"Yes, I'm sure you were right to do that."

It feels unusual and not really good that Sarah Mammoth asks me what I think, I mean, I'm Erik Gecko, I'm only a customer who buys cigarettes in the tobacco shop, what can I say about whether she should say one thing or another to strangers who call and ask about lizards? But Sarah lights her pipe and continues staring at me while she produces large puffs of smoke, she is staring in a way that makes it quite clear that I should say something, that I should confirm or deny something, and I swear, even if it sounds silly, that only then do I understand that the lizard Sarah thinks the party who called is asking about is . . . me.

"Someone called and was looking for me?

"No, it's absolutely not . . .

"No, I have absolutely nothing to . . .

"Yes, you can do that. If they call again."

For I have nothing to hide, I think it's important that Sarah understands that, because the opposite would suggest that I've been fooling her all these years, that I've been carrying on some kind of double life, but I haven't. Sarah is my only confidante in this city and she must know that I am nothing other than who I've made myself out to be, and as far as I'm concerned she can talk about me to anyone at all, for the simple reason that no one is going to call and ask about me . . .

"Yes, really," I repeat with emphasis, so that she understands, and she nods and produces even larger puffs of smoke and we stand a moment quietly and look at each other to confirm that we've both understood, and then I leave the cramped, aromatic tobacco shop for the day.

Day out and day in and I'm trying to be good and do good and not let the self-loathing take over, I am working my way up from the bottom every morning and distract myself by doing things, finding chores that help me avoid thinking that I'm alive, because I know that what shapes us stuffed animals is a single mistake for a few inattentive seconds, and then we're forced to carry it with us for the rest of our lives. In my case I'm standing in the hall, I'm six years old, Mom has burnt up, someone knocks on the door and I open it, on the stairs outside is a police officer, I know I should be afraid of police officers and make myself scarce, but I don't know any more than that because I'm a silly little idiot, six years old, and when the police officer asks me if Dad was home yesterday evening I answer that no, he wasn't home, whereupon the police officer shoves me aside and enters the house, and after him come a couple more police officers, and they run up to the top floor and pull Dad out of bed and drag him down the stairs, and when he catches sight of me he screams that a squealer is the most worthless of all stuffed animals. The police carry Dad through the hall and Dad screams that a squealer is a failure of Magnus, a squealer isn't worth anything other than scorn and contempt, he will never be loved by anyone, and a squealer, that's what I am, and Dad is screaming all this while the police drag him out of the house and he never comes back and I don't know where he's gone but I know what I am, afterward I know exactly what I am: I am the low-water mark of creation, I'm a lizard who lets his mom die and who squeals on his dad, I'm not worth anything, I am nobody.

It's a Saturday in the middle of the day, my brothers are awake and I can hear them upstairs awhile, but they haven't come down to breakfast yet, even though everything's ready and set out. As usual I'm trying to keep the porridge hot by stirring it just enough (you shouldn't stir too much because then it gets too runny, and Rasmus loathes that), while it's the opposite with the eggs, neither of my brothers likes eggs that are warm, so I've set them to cool in a saucepan of cold water—which makes them easier to peel besides—and I'm waiting to squeeze the juice until I hear footsteps on the stairs, otherwise the pulp sinks to the bottom, and nobody likes that.

When the doorbell rings I assume it's some annoying cubs from the neighborhood, no one would dare disturb us for real, and it can't be acquaintances because my brothers have no friends—at least no friends I've heard about or met—so I ignore the doorbell and continue stirring the porridge and when it rings again I decide to give the rascals a lesson. I go quickly into the living room, open the window, and lean out. From there you can see the stairs up to the front door, and my idea is to really scare them by shouting that Leopold and Rasmus know who they are. But when I open the window and lean out, I see a well-dressed female with her back to me, she has high-heeled shoes and a long coat that is narrowly cut, and I am so surprised that I forget what I was doing, while the female has heard the window being opened and turns around.

Perhaps it's due to the fact that I'm already surprised that it takes a few seconds before I realize who is standing outside the door on Carrer de Carrera, but I get a kind of blackout, something goes off in my head and my mind goes blank, and when Sparrow Dahl from the TV building (the one I met on the bench, who made sure I got to do my test) rings the doorbell a third time I hear one of the brothers open the bedroom door upstairs with a bang and shriek at me that I should chase them away, because he also thinks it's some cubs.

I can't move, it's incredibly unpleasant, I'm actually trying to do something: close the window, go out in the hall, open the door and ask her to go away. I'm trying to think how I should express myself, both to her and to my brothers, but all these thoughts lead nowhere, I remain paralyzed until I hear Leopold roar for the second time from upstairs, and then finally I run out into the hall and open the door.

Sparrow Dahl smiles when she catches sight of me. She nods and asks if she may come in just as Leopold screams from upstairs and asks who wants a punch in the mouth, he still thinks it's the neighborhood rascals we're dealing with, and I don't know what I should say. I take a step to one side so that the sparrow can come in, at the same time I hear Leopold on his way down the stairs, and I follow her into the living room.

"What the hell is going on?" Leopold shouts. He's out in the hall and comes crashing into the living room, where he catches sight of the sparrow, who is already standing over by the TV, and she turns around, smiles at him the same way she did to me, and he stops short, remains standing with his jeans unbuttoned and his upper body bare, he just got up.

I've advanced, I think, and at the same moment I realize that this is the thought that has blocked all the other thoughts the last few minutes, that I've advanced, I did the program-host tryout and they thought I was so good that I advanced, I'm one of the chosen candidates who is going to compete on *New Mornings*.

Sparrow Dahl smiles and talks quietly, but she sounds very definite, and because I turn away, I'm looking down at the floor, she directs herself to my big brother, who hums and nods and interjects brief questions, and what she says is exactly this: that I've advanced in the program-host tryouts to *New Mornings* after my successful audition, and Leopold reacts at last and says the hell I am. There must be some mistake. He turns to me, his eyes are black as coal, and he asks the question directly to me . . .

"No, of course not!

"I have no idea."

Sparrow Dahl protests, and now she also asks me the question, but I insist . . .

"I've never done any tryout.

"Maybe you're confusing me with someone else?"

The sparrow stops short when I deny having done the tryout, and the thought that TV has confused me and Leopold makes my big brother just as outraged as hopeful, it might be that way, he thinks. But the sparrow explains that it's not that way at all, she knows that both Leopold and Rasmus were at the tryouts, that unfortunately neither of them has advanced, but on the other hand I, Erik Gecko, have . . .

"No.

"No, I promise, Leopold, I never did any test, I've never been there except with you and Rasmus. You're wrong, Sparrow, I don't know why you're coming here and accusing me of things I haven't done, I don't know why."

Leopold nods gloomily, lowers his voice and talks seriously with the sparrow, explains how it actually is: that his blockheaded little brother Erik Gecko is so damn stupid he can barely sit up, you only have to look at me now and see how my upper body sways back and forth like a damn reed in the wind, and to think that he could sit up straight in front of a camera and be someone you should trust, that's so damn stupid it's not even worth mentioning, or what, and even if my stupid little brother might have done something good for the first time in his life, then he would still not want to be part of that shitty program, that everyone here in this house hates like the plague . . .

"But it wasn't me, Leopold, it wasn't me. You have to believe me.

"It wasn't me.

"There are hundreds of lizards around here it might have been.

"Because it wasn't me.

"You're wrong, Sparrow, you'll have to look somewhere else."

I finally dare to look up and meet the sparrow's gaze, and we stand staring at each other for a moment—the longest I've ever experienced—and Leopold studies me carefully, in detail, but I don't reveal anything and the sparrow suddenly decides and quite unexpectedly for both my big brother and me she says well then, she must have been wrong, and then she leaves us in the living room, and we hear the door shut.

"I promise, Leopold, I promise.

"I don't know why she was here."

Leopold, Leopold, my beautiful spotted big brother, is at a loss, but decides—this, too, is surprising—that he should trust me, and he says he's hungry and asks why the hell it smells so bad from the kitchen, and I realize that the porridge has burned.

EPILOGUE

For years my girlfriends have been nagging me to move on. That's easy to say, but to move on there has to be a reason. You have to want to go from something to something else. I have no such desire. In contrast to many of my girlfriends I don't identify with work that way. I realize they draw that conclusion because I live alone and devote most of my waking hours to my job, but it's a matter of duty and desire. I'm still developing as a stuffed animal, even if the job no longer·offers the same challenge.

I was part of the project group that came up with the program concept for the channel management, I worked as a news editor on the team that made the pilot episodes and over the years I've had most positions, the last four seasons as executive producer of *New Mornings*. It has been an amazing journey. After a few tough years at the start, our program has become an institution, something as improbable as a sure success. Besides, a lot of good TV animals started their careers on the program, Kara Marmoset and Garcia the Swan, just to name a few.

The work is currently characterized for the most part by professional routine. If you work with TV there's always an uncertainty factor of course, ordinary stuffed animals are, after all, the starting point for *New Mornings*, but after all these years we've learned to handle most things.

Sometimes, at a dinner with close girlfriends and a few glasses of red wine, I've complained about this. That the excitement is gone, repetition has taken over and the challenges are few. I realize that such comments may cause some to think I ought to move on. Find some other job in the TV building, because I absolutely believe I can get one. Yet I have no desire. And it's the moment when Erik Gecko sat down in front of the TV camera that makes me stay put at *New Mornings*. It's the surprise and the magic in such moments. Then all the routine is blown away. Then it's worth all the boring administration and predictability.

I don't know what it was that made me realize his potential when I sat down beside him on the bench in front of what we in the TV building call the "Garden of Eden." Intuition, I assume, developed after many years in this profession. I immediately felt that he was special, that there was something extraordinary in his charisma, in his gaze, and I knew the cameras would see it the same way I did, and communicate that via the TV screens to homes in Mollisan Town.

When he recited his nonsense text I also knew he was this year's winner. He was distinct and credible, calm and factual, but in his voice there was an undertone of urgency that is common to all the foremost newscasters. Some have it while others never will. It's no more difficult than that.

Every year we have a few "wild cards" that we've run into between seasons, and who we think may fit the program. So Erik was not unique, and I took for granted that he would appear on Monday and read before the camera. In the TV industry we always assume that everyone wants to be on TV.

I didn't think it mattered that Gecko hadn't filled out any

application forms and for that reason we didn't have his address or full name.

I am seldom present at the tryouts because, to be honest, it's unbearably boring to suffer through all the amateurs whose mediocrity is not at all entertaining. But because I had invited Gecko I was there that morning to meet him. He looked terrible. He was shaking with nervousness, and had put on a pillowcase that he'd re-sewn into a jacket. It was a striped pillowcase, and it made his already narrow shoulders almost disappear completely. I admit I regretted it then, and thought I'd been wrong, but then when he sat down in the studio, looked into the camera and started reading, I knew again I'd been right. Then I knew just as certainly as I'd known before the weekend that he would be the year's victor.

It came as a surprise when he got up and ran out of there. No one on the team had time to react, and I only managed to catch hold of his jacket, which of course fell apart, before he was gone. There I stood, with a bottle cap lying on the floor, which later would be my first clue, wondering what got into him. And during the days that followed I was so certain that he would contact the program that I didn't even bother searching. Then I realized that something had happened.

You didn't need to be a detective to figure out that the bottle cap came from Carlsweis, so we phoned the brewery and asked if they had any lizards working there. We got a list of five names, but no addresses or contact information, and it was unclear whether that was due to some internal policy or whether the information was lacking.

On the test video we discovered a burn mark on Gecko's striped jacket, and it looked as if the mark came from a cigarette. So we called around to the tobacco shops that were in the vicinity of Carlsweis brewery, and ended up at last with a mammoth who indicated she knew what lizard I was talking about, a gecko whose name was Erik. This detective work had not taken the office more than a couple of hours, and I decided to go down to the address, in the southern part of Yok, the following day.

That proved to be an absurd experience. I rang the doorbell at a little house on Carrer de Carrera, Erik Gecko opened the door but pretended not to recognize me, and also denied that he had ever been in the TV studio. According to our own files, both Leopard and Panther—with the same address—had applied for this year's tryouts without being chosen, and I admit I was a trifle perplexed. Was I mistaken? Something strange was going on in that house, and I had an ominous feeling of danger, so I decided to leave.

Later in the afternoon I had almost forgotten that foreboding, and when the following workweek began we had the usual problem of too many applicants, not too few, so I put the lizard aside for a couple of days. It was only toward the end of the week when we made an assessment of possible winners that he came up in the discussion again and I decided to make a final attempt. Deep down I was of course certain that Erik Gecko was our lizard.

I decided to return to the house on Carrer de Carrera, wait out the three brothers and snoop around in the rooms on my own to see if there was any evidence that Erik was the same stuffed animal we had on tape. It may sound melodramatic, but we had been on similar adventures before. I took a camera team with me and filmed the episode, with the ulterior motive of perhaps being able to use the material later on *New Mornings* if and when Erik Gecko advanced. I was thus neither alone nor directly worried.

We arrived in our van early in the morning, and first saw Erik leave, to his job at Carlsweis, we assumed. His older brothers did not leave the house until after lunch. Then we slipped in.

After only a few minutes I discovered the blue-striped pillowcase in the living room; it was surprising I hadn't seen it when I was there before. But it was only when one of my assistants found Erik's wrinkled jacket in a storeroom in the cellar, with a thread that showed where the missing button had been, that we knew we had the right lizard. We left the house and waited in the van with the camera ready, for Erik to come back.

I already suspected, of course, that this was about a sibling conflict. The two other brothers had tried but failed to be selected, and Erik had succeeded without even really wanting to. It must be hard for the older stuffed animals, so my plan was not to talk with the leopard or the panther before I had spoken with Erik.

When the Breeze again started blowing and the Evening Weather announced its arrival, the brothers came back, but there was still no trace of Erik. The panther and leopard stayed in the house for a while, perhaps half an hour, and then left again. The camera team and I gave up when the day started to darken and Erik Gecko had still not come back from work.

The following morning I decided on a new tactic. Perhaps it was easier to talk with him at his workplace, I reasoned, where I didn't need to worry about the brothers and their internal conflicts. Besides, we had already filmed his house. So I took the camera team and went down to Carlsweis.

At the workplace they informed us that Erik Gecko had not clocked in either yesterday or today. It was a polecat we talked to, and he let it be known that this was the last time Gecko would be absent; as of now he could consider himself unemployed. I am ashamed when I admit that I thought this would be really good on TV.

We identified the tobacco shop I had phoned, and the mammoth who said she knew Erik Gecko, but she had nothing further to tell us. I still refrained from bothering the brothers, but when two days later we had still not seen a glimpse of Gecko I went down to Carrer de Carrera in the evening with my team, and rang the bell. The leopard opened.

"Hello, my name is Sparrow Dahl, I work as executive producer for *New Mornings* and I'm looking for Erik Gecko."

"Weren't you here before?"

"That's right. For the same reason, I'm looking for Erik Gecko."

"Well, good luck with that!"

"What do you mean?"

"He split, the little creep."

"Split? What do you mean?"

"He's not here, damn it. Get it? And if we find him, I promise he's going to get a beating you wouldn't believe. But he's gone."

"Gone?"

Yes, the conversation with Leopold Leopard went on this way for a while, and I was forced to accept that Erik Gecko really had disappeared.

On a few occasions during the autumn I made renewed attempts to get hold of the lizard without success. I was disappointed, of course, but that was nothing compared with the brothers' reaction. I heard, in a roundabout way, that they were more or less on a full-time hunt for their little brother after he disappeared, but that led nowhere. Then I put the lizard out of my mind. If you want to, you can disappear in Mollisan Town, and modern surgery can re-sew a stuffed animal beyond recognition.

To be honest the ninth season of *New Mornings* was an off year, but it can be that way and I'm looking ahead. It feels like I still have things undone with the program. Even if I complain sometimes I intend to continue, as long as TV allows me, and as long as that moment with Erik Gecko on the bench makes me remember why I first started.

CORBOD

1.

Mike Chimpanzee held the slender neck with both hands, swinging the guitar over his head; the next moment the instrument shattered against a Lanceheimian gargoyle from the fourteenth century. Splinters flew, the strings sang and the ape's pulse was pounding in his ears. He was high on grass, low on booze, and feeling extremely sorry for himself.

At the same time, he thought a photographer should have been present. Now they would see him: Now he was rock and roll. In boots and worn jeans, his shaggy brown upper body bare and guitar parts flying through the room. He peeked at himself in the large mirror by the sofa bed: raw power, attitude, and energy. His bright blue eyes radiated pain. The dark interior of the antique store was an excellent stage set, with old rugs hanging on the walls and dark cabinets with carved doors forming narrow corridors where the light from dusty chandeliers barely reached. An enchanted, mysterious, and yet curiously glamorous place.

He collapsed onto the gargoyle, letting go of the guitar neck. He wanted to feel uncompromisingly destructive, but he had smashed the guitar he never used, while the guitar he'd been playing last night still stood untouched in its place over by the desk. Even so, his anxiety was sincere, there was no mistaking that. An antique plaster cat with a price tag for a thousand sat atop a turn-of-the-century drop-leaf table, smiling slyly at him.

The antique store had been Mike Chimpanzee's home for the past six months. He slept in a wooden sofa bed, used a tiny refrigerator in the cluttered office to keep beer cold, and didn't care that the restroom had no drying cabinet. He had moved around quite a bit the past year; as soon as his fans discovered where he lived, they set up camp outside the building in question. After his breakthrough Mike had become public property. Admirers of all sorts, ages, and genders pursued him night and day, heedlessly throwing themselves at him, asking for autographs, swearing their love, and offering him . . . most everything. At first it had been marvelous. All the love that came his way, all the adoration, had been bewildering and endlessly confirming. He was amazed by it and couldn't get enough of it. He abused it and surrendered himself to it.

The months that followed, on the other hand, were unbearable. The attention was so overwhelming that he felt ashamed. He was not worthy of their adoration. He was not worthy of their love letters, their underwear, or their unconditional trust.

And besides, love didn't pay any bills. He was a star, but an impoverished one. The advance the record company had given him was already spent. Good drugs weren't cheap. Ingratiating friends were expensive. With more money maybe he could have more easily handled the excitement he provoked as soon as he appeared on the city streets, but when you didn't even have money for a taxi . . . Better to stay out of sight.

No one had uncovered this humble antique store yet. The rhinoceros who loaned him the use of the store was a devoted admirer with many shops around Yok, and he didn't ask for any rent. Mike's only return service was to answer the phone when it rang, but so far it hadn't. At least, he hadn't heard it.

Slowly he got up. He cast a disdainful glance at the pad and pen still lying on the desk, a reminder of the night's failure. With a deep sigh he went over to the row of sideboards, searching for the whiskey bottle he recalled having seen there some time around midnight. The antique store was chock-full of stuff, everything old, bad-smelling, and expensive; it was easy to misplace things in the excess. He hummed his newly composed chorus, still feeling satisfied. He often mixed up the latest attempt at a melody with one of its hundreds of predecessors— the ones that had always made him so disappointed—but this time it felt different.

Mike sneered to himself; it always felt different.

No, it wasn't the melody but the disastrous attempts to write the words that finally caused him to smash the old guitar. Lyrics were usually his strong suit, but last night he got stuck. He'd had an idea to write about the forest, making it dangerous in an exotic, seductive way, and in the chorus maybe list some of the trees and bushes whose names he always found lyrical. But when dawn came the lyrics just felt silly, and furiously he tore the pages with crossed-out lines, where "mist" rhymed with "kissed" and "willow" with "pillow," out of the pad.

Mike sighed again. Absentmindedly, he picked up a small blue glass ink bottle sitting on a shelf with glass objects, and with his thumb he carefully wiped dust off its rounded belly. He hummed quietly:

> *Do you believe what they're saying?*
> *Do you know how it feels?*
> *'Cause freedom is / freedom is / freedom isn't here.*

Where did that come from?

With the little ink bottle between his fingers, Mike let the echo of the words ebb away in the stuffing in his head. That was actually not that bad. Not bad at all. He sang the lines again, and found that they fit the melody perfectly.

In the meantime, his gaze was involuntarily caught by the swollen belly of the little blue glass bottle, and at first Mike thought he was imagining things.

When he sang, it was as though something was vibrating inside the bottle.

For the third time he repeated the lines about freedom, and now he concentrated on the ink bottle.

Yes, there was something moving inside.

In contrast to the other ink bottles whose caps were adorned with gilded penholders, a simple cork was in the blue bottle. Mike Chimpanzee didn't hesitate and pulled the cork out of the bottle.

There was a *pop*. A powerful *pop*, like a hard blow against a snare drum, and smoke poured out. Mike stumbled backward in a cloud that smelled faintly of ginger. He got smoke in his lungs, as he coughed in exasperation and waved at the air in front of him. It was impossible to see how such an intense cloud of smoke could come out of such a little bottle.

He turned around, and in the thick, gray fog he stumbled over to the outside door of the shop. He opened it, coughing out on the sidewalk until the Morning Breeze took away most of the smoke over indigo blue Calle Gran Via and he went in again. Back in the store, next to the blue bottle, a cloud in trousers was waiting.

This was Mike's thought, quite clear and definite:

A cloud in trousers.

The being—the cloud—was impatiently stamping his foot. His feet resembled Mike's, but consisted of white smoke. Around the smoke was a pair of simple, white sandals. The trousers were broad, thin, and blue; the same color as the glass of the small ink bottle. The upper body and arms were white, diffuse in their outlines, and the body seemed to lack substance. The face, too, was more cloud than matter, but there were features that resembled a feline, and the small puffs of cloud standing straight up from his head could easily be mistaken for a pair of ears.

"Mike Chimpanzee," said the cloud. "Mike Chimpanzee, if you'll excuse me for saying it, but this wasn't a day too soon, was it?"

Mike stood frozen to the floor, as if he were one of the antique objects for sale. The cloud's voice was strong and deep. Pleasant, without a doubt, but also with a definite tinge of superiority.

"Mr. Chimpanzee," the cloud introduced himself, "my name is Fredrik, and I am the best thing that has happened to you."

Fredrik the cloud looked around the antique store with distaste, and nodded with emphasis.

"I am truly the best thing that has happened to you," he repeated.

Mike stood quietly in the passage between the sideboards and let the cloud maneuver around him.

"Ah," said the cloud with pleasure. "You can't understand how it feels to have a floor under your sandals after so many years in a bottle."

"In a bottle? Was that you . . . in the ink bottle?"

"My usual bad luck," said Fredrik with a friendly smile that was soon transformed into something else; his facial features flew around in an unpredictable way. "I haven't exactly ended up with the intelligentsia, have I? But, nonetheless, it was you who pulled out the cork?"

Fredrik the cloud made a stage pause, sitting down in the chair at the desk where Mike had been writing during the night.

The chimpanzee nodded. "I pulled out the cork."

"Not that it sounds especially difficult when you describe

it," Fredrik said, as if he were talking with a mentally handi-capped stuffed animal, "but one thing I can promise you, Mr. Ape, from inside it was impossible to open!"

Mike Chimpanzee just stared. In his hallucinatory moments, high on chemicals from dubious laboratories, he had seen stranger things than this. Could it have been the smoke he ingested when he opened the bottle?

"I would gladly make it easier for you in some way, sir," said the cloud, "but this is how I look. I'm a genie. You'll just have to accept that. You know how it works, don't you?"

"Works?"

The cloud sighed theatrically and rolled his eyes.

"No? You have three wishes that I must fulfill as thanks for freeing me. Until that is done, I remain like this, in this . . . cloudlike form. It's only after I've repaid my debt that I become myself again."

"Yourself?"

"And there's no point in asking, sir. After a couple thousand years in what you call an ink bottle I don't remember what I was. Exciting, isn't it? But, Mr. Ape, doesn't it smell in here?"

Fredrik the cloud sniffed the air. Mike did the same, but noticed nothing.

"When did you last scrub these floors? I mean, really scrub?"

Mike shook his head. Scrub? He couldn't recall ever having scrubbed a floor. Maybe put the bedspread on sometime in his teens when Mom yelled at him; cleaning was not one of his interests.

"I don't intend to live in filth," Fredrik the genie explained, throwing out his hands in a gesture that included everything in the antique store. "We'll have to try to take care of this wish business quickly. Have you thought of anything?"

Was this a joke, some kind of *Candid Camera*? Mike looked around, as if he would find a concealed TV producer next to the three mosaic bathtubs.

"Maybe that's an idea," Mike answered, going over to the door. "That you clean up here, scrub the floors?"

"Not that I want to make it difficult for us, sir," the genie laughed haughtily, "but I suggest you think a little before you start. You don't need me for scrubbing floors. Try to be serious. You have only three chances."

In the display window Mike had set out a small living room set. A round mosaic table from the early 1900s and around it four chairs designed and built by Cordodidier. The point wasn't to attract customers; on the door there was a large sign pointing out that you had to call to schedule a visit. No, Mike had put the furniture out for himself. The store faced north, and the display window was the only light opening in the long, narrow space.

He almost expected to see a camera team sitting in the chairs, but no one was there. Still, the cloud must be some kind of projection, maybe a hologram that clever technicians were able to maneuver?

"Listen, Cloud," said Mike. "I don't have time or the desire to play games with you. I don't know who you are, I don't know if you're anywhere besides in my head, but can we see to it that you disappear as fast as possible?"

The cloud sighed audibly, again rolling his eyes and sitting down across from Mike. He seemed to hover over the chair rather than sit in it, but the intention was clear.

"Gold?" he said. "Let's talk seriously now, Mr. Ape. Jewels? Or a single diamond, forty carats or bigger? Or a glowing ruby, the most beautiful and largest that Mollisan Town has ever seen? That you can give to your dog?"

Mike started. How did the cloud know about Cocker Spaniel? Whoever was behind this trick must have done their research.

"Cocker Spaniel has all the rocks she needs," said Mike.

"You are a truly naive ape, you know that?" The cloud sighed. "But I don't really have time to be a love adviser. Let's try something else. The biggest, fastest Volga the city has seen? Equipped with four-wheel drive, hydraulic shock absorbers, and a music system that will make any nightclub sound like a transistor radio?"

"For someone who's been trapped in a bottle for thousands of years, you're pretty up to date," Mike noted drily.

"But you have a good idea there, sir!" Fredrik exclaimed. "A journey in time? Where in history do you want to go? A thousand years, a hundred years, ten years ago? What do you say? Possibly I can negotiate two trips for one wish? That doesn't sound bad, does it?"

"Give up. Do you think I'm an idiot? And that I'm going to make myself ridiculous in front of a camera that you've hidden up in the rafters? Listen, I'll tell you what I want: marijuana to last a month. Pre-rolled, neat joints. On this table. Now."

Fredrik the cloud looked suspiciously at his liberator, shook his head so that all his facial features ended up in the wrong places for a few seconds, and then nodded curtly to put them back.

"Let me see if I understand you correctly, sir," the genie said slowly. "You can wish for anything you want, exactly what you want, and you want marijuana for a month?"

"Stop talking," said Mike. "You've heard my first wish, 'genie.' And if I understand correctly, it appears you can't deliver."

The genie sighed.

"And why should I make it hard on myself when I ought to be happy that . . . an unimaginative type pulled out the cork?" he muttered to himself. And suddenly on the table in the antique store's display window there were 120 narrow, white, hand-rolled cigarettes, packed with marijuana.

"They won't run out," Fredrik commented drily. "If you manage to smoke all these in a week, there will be just as many left for the rest of the month."

2.

Mike's head was bursting. Laboriously, his awareness crawled up out of the colorful fragments of an abstract dream. There wasn't anything wrong with the cloud's weed, it was only Mike who had overdone it. He wanted to test if it was true. And unbelievably enough, despite all he'd smoked, there was just as much left on the table in the display window at dawn. The consequences of the experiment were now aching between his temples.

The daylight barely reached the sofa bed but would still poke like two darning needles if he opened his eyes. Mike put the pillow over his head. It felt cool. He tried to recall if he had to be anywhere at a certain time. Tonight he was supposed to have dinner at the Rozenblatts, he remembered. He moaned loudly. He was not looking forward to that.

After having failed at a serious attempt to go back to sleep, Mike pulled off the covers in a sweeping motion. He sat up carefully before he finally opened his eyes, and got a shock.

"Good morning, sir," said the cloud, making the word "sir" quiver with irony. "The weather has passed lunchtime. Are you ready for your second and third wishes?"

The genie was sitting on the desk. The desk lamp was sticking up through his thigh. He was dressed the same as yesterday, but seemed more compact today, as if he had practiced holding his diffuse body together during the night.

Mike fell back down on the bed. He closed his eyes again. This cloud in trousers, this figment of his imagination who possibly originated from some past bad drug trip, had apparently come to stay. But the joints that were inexplicably on the table yesterday had been good weed. Instead of questioning, Mike was forced to accept that. For a fraction of a second he regretted having only asked for a month's worth when he could have asked for a lifetime supply. Then he dismissed the thought. He had bigger problems to worry about.

"In line with your first, ingenious wish," Fredrik the genie continued in what Mike was learning was his customary, ironic way, "perhaps your second wish could be a croissant and coffee in bed?"

The genie let out an unnatural giggle that was presumably meant to provoke.

Mike sat up again, and was about to give the annoying cloud a piece of his mind when the door to the antique store opened with a bang. In the daylight that fell along the floor a familiar, terrifying silhouette was outlined.

"Mom?"

"My little cotton troll!"

Ilja Crocodile stormed into the store. It was her natural way to make an entrance; she marched in wherever she went. She was at his sofa bed in a few seconds, and embraced Chimpanzee before he could defend himself.

"My little cotton troll," she repeated lovingly.

"Mom, don't call me 'cotton troll,'" Mike pleaded, but it was impossible to hear because she was holding his head pressed against her voluminous bosom.

She had on her tall hat and the thick, dark red coat with fur trim that she bought for herself as a present on her fiftieth birthday. She reeked of perfume.

This really wasn't what he meant when he had complained in the past that she was suffocating him.

"But . . . you're not dressed yet?" she exclaimed. "We don't have much time! We have to go to the tailor's. Oh, I'm so happy. For your sake."

Finally she released him, and panting he caught his breath.

"And I'm so happy for my sake," she added.

"That's nice, Mom," he said, getting up on weak legs.

"Now Mrs. Rosenthal won't know what to say," Ilja Crocodile declared. "I know what she said last summer about my little darling. But this will shut her up now."

"That's nice, Mom," he repeated.

He slept in his underwear, and now he took a detour around the sofa to find the jeans that must be lying somewhere on the floor.

"She was so stuck-up about her rat, who's become a looooyer and is so fiiiine. But it's not her rat who's going to get married in May. No, it's my own little apesie-papesie-sweetie."

For some reason that he didn't remember, he had hung the jeans on a pewter statue that represented a marten. He took them down and pulled them on.

"Mom, it's not a competition," he objected.

"My sweet cotton troll, it sure enough is!" Ilja exclaimed. "Come along, the tailor won't wait all day."

The dining room was small, the walls dark green. Heavy, brown velvet curtains hung from ceiling to floor alongside the windows, oil portraits of stuffed animals stared gloomily down from inside their broad frames. Candles were lit in the chandelier, light blue carnations dominated the flower arrangement on the table, which was covered in a white linen tablecloth. There were eight padded, clearly rococo-inspired chairs around the table, but only four stuffed animals were having dinner.

"But I still don't understand," said Mrs. Rozenblatt. "Why does he have holes in his trousers?"

"They aren't big holes," Mr. Rozenblatt pointed out.

"But . . . his trousers are torn," Mrs. Rozenblatt insisted. "Why is that?"

"He wants to be an artist," said Mr. Rozenblatt. "Artists behave incomprehensibly sometimes. That's just how it is."

The lovely Cocker Spaniel, a light brown dog with a pink silk nose and long, alluring eyelashes, was dressed for the evening in a white dress with a round neck and puff sleeves. She looked at Mike Chimpanzee, rolling her eyes theatrically at her parents.

Mr. Rozenblatt sat at the end of the table and his wife to his right. They talked casually about Mike as if he wasn't there. In Mollisan Town in general and in Yok in particular, it was very unusual for stuffed animals to take each other's surnames. Mike thought it was funny to think of an entire family as the "Rozenblatts"; something he had indiscreetly said at a previous dinner and was then punished with a lecture about the deteriorated family values of the day.

"Artist?" Mrs. Rozenblatt answered guardedly. "Plucking a little on a guitar? Besides, what does that have to do with trousers?"

"I don't have any others," said Mike.

But they didn't hear him. In the Rozenblatt family, youngsters only spoke if they were spoken to.

The Rozenblatts lived in a town house in south Amberville that was smaller than they wanted to admit. On the way there Mike thought he had figured out how he could be rid of the nagging genie: Fredrik seemed to be a shy type.

When Mom stormed into the shop the genie had disappeared, and he'd stayed away the whole afternoon during the visit to the tailor and on the way there and back. He made himself known when Mike returned to the shop to change for the evening, but disappeared again on the bus on the way to Amberville. Then he was waiting at the bus stop where Mike got off. He had put on a long, beige coat that concealed his insubstantial body and made it less obvious that he was hovering a few centimeters above the sidewalk without standing on it. Together they walked the four blocks to the Rozenblatt house, and during that time the genie managed to offer more than ten suggestions for exotic travel destinations. Then Mike rang the Rozenblatts' doorbell, Cocker Spaniel opened, and sure enough, Fredrik had vanished without a trace the moment Mike entered.

"I see," said Mr. Rozenblatt, who now thought it was high time to let "the artist" into the conversation. "And now, if I understand this correctly, is Reuben Walrus going to lose his position in the Academy? For the sake of a silly little skirt. It's bewildering, isn't it, Mike?"

"Walrus?"

Mike didn't know who Walrus was. Rozenblatt assumed that all musicians were interested in the Music Academy; personally he was extremely interested in the subject. Within the Academy there were scandals all the time, and in circles that Rozenblatt willingly acknowledged were among the better.

"She can't be more than twenty. And he's over sixty. To think that she would have him?" he continued with a certain degree of envy in his voice.

"Walrus's little skirt is the daughter of Director Carlsen at the Savings Banks Bank," Mrs. Rozenblatt informed him.

"Carlsen? Was he the one who had cubs in sailing school along with our little darling?" Mr. Rozenblatt asked, taking the opportunity to give Cocker Spaniel a loving glance. "Carlsen?"

"Exactly," Mrs. Rozenblatt nodded, also turning to her daughter. "Do you remember her, honey?"

"Of course she remembers. It's only three summers ago that we—"

"Excuse me, dearest," Mrs. Rozenblatt objected, "but it's actually four summers ago. At the same time that Lily got her cub."

"No, my dear," protested Mr. Rozenblatt, who loathed being corrected. "I would have remembered that. It was three years ago, the same year your mama glued her beak shut."

"The beak operation," said Mrs. Rozenblatt, no longer able to conceal the irritation in her voice, "was only two years ago. Have you already forgotten that? Mama should hear about that."

"She only hears what she wants to these days . . . ," Mr. Rozenblatt muttered.

How could words become so inane, Mike asked himself. How could a conversation go on without anything being said? It filled him with both fear and longing. In a way, it was a sublime art form, this empty babble that concealed lifelong frustration, envy, and control. What was he doing here? He longed for one of the genie's narrow rolled cigarettes.

He sneaked a glance at Cocker Spaniel. She was attentively following her parents' conversation, and Mike was pretending to listen, but he soon started removing the prudish dog's clothes in his imagination. He let it happen slowly and sensually, and when he suddenly heard the silence around the table he had no idea how long they had been staring at him.

"Yes?" he said cautiously, because it was obvious that he was expected to say something.

"But didn't we have an agreement?" said the lovely Cocker Spaniel.

"Sure, sure, but we still do, don't we?" Mike answered.

"You see!" Cocker Spaniel exclaimed, glowering furiously at her parents.

"I've never heard anything like it," Mrs. Rozenblatt snorted.

"Champagne with the main course?" Mr. Rozenblatt agreed with his wife. "Is that really what you want?"

Mike Chimpanzee nodded firmly. Now he understood what the conversation was about. His intended had very strong opinions on the subject. The friends Mike had invited to the wedding—a carefully selected little group that was barely noticeable on the long invitation list—would gladly drink anything at all, as long as it was free. But Cocker Spaniel explained how glamorous it was to serve champagne throughout, and the future bridegroom had no opinions.

Even though he really loved her, he couldn't exactly remember why they had decided to get married. But it was too late to back out now, and Mike's mom, Ilja, was happy as a lark.

"Champagne is what we want," Cocker Spaniel confirmed. "And that's what we've agreed on."

"Will you excuse me a moment?" Mike asked, getting up from the table before anyone could protest.

He slipped out into the garden—in southeast Amberville, all town houses had a small garden in back—and consoled himself with genie-grass. In the shadow of a large apple tree he could observe the Rozenblatt family through the windows without them seeing him. Mr. Rozenblatt sat at the table making large, self-satisfied gestures. Mike knew he ought to despise the narrow-minded paterfamilias, but for some reason he couldn't.

"There's a champagne from the thirteenth century," said Fredrik the genie.

Mike jumped. The genie sat perched in the tree, on one of the lowest branches. He was smiling.

"Priceless, of course. Sir, perhaps that would be something to give the bride before the wedding night? Or during the wedding night?"

But before Mike had time to answer, Cocker Spaniel appeared on the terrace, and the genie cloud dissolved and disappeared.

"Mike?!"

He took a step out of the shadows so that she could see him.

"Mike, what are you doing?"

He put out the cigarette in the grass, shivering at the same time. The Evening Weather was cool, and he only had a shirt on.

"This is really shit," he answered. "Now we've known each other, I don't know, a long time. And your parents still can't respect me. What's wrong? What am I doing wrong?"

"You're not doing anything wrong."

"Your dad . . . doesn't he get who I am? Why does he talk about the Music Academy all the time? Is that some kind of gibe? Does he think he's better than me just because he listens to string quartets?"

"He's just old-fashioned, Mike," Cocker Spaniel answered. She went over and hugged him, holding him close to her.

"Something smells strange here, doesn't it?" she said.

"What do you mean, old-fashioned?" he asked, extracting from her embrace. "I've always behaved. I mean, he's boring and square and represents everything I despise. Still I come here and sit quietly and eat his disgusting food and listen to all the bullshit. The least I can ask for is respect."

"He respects you, Mike. In his way."

He heard that he was making her sad, and he regretted it.

"Sorry, sweetie," he said. "Forgive me. It's been a bad day today. Mom and the tailor . . . it was a nightmare. Forgive me. Go in, I'll be in soon, I just need to be alone."

She looked at him with her big eyes, nodded at last and went into the house. He intended to follow her, but the thought of returning to the heart of middle-class respectability was so repugnant he could not even try. He would have to call tomorrow and explain. Besides, he doubted the Rozenblatts would miss him; this wedding was being planned by forces much stronger than Mike Chimpanzee's will. Along with his genie, he sneaked out through the gate at the back.

3.

The next day Mike Chimpanzee, guitar in hand, hesitated on oil black Boulevard de la Vilette outside Brown Brothers' main office. The sun was high, the traffic dense, and the smell of diesel and garbage typical to Tourquai was impossible to ignore. Before him rose the S-shaped skyscraper paid for by performers' historic successes. The building was clad in black glass and red aluminum and the record company's rainbow-colored logo—synonymous with rock and roll in Mollisan Town—shone above the entry. In the large windows facing the street were posters of Johnny Badass & the Bleak Leeks; Mike had heard they would be going out on a club tour later in the spring. Someone said their new sound was more mature. Ominous, thought Mike; Johnny's only good point was his lack of maturity.

"Sir, I'm sorry to have to point this out, but for being a creative monkey you seem to lack ideas," the genie commented.

Fredrik the genie was still wearing his long trench coat. He had been nagging Mike about his second wish from the moment Mike woke up that morning.

"I don't want to be so presumptuous as to criticize you,"

the genie explained while freshly washed cars rolled past on Boulevard de la Vilette. "But now you've had a whole day and night to think about it, and you must have come up with some inkling of an idea? Mr. Ape?"

It had been the ache in his chest that woke the monkey. First he thought it had to do with the genie's weed; for the second night in a row he had once again overindulged on marijuana. Then he felt the customary anxiety and the feeling of barely being able to breathe. This had gone on for several weeks now, since the recording sessions started. He remained lying down and tried to meditate out of the black hole, but it hadn't worked.

When he finally got up, the antique store smelled of soap and cleanser. The genie had been visibly pleased.

"It looked disgusting, sir. I'm sorry to say it. I'm afraid you're not living a healthy life, Mr. Ape. I took the opportunity to tidy up a little while you were sleeping. A small shovelful in a gigantic manure pile, you may object. But someone has to take the first shovelful, don't they?"

It was during the morning that Mike decided to show up unannounced to Gavin Toad's office. The idea had been floating around his mind, but possibly it was Fredrik who indirectly helped him make the desperate decision. The genie's uncommon insistence could drive anyone mad. So now he was standing on the street outside Brown Brothers.

"If it's not too much to ask—and it's not—I'm begging you to give me something to work with. A hint? A suggestion?"

Mike ignored the irritating cloud. Pretending like it wasn't there was the only strategy that remained after the morning's many attempts to free himself from the nagging.

"Give me something, just a little something?"

They both turned and looked over toward the dark glass doors in front of the lobby.

Mike did not recall exactly when he had been here last, but it must have been more than a year ago. That time the shame had followed him down in the elevator. Defeat had tripped him up as he stumbled past the café in the lobby, where the decision makers at Brown Brothers relaxed with gossip and croissants between launch decisions and discussions about recording budgets. In the record company building rumors spread in no time, and they had probably already heard that Gavin Toad had just mocked Mike because the new songs, once again, were too deep and too long for the general public.

At least according to Gavin Toad.

Now, more than a year and a lifetime later, Mike and the musicians got to hang out in the studio a few blocks away. He usually met with Toad in the city or at the antique store, never up at Brown Brothers' main office.

Mike Chimpanzee closed his eyes, took a deep breath and hummed to himself:

> *Do you believe what they're saying?*
> *(Every life its outer limit)*
> *Do you believe what they're saying?*
> *(Do you know how it feels?)*
> *'Cause freedom is / freedom is / freedom isn't here.*

And with the successful chorus echoing in his head, he let the glass doors glide open and stepped resolutely into the lobby, taking firm hold of the neck of the guitar and making a silent promise not to give in, whatever happened.

He waved to the security guards far off in reception. They recognized him and waved back. Involuntarily Mike looked around, but the trench coat–draped genie remained out of sight.

Mike stationed himself to wait by the elevators that went to the thirtieth floor and higher. Gavin Toad's office and Brown Brothers' department for contemporary R&B were on the thirty-seventh floor, and the whole way up he continued humming his chorus; it gave him strength.

The first animal he ran into when the elevator doors opened was Barbara Ladybug.

"Mike?"

"Hi, Barbara."

She looked like he remembered, with a pair of tight blue jeans; a worn but expensive T-shirt; and around her neck she had wrapped at least ten necklaces, all of which were large, colorful, and rattled when she moved.

"Where did you go, Mike? You promised to come by the morning after?"

"Barbara, I swear I tried. I wanted to. But life doesn't always give us the right to—"

But before Chimpanzee had time to wrap himself up in an explanation that probably wouldn't have fooled anyone, he was interrupted by a young donkey looking out from one of the dozens of cramped cubicles where stuffed animals sat and worked; the worn moss green office landscape was not as glamorous as it should have been.

"Did you bring your guitar, Mike?" asked the donkey. "Are you thinking about playing?"

And the question created a murmur that spread across the workplace with an inexplicable speed, and suddenly a buzz, vibrating with expectation, hovered over the exhausted office workers.

In his large office at the southeast corner of the thirty-seventh floor, Gavin Toad heard that something was happening out in the cubicle area. He was in the middle of an important phone call—there was no other kind—but slammed down the receiver and got up from the desk to find out what the frenzy was about. Under the lines of framed gold records on the wall was a large mirror, and he took a quick glance in it. In the breast pocket of his gray suit jacket a pink handkerchief fluttered. It matched his socks. He was at once strict, elegant, and a little crazy. He nodded to himself and tore open the door. Toad was the first to admit his unnatural need for control, but everyone had to live with his defects, and in Toad's department at Brown Brothers he was the one in charge.

As soon as he came out of the office he heard Mike's voice. Chimpanzee may never have had the ability to write songs, thought Toad, but there was nothing wrong with his voice. The record executive advanced quickly along the narrow passageway between the cubicles. Those who were still working fell in place behind him. Seeing the toad puff up always provided a momentary diversion.

Mike Chimpanzee was in the middle of the chorus of one of his old hits when Gavin Toad reached the improvised concert stage outside the elevators.

"Enough now!" he cried out. "Back to work, everyone! Mike, what kind of flipping antics are these? We have better things to do than listen to your semi-rotten songs. Royalties have to be calculated. Sales tax has to be paid. Invoices have to be drawn up. Taxes have to be avoided. This is an office, not a flipping rock club!"

It wasn't possible to keep singing when Toad screamed. Toad loved to harass his artists. The final proof of Brown Brothers' dominance in the music industry in Mollisan Town, and thereby evidence of Toad's own standing, was how mean and yet nonchalant he could be to performers like Mike. As it turned out, the worse he behaved, the stronger he tied the rockers to the company. If he acted like they needed him more than the other way around, the poor souls believed it.

Chimpanzee stopped playing, the small audience scattered and Mike followed the wildly gesticulating Toad back to his grandiose corner office.

"Easily entertained idiots," the toad scolded loudly. "A silly little rock star, and you immediately forget your duties. What if I was to do the same? Around the twenty-fifth of every month?"

Toad held open the door for the chimpanzee, simply to be able to slam it behind him with a loud bang.

Gavin Toad sat behind his large desk, and Mike sat down in the visitor's chair opposite. Behind the toad's back Mike could look out through the floor-to-ceiling windows over all of north Tourquai, from the financial district up to the forest. It was a magnificent, terrifying view for someone who lived in a dingy antique store in Yok, even if it was located in Corbod, the tidiest district of the most miserable part of town.

"There are bad vibes in the studio, Mike," Toad began. "Bad vibes mean drawn-out sessions, and drawn-out sessions mean money burned. And I really don't like burned money."

Mike fumbled in his inside pocket, and got hold of one of the genie's joints. He took it out and set it on the desk while he searched in his jeans pockets for the lighter.

"Grass?" Toad exclaimed. "You intend to sit in my office and smoke? Are you completely flipping crazy?"

Mike mumbled an apology, put the joint back in the inside pocket, and instead found a cigarette in a crumpled pack that had been with the lighter in his pants.

"I'm cooperating, Gavin," Mike mumbled as he got the cigarette going, "and I don't mean to complain, but Lancelot is not exactly—"

Toad got up so suddenly that the chair almost tipped over behind him. He aimed a long, green finger at the ape.

"Idiot! You're acting like a little cub. Do you think I don't know what's going on? If you don't straighten up he's going to get tired of you, don't you get that?"

"Sure, sure"—Mike tried to calm the record company executive—"but you have to admit that—"

"I'm not admitting anything," Toad declared, going around the desk to have room enough to deliver his reprimand. "I never admit anything. It's a matter of principle. Now you listen carefully to me, Mike."

And for the tenth time in as many days, Gavin Toad explained why Lancelot Lemur was Mike Chimpanzee's salvation from a life as a has-been.

"You have the voice. You have the charisma. But you have

flipping poor judgment, Mike. Your songs are shit. Lancelot's songs reek of money."

"But there's a song missing," said Mike. "We agree on that. The album needs one more song before we're done. And Lancelot has no obvious candidate. I'm working on a song. About freedom. I think it can be nasty. I don't have the verse quite right yet, but it's on its way. The chorus is amazing. I'll—"

Mike picked up the guitar and started playing before the toad could protest. *Freedom is, freedom is, freedom isn't here*, sang the chimpanzee, all while Toad waved more and more intensely.

"Now stop, for crying out loud!" the executive screamed, almost running around the desk to be able to aim his long finger right between Mike's eyes. "I don't intend to listen to any more of your miserable songs. Get it?"

"It's not done," Mike defended himself. "It's more like a foundation, a base to build the house on. I'll be working on it more, don't you understand?"

Mike Chimpanzee's album *40 degrees* had been one of the best-selling debut albums released in Mollisan Town. After an initial lukewarm reception from the critics, Gavin Toad convinced the producer of the popular TV show *Menus of the Stars* to let Mike play before dessert. That was all that was needed. The next morning, success was a fact, and the first pressing of the album sold out over the weekend.

Mike had been eighteen and unprepared for the breakthrough; unprepared in the sense that for several years he had fantasized about everything that was now happening for real. But it had never been fame he was after, only confirmation.

The record came out after a few months of intensive songwriting, mostly at night, and during that time hardly anyone knew what he was up to. True, Toad had turned down his songs, but gave him ten new melodies to write "profound" lyrics to. A turbulent month in the recording studio, as studio musicians came and went without Mike understanding which songs the various tracks belonged to. There were saxophones and choirs and transverse flutes that he never would have dreamed of. As if out of charity he got to listen to the daily takes, but if he expressed an opinion no one listened to it. Somehow the lyrics managed to survive the harsh treatment, mainly because no one seemed to care about them. In Gavin's world, these lyrics, over which Mike had agonized during intoxicated, angst-ridden nights, were only syllables to sing in the chorus. For Mike it was the soul of the song.

Toad returned to his desk chair. He leaned back and set his expensive, black patent-leather shoes on the desk.

"It worked last time, Mike," the executive reminded him. "Thanks to me. And it's going to work again. Thanks to me. And Lancelot. You don't touch the songs, and he won't touch the lyrics. That was the agreement, Mike."

"But I—"

"No. No buts. Just that."

Mike took a few quick puffs on his cigarette. With the perspective that time provides, he could later state that he had been unable to be sufficiently present during the year that passed after *Menus of the Stars*. He would end up appearing on TV sixteen times, he did twenty-three concerts in the course of thirteen months, and seven of a total of eleven songs on the album became singles and reached the top of the charts.

The number of parties? He didn't remember. The number of new friends? They vanished just as quickly as they came. The number of females? He didn't want to think about that. The drugs? Wherever he turned. The money? He still didn't know whether there had ever been any.

Life became incomprehensible.

Before the breakthrough he had struggled with his identity, like all other teenagers, and by way of betrayed ideals, existential crises, and bleeding hearts, he had created an image of who he was. In the eyes of the fans and the media he became someone completely different in one stroke. And it wasn't worth it to protest, it didn't sink in. Gradually he was transformed into the one they wanted, and then he became more than that. As he stood on the stage there was just rhyming strings of words left of the lyrics that had meant so much. The audience cheered. He did not deserve a tenth of the love they gave him. There was not a chance in hell that he would dare turn himself in for detox.

The dream ended with a crash. He had as little recollection of it as of anything else that year. He woke up in a display window, with glass all over his fur, cotton sticking out through large tears in his belly and across his legs, and around him hundreds of flowers. Blue carnations, white lilies, dahlias in all the colors of the rainbow. Had someone thrown him into the flower shop? Had he thrown himself through the window? It would never be determined. The pain came later, in the ambulance en route to St. Andrews. It was only in the hospital emergency room that the doctors discovered that his nose was loose; a considerably more serious condition than the tears in his body.

The operations would prove to be the lesser problem. The display window had been smashed, and tiny, tiny pieces of glass had drilled in through the chimpanzee's fabric and disappeared into his cotton stuffing. Worried, the doctors had considered the possibility of totally re-stuffing him, but such an intervention was far from risk-free. Instead they let nature take its course, and during the weeks that followed the pieces of glass came out in a natural way. The pain and discomfort were mitigated by morphine, but somewhere inside his pleasant delirium Mike knew he had reached the end of the road.

When he was discharged after two weeks at St. Andrews, he made himself a promise: He would never betray himself again.

Now he was sitting in Gavin Toad's office, being humiliated. After rejection upon rejection Toad had finally thought of the solution with Lancelot Lemur.

"It's not done yet," the chimpanzee repeated. "The song about freedom—"

"Go to hell, Mike!" Toad answered jovially, turning his attention to one of the many papers on his desk.

Mike left the office; he was stubborn, but not stupid.

4.

Down on oil black Boulevard de la Vilette, Fredrik the genie was waiting.

"Finally." The genie sighed. "Mr. Ape, I beg your pardon, but after thousands of years in a bottle one doesn't have much patience left. What were you doing? Did you take a wrong turn in the elevator?"

"Go away," Mike answered, starting to walk south.

The Afternoon Weather was on its way in over the city, and Mike was longing to be back in Corbod; he wasn't made for the broad, clean streets and pulsating traffic of Tourquai.

"Sir, I realize that mental exertion is not your strong suit, and I have complete respect for that, of course, but can't we think of something?" the genie insisted. "Now that you've had a little time to yourself to think it over?"

"Shut up, Cloud," Mike said. "Leave me alone."

Deep inside Mike Chimpanzee's head sounded an ominous tone that was barely perceptible, but irritated him anyway. He was ashamed of himself. He had played the chorus for Toad, but couldn't stand by it. He had apologized immediately, and promised improvement. That was disgraceful behavior, and it was because far too much was at stake. Getting a song of his own on the record, a song that wasn't programmed out of one of Lancelot Lemur's self-playing computers, meant more to Mike's ego than he dared to admit.

Right from the start the record company had reduced him to a singing puppet, but now he got the feeling that this pointless floundering was exactly what they expected. That they were sitting in their skyscraper, laughing at his predictability.

With the faint sound in his head came a headache. Mike stopped by a crosswalk and let the seemingly endless stream of dark Volgas rumble past while he leaned the guitar against the stoplight and lit the joint that Toad had just denied him.

"Sir, isn't it true that drugs stimulate creativity?" the genie asked rhetorically.

The genie was hovering around in his impatient way, and the headwind from the cars caused him to sway even more.

"If material things don't interest you, you can always consider experiences. You, the one who likes marijuana? Only the imagination sets the limits?"

"My own dealer genie," Mike mumbled, crossing the street. "Leave me alone now, then I'll—"

The genie took the opportunity with one motion to remove a couple of cigarette butts from the sidewalk to an ashtray hanging on the light pole, and then he caught up.

"Unfortunately, Mr. Ape, that's not how this works," he informed him. "You make three wishes, I'm free. If you don't make three wishes, I'm not. So, you have two wishes left, and then I'll leave you alone."

"Mm. But right now," Mike said, taking a high step up onto the sidewalk on the opposite side, "right now I've had enough of you. If you leave for a while, I promise to think about it."

"Given the short time we have spent together, I have a hard time attaching too much importance to such a promise," the genie noted drily.

"Shut up," Mike said. "Shut up, leave me alone. I've had enough of you right now."

A vacant taxi was heading south, and Mike waved with his guitar in the air. As he sank into the backseat of the car with a throbbing headache, the genie was gone, of course, and Mike closed his eyes. He asked the driver to take him down to Yok and then just drive around for an hour; he needed to think. If Gavin Toad didn't want to listen to his songs, at least the record company executive would not escape his taxi receipt.

As the Evening Weather settled over the city, Mike Chimpanzee was still in his taxi, and he didn't want to go home. He was neither hungry nor tired. The thought of the genie waiting in the antique store nauseated him. The taxi had been driving in circles around Yok, and the ominous tone in his head refused to go away. At first he thought it was the tires of the car, but then he recognized it. A sign, he thought.

But he didn't know how he should interpret it.

At last he asked the taxi driver to drive to Scheherazade on sludge green Cle de la Bola, a crooked stone's throw from the antique shop on indigo blue Calle Gran Via, and ten minutes later he entered the restaurant with an imposing taxi receipt in his wallet. The genie was visible as Mike got out of the taxi, but disappeared just as quickly again when he opened the door to Scheherazade. The storm had abated, and night had officially arrived in Mollisan Town.

There were an unusually large number of stuffed animals in the restaurant, and Mike had to elbow his way to the bar. Since his breakthrough he was accustomed to always being noticed, but inside Scheherazade only rarely did anyone bother him. It was more likely that females at the bar pretended not to even know who he was, when they asked for a light or a little passion for their fading lives.

Tom-Tom Crow saw him at a distance, set out a large beer

and changed the music to Nikki Lee and the Suspects. The grating electric guitars fell like a curtain behind the swaggering fortune-hunters drinking red wine in the bar. The cigarette smoke was like a haze over a battlefield. Tom-Tom had no time to give the rock star any further attention because other—paying—customers were making demands.

Mike managed to commandeer a bar stool, and sipped his beer. He recognized many, but knew no one. He was grateful for that, because inspiration was unexpectedly flowing. He picked up his black notebook and leafed quickly through it. The notes were written and arranged based on a flow of associations that was hard to re-create. Introverted song lyrics were juxtaposed with simple diary entries. Shopping lists, pasted-in receipts and dry-cleaning tickets for clothes he never had the money to pick up. Here and there addresses and telephone numbers without names, or names without addresses and telephone numbers. When there was no room, he wrote over things he'd written earlier. On other pages the blankness itself was the point. At last he found an unused page, and quickly wrote a whole verse without raising his pen:

> *Down South Avenue, as darkness starts to fall*
> *in a car your Mama gave you when you turned*
>   *twenty-one*
> *You're the king of the bar, and you buy drinks for all*
> *and later take home someone who'll have to leave at*
>   *dawn*

Scheherazade faded in the cigarette haze. Mike no longer heard Nikki Lee's scratchy, desperate voice, he was so absorbed by his verse making. The minutes flew past, the beer mug was emptied once and then twice, and soon there was another verse in place in the black notebook:

> *This life you want to live is getting too intense*

planning is believing you know the way to go
but a little spark becomes a fire, a little thorn becomes
  a tear
freedom's letting go, say the ones who know.

He closed the notebook and nodded. This wasn't bad. This might be the verse to the song about freedom.

He looked around; the restaurant was quickly emptying out. Sam Gazelle came out of the kitchen, and only now noticed the chimpanzee.

"Mike!"

The gazelle dried his wet hooves on an apron where the food stains told the whole story: A little more than a year ago Sam, along with his friend Tom-Tom Crow, had taken over the restaurant on sludge green Cle de la Bola in Yok. It was no shopping street, but it had its charm. Across from the restaurant were the ruins of an apartment building from the fifties. Dark green, blossoming clematis had buried the razed exterior walls under billowing greenery, and when the Afternoon Rain fell and the sun was turning homeward, thousands of leaves glittered like stars in the night sky.

Rumor had it that an elderly widow had willed the place to Sam at a point in his life when more than ever he needed a roof over his head. So he moved in, with his chemicals and herbs, and realized after a few weeks that he needed help. The unusually large stuffed animal Tom-Tom Crow was not hard to convince. Together they painted the walls of the restaurant turquoise. The dark wooden tables and bar remained, while the crow set about sewing new white covers for all the chairs; on some he embroidered skulls with little red sequins. Besides the bar and the five window booths, there were a total of eight tables with room for thirty guests. They christened their restaurant Scheherazade.

Sam Gazelle went up to the bar and gave Mike a hug, whereupon Mike as usual felt uncomfortable. The poor chimpanzee could not defend himself against the gazelle. He had always attracted homosexual stuffed animals; perhaps it was his confusion that was enticing? Mike Chimpanzee pulled his shirt higher up on his hairy chest; Sam took a slender, hand-rolled cigarette out of his breast pocket.

"Not the best quality," he commented, handing it over.

"I've got my own," Mike said, taking one of the genie's joints out of his breast pocket.

"You do? Did you get an advance?" Sam asked.

Chimpanzee not bumming drugs off the gazelle was a minor sensation.

"You might call it luck," Mike answered hesitantly.

Sam took off the apron and set it over the back of the bar stool. Under it he had on a white ruffled shirt unbuttoned down to the belt line; the buckle depicted a withering rose. He had dark blue kohl around his large, round eyes, and he smelled of a perfume that Mike recognized but could not place. The limits of vanity, Gazelle maintained, were at repairing the broken-off right horn on his forehead. The stump of horn had become his trademark.

Mike's impulse had been to tell Sam and Tom-Tom about the annoying genie who had invaded his life, but now that felt impossible. The story was too ridiculous, and too unbelievable.

Crow set out two glasses of white wine, and Sam and Mike toasted in silence. Apart from a python who had curled up and fallen asleep in one of the booths, the restaurant was now empty. Nikki Lee's distinct voice was still coming out of the speakers, accompanied by a careful brush that caressed the cymbals.

"Be my guest, dears," said Tom-Tom. "My goodness, damn, what a night!"

"We're talking record-breaking, darling," Gazelle agreed.

Scheherazade, under its new owners, got off to a slow start, but because there were few customers, the crow and gazelle could practice their new roles as headwaiter and chef in peace and quiet. Soon they surprised themselves by managing to prepare and serve food from a solid menu; besides, the inexperienced restaurateurs paid the suppliers' bills with such regularity that the supplies didn't stop.

Now the crow disappeared into the kitchen to do the final cleanup before they could go home. Sam sat down at the bar next to Mike. They could glimpse themselves behind the forest of liquor bottles of various sizes and colors on the glass shelves in front of the bar mirror. Mike thought he looked lost. And the next moment the tone in his head was back.

"Oh dear," said Gazelle. "Did something just happen?"

"No worries," said Mike, trying to cheer himself up. "A dip. Already on the way up again. Maybe low blood sugar?"

"It has been better for a while, right?" Sam asked, sipping his wine.

Mike hated feeling like a mental case. True, Gazelle had become somewhat of a therapist during the past months, but that didn't give him carte blanche to console. The ape shrugged his shoulders.

"It's this damn neighborhood," he said. "It's suffocating. It's like a closed room, an ecosystem under a big glass dome. Whichever direction I run, I hit my head against the wall. And if you don't want to sit still? It drives you crazy, thinking like that."

"You shouldn't think that way, darling," Sam suggested. "It sounds corny when I say it, everything sounds corny when I say it; I'm that sort of gazelle. But it's more profound than you think. Choose what to think about. And think about something else."

The gazelle searched in his pants pocket and found a green pill, which he put in his mouth. He was full of chemicals, smoked tobacco, herbs, and powders, and seldom knew exactly what he was taking; he combined colors and forms in ways he hoped were balancing. Where alcohol was concerned he was very limited, however; a glass of white wine on special occasions, nothing else, which mainly had to do with his fear of gaining weight.

"You've had it too easy, darling," Gazelle said, as he placed a consoling hoof on the ape's shoulder.

"That's good," Mike said. "I'll remember that next time I'm considering drowning myself."

"How old are you, Mike?" asked Sam, now less sympathetic. "Twenty? Twenty-one? Doesn't matter, you're too young to be bitter, honey, and to be honest you sound a little ridiculous when you want to be disillusioned. You know that I love you, but this has to be said."

Sam slid down from his tall stool and rounded the bar. He moved quickly and softly.

"Sweetie, this is how it is," said the gazelle, rooting in the drawer of the cash register, where he hid small, white tablets that made him melancholy. "You are loved by everyone. I love you, your mom loves you, hundreds of thousands of teenagers in this city worship the colorful asphalt you walk on. It's true that you've spent all the money, but, darling, there'll be more. You're making a new record with Lancelot Lemur and you're getting married to the love of your life. You're, like, not believable as suicidal."

Tom-Tom came out of the kitchen, so Mike avoided answering.

"Now damn it, all that's left is to go home," the crow called out.

He and Gazelle lived in the apartment above the restaurant.

"Do you want to spend the night at our place, Mike?" he asked. "I can toast bread for breakfast."

Mike weighed the invitation. In the one scale was avoiding the genie, in the other Gazelle's intolerable snoring.

"Thanks," he answered at last. "But I think I'll toddle off home. Another time?"

Crow laughed happily and patted him hard on the back. It was the bird's way of showing his appreciation.

"Do I owe you anything?" Chimpanzee asked.

"An answer," said Sam. "But we can deal with that later."

Mike nodded. He had already lost focus, forgotten the crow and the gazelle, and instead was back at the verses he'd written. As he stepped out onto the sidewalk he completed the chorus in his head:

> *But do you believe what they're saying?*
> *(Every thought has an end)*
> *Do you believe what they're saying?*
> *(Every life its outer limit)*
> *Do you believe what they're saying?*
> *(There's no way out again)*
> *Do you believe what they're saying?*
> *(Do you know how it feels?)*
> *'Cause freedom is / freedom is / freedom isn't here.*

5.

"Did you hear what Mike said?" Mr. Rozenblatt laughed out loud. "He suggested sole!"

Mrs. Rozenblatt, dressed for the day in a small pillbox hat, chimed in with strained but grandiose laughter, whereupon even Ilja Crocodile giggled and Mike himself smiled a little, even as his heart ached.

Mike Chimpanzee truly wanted Mr. Rozenblatt to like him. It might be put more elegantly, but it was just that simple. It was a wish the ape hardly dared admit to himself, and amateur psychologists could bicker about the reasons behind it. But it meant that Mike exerted himself much too hard, and fell even further down in Mr. Rozenblatt's eyes.

"There's nothing wrong with sole, is there?" Cocker Spaniel defended her intended.

This caused Mr. Rozenblatt to laugh even louder; he snorted derisively and slapped his belly.

"No, no, I was only joking," said Mike, trying to make himself heard. "It's clear, darling, we can't have sole, can we?"

They were sitting around a pastry table at La Cueva. The

legendary chef Jan-Henrik Swan sat at the end of the table, and he was the one who had just suggested fish as the main course. Over by the stoves the cooks were doing prep work for the evening; again and again Swan cast worried glances in their direction. He was having a hard time concentrating on the wedding planning and it was obvious he would prefer to end the meeting as quickly as possible.

"No worries, Mike," Cocker Spaniel whispered, placing a consoling paw on Chimpanzee's shoulder. "He's only making a fool of himself. Of course you can have sole."

Mike felt extremely irritated by this kindness. In her father's eyes the fact that Cocker Spaniel intervened and tried to rescue the situation hardly strengthened Mike's stock. But snapping at his intended in this situation would only make matters worse, so carefully he shook off her paw.

"I was imagining an organic salmon pâté," said Chef Swan, unaffected by the stuffed animals' peculiar conversation, "with a whitefish roe sauce and my award-winning Brussels sprout risotto. For dessert a blueberry soufflé, resting on a bed of blackberries and raspberries, served tentatively with a young sauvignon blanc."

"Oh, that sounds marvelous," said Mrs. Rozenblatt.

"Dear Swan, you are a true artist," said Mr. Rozenblatt.

Cocker Spaniel smiled happily, and Ilja Crocodile struggled with her saliva production.

"Perhaps we could replace the raspberries with cloudberries?" Mike suggested.

The words felt like slaps; that was how the Rozenblatt family understood the comment. Terrified and furious glances were aimed at Chimpanzee. He knew what he had done; he had wagered everything on a final, desperate card; after having been reduced to an ignorant lout time after time by Mr. and Mrs. Rozenblatt, this was how he sought revenge.

The silence was only broken by the clatter of the cooks at the stove.

After having stared at Mike with fury and contempt, the company turned their pleading eyes to Jan-Henrik Swan.

But the chef shrugged one wing without interest, and said, "Well, cloudberries instead . . . that might not be a bad idea."

And thereafter he declared the meeting over and returned to his proper element, where his colleagues were waiting.

A few hours later Mike Chimpanzee still had a hard time letting go of Mr. Rozenblatt's condescending attitude, but he did his best to focus on the moment and aimed his light blue gaze at the lovely deer.

"Doll," he said in a voice so smooth it made the Breeze outside seem pushy, "I'm always going to love you."

Tears were running down her cheeks. The sun settled in her lap, the weather was midday and they were sitting across from each other in one of the booths at Scheherazade.

"Mike Chimpanzee," she answered, "you are a swine."

He smiled a tired but loving smile and shook his head almost imperceptibly. He could not help it that the music playing in the background claimed all his attention for a moment, the syncopated eighth notes on the rider just as the bass line ground on in quarter notes; only Nikki Lee and the Suspects could rock like that.

Then he again recalled the lovely deer, on whose cheeks the round roses had been sewn with a master's hand.

"We're torn apart, you and me," he said seriously. "We don't have the ability to make ourselves whole."

She looked at him as if he were the last, disintegrating bite of a hamburger with too much mustard and mayonnaise.

"You're a cowardly, miserable wretch, Mike Chimpanzee," she spat out.

"That I am," he exclaimed. "Guilty. Have I ever said anything else? I'm cowardly and I'm miserable. But a hope lives in my heart, a hope that one day you are going to understand, and forgive."

The scent of burnt almonds and marijuana drifted past the table. The chimpanzee twisted his head to hold it back a little while before it disappeared out on the street. Behind the bar stood Tom-Tom Crow, drying glasses. From the kitchen Sam Gazelle was heard trying to sing harmony to Nikki Lee. The muffled sound of the gazelle's carving knife against the cutting board—Sam was slicing cucumber, leeks, and carrots—kept time with the beat.

Mike was sitting parallel to the table, his feet on the bench and back against the wall, and looked her deep in the eyes. They had not known each other more than six months, but until now he had always been able to persuade her.

Not today.

"I'm not coming back," she said.

Her tears had dried, and he heard how angry she was.

"Doll, believe me," he said.

"The last time you called me. And I came. But that's not happening again."

"Doll, I would never—"

"And stop calling me 'doll,' damn it!" she screamed.

He held his hairy fingers up in the air in an attempt to defend himself. Scratched his ear and placed the other hand on his chest.

"It hurts," he stated.

The intent was to show that his heart was bleeding, but she misunderstood him.

"In your ear? I don't give a damn about that," she hissed.

She slid quickly out of the booth and remained standing for a moment in front of the table to heighten the drama. Then she left the restaurant with furious steps. At the bar Tom-Tom Crow continued drying glasses, unconcerned. He was not the most sophisticated stuffed animal in Yok, but there was something mysterious in the crow's small porcelain eyes that made you want to gain his sympathy. Now he mostly appeared bored. Through the open door to the street the sound of the deer's high heels was heard as she ran down toward flax yellow Piazza di Bormio. The chimpanzee could not help noticing that her running was not in sync with the music.

"Sam!" Mike called out toward the kitchen. "Today you'll have to share the weed!"

But the hacking from the kitchen counter did not stop.

Mike leaned his head back, against the window, and closed his eyes. He had let it go on far too long. He should have ended it the same evening he proposed to Cocker Spaniel, but he hadn't been able to. The deer was too beautiful, her eyes too large. Yet they had never been meant for each other, him and her. Mike sighed. He did not understand how he could love so intensely—which had actually been the case with the deer—and lose so easily. Was it pain he was looking for, this self-contempt that caused him to literally feel sick?

The anxiety then increased when he thought about the pink rosettes in his lovely Cocker Spaniel's ears and her moistly glistening glass nose.

"Sam!" Mike called again. "I have my own at home, but I didn't bring any with me. You've got to share!"

Sam came out of the kitchen. He untied his apron and set it over a bar stool. Under it he had on a light blue ruffled shirt that was much too small.

"You may be worth a break, honey," he said, gliding down on the bench in the booth where the deer had just been sitting. "Have you made someone sad again?"

Sam Gazelle lit two joints, and with studied slowness he pouted his full lips around one before he gave it to Mike, accompanied by a long look.

"I'm the one who's sad," the rock star answered, ignoring the gazelle's seduction tricks. "I'm not in control of my own feelings, Sam. I can't help it. I know I've hurt others, but most of all I've hurt myself."

"Poor silly little you." The gazelle sighed, smiling wickedly. "You run off with a beautiful deer, dump her because you're going to marry someone else, and feel endlessly sorry for yourself. Honey, you know that I love you, but—"

"It's not like that!" Mike protested, letting the cigarette paper flare with a deep puff. "I don't know why I . . . I guess I thought that . . . it's like never the idea that I . . ."

But he didn't know what he wanted to say because he didn't know what he felt.

"You're so young," said Sam, and the gazelle's voice was suddenly serious. "I've seen it happen with others, too, darling. It gets to be too much. Overwhelming. Honey, your enormous success, it was not about whether you did or didn't deserve it. And no one can blame you for wanting it to happen again. What stuffed animal wouldn't? Of course you'll have to toil hard to get this record to work out as well as the last one. But when that happens, remember it was something you wanted. Something you struggled for. That it was okay to want that. And that it's okay to enjoy it. It's not you they love, Mike, it's what you've achieved. It's absolutely not the same thing. But it's okay to let them love what you've achieved."

Mike nodded. And smoked. And nodded again. Then, unexpectedly, a tear fell from his eye.

"Are you crying? Darling, are you crying?" Sam Gazelle exclaimed, and his emotions overflowed.

The gazelle was about to slide off his bench to throw himself around the table and hug the poor star, but Mike—who realized what was about to happen—was just as quick from his side. Before Gazelle was able to exploit this golden opportunity, Mike was standing by the door, waving to Tom-Tom at the bar.

"Got to go now," he said. "Tom-Tom, Sam, see you soon. And, Sam? Thanks."

6.

Brown Brothers' showcase recording studio was in the attic of the National Bank offices on cucumber green Place St. Fargeau. Hundreds of superfluous square feet of white-glazed oak parquet, daylight streaming in through the skylights, casually placed, oversized white lounge suites and walls black with guitar and bass amplifiers. There were freestanding kitchen islands encircled by bar stools, and housing refrigerators stocked with ice, beer, and pop next to cabinets full of alcohol and chips. Musicians could move in here for weeks at a time to torment themselves through monotonous rehearsals and recording sessions that in the end gave the record company twice as much money as the musicians themselves.

"It's in the silences that you get the groove." Lancelot Lemur nodded. "You know, *ticka-ta-tick ticka-ta-tick, cha-cha.*"

They were each sitting in an overstuffed black leather armchair in front of the massive mixing board in the studio. The number of slide controls and knobs gave Mike a headache, thinking of the possible combinations. Lemur nodded four beats and let his long fingers indicate the rests; the silences he was talking about. He had on a black, see-through shirt and a pair of tight, black leather pants. His silver armband with a dozen skulls rattled as he moved his hands, the music streamed out of the speakers; they were listening to the afternoon's recordings.

Mike mumbled a confirmation: Sure, he felt the groove.

They smoked in silence. Both of them tore the filters off their cigarettes, both had double espressos, and though they had never worked together before, they felt a connection from the first day. Lancelot Lemur was one of Mollisan Town's most successful producers; earlier in the year he had made the Screaming Canaries a phenomenon, but his career was as long as it was legendary.

Gavin Toad maintained that Lemur was fired up at the chance to work with Mike. That couldn't possibly be true, but all the same Mike was secretly flattered to be sitting here discussing pauses with the great Lancelot Lemur.

"Gavin only heard the chorus," the chimpanzee now explained, "and it wasn't even quite finished. Now it is. The verse, too, more or less. I'm still polishing a few things, but . . . it's going to be . . . well, you can listen yourself. I really think I'm onto something."

"I don't remember, did you write anything on the last record?" Lemur asked.

The producer had asked that question many times the past few weeks, but he wasn't interested in the answer; he wasn't interested in anyone other than himself.

" 'Moon over Lanceheim,' " Mike answered. "It opened the last record. That one was mine."

Lemur shrugged his narrow shoulders.

"You know," he said gravely. "If Gavin wants, we'll put in one of your songs. I can transform any kind of shit into shit that will top every list in this city. It's a gift I've got."

The demon producer took a puff on the cigarette, picked a few flakes of tobacco off his lip, and sampled the espresso without appreciating it.

"Not that I'm calling your songs shit," he added. "But you get what I mean? Give me a little time, and I'm magic."

"This song I'm writing now, about freedom, it's magic, too," said Mike, regretting it at once.

It made him sound like a little cub.

"Cool," Lemur answered, rocking his whole body to reinforce his ironic, contemplative nods.

"It's important to me," the chimp explained. "I have to be able to stand by what I do."

"Great, great." Lancelot nodded, leaning over the board to correct a drum sound at the end of the song they hadn't listened to. "Personally, you know, I could care less where I stand. But cash is cash. Well, nothing personal, you get what I mean?"

Just as the sun was rapidly sinking into the horizon and the Evening Weather was cooling down the city with its darkness, Mike Chimpanzee slipped away. The checkered Nils Gull—more than twice as old as the ape, he'd played with Owl, Bill & Trash in the early days of rock and roll—was adding guitar licks to "It's Not Over ('Cause It Never Happened)." The gull was a perfectionist, and as he was rejecting the eighth retake, Mike picked up a wide-brimmed hat and took the elevator down to the lobby. During the Evening Weather was Mike's best chance to take a walk undisturbed. For one thing, there were fewer stuffed animals out on the streets in the evening, and the shadow of the wide brim kept him from being easily recognizable.

He opened the heavy outside door, put on the hat, stepped out onto the sidewalk, and started walking east, along the imposing stone facade of the National Bank. Right on schedule the genie showed up at his side. He, too, was wearing a hat.

"Sir, don't get mad now, I don't intend to say anything," said Fredrik. "I only intend to walk here beside you, trying to keep from noticing that you haven't tucked in your shirt and from reminding you that everything you wish for you can have."

On the other side of the street was Parc Clemeaux, with its pruned boxwood bushes and artfully shaped arborvitae and cypresses. When Mike discovered the garden a few years earlier he had been astonished and spent hours along the labyrinthine pathways. But the pleasure of novelty soon faded, and now he hardly cast a glance across the street.

He should have.

Somehow the rumor had spread. It might have been someone up in the office at Brown Brothers, or one of the musicians in the studio. It might have been pure chance, a stuffed animal who had seen him use the door a few hours earlier, or the kind of cunning espionage the tabloids excelled in. But whatever the cause the fact remained: There were two dozen stuffed animals behind the boxwood bushes in the park opposite, following Mike's and Fredrik's every step.

It was the genie who discovered them first.

"Goodness," he said.

The next moment he was gone.

This caused Mike in turn to stop and look around, and just then the horde of stuffed animals on the other side decided to attack. They ran right out into the street, cars honking and swerving with screeching tires, but this did not stop them.

Mike reacted instantly. He took to his heels. The big hat went flying.

"We love you!" his fans screamed, running after him.

"We want you!" they shouted after him.

"Mike, stop!" they screamed.

But Mike managed to throw himself into the entryway out of which he had just come, right before the devoted fans caught up. He ran up the stairs and pounded on the door to the studio. Listened for steps in the stairwell, but heard none. Lemur opened with a raised eyebrow.

"When did you leave?" he asked. "Why are you out of breath?"

Mike didn't answer. He dragged himself across the threshold with rainwater dripping from his body. There was a large drying cabinet in the bathroom behind the sauna, and that was where he headed.

Nils Gull was sitting on a bar stool at the closest kitchen island, skimming a newspaper absentmindedly when Mike Chimpanzee came out again, warm and dry. The checkered old guitarist was drinking whiskey with a straw. From the studio, a technician was heard putting in the sound from a cymbal, and through the skylights Mike could see in the night sky that the Storm was approaching. Lemur was not to be seen.

"Lancelot?" Mike asked.

"He split," Gull answered. "Went to some meeting. Back in a couple hours, he said. You want some?" he asked, gesturing to his glass.

"A meeting? Now?"

Gull aired his feathers to explain that he didn't know more than that, and held up the whiskey bottle. Mike nodded and sat down on the other side of the island. They didn't know each other very well, had only met a few times before, and yet not many minutes had passed before Mike started telling about his songwriting. How dependent he was on inspiration, how authentic his sources of inspiration were, how different his process looked. It was in creation, Mike Chimpanzee said to the checkered gull, that he became whole; it was his only way to put together the fragments of a life that was constantly cracking.

Nils Gull listened attentively. He had met hundreds of performers like Mike Chimpanzee, good-looking types who earned piles of money but still whined about artistic integrity; they all thought they were geniuses. At the same time, Nils was a professional musician and knew who paid the bills.

"You need something like Nikki Lee's guitar pick," he said.

"Nikki Lee's guitar pick?"

"Now I feel old." Gull sighed. "You mean you've never heard of Nikki Lee's guitar pick?"

"Do tell," Mike asked.

"Nikki Lee . . . you know who that is?"

Now Mike blushed with shame and fury.

"I haven't heard the story about the guitar pick," Mike repeated. "But Nikki Lee and the Suspects is the reason I started playing. She's my role model. In many ways."

His voice quivered with indignation. Gull nodded indulgently.

"When Nikki Lee was fifteen she was already, you know, something out of the ordinary," the guitarist said. "She had a voice like . . . well, you know what I'm talking about. Today everyone knows what I'm talking about. But at that time she only sang a little. Not very often. It hurt too much. It cut like knives in her throat. She told her parents, but they thought it had something to do with her vocal cords. She was scratchy and rough even then. It wasn't strange, they thought, that it hurt. At the same time it was a shame, because she sang so amazingly."

"Amazingly." Mike nodded in agreement; Nikki Lee's voice had always been one of his guiding lights.

"Everyone who heard her sing loved her," Gull continued after a sip from his straw, "and encouraged her in every way. She learned to play guitar unwillingly, and tried writing songs, but it was a no-go. Not because she couldn't. And, as I said, she sang like a goddess. But it was . . . mediocre. Half-baked. Nothing that stuck out."

"I know what you're talking about," Mike admitted, sipping the strong booze. "Hell, I know exactly what you're talking about."

"Besides, her throat only got worse and worse. She tried whispering her lyrics, whistling the melodies, but that didn't work. Finally she went up to the record company to do her big audition. Halfway through the song her throat hurt so much that tears welled up in her eyes and she fainted."

"Is that true?" Mike whispered.

"She woke up in the hospital," Gull continued. "In comes the doctor who did the operation, and in his claws he's holding a little piece of plastic."

"A guitar pick?"

"A small piece of plastic, which had been in Nikki Lee's throat the whole time, probably ever since she was manufactured. A piece of someone else's nose, or someone else's claws. She goes home after a few days in the hospital, and takes the piece of plastic with her as a memento. When she feels good enough, she sits down with the guitar. She remembers the piece of plastic, gets it, and uses it as a guitar pick. It's not just that her voice holds; after the operation she can sing without feeling pain. More important yet, with her new guitar pick she writes the songs that you and I and everyone else have loved since then. The classics."

"Unbelievable." Mike sighed.

"You need something like that." Nils Gull nodded. "Something that makes it happen."

"Makes what happen?" asked Lancelot Lemur, who had just come in the door.

"Nothing," Mike hurried to say.

He had no desire to take the role of a wretch once again, even if he felt like one.

7.

The tears welled up in Cocker Spaniel's eyes, gathering as heavy drops on her long eyelashes. If she were to blink now, they would roll down over her cheeks.

"Don't be sad," Mike pleaded.

He regretted it bitterly, and it felt like someone was squeezing his heart into a hard little ball.

"I thought it would be so . . . special," Cocker Spaniel said quietly.

"But isn't it obvious that it's special?"

"But I thought you wanted to have a chain, too."

"Darling, of course I want a chain. It's just Gavin who— oh, forget about him. Of course we'll buy matching chains."

A devout stillness prevailed inside Vulgaeri. Voices were naturally subdued by dark blue wall-to-wall carpet under the many beautifully illuminated counters of brushed steel and glass. For security reasons the store had no windows. The walls were clad with red velvet wallpaper, and the classical music was playing so faintly that it was felt more than heard. The well-known jewelry store was on sand white Glöckleinsgasse, one of the more out-of-the-way streets in Lanceheim, and Mike and Cocker Spaniel were sitting in front of the counter with wedding chains. Not all stuffed animals had necks, but they all had a head, and the chains could be made as long or short as you wanted.

"I don't want to force you into anything," Cocker Spaniel sniffed. "I guess it was stupid of me to think that—"

Mike realized that this moment would follow him throughout the marriage. Due to some unguarded words, equally sincere and thoughtless.

"Darling, forget that now," he repeated. "That was just silly. Do you like the one with diamonds better?"

But she had lost the desire to choose and shook her head.

"We'll take the simple one. It's more truthful."

On the glass counter there were three chains that remained after an hour of deliberation and testing: a narrow one in white gold, another equally narrow chain but strewn with diamonds, and finally a thicker variation in red gold with a beautiful silver clasp. Mike had thought out loud, and stated that onstage Gavin Toad wouldn't allow him to wear any of them: The chains weren't rock and roll.

"But you preferred the diamonds, didn't you?" he insisted.

"We can't afford it."

"We'll be able to afford it when the record comes out."

"You don't know that."

"It's the sort of thing you feel."

But that was a lie, of course. The work on the record was in a phase when he felt less certain than ever about Lancelot Lemur's genius. Last night he had continued working on the song about freedom; that was his method, working over and over again, and he thought he'd made a bit more progress. To surprise himself, after a number of genie-cigarettes, he had unexpectedly chosen F minor, a key he never used. This freed him. Suddenly it became possible to exchange the most obvious chord progressions for alternative suspended and diminished chords, to mix keys and not get stuck in stolen riffs. With his guitar in his lap he felt smarter than he had in a long time.

With these thoughts a powerful urge came over him, and he wanted nothing better than to leave this store and return to the black notebook and the melodies.

"Besides, your dad isn't going to like it if it's too simple," he said. "We'll take the one with diamonds."

But Cocker Spaniel Rozenblatt was not in the mood for gibes about her father, and because he—Dad—was going to pay for it anyway, she bought the simplest variation. They left the store in silence, and went to wait outside on the sidewalk. A coworker would come and pick up Cocker Spaniel and drive her directly to work. She was a real estate agent in Tourquai, and reasonably free to arrange her time as she wanted.

When she turned toward him with tears in her eyes and fell into his embrace, Mike realized in shame that he had already forgotten their conflict; instead in his thoughts he was in an intro that might work with the verse.

"Mike," she wept. "Forgive me?"

"Yes, no, that is, I was the one who was stupid," he answered.

Her soft body against his, the tears absorbed by his shoulder, the scent of fabric softener, her breath that smelled of cotton and mint . . . He was back, again fully and mentally present on the sidewalk on Glöckleinsgasse.

"My darling," he said, "you know you're going to have to forgive me again and again when we're married, don't you? I'm that type. That has to be forgiven."

And she wept and laughed in turn, nodding at the same time.

"I know," she said. "I'm sure it's because I love you so much, which I am never going to admit again."

"I didn't hear a thing," he whispered.

"Good."

And with perfect timing, a red Volga Mini pulled up by the

sidewalk, and Cocker Spaniel's colleague Karin Lion rolled down the window.

"Turtledoves!" she called. "You'll have to wait with that for a few weeks. So there's something left for later."

Laughing, Cocker Spaniel got into the car, and as they drove away she stuck her head out and threw air kisses after her. Her long ears fluttered in the wind, and he waved back.

Mike had fallen in love with the idea of falling in love with Cocker Spaniel Rozenblatt even before his first record hit the shelves and he was blessed with stardom and a year in the fast lane. When he saw her for the first time, she was doing volunteer work at his school, helping out the overworked staff during breaks and lunches. He had never seen anyone like her before, with her pearl necklace and ironed skirts down to her knees. Not to mention that she was a few years older than he was. She was acting like the cubs in the Corbod school were not of lesser means but of lesser minds, and she talked very slowly so everyone could understand what an animal from the better part of town was saying. Mike was as provoked as he was fascinated. She didn't seem like a stupid animal, so why did she act that way?

When they started dating—in the beginning she refused to call their meetings "dates"—Mike understood that to Cocker Spaniel, poverty was completely unknown. She acted with caution like any true explorer would in a hostile environment. And that perspective, along with the way she pronounced "Tourquai" and how her world consisted of "who-said-what-to-whom," while the most common existential and political dilemmas seemed to make no sense to her: Mike envied it all. He pursued their relationship, he himself became an explorer, and he accepted that she went along with it for the same reasons. He was everything her father was afraid of. And the years passed and now he was standing on this sidewalk, waving to her with a wedding chain in his paw. In many ways, it was incomprehensible.

———————

Mike Chimpanzee took the wedding chains home with him because he was the one who would present them at the wedding ceremony, and during the day's obligatory phone call with Mom—she called around lunchtime every day to make sure he was alive and dry—Mike happened to mention the visit to Vulgaeri. Ilja threw herself into her old, automatic transmission Volga and stormed into the antique shop ten minutes later.

"Where are they, let me see them!" she called out halfway across the threshold.

He showed her the chains, which for her taste were much too minimalistic, but she sighed heavily anyway and shed a large crocodile tear that thankfully fell to the side of the expensive velvet case.

"Now I believe it, my monkeychin, my own little candy troll. Now I believe it. My own little chimpy-wimpykins has become a big ape and is really going to get married. Mrs. Rosenthal can choke on that for real."

"Mom, can't you just call me 'Mike'?"

When his mom left, the genie would not leave Mike alone. The frustrated Fredrik had decided to dial up the intensity a few notches, and out of his diffuse mouth bubbled a cavalcade of possibilities that would have aroused unbridled avarice in any stuffed animal: gold, securities, and lotteries with guaranteed winnings. Exclusive wardrobes, classic guitars from Mollisan Town history, handwritten manuscripts by the great masters, horns of plenty, and luxury villas in the resort town of Hillevie. If nothing else, Fredrik demonstrated an imagination born out of his own desperation, and which for that reason lacked limits.

Mike demonstratively remained lying in bed. When the

genie addressed him, he stared down at the pages of a random paperback without turning any. The genie was not so dumb that he didn't notice this.

"Mr. Ape," Fredrik said at last, "it seems as if we're both stuck. Or, which perhaps is closer to the truth, it seems as if you're stuck, both as far as your reading and making a decision is concerned. A little air will do us good so I can take the opportunity to show you instead of telling."

And so involuntarily, Mike accompanied the genie to the sidewalk outside the store. The afternoon sun was broiling hot from a blue sky, and the chimpanzee did not need to be in the studio until evening, so he actually had all the time in the world. As usual, he assured himself that the street was empty before he went out. If an admirer saw him coming out of the store, his secret residence would be discovered, forcing him to flee.

Otherwise the Corbod neighborhood in Yok was a good place to live for someone as well-known as Mike Chimpanzee. In Corbod, as in Yok in general, you minded your own business, and knew to look away when things happened that didn't concern you. For that reason no one in the neighborhood would claim that a beautiful fifty-foot sailboat was suddenly on a trailer outside the antique store, even though the boat's newly varnished wooden hull glistened in the sun. The boat then disappeared a few minutes later, as if in a fog.

The silver-gleaming truck pulling a trailer with the city's most modern recording studio—complete with instruments and cover press—did not attract any attention either, even though it drove up hissing and groaning. The genie forced Mike to enter this technical sound paradise, but from the ape nothing was heard other than a heavy sigh. Fifteen minutes later, the truck and trailer drove around the corner, and seemed to disappear down into a tunnel that faded away the moment after.

It was one thing that the rootless stuffed animals in the

neighborhood knew to show disinterest, but it was even stranger that Mike Chimpanzee remained so indifferent to what Fredrik presented, and this included a diamond whose like had never been seen before, or since, in Mollisan Town. Back on the sofa bed Mike cast a distracted look at the stone and shook his head.

"But, sir, I don't know if you understand," Fredrik said. "If you only say the word, it can be yours."

"A diamond? Sorry, Cloud, you'll have to forgive me, but I have other things to think about."

"Maybe that's the problem?" the genie said. "You still address me as 'Cloud.' Are you really sure you've understood? I'm a genie. I can fulfill three wishes. Any whatsoever. Shall we start again? This diamond is the most significant precious stone Mollisan Town has ever seen."

"Shut up now, Cloud," said Mike. "I have to finish so I have something to show Lancelot tonight."

And with those words, the chimpanzee picked up his notebook, unmoved by boats and diamonds, and stared down at the pages without reading a line.

8.

Fredrik the genie sat on a rocking horse from medieval Lanceheim, watching a mop scrub the wood floors in the antique store. It wouldn't help, he sighed to himself; the filth was ingrained in the floor. But he was forced to do something. He did not consider himself a perfectionist, but it was impossible to stay still, even for a genie.

Mike Chimpanzee was still asleep, even though the Morning Weather had advanced far toward lunch. Using telepathy, the genie dipped the mop in the scrub water, letting it make majestic sweeps under the sofa bed on which the ape was lying.

The genie's master slept often and a lot, which went along with the fact that he smoked or drank all the time. When he came home from the studio in the dawn hours he was thoroughly tipsy. Fredrik shook his head. He shouldn't have done that. His already diffuse, cloudlike facial features came undone, one eye ended up on his cheek and his nose exchanged places with an ear. It took a few seconds to straighten out the puffs of cloud, and instead of repeating the maneuver he sighed heavily.

Any stuffed animal in Mollisan Town would have rejoiced at the opportunity to make three wishes. With very few exceptions the same stuffed animal would have leapt at the villa in Le Vezi-not, a golden drying cabinet, or King Carl's spurs. But the genie understood that Mike Chimpanzee would never wish for mate-rial things. Perhaps it was after the breakthrough as a star that he realized how fleeting success could be. That for a brief period he had money to buy anything at all, which he did, but real-ized that, basically, this really didn't change anything. The genie didn't know, nor did he search for explanations. Instead he tried to understand what Mike wanted most of all, and it quickly became obvious: More than anything else, Mike Chimpanzee wanted his song to be on the impending album.

So why didn't he wish for that?

On two occasions the genie had suggested that Mike ought to wish for a song on the album, which made the chimpan-zee positively aggressive. The first time it was mostly shouting and unbelievable quantities of vodka. The second time the ape picked up a blow-dryer and went on open attack. It took the genie several minutes to put himself back together. He could not say that he understood Mike's reaction, but he understood that the suggestion must be handled carefully. And if it was brought up again, it had to happen on Mike's terms.

Mike Chimpanzee was a mystery.

The ape had everything. Everyone loved him, and he was recording an album that would most likely consolidate his position as one of Mollisan Town's foremost performers . . . and yet, he seemed mostly depressed. Restless, ungrateful, and gloomy. Searching, confused, and afraid. He seemed to iden-tify himself completely with the role of failed songwriter.

Even more problematic, and threatening for the genie, was that the chimpanzee was uninterested in his remaining wishes.

The genie was convinced of his own inexhaustible imagina-tion and his verbal abilities; his description of the opportuni-ties would have enticed the most recalcitrant. He was a genie, after all. Everything was in his power and he could satisfy them all: the materialist, the humanist, and the idealist. Ser-vices, experiences, or things; egotism, altruism, or dualism,

Fredrik felt no limitations. Yet he failed where Mike Chimpanzee was concerned. Because the cursed ape simply seemed so absorbed by his own miserable spiritual life, he didn't even have the sense to listen to the genie's enticements.

The previous evening the genie thought he had come very close to granting a second wish, but for some unfathomable reason he had not succeeded in getting all the way to a decision. Mike came home at dawn, intoxicated, and as usual sat down at the desk with the guitar on his lap. The genie spent the night brooding, ready to attack the ape from a new angle. He was exhausted in a way that he assumed was typical for genies; more frustrated than tired. Outside the night sky watched over Corbod and a massive convoy of heavy trucks rolled past on Calle Gran Via in the protection of darkness and the clouds of dust they stirred up.

"If I say Rozenblatt," the genie said, "what do you say?"

The dear and feared name Rozenblatt appeared so suddenly that Mike stopped playing. He set aside the guitar, looked inquisitively at the genie, and went into the office to get a beer.

"What do you mean, Cloud?"

"Dear Mr. Rock Star Ape," the genie said formally, "many are the stuffed animals you have managed to dupe, but not your future father-in-law, isn't that right? Because he has seen through you. Your stock is not particularly high there, is it? He knows you can't do dishes."

Mike opened the refrigerator door and noted there were only about ten bottles left. He would have to ration in the dawn hours.

"I'm not getting married to Mr. Rozenblatt, Cloud," he answered. "And even if I couldn't do dishes—which of course I can—that's hardly why Cocker Spaniel wants me. She wants me because—"

"Sir, let's not go into that, if you please?" the genie interrupted in horror, adding: "But permit me a certain forwardness, anyway. Being an accepted stuffed animal like the Rozenblatts, that does seem to have a certain significance for you?"

"Bullshit."

Mike twisted the cap off the bottle and put it to his mouth.

"Really?"

"Bullshit."

Inside, Chimpanzee was shaken. Up to this moment he had not even admitted to himself what the genie was hinting at: that he actually longed for the acceptance of the Rozenblatt family in a way that went beyond the fact that Mr. and Mrs. Rozenblatt were his future parents-in-law. He drank from the beer bottle. It was not only inconceivable, it was degrading.

"Being accepted by Mr. Rozenblatt," said the genie, interrupting Mike's train of thought. "Being respected by Mr. Rozenblatt . . . that would feel good, wouldn't it?"

Mike shrugged his shoulders, but he was no actor.

The genie chuckled to himself. It was obvious that he had guessed correctly; this meant a lot to Mike.

The ape took a few more gulps of beer and returned to the desk, where the glow of the lamp fell down over the black notebook open on the underlay. He picked up the guitar. By his body language it was visible that he had yet another worry to bear.

"You only need to ask me nicely," clarified the genie, who amused himself by hovering out from the office instead of pretending to walk. "And don't think about the wording itself. I'll gladly assist. Shall we call it respect, love, or maybe unconditional admiration? Does it concern both Mr. and Mrs. Rozenblatt, or just one of them? You wish—when I think about it, you don't even need to ask particularly nicely—and then the matter is done. Mr. Rozenblatt will be your latest admirer."

Mike stared at him for a long time, but then leaned over the guitar and started again plinking the same chord progression that the genie had been forced to listen to many nights in a row. And the moment had passed.

The rest of the morning was as usual; Mike played and the genie nagged. Much could be said about the self-occupied rock performer, but he had an impressive capacity to ignore something if he wanted to.

Fredrik got off the rocking horse, considered pouring the murky water in the bucket over the sleeping chimpanzee, but thought better of it. Acting out his frustration would not help him, and besides, he couldn't raise his hand against his master.

According to the unwritten rules of genies, Fredrik was forced to carry out his master's three wishes. Nothing required him, however, to like his job. Or to like his master. Mike Chimpanzee didn't fold his clothes, he didn't brush his teeth, he didn't scrub floors, didn't dust shelves, and didn't change the sheets. He put out his cigarettes in the leftovers on his plate. The fact that Fredrik tried with such energy to get Mike to come up with a couple of wishes was not only connected with his longing to resume solid form after thousands of years as a cloud; he feared that he would soon not be able to put up with the stuffy, dark, and dirty antique store any longer.

More and more often he tried to get away from there; he was limited neither by space nor by time. At first he felt guilty when he took his excursions. His only purpose in Mollisan Town was, after all, Mike's three wishes. At the same time, the chimpanzee was not coughing up a single miserable suggestion even if Fredrik nagged, and for that reason, every day, he ventured farther and farther away from Calle Gran Via.

He flew out over the forests and smelled the odor of pine and dampness, he hovered high above the sea and smelled fish and salt air, and in his most dissolved form—when for a stuffed animal's eyes he was no more than steam—he could even spend time on streets and squares; consistently in search of an idea for a wish that Mike Chimpanzee might conceivably want to make.

Sometimes Fredrik seemed to recognize something: a square or a tree or a tone of voice; and a nostalgic quiver went through his condensed exterior. Under the focused surface were memories about to return, the physical feeling that at one time he had been a stuffed animal like everyone else. The longing he experienced to return in solid form was nothing other than an instinct of self-preservation, the only instinct he had left as a genie. Then this caused him pain, and he dissolved in atoms and had a very tough time fusing together into a cloud again.

How he had learned these genie rules—how he knew that he had to make himself invisible to everyone except Mike, how he could fly or conjure forth diamonds and cars—he himself didn't know. Was there some kind of course included in the bottle where he had lived for thousands of years? A pedagogical voice that echoed through the centuries and was implanted in his awareness? He didn't know, and it was just as pointless to speculate about this as to try not to.

But more often than wondering about how he could get a meadow of poppies and hemp to grow in an antique shop, he brooded over what terrible deed he must have committed to have been sentenced to lifetimes inside a bottle. Fredrik thought about it morning and night, but discovered not the slightest trace of the evil of which he evidently must be capable. And consequently, a suspicion awakened in his overactive brain: What if he was innocent? What if he had been a victim of a conspiracy or simply of chance circumstances? No one, neither stuffed animal nor genie, wants to see himself or herself as evil, and therefore he often fantasized about his innocence. It was both terrifying and consoling, and sometimes he felt a desire to discuss the matter with someone.

"Sir, from the impressions you've had of me," the genie had asked the ape as they had a late breakfast together yesterday, "even if perhaps they aren't the best, I realize of course that I nag and so on, I wonder, do you see any potential evil in me? Don't I seem like a decent chap?"

"A decent chap?" Mike Chimpanzee seemed to think about it, and after a long silence he answered, "You seem obsessed with stuff."

"Hm, meaning?"

"You seem fixated on things, very preoccupied by money and objects. But if that makes you into a cloud, I don't know."

"I would appreciate it if you didn't call me 'Cloud,'" the genie pointed out. "If there's no objection, can you please say 'Fredrik'?"

"Fredrik, there's more to life than material things," said Mike.

9.

When the full moon became half and the night entered its last quarter, Mike took out the guitar. The genie sighed heavily and meaningfully. They had made a pact: Between midnight and dawn the genie promised to keep quiet. The chimp's service in return was to really listen and make a decision on the suggestions the genie would present the following morning. Maybe, thought Fredrik, this was playing to the gallery, but that was better than no play at all.

To make sure that this night's songwriting session would not be yet another in a long series of repeated failures, Mike had changed the prerequisites. He used a different desk chair—a baroque-inspired variation on wheels that was inside the office, originally bought by the shop's first owner—and he turned on a couple of the antique floor lamps at the back of the store. Their warm light was now reflected in the reddish yellow lacquer of the guitar as he started to play. He had passed the limits of fatigue and physical autopilot took over.

But do you believe what they're saying?
(Every thought has an end)

Do you believe what they're saying?
(Every life its outer limit)
Do you believe what they're saying?
(There's no way out again)
Do you believe what they're saying?
(Do you know how it feels?)
'Cause freedom is / freedom is / freedom isn't here.

He played the usual chord progression again. The experiment in F was over. He pulled out a G major, D major, E minor, and C major. His long fingers danced over the neck of the guitar. He sang the melody he had given the lyrics yesterday, but it didn't take off. He lit a joint, letting it hang from his lips while he hummed the notes that followed one another in a far too predictable sequence. It was too docile, not interesting enough.

He exchanged D for B minor, and finally something happened. He tempered the C chord by letting the bass notes go down, through B and Bb to A minor. This progression was too depressing, and he saved himself by returning up to D before tying the loop together with his original G.

In the meantime he continued humming, changing, and improving. He put out the cigarette. Was this really a chorus? Did it have the needed lift? If he transposed the verse to F sharp, would it take off thanks to the lower key? To further leave his secure base, the ape threw in an A major and broke the harmony. Sang his way to a partially new melody. Was this the cursed hook Gavin was harping about?

After another half hour Mike set aside the guitar and retrieved the tape recorder from the bottom drawer in the sofa bed where he stored valuables. Turned it on, set it on the desk, and played and sang. Turned it off, went into the office, got a cold beer from the fridge. Every time a sound was heard from the genie's direction—sighs or moans—Mike raised a finger ominously. Not a word. The genie's frustration soon became too much for him, and before the chimpanzee's eyes he dissolved and disappeared. Where he went did not interest Mike.

When Mike Chimpanzee thought sufficient time had passed he returned to the desk, sat down, and placed his index finger on the tape recorder's play button. But he did not start the machine. He didn't need to. He knew exactly what would happen when he played what he had just recorded.

He felt the shiny, cold metal under his finger, and remembered how it had been yesterday. And the day before and countless nights before that. He closed his eyes, and saw in his mind how he would listen and feel pride and joy. How he would rewind and play the chorus again, over and over. Every time the melody would sound better and better. And when at last he went to bed just as the sun was rising, he would be certain that now, now he had finally done what Gavin Toad always harped about.

The next morning he woke up with the memory of his nighttime success, but still hesitated before calling the record company. He avoided the tape player until noon, when he could no longer withstand the need of a final confirmation. But then, when at last he listened to what he had accomplished the night before, it was his own mediocrity he heard.

The little tape player represented self-deception and false pretenses.

Mike Chimpanzee swallowed a few times, lit another joint, and pressed the play button.

> *Do you believe what they're saying?*
> *(Do you know how it feels?)*
> *'Cause freedom is / freedom is / freedom isn't here.*

He turned it off. Closed his eyes. Got up from the chair, took the tape player, and threw it with all his might against the wall. It struck against the brick with a sharp crack, after which electronic parts rained down over the floor.

Mike screamed.

He collapsed on the floor next to the desk. The tears flowed, a howl that soon changed into a painful whimper forced up through his throat. His head was bursting, thoughts refused to appear: The truth was dangerously near, and it would first destroy his ego and then his life.

"Moon Over Lanceheim" on the first album was—even though it was his only recorded song so far—not much to brag about. Even then he had been aware of that. But when he recorded it, its mediocrity had not worried him; the song had been a starting point, and you have to start somewhere.

But it also ends somewhere.

An anxious whimpering filled the room. The sound of capitulation. The thought was formulated, and with that he could never deceive himself again.

He struggled up from the floor and sat down on the bed. His head in his hands, his back bent, and his eyes closed. Emptiness. He was an artist, unable to create art. He was a poet without poetry. He was not who he had always believed himself to be. But then . . . who was he?

The haze of the Morning Weather concealed the dawn with a white fog that lay heavy and damp over the city's still empty streets. Mike was sitting on the edge of the sofa bed with his head heavy in his hands when he made his decision.

"Fredrik!" the ape called.

"Sometime has to be the first, sir," replied the genie, who had materialized out of nothingness without delay. "In no way should you be ashamed that you called on me."

"Why should I be ashamed?" Mike asked.

"No, that's my point, sir."

"Which?"

"That you shouldn't be ashamed."

"About what?"

The genie sighed. This conversation was going nowhere.

Had Mike Chimpanzee called him there to tease him? Or was the ape once again so high that nothing more reasonable could be expected? The genie was about to give up and leave, when Mike said the liberating words.

"Genie, I have a wish. A second wish."

"A wish?"

The genie stopped short. Bewildered and surprised. He realized when he heard the words that unconsciously he must have written off the possibility that Mike Chimpanzee would ever wish for anything at all. Without wanting to, he dissolved into atoms and rained down over the astonished Mike Chimpanzee and his antique store.

"Pull yourself together, Genie," said Mike. "We're leaving."

10.

"Cancelled?"

The word echoed in the boutique. The dozen or so stuffed animals fingering shirts and sweaters turned toward the entry, where a furious crocodile in a thin red coat with a shawl collar was coming in.

Mike Chimpanzee, who was in a fitting room about to pull on a pair of jeans and a pale rose-checked piqué sweater, recognized the voice. For a fraction of a second he considered staying in there, out of reach of Mom, but gave up the idea. She would find him anyway. Here or somewhere else. He pulled the heavy drapery to the side and came out. From the outdoor clothing department she was on her way through the store right toward him.

"How," he mumbled to himself, "did she know I was here?"

But Ilja Crocodile had built up a fine-meshed network of informers around Corbod, and Mike had resigned himself long ago—escaping from Mom was impossible.

The crocodile rushed through row upon row of tightly packed racks of clothes. Vechado was a boutique chain that specialized in vintage clothing. They donated a quarter of the profits to the charity A Helping Hand, and in exchange got the majority of their garments from them.

"Cancelled!" Crocodile shouted again.

Mike stood paralyzed outside the fitting room watching his mom rush toward him, like a torpedo through a launching tube.

"Cancelled!" she shouted a third time, but now added, "What have you done, you good-for-nothing!"

And when she reached the fitting room she smacked him across the head with her handbag. Surprised and unprepared he was thrown sideways, landing on the armrest of an over-stuffed armchair where a customer or bored companion could wait during the clothes fitting.

"So you didn't intend to say anything about it?" she screamed.

Mike pulled himself up so that he was half reclining on the armchair, staring up at the green monster that was his mother. He tried the pleading, helpless look that most often appeased her.

"What?!" she screamed, unaffected. "Didn't you think we should talk about it?"

"Mom," said Mike quietly, "I don't know what you're talking about."

"Cancelled!" Ilja repeated desperately, staring ominously down at her son. "After we've invited all our friends, the neighbors, your father's chattering aunts, the Rosenthals, everyone! And then you cancel! Do you understand what I've gone through? Do you understand what you've subjected me to? The shame that's awaiting—"

"Mom, I don't know," said Mike. "Cancelled? I'm sorry, but—"

"*Sorry!*" Ilja Crocodile exploded. "Sorry? I'm the one who's sorry, Mike. I'm the one who's sorry. Sorry about not having done better with you. It's my fault, of course, everything is always my fault. That you never mature. You can't take responsibility, Mike, you refuse to grow up. And it's my fault. I've been there for you all the time. I've cared too much about you. My love has been too great for us both. You're not the one who's done this to me, I'm the one who's hurt myself!"

During this harangue Mike had crawled up in the armchair and was now sitting normally. He still didn't know what she was talking about.

"But, Mom," said Mike, "you shouldn't take it all on yourself—"

"When you arrived, I was so happy," Ilja continued; her tone was high and shrill, everyone in the store listened to her. "I couldn't have been happier. Of course your father didn't understand a thing, but I knew. You were chosen, Mike, you were special. Your musicality, your charisma, even when you started school it was clear that you would become something special. At the same time I knew you had a heavy disposition. You didn't get that from me; this constant questioning and brooding comes from your father's side of the family. What good has that done, tell me that? Why can't you ever be content? Was the Rozenblatt family not fine enough for you?"

"But, Mom, the Rozenblatt family . . . I love Cocker Spaniel, and . . ."

"With all your prospects," Ilja Crocodile went on. "You could have anyone, Mike, anyone at all. There isn't a female who wouldn't run to the altar if she knew you wanted her. And then you can't even make this happen!"

"Mom, we're getting married in just a few—"

"Nothing will come of that, Mike," Crocodile howled unhappily. "I get sad when I think about it. You have made your mother sad. Are you happy now? Are you proud of that? Seeing me like this, in tears?"

"Mom, why are you saying that nothing will come of—"

"But I'm angry, too!" Ilja shouted, almost surprised. "Really furious!"

She raised her handbag to give her son another beating, but he jumped up from the chair and took a few steps away.

"Mom, what are you talking about?"

"Don't put on airs," Crocodile hissed. "Mrs. Rosenthal called. They're cancelling the wedding. You good-for-nothing. What have you done?"

Mike Chimpanzee stood outside the Rozenblatt family's well-maintained town house in Amberville and pounded on the door. The narrow gravel walk up to the house from the gate was neatly raked, the sun was shining from a clear blue sky, yellow hollyhocks stood at attention in the flower beds on each side of the stairway, and the neighborhood rested in deep harmony. Mike's panting disturbed the calm. He had already terrorized the doorbell for a few minutes, without success. He knew someone was at home; he'd seen a movement behind the curtains in the kitchen just as he arrived.

What had happened? On the way from Vechado to Amberville Mike could not make heads or tails of what his mom had said. Had she been drinking? Was it the start of dementia? It seemed completely crazy that the wedding was cancelled and no one told the groom?

"Open up!" he shouted at Cocker Spaniel's closed door. "I see you're in there!"

Being noisy ought to be effective. If Mike knew the Rozenblatt family, there was nothing they feared more than being scandalized in front of the neighbors.

"Open up!"

Behind Mike Chimpanzee, a car pulled in with screeching tires. When the ape turned around, he saw that it was Mr. Rozenblatt parking his dark green Volga. His face beet red, Rozenblatt threw open the car door and ran up the well-raked path to the steps, where the chimpanzee was shouting.

"Now you shut up!" Mr. Rozenblatt yelled.

Mike realized what had happened. Someone inside the house—Mrs. Rozenblatt or Cocker Spaniel—had called Mr. Rozenblatt at work and asked him to come. Averting the conflict with the chimpanzee was a task for the head of the family, and here he was now, Mr. Rozenblatt, the knight in shining armor who would rescue his daughter from the wicked rock star.

"What are you up to?" an indignant Mr. Rozenblatt thundered, taking a few steps up the stairway. "Are you out of your mind? Get out of here!"

Mike proceeded carefully.

"My mom told me you called and said the wedding is cancelled," he said calmly. "That sounds completely crazy, but I wanted to—"

"Everything is cancelled!" Mr. Rozenblatt confirmed.

Rozenblatt took the last step up to the top of the landing, and without thinking about it Mike took a step down. This reversed their positions, and Mr. Rozenblatt felt more comfortable.

"But—"

"And it's not even because of me," Rozenblatt added ironically. "Cocker Spaniel is crushed. And even so . . . even so I can't help feeling satisfied! I knew it, Chimpanzee. That you would break her heart! You're a wretch!"

"Break her . . . but what happened?"

"My wife, Mrs. Rozenblatt, gets her claws painted once a week, do you understand, Chimpanzee? Does that ring any bells?"

Mike didn't know what Mr. Rozenblatt was talking about, and admitted so.

"Mrs. Rozenblatt has gone to the same claw sculptress for many years," said the satisfied Mr. Rozenblatt. "A charming little stuffed animal. But yesterday she was sad."

Mike shook his head. Everyone seemed to be talking in riddles, as if there was an agreement among the parents.

"Yesterday she was sad, Chimpanzee, my wife's claw sculptress, because a ruffian had broken her heart. Can you imagine that, Chimpanzee, breaking such a sweet deer's heart? It turned out that the ruffian . . . he'd had several relationships at the same time, and one of the females he was seeing he intended to marry!"

Mike's heart stopped beating.

"But we can make the deer happy about that, at least. That there won't be any wedding. Get out of here, Chimpanzee, and don't ever, ever come back!"

Voices conversing, dishes clinking, the stuffy warmth that smelled of nicotine, grilled meat, and heavy perfume. Through the loudspeakers Larry "Car Crash" Hyena howled to the painful climax of the warped guitar. The HateLites rocked on to the best of their ability; the drums rattled out a rolling rhythm that the bass transformed into a tightly wound carpet of sound. Plopping and dripping synth sounds dotted the carpet and above it all was Larry's scratchy voice.

Mike nodded gloomily to himself. Lancelot Lemur must despise the HateLites, he thought; they were much too intellectual for a hit machine.

"Another?"

Mike nodded. Tom-Tom Crow filled the glass to the brim. The whiskey smelled smoky, the joint tasted sweet, and life was bitter.

"I'll be damned," said Crow. "So it's all over now, huh?"

It was the third time in as many minutes that Crow had said just those words. Mike nodded. Even he had a hard time believing it. Yesterday he was engaged, today he had been dumped. Yesterday life had been mapped out, today it was unpredictable again.

Mike drank. He was already drunk, but he could get drunker. Larry croaked on in the background.

"Mike, darling, I heard . . ."

Sam Gazelle came running from the kitchen. He hugged the surprised ape hard and much too long, not releasing his hold until Mike freed himself with controlled force. Sam's eyes were shiny with tears, his eyebrows raised in empathy.

"You must be crushed!"

Mike mumbled in agreement.

"Oh, honey," said Sam, who mistook quietness for sorrow, "what a bummer. She was really pretty."

Mike nodded.

"But the family, Mike? At the same time, you got rid of her mom and dad. There's always something to be happy about. Do you want any pills?"

Gazelle dug in his pants pockets and pulled out an impressive number of colorful pills and vials. But Mike shook his head.

"But you have to stay here with us tonight," said Sam. "We're not letting you be by yourself. If you try to leave here, Tom-Tom is going to carry you back, honey. Oh, Mike, what a bummer. She was the one your heart had chosen, wasn't she?"

Mike mumbled something and emptied the glass. He hated being reduced to a victim. But he didn't dare protest. Cocker Spaniel had been his betrothed, they were going to be married in only a few weeks; these were unequivocal facts. Sam Gazelle's concerns were logical. Mike ought to feel abandoned and rejected. He had reason besides to be ashamed. It was his own infidelity that was behind all this misery.

"I don't intend to do anything stupid, Sam," he said. "I'm not the type, you know?"

"Under circumstances like these, you never know," Gazelle replied. "Right now we're standing here, in a well-lit bar with lots of stuffed animals around. But tonight, when you're alone . . ."

Mike Chimpanzee gave his genie a thought, and thought that alone would be marvelous.

" . . . when you're alone," Gazelle continued, "then perhaps everything will feel different. That's why we want you here."

Mike nodded. Maybe the gazelle was right, and Mike almost wished that were the case. Because when the shock subsided after the visit to the Rozenblatts in Amberville, it was not despair that was visible behind the fog of emotion. Instead, Mike had experienced an unpleasant feeling of liberation. It was as unexpected as it was intense.

And Mike would not dare admit that even to Sam Gazelle; he felt relieved to escape the wedding and Cocker Spaniel.

11.

At home there was a small, black piece of plastic on the desk. It was almost triangular, chipped on the corner with a white line that went from edge to edge.

Mike Chimpanzee couldn't help it, but when he returned to the antique store on Calle Gran Via the next morning—in the end he had been forced to stay with Tom-Tom and Sam— he did so at a run. Cocker Spaniel and the Rozenblatt family had intruded, distracted him, and caused him to think about other things. But when morning dawned and Mike came to life, with a bursting headache and a tongue that felt like it was dipped in acetone, it was not the wedding that was on his mind. Instead it was the second wish that the genie had granted him. And this caused his pulse to race.

The genie flew right behind him on the indigo blue sidewalk, trying to calm him.

"Sir, there's no danger, I swear. I was there the whole night. Took the opportunity to change the sheets on the bed, it must have been a while, why don't we burn the old ones? Then— and I'm sure there's a proper reason, but let's not go into that—I threw out all the cigarette butts in the desk drawer. I've had the situation under control the whole time."

But Mike continued running, threw open the door to the store, and hurried over to the desk.

The piece of plastic was still there.

He sank down into the desk chair, out of breath. Thought a moment. And could state with confidence that he didn't regret it at all.

When at last he had dared to wish for Nikki Lee's guitar pick, the magical piece of plastic that would transform his life and give his pathetic songwriting the lift he couldn't achieve on his own, he had been worried that he would regret it the next day. But . . . Mike breathed slowly and closed his eyes . . . no, nothing.

Ever since Nils Gull told the story about Nikki Lee, the idea had been there. Integrity had hindered him. There were no detours to finding his artistic expression. To express the contemporary version of Truth and Pain, you couldn't use the help of ancient genies. Call it pride or madness, but at first Mike had not even given the idea any serious thought. It was more the enticement of personally finding a counterpart to Nikki Lee's guitar pick that incited him.

But night after night after night, he had failed in his attempts. The songs didn't work, and he didn't know where he should start looking for his good-luck amulet.

Then the idea occurred to him: What if he asked the genie?

Mike pulled out the phone jack, turned off his cell phone, made a pot of strong coffee, and sat down at the desk with the tape recorder ready, notebook open, and guitar in his lap. Solemnly, he took the guitar pick between thumb and index finger, raised it in the air, and turned it slowly in the light from the desk lamp. It was impossible to imagine that this piece of plastic had been in Nikki Lee's throat the day she was delivered to her parents. Mike had asked the genie if there might be two identical pieces of plastic in Mollisan Town, or if Nikki Lee had lost hers, but the genie had not answered in a way that was comprehensible.

Whatever.

Mike Chimpanzee would finally write the songs that would outlive him.

He set the guitar pick carefully on the top E string, let his hand fall and listened to an E minor that sang in the guitar in a way he'd never heard before. He was on his way.

Mike worked without interruption for ten hours. Not even the genie disturbed him. Possibly Fredrik felt sufficiently satisfied to be one wish closer to his own freedom, or else he kept silent out of respect. Chimpanzee had never before radiated this sort of focused energy.

Over and over and over again, Mike hummed to the guitar chord that filled the room with its metallic roundness. *Over and over and over again*. It was so simple and so clever at the same time.

When the Evening Storm waned and darkness fell, Mike pulled on a jacket and walked quickly around the corner—he carefully avoided Scheherazade—to Reza's ToGo, where he bought a kebab and a cola. Then he continued working until he literally fell asleep at the desk a few hours after midnight. He woke up early with a nasty pain in his back, and considered lying down on the sofa bed for a few hours' proper rest. He saw his notes out of the corner of his eye and was again seized by the frenzied joy of creation.

Mike Chimpanzee was experiencing the most intense surge of creativity. To say that he found himself in a blessed flow was to reduce his condition to something general and familiar. He actually felt that he was in direct contact with Nikki Lee, that an invisible line of communication had been drawn from her soul right into his guitar, and that out of her life and suffering he was granted a wisdom and intuition that he had never been close to.

Over and over and over again.

Something inside him also said that this was urgent, that the power he was experiencing would end and that the genie's "theft" must soon be discovered and punished. He worked to keep up with his brain's energy.

When the haze settled over the city after lunch, Mike Chimpanzee was done. The silence was so sudden that the genie, who was observing a feather duster clean the thousands of decorative objects in the glass display case, lost his concentration, and the duster knocked over a porcelain dolphin.

"Done," said Mike.

"Done?"

"Sincerely, Genie, even you have to admit that this turned out to be something really special. Something sensational."

The genie had not been listening. He thought that all Mike's clinking and gaping was borderline unbearable.

"Sensational, Mr. Ape," he confirmed. "Sublime, but not difficult. Captivating without being ingratiating."

"You think so?"

"I really think so," answered the genie, who in his spirit vows had never promised not to lie. "Now of course I can't tell one song from another on the radio. I get more enjoyment from . . . hearing a third wish?"

But Mike had stopped listening. He was already on his way out to the street, with his guitar in hand and the black notebook stuck into his coat pocket. He ran north out onto Calle Gran Via in the hope of finding a taxi on ash gray Carrer de la Marquesa, the street that divided Yok into a northern and a southern half. Mike felt that he was flying along, just like the genie; never before had he moved so easily. He left Nikki Lee's guitar pick on the desk; he didn't need any more help to play the song, and he didn't dare risk losing the guitar pick somewhere in the city. In his head the chorus that he had just created out of his undistilled desire was still playing:

Over and over and over again, he sang to himself. *Over and over and over again.*

How he made his way up to Tourquai and Brown Brothers he didn't remember. During his crazy year after *40 degrees*, he had been high on everything there was to be high on, but none of the kicks were even close to what he experienced today. He imagined that it was he, not the elevator, who climbed the thirty-six stories up through the building. When he stepped into Gavin Toad's office with the marvelous view of Tourquai's spiny skyline, he began by explaining that he refused to play until Lancelot Lemur was there.

"You refuse to play?" Toad exclaimed in surprise, sitting behind his shiny desk puffing on a fat cigar. "As if I would want to hear you play? What the hell have you been taking today?"

But Mike Chimpanzee strutted around inside the toad's office, with his guitar in hand and such consummate rock-and-roll attitude that at last Toad could only shake his head, pick up the phone, and call Lemur. During the twenty minutes it took for the demon producer to get there, Chimpanzee did not sit still for more than a few seconds at a time. He threw himself onto the toad's elegant visitor's couch, sat in every one of the armchairs, and exercised his fingers with scales on the guitar. Toad eventually had enough and left the office to wait for Lancelot by the elevators. Mike twirled twenty turns in each direction in Toad's office chair.

The whole time Mike was singing the chorus to himself. Listened and smiled at the thought of the clever transition to the verse, felt the bold riff vibrate in his fingertips. He could not hold back a laugh when in his imagination he saw the toad's and the lemur's surprised faces.

Over and over and over again, he sang. *Over and over and over again.*

"Okay," said Gavin Toad brusquely, plopping down on the outer edge of the couch. "I really don't have time for these pranks. And you don't either, Mike, because expensive studio time is ticking."

"I have all the time in the world," Lemur explained, falling down on one of the deep armchairs that looked even more comfortable when Lemur was swimming in it. "All the time in the world. Because you're the one who's paying for it, Toad."

Lemur was smiling, but it was hard to say whether the smile was ironic or obsequious or if he was simply thinking about something else. He absentmindedly rattled the skulls on his armband.

"I'm calling it 'Over and Over Again,'" Mike said.

He sat in the visitor's chair. He had placed the notebook with the lyrics on the desk because he hadn't had time to memorize it all. He struck a chord, cleared his throat quietly, and then he was off.

The energy from last night and this morning carried him over verses and bridges. There was a sense of triumph in his voice that made it clearer and sharper than ever before; the chorus was so great that he felt he could repeat it as many times as he wanted:

Over and over and over again, he sang proudly. *Over and over and over again.*

Not once did he observe his audience, he was so filled by his own performance, and when he was done and the silence slowly settled over the room—like a newly laundered sheet falling down over a mattress—he finally looked up.

To his total surprise.

Toad was looking in a folder. Lemur appeared to have fallen asleep.

"What?" said Mike.

"Huh?" Lemur replied, looking up.

"Are you finished?" Toad asked.

Mike nodded.

"That was shit," said Toad. "As usual. It sounds like something you shoved up your ass that you couldn't get out. Mike, forget about that now, and record the songs you have."

"I wasn't listening that carefully, Ape," said Lancelot, "but if you want I can run it through my hit machine. Maybe something really cool will come out on the other end?"

Things were getting dark in Chimpanzee's eyes. It was as if the air was being sucked out of him, as if he were becoming a compact package of cotton without heart or soul, and without listening to the toad and lemur's continued discussion he left the office, with guitar in hand and hope smashed into tiny fragments.

The genie walked beside him along the deserted sidewalks of Tourquai.

"You shouldn't worry about them," said Fredrik. "Some like one thing and others like something else, isn't that right?"

It was not only for his own purposes that the genie was trying to console Mike. True, a deeply depressed chimpanzee would never manage to formulate one last wish, but the genie also felt sincerely sorry for Mike's sake. He if anyone knew how deep down the second wish had been, how much hope the chimpanzee had attached to the little piece of plastic, and the fiasco hurt even from a distance.

"Toad isn't exactly the most sophisticated judge of taste, is he?" said the genie.

But Mike wasn't listening.

It took him a few hours to walk home to the antique store from Brown Brothers' skyscraper in Tourquai. He could not recall ever walking so far before. If he'd had the idea that physical exhaustion would dampen the spiritual flattening, that came to naught. He was completely used up, but still just as depressed.

The month of free marijuana was over, but he found a few cold beers in the fridge. He sat down heavily on a Renaissance armchair and let his fingers caress the embroidered peacocks on the armrest. The genie continued trying to cheer him up, but Mike was not receptive. Toward twilight the ape fell asleep, and woke up a few hours later with drool running down his chin. He felt stiff and cold, and on his way over to the sofa bed and the soft, warm down comforter, he plugged the phone jack in again. It was more a reflex than a conscious action; he wasn't expecting any calls.

It rang just as he lay his head on the pillow.

He listened to five long rings without reacting, but when the phone kept ringing he forced himself up to answer. He expected his mom's angry voice. A lifetime was far from enough for her to forgive him for the cancelled wedding.

It was Gavin.

"Hey, you poor bastard," said Toad. "Lancelot and I talked about it when you left. You looked like you intended to burn yourself up. Damn, Mike, if this is such a big deal . . . Lancelot said he'll include the song about freedom on the album. This latest thing was unbearable, but the freedom song had something. We'll take it."

Pause.

"Mike? Did you hear? We'll include your freedom song."

"Are you sure?"

"Yeah, what the hell, Lancelot promises to make something good out of it."

"I don't know what I should say," said Mike.

"Write something nice about me in your memoirs," said Gavin Toad, hanging up.

Mike stood with the telephone receiver against his ear, staring vacantly ahead. Word for word he went through the telephone conversation as he slowly hung up the phone. The genie was in front of him, quivering with curiosity.

"What just happened?" asked the genie, and a damp cloud of expectation emerged from his mouth. "What just happened? What did he say?"

"He's putting 'Freedom' on the album," said Mike.

"That's amazing, isn't it? Mike? Why do you look so glum?"

"He said he thought 'Over and Over Again' was unbearable."

"Yes . . . but . . . you'll get a song on the album? Isn't that what you wanted? A song on the album?"

"Unbearable," Mike repeated. "The song that I wrote with Nikki Lee's guitar pick. He's out of his mind, that bastard."

"But, Mike . . ." the genie began, but the chimpanzee had already picked up the guitar pick and fetched the guitar.

"I'll show him," said Mike. "It's the verse that doesn't add up. I'll rewrite the verse, maybe fiddle with the riff a little . . . it's a good song, I know it."

"But, Mike, didn't he say that—"

"He said he didn't like Nikki Lee's song," Mike repeated. "He's out of his mind."

12.

Sometimes on weekends, when Mike Chimpanzee was a little cub, his dad would take him to Plaza de Bueno, the rain forest park. That was while his dad was still transforming into the pale shadow who, as Mike was growing up, would live a few steps behind Ilja Crocodile, at the periphery of the family's life, before finally disappearing without a trace.

The park was one of Yok's neglected treasures; most stuffed animals hated getting wet and avoided the artificially humid atmosphere. Mike and his dad would walk on the path between the mangrove trees up to the pond where the water lilies blossomed, sit down on a bench, take out the finely chopped leek and liver sausage sandwiches they brought with them, and eat in silence.

That was where Mike Chimpanzee made his way after Gavin finally yielded and accepted "Freedom" on the album. To escape the genie's nagging, Mike asked Tom-Tom Crow if he wanted to come along, and now they were sitting on a bench in the shadow of a massive magnolia, looking out over

the quiet, still pond. The sun was high in the sky, the faint
Breeze made the rain forest breathe carefully.

"How did it happen," Mike asked his large friend, "that
regardless of the circumstances, from the existential questions
of youth, that unfathomable orgasm of acknowledgment after
the previous album, to all the sudden changes of the last few
days, the anxiety is still pretty much the same?"

"Damned if I know, Mike," Tom-Tom answered. "Who
knows? Do you mind if I knit a little?"

Crow had brought some knitting with him in a plastic bag.
He was working on a white cardigan sweater that he intended
to give to Sam as a Christmas present.

"No, no, go ahead and knit," Mike said distractedly.

The chimpanzee was tired after the night's session. In a
frenzy he had stayed up past dawn, striking the strings of the
guitar harder and harder with Nikki Lee's pick. He had recorded his attempts after he was finished; he had listened and
rejected them all. It didn't work. It just wouldn't work. Every
melody line was predictable and uniform. There was no point.

Mike's head fell down between the torn knees of his jeans
and closed his eyes hard. Crow's knitting needles clicked
against each other. The scent of the rain forest's dampness
obstructed his nose. Melancholy seized him, tears welled up
unexpectedly in his eyes, and the emptiness sucked the life out
of his chest. He suddenly missed Cocker Spaniel Rozenblatt
with a physical intensity that made him dizzy.

He had never loved her. He could never even say the words.
On the contrary, it was her love that he had expected; it should
have been enough for both of them. But it had proved to be
fragile.

"We all have a right to be loved," he said. "Don't we?"

He made an exception to the overwhelming, collective love
his fans gave him every day. True, it was unconditional and
made no demands, but at the same time impossible to take in.

"I love you, Mike," Tom-Tom Crow answered, without

looking up from his knitting. "And Sam loves you to death. Although in a different way."

Mike nodded. That's how it was. Useless.

Why couldn't anyone accept him for who he was? Why did his rock star status stand between him and the world? It was as if for every emotion he declared, every truth he delivered in lyrics or interviews, nobody heard what he said, they were all preoccupied with the way he said it.

Mike Chimpanzee thought he was screaming, but no one listened.

"And Mom, Mike," Tom-Tom continued his own thought. "Your mom loves you, too, damn it."

Mom. Presumably the root to what was bad was in cubhood, Mike thought bitterly, in Mom's intense coddling, which would never end either.

The fatigue that he felt so acutely as he sat beside the large, knitting crow was born out of the feeling of never being sufficiently loved, never feeling sufficiently talented and appreciated and . . . everything else that Mom got him to believe over the years that he had a right to. It was Mom who, through her unexpressed expectations, her sky-high pedestals, created the needs that constantly pursued him; his striving to exceed every conceivable expectation. There wasn't a psychotherapist out there who could settle accounts with Mike's adolescence.

"Mike, I was going to stuff pilsner sausage this afternoon," said Tom-Tom. "Do you want to help?"

"That's nice, Tom-Tom," answered Mike, who realized the crow was trying to cheer him up, "but I think I'll pass. I didn't sleep at all last night, and I have to get a few hours' sleep before tonight."

Mike got up from the bench, carrying the gloom on his shoulders. He walked back down the hill, leaving the crow behind. The overgrown flower beds on the side of the path rustled. Along with the damp fog that constantly rested over

Plaza de Bueno, the day felt enchanted. Mike found himself looking for the genie, but Fredrik was not to be seen.

The idea grew during the walk home. With each block, Mike Chimpanzee's pace quickened, and when he reached indigo blue Calle Gran Via there was no doubt remaining.

He opened the door to the antique store and called to the genie. Fredrik materialized instantly.

"Now I know," said Mike. "I wish to be free."

"Free?"

"I'm tired of never feeling like I measure up. Tired of the demands. I want to be free for real."

"Excuse me, sir, but I don't really think that . . . whose demands are we talking about?" the genie asked.

"The demands!" Mike exclaimed in irritation. "Everyone's demands. Stuffed animals in the city who stare and expect . . . something. Toad's demands. Mom's demands. The demands!"

The genie pretended to furrow his brow in deep folds, but of course that was wasted effort.

"And you want to be free?"

"Lose this damned stress and anxiety I wake up with in the morning and go to sleep with at night." Mike nodded.

"That is your third and final wish?" the genie confirmed.

"I know that," Mike replied. "And that's what I want. Freedom."

The genie nodded.

Before Mike Chimpanzee's eyes, the transformation began. The cloud of diffuse outlines that Mike had become accustomed to seeing under the genie's clothes successively took more solid form. The grayish white cloud yellowed and became furry. What had been air became a body. Out of the implied facial features a nose appeared; whiskers grew out, and the puffs of ears became thick and hairy.

Fredrik was a lion.

"At long last," he whispered.

He stretched himself, stroked his belly and shoulders with his paws, let his tongue investigate his lips, and filled his lungs with air.

"At long last," he repeated.

Then he took a few steps over to the glass display case and found the small blue glass bottle where he had lived for so many years. He pulled the cork out, and at the same moment Mike Chimpanzee felt something happening to him. It was not pain, more like a kind of ache. It started in his feet and quickly rose up through his body. It dematerialized body part after body part and left behind a lovely vacuum; he leaned his head forward and discovered that his feet no longer were feet, only clouds.

The insight was momentary.

"I'm becoming you," Mike panted.

"You're free, Mike."

Fredrik held the blue glass bottle up in front of him, and in only a few seconds Mike had been sucked in through the opening. The former genie put the cork back in the bottle, and placed it back on the shelf where it had previously stood along with other antique writing implements. Then he left the antique store without looking back.

MINDIE

PART ONE

N ame?"

"Vincent Hare."

"Age?"

"Twenty-two years, 150 days, 4 hours, and about 20 minutes."

"Are you kidding me?"

"It is our cursed duty to keep track of how much time has passed," the hare answered without a trace of irony.

Vincent Hare was a light yellow stuffed animal with a crocheted nose. The inside of his long ears was covered with warm pink silk. He went on.

"At the moment the Deliverymen bring us, it's like a great devil's paw turns over the hourglass, and the countdown has begun. I hear the sand running every morning when I wake up and every night when I go to bed. Shh! Do you hear it?"

Vincent pricked his long ears.

Falcon Ècu wrinkled his well-polished nose, dissatisfied with the answer. A few months before he had been reassigned to this police station in Mindie in Yok and, while not happy, was trying to make the best of the situation.

"Address?" asked Ècu.

"Calle de Serrano, 25."

"Occupation?"

"Philosopher."

"Philosopher?"

"Or," said Vincent, "forget philosophy. Just say 'artist.' "

"I'll write 'student,'" Ècu said.

"If that's easier for you to spell." Vincent nodded, shrugging his shoulders. "And that's not necessarily wrong. I study myself and life. The sand runs, time passes, and we have an obligation in life to try to understand why we're here. Do you understand?"

"Do I understand why we're here?"

Vincent nodded.

"We are here," said Ècu, "because you have to answer my questions."

The room was big enough to accommodate two chairs on either side of the white table. White walls. A badly worn wood floor. Behind the police falcon there was a wide mirror along the short wall. The light of the ceiling lamp was sharp and cold. Ècu was not a friend of typewriters, and it was slow going to peck out "student."

"I'm in a bit of a hurry," Vincent said.

Ècu looked up from the typewriter, shaking his head and leaning back. The motion released an aroma of soap and fabric softener.

"No, I don't think so," said the police officer. "You don't seem to get what this is about. You've been brought in for interrogation. You're going to stay here until we're done."

"I'm in a bit of a hurry," Vincent repeated impatiently. "Because my life is running out—yours and mine—and the day the Chauffeurs arrive, neither of us is going to remember this meeting, these minutes in this room. Because of that, this conversation is wasted, and we're both in a hurry. This is not how we find out what we really should be doing."

Vincent threw out his arms, indicating the cramped room. The knot of his tie was small and hard, the polyester of his light blue shirt shimmered and the lapels on his jacket were narrow. For being an impoverished student from Mindie he was remarkably well-dressed, Ècu noted.

"Listen up!" said Ècu, raising his voice. "Now I think you should—"

"Wait!" Vincent shouted, raising his paw. "Do you hear it?"

Ècu listened, but heard nothing.

"It's the sand running," said Vincent. "It's time that's passing, Falcon. While you sit here tapping on that machine, time passes, and you don't seem to be running, Falcon. You seem to sit still. But I have to run. You have to catch up with yourself before it's time for the finish, Falcon. We're in a hurry, it's a race."

Falcon Ècu tiredly observed the vain hare.

"You're twenty-two," Ècu pointed out. "And you're acting like you're twelve. Now shut up, and just answer my questions."

"Ask them quickly," said Vincent.

"We know you were outside the loading dock at St. Andrews Hospital at twilight two days ago," said the police officer. "We know you were serving as a lookout. We're prepared to let you go if you tell us who was in the car and where you were taking the stuff."

The police in Mollisan Town were organized in three divisions. At WE, crimes committed in wrath or envy were handled, that is, the majority of violent crimes. GL took care of criminality due to gluttony and lust, primarily sexual offenses. Vincent Hare had been brought into the third division, PAS, which was the largest, because it was assigned pride, avarice, and sloth, and investigated all the robberies, thefts, and swindles in the city.

"I'm not sure," answered Vincent, "whether you already

know you've made a blunder, or you're taking a chance, or whether you're mixing me up with someone else. But, no, I haven't been at any hospital."

"We know you were there," said the falcon, sighing. "There's no point in denying it. Who was driving? Whose idea was it?"

Vincent snorted, adjusting his cuffs.

"This is turning into a pretty boring conversation," he said, getting up. "Can I leave now?"

"Sit," Ècu ordered.

But Vincent remained standing, and demonstratively placed one paw on the door handle.

"Listen now, cop," he said. "I don't know what you think I've done or why you've brought me here, but if this is about a hospital I can't help you. Sorry. I'm leaving now. Vanishing back into the haystack."

"You arrogant little shit," said the falcon, but without energy. "Sit down and shut up. You mustn't take that tone just because you dress like a rich kid. I know who you are and where you come from."

Vincent opened the door. It wasn't locked. Without hesitating he left the cramped interrogation room, turned left in the corridor, and headed toward the exit. Ècu did not follow. There were no grounds to hold Vincent.

At the café in the entryway to the police station, Vincent sat down at the counter, ordered an espresso, and took a gray notebook out of his inside pocket. He had not been lying to the police. He heard the sand running in the hourglass of life every morning when he woke up and every night as he fell asleep. It was a miracle, he thought, that he hadn't gone crazy.

The gray notebook was a kind of existential account book. He imagined three accounts. Under the first account he tried to summarize the meaning of life in Mollisan Town. The second one he called the Knowledge Account, and here he gathered clues that might lead to answers in the first one. The third and final account was the Bank Account.

He sipped his espresso, and wrote:

1. *Meaning of Life: Still no idea.*
2. *Knowledge Account: Won't become a police officer.*
3. *Bank Account: Zero.*

Casino Biscaya in northwest Tourquai was a place without ambition. Here you would never catch a glimpse of the rich and beautiful; instead, anonymous stuffed animals sat huddled in long rows, feeding one-armed bandits without looking up when the winnings occasionally clattered out of the machines. The money was used to buy more time; the alternative was to return home to solitude.

At the bar were those who made drinking the main event. They didn't drink to get drunk, to forget or celebrate; they bought a place at the bar by paying for the next drink. They were all regulars who despised one another because they were the mirror images of one another.

The casino's card-playing section was a half flight up, to the right of the financially shaky restaurant. There were six tables on a platform bordered by an elegant leather railing: two tall, half-moon-shaped blackjack tables and four round poker tables. At one of the poker tables there were six players, one of whom was Jack Dingo. The table felt was green; the liquor brownish; and the chips red, black, yellow, and blue. Thin layers of cigarette smoke curled in the feeble light from the ceiling, but the light did not reach beyond the circle of the green table.

Dingo had two pairs with tens high. He let his long, transparent glass claws drum impatiently against the table, decided his move, and threw in a pair of fifty markers to see the cockroach across from him. The cockroach folded and shrugged his wings. Dingo gathered up the pot.

"That's enough for tonight," he decided, leaving the table.

No one had any objections. Dingo had lost about as much as he won.

In the bar Vincent Hare and Gavin Zebra were waiting. Hare was 23 years, 234 days, 18 hours, and about 10 minutes old. He was dressed in a midnight blue suit, blue shirt, and cream white tie. Zebra was wearing jeans and a T-shirt.

"I'll treat to a round," said Dingo, as if he had won at the gaming table.

Hare and Zebra nodded. Neither of them was interested in gambling. They had gone to high school together, but never been close friends. In the last year of high school Gavin Zebra discovered the author Fernandez Armesto, and read *Solitude* four times in a row. It was one of Vincent's favorite books, and for a few weeks he and Zebra had something to talk about. After his entrance exams Zebra's passion for Armesto waned, but for Vincent, the trilogy, starting with *Solitude* and continuing with *Exposure* and *Meaninglessness*, remained one of the most important things that had happened to him. When Vincent and Zebra were later accepted at the College of Architecture, they resumed their superficial acquaintanceship, but never found any deeper kinship.

"Thought about heading up to Bois de Dalida this weekend," Dingo reported as he paid for the mango drinks with vodka. "Anybody want to follow along?"

Jack Dingo spoke loudly to be heard over the music, making the stuffed animals at the bar twist their heads. He rustled his thick gold armband and acted like he owned the casino. He always hinted that he had connections all over. Neither Hare nor Zebra was sure this was true. Why, in such case, did Dingo hang around at a place like Casino Biscaya? Or with stuffed animals like Hare and Zebra?

"I'd like to," said Zebra, "but I promised Jeanette—"

"Sure," said Dingo, without hearing the excuse. "And you, Vincent?"

"Dalida? Sure. The forest? Who's going?"

Dingo named a number of stuffed animals that Vincent didn't know. Zebra lit a cigarette, Dingo ordered more drinks and told about a Volga Sport Delay being built in a limited edition of one hundred, and that he was in line to buy. Zebra showed some interest in the car model, which he'd read about, but Vincent stopped listening. He sipped his second mango drink and listened to the sound of the sand running through the hourglass.

"What the hell are you staring at?"

The words made all three react. A bald eagle in a worn leather jacket was pointing at Vincent. The eagle's pupils were big as plates, his sharp claws only a few inches from Vincent's nose, and on the chest pocket of the leather jacket was a monogram that read SS5.

Without meaning to, for the past few minutes Vincent had been staring at Eagle's embroidered ears. His gaze just happened to settle there.

"Me?"

"Yes, you, you ugly ball of cotton. What the hell are you staring at?"

Everyone knew what SS5 was—the private security force used by the stuffed animals who controlled the organized prostitution in Tourquai, and notorious for their brutality.

"What am I staring at? Nothing," answered Vincent slowly. "Absolutely *nothing*." And he stared even more intensely at the enraged eagle, while Zebra pulled on him.

Vincent was no fighter, but he was always getting into fistfights anyway. He never hit back. He let them hit and tear until they were worn out, and sometimes—but not always—he felt liberated afterward. Pure from pain, pure from humiliation; he could not explain it.

"Forget about him, Vincent," Zebra whispered.

"What the hell are you saying?" asked the eagle.

"Let's go, Vincent," said Zebra.

"Like those freaking ugly ears are worth staring at," said Vincent. "I've never seen anything so ridiculous. How did they get there? Was your mother cross-eyed?"

"What the hell?"

Zebra threw himself forward and placed himself between the eagle and the hare. The eagle pushed Zebra aside with no effort.

"Do you want a beating?" asked the eagle.

"From you and your friends?" Vincent asked. "Oh, excuse me, of course you don't have any friends—"

Eagle's reaction was instinctive. His wings shot forward, he wrapped his claw around Vincent's neck and pulled him down from the chair. No one dared intervene. Dingo was gone. Zebra staggered to his feet, and while the eagle pulled Vincent across the floor of the casino the zebra ran after.

"Let him go!" Zebra pleaded. "He didn't mean any harm."

"You shouldn't be ashamed because you're a bird." Vincent continued peeping his provocations. "Some birds have brains. And I'm sure you're . . . a friendly soul."

"Shut up, Vincent!" Zebra shouted.

The eagle stopped and pounded the hare's head against the floor a few times to get him to be quiet. Then he continued toward the exit. He was holding Vincent by the ears, dragging him behind like a rag.

"Or to say you have a soul," Vincent slurred. "Perhaps that's saying too much?"

Eagle tore open the door and threw Vincent out on the street.

"You're afraid to fight, huh?" Vincent shrieked from where he was lying. "Maybe you're afraid your nice jacket will get torn?"

Eagle sighed, bored now. The lesson must be given, however, even if it didn't feel truly motivated. He took a step out onto the street.

"When you see this monogram next time, you'll know to keep your trap shut."

The eagle gave the hare a kick in the belly that made him fly into one of the parked cars along the sidewalk. The eagle went slowly after, and the next kick hit the hare's head. After that, the hare did not remember anything.

The moon was half and the Breeze faint when Vincent came around again. He was sitting against the wall of a building, and he could smell sewage and asphalt. Zebra was crouched in front of him. Tourquai was deserted and abandoned. They were no longer outside the casino.

"What a nobody," Vincent mumbled.

"I'll help you home," said Zebra. "Do you still live on Calle de Serrano?"

Vincent nodded. Zebra placed Hare's arm around his neck and helped him to his feet. They had no money for a taxi, and crossed the street to the bus stop. The fatigue made Vincent dizzy, the emptiness made him light. He had not eaten since yesterday morning. He discovered that his jacket was torn. One sleeve was missing and the lining torn out. But Vincent made his own clothes, and the jacket could be fixed. When the night bus finally arrived, Casino Biscaya was already a memory, a peculiar dream. Vincent sat down heavily on the seat, leaned against the window, and fell asleep. When he woke up fifteen minutes later, they were back in Yok.

"What were you up to, really?" asked Zebra. "You were completely crazy. You know you didn't have a chance. You weren't even trying."

"No," Vincent agreed. "I don't fight."

"What were you trying to prove?"

"Nothing," Vincent answered.

The bus lurched as it drove over one of the many holes in the asphalt—no one maintained the streets in Yok—and Vincent moaned in pain.

"You can't say you like taking so many beatings?"

"No," answered Vincent, holding his head.

Zebra peered out at the dark blocks, and pressed the button on the strip under the window for the next stop.

"So why were you provoking him?"

"Because it has no meaning," Vincent answered. "That's just the point. It's all the same. Get it?"

Zebra did not understand, but chose not to say anything. The bus glided toward the sidewalk and stopped. The two companions rose and got off.

There were a couple of blocks to walk from the stop. When they came up to the entryway of the hare's apartment complex, the sky was colored pink by the first light of day. A shimmer fell over the roofs of the buildings, and it made them calm.

"Come on in and have a cup of coffee," Vincent suggested.

Zebra had a vague memory that Hare's parents were no longer alive. The mother had not been in the picture for many years, and the father was gone, too. But that was later, in high school. Hare seemed to be living in the same apartment, however.

"Okay," Zebra answered, because the night was used up and the day already disturbed.

The apartment proved to be considerably larger than Zebra remembered. A narrow, dark corridor cluttered with moving boxes connected the bedroom, a kitchen and a large bathroom with a studio-like living room at the other end. There were half-finished oil paintings stacked along the walls. On an easel in front of the window was a canvas that Hare apparently was working on right now. Zebra would describe it as abstract expressionism, a furious explosion of color that was impossible not to be drawn into. Zebra remained standing before it, captivated.

Vincent was not interested in talking about or explaining the strikingly large number of paintings in the room. He had taken a couple of pills that he said were pain relievers. He was semi-inclined on the large couch in the middle of the floor, where by turns he slept and for short periods woke up and had some of the coffee he'd made. Zebra walked around looking at the pictures.

"Now I get it," said Zebra, mainly to himself.

Zebra was proud at having been accepted to the College of Architecture. He was an industrious student who would get his degree in the stipulated time of four years, and with distinction. Hare was his opposite. So far Hare's time at school had been sporadic and unsuccessful. He could not add two and three, and without a talent for mathematics it was tough to study architecture. The fact that the college accepted Hare was a mystery to Zebra, but now there was an explanation. The longer Zebra walked around, picking up the various paintings all over the room, the more clearly he realized that Hare not only had talent, he was already a great artist.

"Have you contacted a gallery owner?" Zebra asked at last. "Have you tried to sell anything?"

"Thieves, the whole lot of them," Vincent answered thickly from the couch. "Had an exhibition, got mentally ripped off, I'll never do that again."

"You must do it again! These are amazing," Zebra said.

But Vincent was pretending to sleep, and as soon as Zebra left he sat up, took his gray notebook out of the inside pocket of the torn jacket, and wrote:

1. *Meaning of Life: Two steps back. No step forward.*
2. *Knowledge Account: There is no wisdom in pain. Meaninglessness is destructive by nature. It is impossible to see your own reflection successfully.*
3. *Bank Account: Negative.*

FALCON ÈCU'S COMMENTS

What was different about Vincent Hare? Is that really my business to interpret? No, I don't think so. I'm not going to pass judgment based on a few isolated occasions, mistakes I am certain that Hare regrets now. Or, it's not certain he regrets them, that I admit; he never gave an exactly humble impression.

There is a kind of stuffed animal, and I don't want to categorize or point to anyone in particular, but you learn over the years that arrogance is an attitude behind which scared stuffed animals hide themselves. Being a police officer is about experience. A professional attitude—that is what characterizes our corps. We have learned to tolerate provocations. Vincent Hare, when I brought him in for questioning the first time, was only twenty-something, and of course he was cocky. What alternative did he have? But should I have let someone of his sort provoke me? No, I don't think so. He was one of many. I can tell you exactly what his problem was: He thought he was something special.

Yes, he was at the station many times. No, I can't tell you why. Getting information from the police archive requires a court order. I know it's long ago, but that doesn't help. Yes,

I remember. Because I knew you would ask, I've done some reading. I keep copies of all the reports I've written in my private safe. Yes, there have been quite a few. If I don't go into detail or reveal anything that may be grounds for any form of violation, of course I can give you an impression.

Vincent Hare was brought in on more than four occasions. I don't want to say more than that. Always in connection with Jack Dingo. But not always as a suspect. What do I mean? I mean that Vincent Hare also appears in our internal documents as a crime victim. No, I don't think that's strange at all. His sort is drawn to trouble. That's just how it is. They are all destructive. That's why they don't fit into society. They don't want to take part in building a better future. They want to tear things down. Hare was like that. He looked for violence, and he wasn't all that smart.

It was as if he wanted to punish himself. He went in search of the worst thugs, the most brutal assassins, and let them beat him black and blue. This happened more than once. I'm no psychologist, but I'm sure there's a label that fits that sort of thing. I don't have a fancy university degree, but I do understand stuffed animals. Vincent Hare thought he was special, and liked to show off. He tried to win respect indirectly by going after the biggest and most dangerous in the gang; stuffed animals have done that all through history. There are simply too many of Hare's sort, that's the whole problem.

No, I don't know what became of him. But I can guess. And it's a qualified guess, because there are many years of police experience behind it. Things didn't go well for him, that's my guess. Like it always does for those sorts of overly smart, superior snot-nosed cubs who don't know what's best for them. Excuse me. I didn't mean to single out Vincent Hare as an individual, I'm only talking about a type. And that is a type whose days in Mollisan Town finally end at King's Cross, at the Garbage Dump or in the sea. It was because of that type of stuffed animal that I became a police officer once upon a time.

Jack Dingo made financial assessments of his customers; he never assessed them morally.

He shut the side door on the van and went around. It was dark in the garage, but he was used to that. The car was a Volga Van with black-tinted windows. An older model, just beat-up enough and with a couple of dents on the bumpers both front and back. He had extra headlights put on, but most four-wheel-drive pickups had them. He had swiped the license plates from a black Volga Van up at a junkyard in north Tourquai. Who Dingo's car was registered to, if the police were to check, he didn't know, but it wasn't him, and the car wasn't stolen.

He climbed up and got behind the wheel. Vincent Hare was waiting on the passenger seat. Vincent was 24 years, 77 days, and almost exactly 9 hours old, and in the darkness of the garage he closed his eyes and listened to the sound of the sand running in the hourglass. The garage door was opened with a remote control attached to the instrument panel above the radio. Slowly the entryway let in daylight. Dingo always delivered his goods in the middle of the day. Carrying sacks and boxes from a black car in the middle of the night aroused suspicion.

"Last night must have been a pretty rough one, Vincent. You look like you're going to die," Dingo commented.

"There are reasons," Vincent answered. "But I don't regret a thing."

Dingo laughed. Hare was young and untested and not much help, but he was entertaining. Dingo had made it a matter of principle not to make deliveries alone; situations could easily arise where he needed an extra pair of paws. Today they belonged to Vincent Hare.

Dingo avoided the avenues, because statistically most accidents happened there, and instead chose narrow streets where red lights constantly stopped him. He was whistling. He was not musical, it was more a way of chasing away the silence without turning on the radio and having to listen to a lot of crappy music. He laughed again when he saw how painful the whistling was to the hungover Hare.

Their first stop was at Doctor Huangho on pinstriped Lennon Lane in south Amberville. In the Afternoon Rain Dingo drove the whole way up to the city line along Fasanenstrasse, which ran parallel to East Avenue. It was a beautiful weekday; he wasn't sure which one, but in residential Amberville the streets were as deserted as on a Sunday. When he turned left onto beige Cle Tortilla he almost ran into a group of preschoolers crossing the street in a long line. He hit the pedal, the brakes screeched, Vincent tumbled down on the floor, and the car glided ahead toward the crosswalk but stopped just in time. A furious preschool teacher shook her claws at them. The students passed, with their raincoats and umbrellas.

Dingo gulped. This was an ominous sign. Vincent swore and crawled up onto the seat, putting on his seat belt. Slowly and extremely attentively, Dingo drove on.

Huangho had been a customer for more than ten years, and in time Dingo had learned to know and respect the wild boar who specialized in eyes. In the basement of a neat town house in one of Amberville's least remarkable neighborhoods, the doctor performed operations without a license. He had no training, but the experience in his field he had acquired made him one of the foremost in the city. There was a whole army of illegal plastic surgeons in town, and Dingo did business with all of them.

Huangho bought pain relievers and eyes. Dingo manufactured the pain-relieving drugs in his own laboratory. The eyes he stole from hospitals or from one of the depots where the city stored stuffed animals who had lost their heads, hearts, or other organs, tragedies that put the animals out of order. As long as the Chauffeurs had not picked up the bodies, Mollisan Town could not declare these mutilated wretches dead, and Dingo had young stuffed animals like Vincent Hare steal body parts for him from the depots at regular intervals.

Dingo also arranged what he called Donation Dates to which society's unfortunate animals could come, get drunk, and have body parts removed by Dingo's minions in exchange for a little cash and drugs. The Donation Dates were unpleasant arrangements, which Dingo never attended himself. The instruments used were neither sharp nor clean. The anesthetic applied was either too strong or too weak. Accidents happened. Dingo's make-believe surgeons were as drugged out as the victims. Dealing with the consequences of these exercises often ate up the whole profit, but sometimes it was necessary to show the customers they could rely on him, even if the profit margin was small. He was building long-term business relationships.

When they arrived at the address on Lennon Lane it was still raining, and they stayed in the car until the rain let up. This morning Dingo had decided to take part in the night's Vol-gaBet, but as he sat there staring at Lennon Lane he changed his mind. Every time he played—and lost—he promised himself never to go back.

At last the clouds dispersed and they got out of the car. Dingo took a position on the sidewalk. In Amberville you seldom saw anyone in the middle of the day. He asked Vincent to keep an eye out anyway, then opened the side doors of the pickup. He took out the black plastic bag, set it over his shoulder, and had Vincent open the gate up to the house. Delivering stuffed animal parts in Amberville was easier than in other parts of the city; here the notion of criminality was distant.

As usual, Dingo and Hare had a cup of coffee with Wild Boar Huangho in the vestibule and talked politics a while before they settled their business. Huangho was outraged about the new proposal for parental leave, and they talked about politicians who didn't understand reality. Hare seemed absent. He was not interested in politics, and his headache made any form of mental activity impossible.

"Do you have any porcelain today?" the wild boar asked.

"Three pairs of blue and three pairs of brown," Dingo replied. "But then it's mostly plastic, unfortunately."

"That works, too," sighed the doctor.

They parted a few minutes later, and Dingo and Hare drove on. They had four deliveries to make before they were done, and when the pickup was full of stuffed-animal parts, Dingo never felt comfortable.

Vincent Hare was dreaming, but the state into which he had sunk could not be called sleep. It was more of a haze, and the fantasies of the haze were more realistic than the fantasies in a dream.

He was lying in his bed on Calle de Serrano, and on the silver screen of memory he was barely five years old. He was lying there, waiting. Outside the window facing the street, a lantern was lit and in the sky the stars were shining. He wanted to fall asleep, he was really trying to, that would have saved him, but fear kept him awake. He was on full alert, listening: the water rippling in the radiator; someone coughing three floors down; his heart beating in his chest; the sighing in his ear as he turned over on his other side. At last he heard the steps on the stairway; the key in the door. Panic flared up in the five-year-old's chest. Desperation tightened his throat.

Vincent heard his mom's voice, but not what she was saying. He heard his dad answer. The voices, one light and one rough, went back and forth at a tempo that got faster and faster. He got out of bed. He had on a pair of blue bicycle-print pajamas. He sank down on the floor with his back toward the door. The voices on the other side were loud. He did not want to listen.

The first blow was a dull smack, followed by his mom's scream. The second blow was another smack, and the third, fourth, and fifth blows were also followed by her screams. Then she was no longer screaming, and at last Vincent opened the door and ran out into the kitchen. Mom was lying by the stove. Dad was standing in front of her, kicking. He turned around when Vincent came in, but then continued kicking. To Dad he was nobody. Air.

Vincent screamed. He screamed and screamed, but Dad wasn't concerned with him. Mom didn't hear a thing. Only when the ambulance personnel broke down the door did Vincent stop screaming, and the emergency medical technicians had to shove Dad aside to be able to carry Mom away. Vincent remained sitting on the floor in the kitchen, crying. Dad stepped over him to go into the bedroom and lie down.

Mom never came back. Dad never talked about her again. Vincent never found out what happened.

In his haze he is lying on the bed in his blue pajamas, and the emptiness in his heart is so great it engulfs the whole house and his whole life and all of Mollisan Town.

It was the stench that woke Vincent. The cold, hard stone floor was incredibly uncomfortable. How could he have fallen asleep there? He must have fainted. It happened sometimes. Pills and vodka were an unpredictable combination. Sometimes it worked out, other times not. The nausea made his stomach turn inside out and he opened his eyes.

He did not know where he was. There had been a time of innocence when he woke up and felt compelled to remember. Experience had freed him from that kind of need for control. Judging by the ceiling height, he was in a garage or a factory. Some kind of industrial space, like always. Carefully he twisted his head. He was not alone. How many were there? Ten, twenty? He didn't know, and he didn't worry about it.

He got up on his elbows. The stench was overwhelming, and when he looked down at his pants he discovered that someone had vomited on him. It could have been him, but he doubted that. He seldom vomited. A yellow green slush had run down over his legs and into the gap over his socks. Into the fabric and stuffing. It was disgusting. It would take days with a heavy, soaking leg to be rid of the smell.

Closest to him was a rat who was usually present at the Donation Dates. Vincent tried to shake life into him, but did not succeed. After a while Vincent got up, feeling unsteady. Outside it was dark, and he realized it was night and not morning, as he had thought. How long had he been lying there? He studiously avoided looking at the other stuffed animals on the floor. He had seen it before, this sea of quietly weeping, shaking, or still-unconscious stuffed animals that slowly realized they were maimed for life; it was a scene he could not get used to. He crouched down, shaking the rat again.

"Where the hell are we?" he asked.

"Lanceheim," answered the rat. "On the outskirts of Nowhere."

Vincent nodded. He went through the space in the opposite direction, away from the scattered stuffed-animal bodies on the floor. His arms and stomach hurt. He found a door and stepped out into the cold night. The air was a release. Against the dark sky the dense crowns of the treetops were outlined, and he realized that the industrial space was on the border to the forest, presumably in the northwest corner of the district where the food industries were located. He started walking south. Soon his eyes got used to the darkness, and he saw the outlines of factories and their massive chimneys.

Even though he had left Donation Dates before, in flight without fleeing, more times in the past year than he cared to count, something different was happening tonight. It was a line out of Armesto's *Exposure* that Vincent suddenly remembered, for the first time in a very long while:

> *Your reality exists in the eyes of others, while in the others' eyes there is only desire.*

When he came up to the barrier gates that he could crouch under (happy not to have to climb over a fence), he could barely breathe. Anxiety had closed up his throat.

He was alive. But the only reason he was able to make his way through days and nights—as if life were an obstacle course—was that he refused to see himself. He had rid himself of the reality that Armesto talked about. In Vincent's life, there were no "others." He was 26 years, 215 days, and about 20 hours old, and had not achieved anything at all. If it hadn't been for his artistic talent he never would have gotten a diploma from elementary school. After school he used his talent to fill exactly fifty canvases with oil paint, paint over them with white and fill them again. The exhibition nauseated him; everything seemed to be a game he tired of before he was even through playing it. The portfolio that was the result of the work and that he sent to the Art Academy was the same he sent to the College of Architecture. He had been accepted in both places and chose Architecture. It was an occupation, anyway. But the college proved to be full of pretentious strivers he divided into two categories: the visionaries and the mathematicians, and he did not belong in either group. He stopped going to lectures. He stopped going to exams. He lost interest, just as he lost interest in life. There was no meaning, anyone could see that, so there was no meaning in discussing meaninglessness.

He walked south, away from the forest, without recognizing where he was. Lanceheim had never attracted him; the district was the city's most anonymous, filled with stuffed animals who lived their lives in forbearance and longing. Sooner or later Vincent would get to a bus stop, and because all the bus lines passed the Star, he could transfer there. The street he was walking on was barely a street, only half paved, the warehouses and factories sporadic, but farther ahead he saw an area of town houses.

It was to this exact point here that life had taken him: to a deserted street in north Lanceheim after a day, or twenty-four hours, in an abandoned industrial space, with pain and degradation and drugs, so that everyone could anesthetize themselves and do what had to be done. This was his life, with a stranger's vomit penetrating the cotton at his shins and anxiety like a lump in his throat. With an emotional life that only came to life from extremes or chemicals.

Vincent Hare stopped.

Did he want to be there?

Had he chosen this?

In a way he had, he thought bitterly and started walking again. He no longer remembered when he first learned to close off, to enclose himself in his own universe where Dad, the teachers, and his classmates were not admitted. There he set his own goals. He created an autonomous world, where he could decide for himself how life would be lived. If the lesson was to page fifty, he could just as well decide that he would read to page one hundred, or not read at all. Instead of being drawn into the capricious hierarchy of social relationships, he learned to be comfortable with solitude. He created his own rules; that was his survival strategy. Only he, and no one else, could know when he was competent and when he was inadequate. The strategy held up until his teens. He was socially wise enough to appear "normal," but he felt he didn't belong. In every situation he could observe himself from the outside.

Enough now, thought Vincent.

Misanthrope or not, he had to start taking himself seriously. The sand was running like a landslide through the hourglass; it was high time.

Vincent walked—no, he marched in the darkness down the empty street, mechanically and without lowering his gaze. He had experienced this moment before, or others very much like it, and yet something was changed. Here, where no one could see him and reality felt so distant, he decided that this time it was for real. The gray notebook was at home, but he knew what he would write:

1. *Meaning of Life: It's not about the present.*
2. *Knowledge Account: It's not the drop that makes the goblet overflow, it happens when you tip the glass. You have to take yourself seriously, however hard that may be. Must do it now.*
3. *Bank Account: A certain hope of replenishment soon.*

JACK DINGO'S COMMENTS

Do I remember Vincent Hare? I remember him well. He was different.

You know, I've always needed help. I mean, unqualified help. A certain kind of stuffed animal who does what I tell them to. Everything has a price. And if they hung around with me, I paid them well. Then they last a couple of years but eventually want too much money. For booze or drugs. Then it's time to dump them, and get new ones.

I would pick up animals on El Torado. I still do. Why change something that works? Late at night at a bar where the liquor is siphoned from the still in the basement it's easy to see who's up to the job and who isn't. That was where I picked up Vincent Hare. He was the perfect age, not yet twenty, no one knew him, and he had no family. Those are the kind I look for. The kind no one will miss.

The only thing that made me uncertain—I remember this because we laughed about it later—was how much he wanted me to find him. It was written all over him. The way he dressed, the way he talked. He was one of those who wanted. What did they want? They wanted to be discovered, I guess. They longed to get away, and they were prepared to do anything at all to escape their sad, confined lives. Or almost anything at all. Hare wanted, and more than anyone I'd seen.

I did my usual routine. I offered him a couple hundred if he met me the next evening and helped out. He said yes right away. That was no surprise. He actually said yes to everything, even the bad stuff; I assume that was a principle of his?

When did I notice he was different? Right away. It was nothing special that happened, mostly a sense, but it couldn't be missed. I had nothing to complain about. He did what I said and learned fast. Many stuffed animals whom I picked out were none too bright, which was usually an asset. Hare was smart. I realized that right away. I was younger at that time, and stupider, and for that reason I liked having someone smart around. When you talked you got a little something in exchange. But in terms of the job itself, it wasn't better. And pretty soon I knew that Vincent Hare was too smart to sit in a car with me or stand watching for cops outside the hospital spare parts warehouse.

But he wasn't one of us. Which us? Us. It was impossible to imagine Hare going in and out of King's Cross. It was impossible to imagine Hare getting hooked on drugs, and carrying on just to be able to buy more dope. It was impossible to imagine Hare getting stuck in everyday life, because it was impossible to imagine Hare getting stuck at all. That was the whole deal. In contrast to all the others, with few exceptions, Hare was always on his way. Forward. He radiated impatience, and in a way that made you understand he would never get there. Do you understand? Others, you saw it in their eyes, would be content in the end. But never Hare. That's why he never fit in with me. He was passing through; I knew that from the start. He was no small-time crook. He was too smart for his own good.

Vincent is dreaming. That he is boarding the train to Hillevie. Walking along a narrow corridor. Finds an empty compartment. The train steams and chugs, whistles and snorts. A dull rumble drowns out the sound of everything he does. He opens the compartment door. Sits down on the seat by the window.

Outside, the platform is deserted. He stares at a bench half covered with graffiti. Next to the bench is a trash barrel. Next to the trash barrel a ticket machine. He didn't buy his ticket there; he had it mailed to him at home.

There are no other trains at the station. No stuffed animals are moving on the platforms. As the train begins to move, he experiences a strong discomfort. He stares out the window. He senses that the train is standing still while the world is starting to move. Faster and faster, buildings and streets flicker past. He tries to focus his gaze on individual objects. He sees a mint green facade with four windows, a reddish advertising sign for toothpaste, and suddenly, at an intersection, in the middle of a crosswalk, he sees his father. He has just raised one arm, and stares at the train. Is he waving? Vincent stares back. Behind his father the world swishes past. Then his father, too, disappears from his field of vision.

The speed is unfathomable. The world outside is reduced to diffuse streaks of color that glide past. He can barely make anything out. Then he feels how the train is taking off from the ground. As if he were sitting in a rocket. The rails follow along up into the sky through the clouds. The speed is extraterrestrial. Moments of calm fill him but prove transient: The insight is sudden. The train tracks cannot be pulled through the sky. Trains can't fly. But he is flying, faster and faster, and Vincent knows that soon he is going to crash.

The architectural firm of Bombardelli & Partners had a grandiose reception area with two modern lounge suites on either side of an oval reception counter constructed so it appeared to hover a few inches above the ground. The colors in the lobby were unexpected: turquoise, mint green, and marine blue. Along with a faint aroma of lily of the valley (which the firm's brand manager added to the scouring powder the cleaning company used on the floors), the room created a reassuring atmosphere.

"Vincent Hare?"

Vincent stood up.

"Please follow me."

Vincent followed the fly into the large conference room, where they sat down at the end of a long table.

"Well, Vincent," said the fly, leafing through his papers. "And how old are you?"

"Twenty-seven years, 3 days, 12 hours, and 40 minutes."

The fly looked up from his notepad with surprise, but since Hare looked like this was a normal answer, he decided simply to continue.

"And you live in Yok?"

"In Mindie, at Calle de Serrano, 25."

"You went to architecture school with Gavin Zebra?"

Zebra had started working at Bombardelli & Partners five years earlier, right after the College of Architecture.

"That was a few years ago. It was Gavin who suggested I should contact you. He said something about a job as an assistant project manager."

Vincent was wearing a tight, bright red cashmere sweater with a pair of wide, white pants and loafers. He had also put on a pair of glasses, whose thick black frames were so conspicuous no one would believe there was window glass in them. Judging by his appearance he was already working at an advertising agency or an architect's office.

"Tell me a little about yourself," asked the fly, who worked for Horse Svensson, one of Bombardelli's two partners.

All Vincent had prepared was to show up at the right time and the right place in good-looking clothes. The rest was improvisation.

But to move ahead in life, to even barely make his way, he had decided to break with Dingo and become a part of taxpaying society. He had to break free from his own life bubble. The only one he could think of to call was Gavin Zebra, and now here he was. It was easy to laugh and say to hell with this ridiculous role-playing and realize that a normal life was not for him. But he remembered the sharp smell of soap that still lingered a week after he had washed off the vomit from the Donation Date, and smiled again.

This was his first job interview, yet he thought he found the right tone. He was arrogant, but not toward the interviewer. He called attention to his deficiencies in order to brag about his strengths. After the interview on his way down in the elevator a tortoise was standing next to him, looking desperate.

"Did you apply for the job, too?" asked Vincent.

Diego Tortoise nodded.

"Me, too. Sorry about that. If I'd known you were going to

apply, of course I wouldn't have come here and swiped it right in front of your nose." Vincent laughed, the tortoise looked even more nervous, and Vincent got a bad conscience.

"We need a reward," said the self-confident Vincent. "The first and last job interview in my life. This has to be celebrated."

The tortoise, in a gray suit, with a serious expression and apparently no sense of humor, shook his head, but Vincent would not take no for an answer.

"We'll swing by Clerk's first," he said. "We're in the neighborhood, aren't we?"

"But I don't think . . ."

The elevator doors opened, and Vincent had already run ahead.

They sat at the bar at Clerk's, where many of the great contemporary thinkers and artists had, according to the newspapers, fallen asleep with their forehead on the wood. Diego Tortoise was surprised by how small the place was, in relation to how often he had read about it. Vincent Hare ordered two colorful pineapple drinks with festive umbrellas even though it was midafternoon, and while Tortoise pretended to sip the alcohol, Vincent told about various ways of lacing pineapple drinks. Tortoise expressed polite interest.

It was soon revealed that Tortoise, like Vincent, had grown up in Mindie. They had even gone to the same school, but because they were four years apart, their paths had never crossed. Besides, Tortoise had a feeling they would not have gotten along very well if they had met.

Vincent ordered another round of pineapple drinks. Tortoise took the opportunity to ask for a glass of water.

Diego Tortoise liked school; mathematics was easy for him and he loved history. Vincent drank and listened with half an ear. Then he pulled himself together, recalled his intentions, and told about his own time in school, which he imagined was the normal thing to do in a situation like this. He lied about athletic achievements and depicted himself as the epicenter of the school balls.

"Vodka with ice," Vincent Hare ordered, without being concerned that Tortoise had barely touched the first round of pineapple drinks.

Continuing studies had not been a given, neither for Tortoise nor for Vincent. In their neighborhood, cubs seldom continued past high school; families in Yok didn't need more expenses. But Diego Tortoise's father had once dreamed of becoming a civil engineer, and encouraged his son to apply to Lanceheim Technical College. Vincent Hare admitted to Tortoise that he was no mathematician, and that he had flunked math in his final exams.

"Maybe I could have passed," he said, "but it was so deadly boring."

Tortoise did not know how to acknowledge such a statement.

"Gin and tonic," Vincent ordered, waving one paw in the air. "And throw in a few olives! And leave the bottle here!"

"I wouldn't mind another glass of water," said Tortoise.

"You don't like losing control, do you?" said Vincent.

"No," answered Tortoise.

The answer seemed natural to him.

"But sometimes you have to," said Vincent. "Try, and see what happens. Life can't be controlled."

"Well," Tortoise answered meditatively, "I don't know if I agree with that. You can probably control most things. I'm not a particularly reactive type."

"Reactive?" Vincent laughed. "That's another way to put it. If you ask me, Diego, reactions are all we have. If we're not good at reacting, we're in bad shape."

Vincent held up the bottle of gin. Tortoise did not understand what he meant.

"Think about it, Diego. You can't control reality . . . I mean, try to control what I'm saying?"

"No, of course I—"

"And at the same time you have to react to everything I spew out. You have to give me some answers. Handle it."

"Yes, but I—"

"So whether you want to or not, it's all about reacting. And losing control, my friend, will be your training. 'Cause that's what life looks like, you know? Uncontrolled. Random. Idiotic."

"Well," said Diego, who did not want to contradict his newfound friend, but not agree with something he couldn't stand for either, "I guess I think that many things in life are logical and rational. Complicated, sure, but not incomprehensible, if you just accept the fundamental conditions."

He spoke in a slow drawl that Vincent found very irritating.

"And perhaps that's even our cause, our mission here in life, to try to bring order to all that you're talking about," Tortoise continued. "What's 'idiotic,' as you say."

Tortoise had been one of the best pupils in his class, and after his civil engineering degree he could pick and choose among job offers. Hare's architecture degree remained unfinished. Even if they were both at Bombardelli & Partners looking for work, they had applied for two different positions.

Tortoise applied for a position in the construction department, after having studied and been fascinated by durability theory in college.

"Good luck bringing order to existence, my friend, and if you succeed you have to call me. Now I want whiskey!" Vincent yelled to the bartender, but it was hard to hear what he was saying because he was slurring. "There's no more of this porridge left."

Hare did not notice that Tortoise still had not had anything to drink besides water.

After the Afternoon Rain more customers appeared, and right before the Evening Weather the bar was full. Tortoise did not dare leave the thoroughly intoxicated hare alone. The stuffed animals at Clerk's studiously avoided watching as Vincent snorted and laughed and shouted and drank; he drank more than Tortoise thought it was possible to drink. When the money finally ran out, Tortoise helped Vincent home. Tortoise lived more or less around the corner from Vincent's red-dotted Calle de Serrano, on cement gray Calle de Padilla. Tortoise hailed a taxi, and when they arrived he helped Vincent up the stairs into his apartment building. The last half hour it had been impossible to make out what the intoxicated stuffed animal was saying, even though he talked constantly.

It was five weeks before Vincent Hare started at Bombardelli & Partners, and by then Diego Tortoise had already worked there a week. Within a few days, everyone had formed an impression of the loud hare. His desire to be liked stopped at nothing. Tortoise did not know whether this was deeply tragic or simply unpleasant.

Vincent's clothing, to start with. Colorful suits that appeared to be a few sizes too small, with handkerchiefs that seemed to gush forth from the breast pocket and were as gaudy as the suits (but in contrasting colors), along with pointed shoes with shoelaces the same color as the handkerchiefs. It reminded Tortoise of a clown running around the office.

Furthermore, Vincent's ingratiation knew no bounds. Every morning on his way from reception to his desk approximately in the middle of the office, he managed to drop more flattering comments than Tortoise would formulate in his entire professional career. The art form was perhaps impressive, but Tortoise leaned over his desk, blushing, to avoid showing how ill at ease he was. Hare himself seemed unaffected.

It was natural that the two sought each other out at first. They were newcomers who started at about the same time, and between them there was also that evening when Tortoise had dragged the dead-drunk hare home from Clerk's. They were opposites, so Tortoise found it more interesting to look for similarities. It turned out that they had both read Gillespie's *On Night in Tourquai* (which Tortoise appreciated while Vincent thought it shied away from the deeper problems), they agreed that the new Volga Mini was a step backward in terms of design, and they both liked pizza, which is why for the first few weeks they had lunch at Gino's, even though it was a bit of a walk.

Surrounded by the heavenly aromas from the open wood-fired oven and the comforting din in the popular restaurant, where a full-bodied red wine was served in carafes with the food whether you ordered it or not, Vincent went into great detail about the internal power structure at Bombardelli, as he perceived it after a few weeks.

"Bombardelli is not just king at the office," Vincent announced as he rolled up a perfectly cut wedge of pizza and stuffed it into his mouth. "The rattlesnake is an autocrat. Dictator. He IS the office. I don't think you understand what that means, Diego. He decides everything. In detail. The pen you are using this afternoon . . . it's not by chance you are holding just that one. Everything is part of Bombardelli's plan."

Tortoise did not drink alcohol with lunch, but Vincent tasted the red wine and it was to his liking, so he took another gulp before he continued.

"And the rattlesnake's partners, Daniela Fox and Horse Svensson," Vincent informed him. "She's thirty-seven, he'll soon be eligible for retirement. This is the kind of thing you have to keep track of, Diego. There is no rule that says there can only be two partners, or that one partner has to retire before Bombardelli appoints a new one."

Tortoise had ordered a Pizza Compastone with no olives but got olives anyway, and picking them out demanded his concentration. Stuffed animals came and went during lunch; at Gino's you sat at a long table, and the hare and tortoise already had new neighbors.

"Don't you understand?" asked Vincent, noticing the tortoise's lack of interest and feeling offended.

"Don't I understand what?"

"But . . . there is only one reason to start at Bombardelli & Partners: It's to become a partner yourself. Everything else is a failure. This is a competition, Diego. Between you and me. A race. We started the same time; let's see who becomes a partner first. May the best animal win!"

Vincent Hare was 27 years, 73 days, 4 hours, and about 30 minutes old and had worked at Bombardelli & Partners for five weeks when he met Maria Goat for the first time. It happened by chance, in the morning, by the coffee machine. He had already set his cup at the designated place in the machine, but took it out again and let her go ahead of him. She had on a red-speckled blouse he liked, and she looked at him with open curiosity. She had an attractive roundness, short legs, and her cream white wool smelled of roses. She pushed the button for "Choco-Tea" and he assumed she had made a mistake. So he said something to the effect that he had pushed the wrong button to start with, too. Thirty-five stuffed animals worked at the office; he had never seen her before and therefore assumed she was new. She answered that she had worked at Bombardelli & Partners for two years, and that she preferred Choco-Tea to the alternatives.

Maria Goat was one of the youngest architects at the firm, and was considered promising. She was not interested in philosophy and lived alone because she chose to. She had Choco-Tea several times a day, she liked Tortoise (whom she considered a model of reliability and solidity), and she had season tickets to the Concert House because she idolized Rachmolotov (whom Vincent had never understood). During the months that followed, she treated Vincent with the same sort of curious interest that was in her eyes the first time; as if he were an odd object, an anomaly at Bombardelli, and he could not decide if he was flattered or bored by her treatment. At some point every day, by the coffee machine, in the lunchroom or in the elevator, they nodded fleetingly at each other, and if they had time exchanged a few words about the particularly interesting and big projects that more or less the whole office was affected by and everyone had an opinion on.

During this time Vincent attempted to adapt to "reality." He thought about the word in quotation marks, even though he tried to refrain, and let the days come and go as they would. After six months at Bombardelli he discovered by chance his gray notebook, long untouched in the drawer in his nightstand. He took the notebook out, and wrote:

1. *Meaning of Life: Repetition = life?*
2. *Knowledge Account: Don't think so much, it feels better that way.*
3. *Bank Account: Looks promising, could be better.*

No one observing the scene from the landing in the ball-room would have believed it was the first time Vincent Hare was at a party where the written invitations had arrived two months in advance. He was dressed in a form-fitting midnight blue tuxedo with a white scarf loosely wrapped around his neck, and a pair of midnight blue patent-leather shoes that set him apart from the crowd. Nonchalantly he held his cup and saucer at waist level and laughed lightly without anyone having been funny.

But in reality he was greedily soaking up every detail, every second, every gesture, and every word he came across. He was 28 years, 105 days, 15 hours, and about 15 minutes old. In life as he had known it so far, nothing surprised or terrified him any longer, but the sound of the sand that ran through his mental hourglass sometimes thundered like an avalanche. That was why this social sphere that he had recently discovered, high above what he was used to, was so important. It was a sign that it was still possible to discover unknown pieces of the puzzle that perhaps might explain or tie together all the seemingly meaningless and disparate parts flowing around in Vincent's life.

Several hundred stuffed animals in evening clothes were gathered in the grandiose ballroom. Dinner had just been taken in the Hall of the Stars directly adjacent. Vincent had not been aware you could hire the National Historical Museum for private parties.

Jack Dingo suddenly showed up, with a broad grin on his face.

"You don't fool me," Dingo said. "You were so turned on by that anaconda you got to sit next to, you hardly knew what you were eating. You were drooling, Vincent."

"Where were you sitting?"

"Where I could see you," Dingo replied. "I never would have brought you with me if I realized you couldn't behave in fine circles."

They both laughed, because it was obvious that it was the dingo who didn't appear to belong among the party attendees. His glass claws lacked a counterpart in Mollisan Town and gave him a certain originality, but there was an expression in his eyes and around his mouth that neither the claws, a white shirt, or a white bow tie could conceal. The dingo's kind of avarice was not openly appreciated by the upper class.

"I see," said Vincent. "These are the finer circles? If you knew where the tip of that anaconda's tail was during dinner, I doubt you would talk about fine circles. But I admit it was hard to concentrate on the food."

Dingo laughed.

"Samuel!"

A plump dolphin went past with a large cognac glass in his fin. He stopped when he heard his name, and lit up when he saw Dingo.

"Jack!" he exclaimed. "Who let you in?"

"Samuel, say hello to Vincent," said Dingo. "He's new here. Take care of him. Where'd you get the cognac?"

Dolphin nodded vaguely toward a corner of the ballroom

where many stuffed animals appeared to be gathering, and Dingo went off to the bar. Dolphin stayed behind. A string quartet started playing on one of the balustrades. The music fell like gentle rain over the gala dresses and made them glitter.

"Well, now. Are you an associate of Jack's?"

"I assume that's the sort of thing I should deny?"

Dolphin laughed.

"I think you're right. We all know him, but no one lets on. If you're not at Rosenlind's level, of course," said Dolphin, throwing out his fin to emphasize the abundance of the evening. "Because then you can associate with any riffraff at all, it just makes you interesting."

"I really don't know Rosenlind except by reputation," Vincent admitted. "He's said to be . . . terrifying?"

"To get anything in this life," Dolphin replied, "takes will. That applies to Lion, it applies to you, and it applies to me. And the will must be strong . . . you know, it can be perceived as unpleasant. I assume Lion frightens some. But look, speak of the devil!"

Jack Dingo came walking with Lion Rosenlind in tow. Beforehand Vincent had done his homework and found out that Rosenlind, besides the boards he was on, not only owned the convenience store chain Monomart—as was generally known—but also for the past ten years controlled the manufacture of Volgas. This meant that he employed hundreds of thousands of stuffed animals in his industries, and that his power over Mollisan Town was considerable.

"Vincent Hare," Lion Rosenlind called from a distance, as if they were old friends. "It is a true honor to meet you. Jack always talks about you. You're a painter, Jack tells me?"

"Well, I needed to pay the rent," Vincent answered with a suitable smile, "so these days I work at Bombardelli."

"An architect!" Rosenlind exclaimed. "Impressive. And how do you put up with that eccentric? Bombardelli is building a reputation. He's gifted, but he pushes the boundaries."

"Who doesn't?" asked Dolphin.

All four of them laughed, Vincent without being sure why.

"It's true," said Rosenlind. "We all live on the edge. But only Jack gets paid for it."

Jack raised his glass and toasted them, but before Vincent had absorbed the thought that Rosenlind was one of Dingo's customers, the lion had disappeared to talk with more guests.

That night when he came home he took out his gray notebook, and wrote:

1. *Meaning of Life: Can it have something to do with physical satisfaction? Why can't it be that simple? When did materialism become a sign of stupidity?*
2. *Knowledge Account: Smile. They like that.*
3. *Bank Account: Everything is relative.*

"Let's drive down to Mindie," said Lion Rosenlind, and he pronounced the name with emphasis on the first and last syllable, the way Vincent Hare had always done.

They were sitting in an anonymous but elegant office, and Vincent had just signed fifty-some documents without having any idea why or what he had signed. Rosenlind stood to the right behind Vincent, and on the other side stood an attorney who supplied Vincent with papers. The last time he had asked what he was signing, and Rosenlind had given him a long, complicated explanation with terms and time perspectives that soon bored Vincent. To run a business in Mollisan Town apparently required piles of permits and signatures. If Vincent had heard right, between the last time he signed piles of documents—a couple of months ago—and this time, he had purchased several chemical industries. Today he sold them again. But he wasn't sure, it could be something else, he didn't really care, he was happy to lend his name. A week ago Rosenlind bought a car for Vincent to thank him. Vincent,

who knew that nothing was free in this city, was still wondering, however, what would be asked in return, because he
doubted that these signatures could correspond to the black
Volga GTI with brown leather seats he was now driving.

The attorney excused himself, threw together his documents, sorted them in plastic pockets, and set them in his
briefcase. Then he quickly departed. As Vincent understood
it, Lion Rosenlind had offices in Tourquai as well as Amberville and Lanceheim, anonymous corner rooms at the end of
long corridors he seldom seemed to visit. Instead of work he
devoted himself to the things he liked: sports and cars, food
and females. Rosenlind's successes had given him a unique
position. There was a rumor that the mayor of Mollisan Town
had the habit of confirming major decisions with Rosenlind,
because the lion controlled such a large part of the city's
industries.

For that reason it was fascinating, thought Vincent, that
the powerful multibillionaire found such childish joy in inves-
tigating Yok.

"Now, let's drive down to Mindie," Rosenlind repeated in
Vincent's accent.

Together they sat in the backseat of one of the lion's limou-
sines, and Vincent had to provide an address where the chauffeur would drive them and drop them off.

The more run-down the neighborhoods Vincent took
Rosenlind to, the greater the billionaire's delight was. In
Mindie, that was a simple task. You only needed to walk a
couple of blocks before you stumbled across traces of prostitution and crime. Rosenlind could spend long afternoons in
brothels where Vincent never would have set his paw, or else
he smoked opium at bars Vincent had passed for twenty years
without going in. The anonymity that Yok offered the dis-
guised billionaire liberated him. He called it his "breathing
hole," and Vincent did not question anything; why should he?

At regular intervals they changed roles, however, and

Rosenlind became Vincent's cicerone in those parts of the city that were the opposite of Yok. The lion presented his unknown friend as one of the most interesting contemporary young architects (though Vincent made it clear he worked as a project manager and nothing more). Vincent got to rub elbows with the rich and powerful in Mollisan Town. The contrast to the afternoon outings in Mindie could not have been greater. Usually they ended up in restaurants and nightclubs, but on a few occasions they went to private parties in one of the enormous houses at Swarwick Park or out in Le Vezinot.

"Are you paying attention?" Lion laughed every time he noticed how impressed Vincent was.

Vincent never knew exactly what he meant.

Before those evenings out, Rosenlind sometimes bought exclusive clothes for him.

"But I already have a dark suit," Vincent might object.

"Unfortunately you can't get away with homemade jackets in Tourquai." Rosenlind laughed, and Vincent felt ashamed.

At the same time he understood that he was doing the lion a service. The rich predator liked feeling generous, and he liked buying expensive but clearly meaningless objects best of all. Six months after Rosenlind bought back the chemical industries, a couple of restaurants were transferred to Vincent for tax purposes, Rosenlind's attorneys explained, and before the signing of these documents, Rosenlind stopped by Grand Divino and bought a ballpoint pen that cost the equivalent of two years of Vincent's salary. It was idiotic.

"So you realize how important these signatures are." The lion laughed.

A week later Vincent lost the pen. It happened at a nightclub where a young polar bear swiped it after writing his phone number on Vincent's business card. Vincent went to confess the loss to the billionaire.

"Easy come, easy go," said Rosenlind, when Vincent suggested they should report the incident to the police.

After such nights, bewildering and crazy, when Vincent at most managed to get a couple hours' sleep, it was sometimes hard to readjust to civilian life, to the everyday routines of work and to meeting stuffed animals whose lives were limited by time and resources. The sand was pressing sluggishly through the narrow waist of the hourglass.

The office layout at Bombardelli & Partners suited Vincent. He considered the architectural firm's diligent employees his audience. He arrived in midmorning, long after the rain had ceased, and never tired of making his rounds among the desks. He smelled of expensive cologne and had a colorful handkerchief in the breast pocket of his jacket. He laughed often and loud. Vincent made a point of remembering whose mother-in-law had been visiting, who had been at the dentist with his cub, who had read *Clouds over Meek Street,* and who was brooding about getting a divorce. He knew what projects they were working on and whom they would have lunch with. He confirmed, questioned, and provoked, depending on individual and need, and there was a single purpose for this daily display: to prove to himself that he could. Vincent's longing after the nights with Lion Rosenlind's friends did not reduce his striving to become one of society's small, insignificant cogs, and perhaps in that way give existence a meaning. Rosenlind's life would never be Vincent's anyway, not even if he had access to the same money and the same power. The fact that Vincent could dress up as one of Rosenlind's equals for a shorter or longer period was another matter. But making yourself blind and deaf, which Vincent realized was a prerequisite for Rosenlind's kind of life, would be impossible in the long run.

The decision to leave Jack Dingo and Jack's whole circus behind to instead become an ordinary wage slave still seemed reasonable after a couple of years. Reality, Vincent knew, rested in the eyes of the surroundings, and he exploited that.

Through the personnel at Bombardelli he was reminded that he had made the right decision, and that he had changed. At night, in solitude or with stuffed animals who only saw themselves, the transformation was less apparent, and that alone was a reason to drag himself off to the office every day. On the other hand he had a harder time taking the work itself seriously. As project manager—already after eighteen months he had dropped the title of assistant—it was about selling ideas. To start with, the firm's ideas for the customer, and then the customer's ideas back to the firm. The latter was always harder, because the customer had less prestige than architects as far as architecture was concerned.

Of all the stuffed animals who worked at Bombardelli & Partners, Vincent Hare remained eager to work with Maria Goat. Out of habit he courted the females he came in contact with, something he had started doing in his late teens. He continued that behavior as he got older, and practice made perfect. But Goat in particular gave him no response. This made his interest grow even further.

Vincent Hare was 30 years, 55 days, 4 hours, and about 10 minutes old when Rattlesnake Bombardelli formed the group that would work on Samuel Dolphin's house, a group led by Goat. She was on an immediate collision course with her principal, Samuel Dolphin, however, and only a couple of weeks into the project found herself in the midst of a moral and professional dilemma. For several days she and the stuffed animals on her team discussed the problem. They often stood around Goat's desk dissecting the question, looking for different perspectives and angles of attack, but Vincent understood the core of the problem as simple. Either you let the customer—in this case, Dolphin—get his way, or else you realized that the architectural concept you—in this case, Goat—had could not be maintained. It had been thanks to

Vincent that Dolphin came into contact with Bombardelli. On an intellectual level Vincent understood how Goat was thinking, but in practice he understood that the only thing was to do as Dolphin wanted.

Samuel Dolphin, who made his fortune on sparkless matches, sought help from Bombardelli to design a house that would be a monument to his successes. He bought four town houses on the same block in Amberville, and intended to raze them all and replace them with his vision, which to a certain degree was Goat's vision: cubistic, deconstructionist, and sparkling green.

But five days ago Dolphin got the idea that all the windows in the building should be removed, closed up, and replaced with a glass roof not visible from the street. He had called from a bar in Tourquai and left a voice message with this order on Goat's cell phone late in the evening. Loud thumping music and shrieks from shrill voices were heard in the background. Then Dolphin left another message early the next morning, in which he demanded that Goat confirm that she received his first message. But the change, according to Goat, would transform a visionary residence into a bunker, even if it had a glass roof, and she refused to put her name on this barn with boxes attached (which, to be sure, retained their lovely forms and colors). For that reason Goat had not phoned back. Dolphin was furious, and on three occasions he visited Bombardelli at the office to tell him what he thought about the firm's professionalism.

Maria Goat was sitting on a chair in worn jeans and a wide-sleeved, white blouse, arguing in a low but definite voice for her cause, often as she was typing on her computer or scheduling meetings in her calendar via phone, and no arguments could budge her.

"But he's paid us," said Vincent, who was leaning against Goat's desk, stretching out his long legs so that Goat was forced to roll her chair aside. "Which means that this is his damned house now, not yours. Those are his drawings. He can do what he wants with them. You've sold yourself, Maria. It's just ridiculous that you don't want to admit it."

He knew that would provoke her, but he couldn't refrain. He recognized himself in her without realizing it. Vincent had always let intellectual ideas turn into compulsive thoughts, had always let principles kill spontaneity. Goat seemed to be similar.

With little interest he listened to her litany of responsibility and artistry and other things that Vincent had given up long ago. He nodded and smiled, mostly so she could get it all out, but the irritation was growing. The other stuffed animals standing around Goat's desk out in the open office layout nodded, too. She could plead her case. A less cynical stuffed animal than Vincent would have been impressed. The afternoon sun fell in through the windows and made the threads in Goat's blouse flash.

"Samuel Dolphin is a friend," said Vincent. "I don't need to speculate. You can think what you want, but Samuel's attitude is simple. He'll be living in the house. Not us. So he's right."

Which made Goat burst out in a new lament. Vincent was the provocateur, the one who poked holes in her argumentation with a quick, clever remark and put his finger on the most tender point. Now he was the one who let himself be provoked. It was an unaccustomed experience, and somehow it pleased him. It proved that he was emotionally engaged.

He let her win the discussion that afternoon. As soon as the other animals dispersed and returned to their places, he invited her out to dinner. He knew she would say yes. After all, he had never had a no. Goat was resistant and a trifle suspicious, but that was part of the game. They agreed to meet in the twilight at Chez Voudrais, and when they parted a few minutes later he was fortunately able to conceal how satisfied he was.

Hare was a practiced seducer, and his main problem had

come to be this very habit. Lack of commitment was a serious sin if you were sitting across from an expectant female who had devoted hours to making herself beautiful; thinking about other things and not being anxious about the evening or displeased about your progress was unforgivable, and threatened the end of the seduction. This had started happening to Vincent. He had stopped being interested. He asked beautiful females out to dinner a few times a month, simply to stay in practice.

Goat arrived a few minutes late. Vincent regretted it as soon as he saw her. The energy of the afternoon had run out of him. He suffered through the appetizers in tormented silence. Toasted with champagne and let his eyes sparkle in the glow from the candle on the table. With the entrée things got more interesting as they gossiped about colleagues at the office. She proved to know more than he had guessed, and the warmth she felt for Diego Tortoise touched him. He was seldom in contact with that sort of genuine devotion, and it made him inexpressibly melancholy without knowing it. With dessert he noticed again that he was running on idle, but then there wasn't much time left.

And it was only at dawn, as he soundlessly slipped out of her apartment and left her naked in bed, with the sheets like twisted rags on the floor, that he noticed the confusion he felt, but did not recognize. He searched for a bus stop, and while he waited he took out the gray notebook and wrote:

1. *Meaning of Life: No. Still no clue.*
2. *Knowledge Account: It must be about putting yourself in situations that you know in advance you DON'T master, as often as possible. But if you end up in such a situation without having planned it? If you don't recognize yourself in the repetition . . . ?*
3. *Bank Account: Why complain?*

MARIA GOAT'S COMMENTS

Did I love Vincent Hare? That's a direct question, but I'm not ashamed to give a direct answer. I loved him. I tried to stay away, but it didn't work. You really should laugh at my situation. For almost a year I observed him from a distance, and more than once I sneered to myself at everything I loved later—his vanity, his need for affirmation, his self-awareness. How he chose bigger and bigger words the more anxious he became. How the pedestal he put himself on sometimes tee-tered, and how desperately he struggled to get it to stand still again.

It was the opposite of love at first sight.

What made me change? His energy, without a doubt. His energy was the key that opened him to me.

This is what I mean: Vincent could be infinitely strong and consider himself superior to everything and everyone. The next moment he was filled by, yes, reveled in, his own bitterness and self-pity and complained in a way that would have made anyone feel ashamed. He could be analytically sharp, more thought-out than anyone I knew, and at the next moment let his emotions steer him right toward the abyss. I did not understand this at all, and found it rather trying. During a meeting he might sit absentmindedly, staring out the window for an hour, and then suddenly throw himself into the discussion without caring where he landed. I asked him about that. He said he always had a hard time concentrating. I think he was lying. There was nothing wrong with his ability to concentrate; it was interest he had a hard time mobilizing.

Then I realized this was all about his energy level. The intensity in everything he undertook was always the same. The introspective brooding. The questioning and the sales talk. The charm he turned on and off like a switch. And then his way of courting me.

From Vincent's perspective I was, like all other females, a conquest. This flattered me more than I want to admit. Few are the males who over the years have considered me a conquest. I'm not that type. I guess I can challenge and attract, but I'm not particularly feminine. Not in that way. In Vincent's eyes I was. Our first dinner made me speechless and surprised, because I had never experienced that before. That kind of cavalier attitude. He treated, even though we both knew I made more. He chose the wine, even though it was quickly apparent he didn't know anything about wine. He lectured on architecture during dessert, even though I was the one who was the architect. He held on to me in the Breeze, even though I wasn't cold. It was so moving I couldn't help but fall for him.

In a reverse way his solicitude aroused my protective instincts. I have never been a stuffed animal who needs to be taken care of. If my friends were to choose a word to describe me, it would probably be "capable." Vincent reduced me to someone in distress, but it was so clear that this was a game to him, a charade, that it could not upset me. The more he exerted himself to show off his maleness, the sweeter he became. I know I wasn't the only one who saw that. In the lunchroom at Bombardelli there were many who sighed in rapture over his manner and his clothes, but the whole time with an undertone of amusement. It was not condescension; it was tenderness. Vincent thought he aroused desire, while in reality he aroused maternal feelings.

And I felt privileged that I was the one he put first, it gave me a different image in the eyes of my colleagues, a dimension was added to who I was. The relationship between Vincent and I became public, we were invited to couples dinners, and it took time before I realized where we were headed.

He could not stop courting me, and he had to outdo himself even though no one required it. It was the same thing at work, with whatever he was doing. If he gave me ten red roses on Friday, he had to increase the number to fifteen the next week. If we spent two hours in bed instead of getting up on Sunday, he kept me under the covers another half hour the following weekend. To begin with I didn't notice this. Then I laughed at it; much of what he did amused me without my daring to talk about it. But at last I saw the destructiveness in his behavior. Then it was too late, for now I was a part of it.

I tried to talk with him, of course. I'm not timid, I have a tongue. But those kinds of conversations were never good. If he sensed criticism, he became incredibly defensive. And aggressive. There was a darkness over his whole life, and you could absolutely not touch or comment on it. He could talk about others for hours, insightfully and analytically. But he did not want to talk about himself. And trying to see himself, from my perspective, or talk about our relationship, he despised that, and he started defending his behavior before I even brought it up.

How well did I know Vincent Hare? What do you mean? I wonder if anyone has really gotten to know Vincent Hare.

Probably only he himself realizes how lost he is. At the same time, when I say this, I know how easy it is for stuffed animals to make Vincent incomprehensible. There is something enticing in mystifying him, but however much we all want to be special, there isn't all that much that sets us apart.

There was in Vincent, more than in others, I think, a greater difference between what he did and what he said. Most stuffed animals say they weigh more than they really do. Sometimes I thought Vincent was the other way around. Perhaps it was his way of pushing limits? He tried a standpoint, a position, formulated himself around it, and then he did the opposite. He could tell about things . . . he had done, which were loathsome. Without my thinking he was loathsome. Is that possible?

Perhaps I forgave him too easily?

But, like I said, I loved him.

Vincent Hare was 33 years, 173 days, 4 hours, and about 15 minutes old when Horse Svensson, one of Bombardelli's two partners, retired. It shouldn't have been hard to figure out, given the large reception that had been held at the office five years earlier when champagne and hors d'oeuvres were served and congratulatory speeches were made on the occasion of Svensson's sixtieth birthday. Yet the news struck like a bomb whose shock wave swept aside all other issues, and for a few days the talk was solely of Svensson's retirement. Some were happy about the change and what it might entail; others feared it. The speculations about what would happen could be summarized in three theses: (a) instead of replacing Svensson, Bombardelli would continue with Daniela Fox as sole partner; (b) Bombardelli would entice a prominent architect from another firm by offering partnership; and (c) Bombardelli would recruit internally, that is, make one of the architects currently working at the office the new partner.

The coffee machine became a meeting place for the most conspiratorial. Vincent Hare, who belonged to this category and who since the news exploded had heard the sand in the hourglass of life running as if it were a rushing river, gathered various groups to discuss the likelihood of the various alternatives. You sipped your coffee and threw out familiar names, which flew through the air to be shot down by criticism and doubt and then fall flat on the ground. Maria Goat usually stayed away, because she had never been interested in gossip. But when the longing for Choco-Tea became overpowering, she was forced to listen to Vincent's theories as she sipped the light brown chocolate.

"You then, Maria," Vincent suggested. "Wouldn't that be an idea?"

"How so?"

Around them stood five or six stuffed animals, and the mood was immediately charged with nervous energy.

"He means you should become a partner, Maria," clarified an earthworm who usually worked with Daniela Fox.

"And you don't think you're disqualified," Goat replied. "Considering that we more or less live together?"

"But that's a good idea," said Diego Tortoise, who was also standing in line to use the coffee machine. "That would make the office younger."

"Diego, there is only one reason the amiable Vincent suggests me," said Maria. "And it's that he wants to promote himself as a possible alternative . . ."

That was their mutual lingo; they liked quarreling with each other in public.

"You're so cynical, darling." Vincent laughed, leaping up and sitting on the counter next to the coffee machine.

When he was sitting like that, his beautifully patterned socks were exposed. Vincent left no part of his deceptively nonchalant clothes style to chance.

"But what about Tortoise?" he said.

"I can't very well be a partner, can I?" Tortoise objected in shock. "I'm an engineer, not an architect."

"Svensson wasn't either," said one of the stuffed animals in the group around them.

"You'd be a good partner," said someone else.

"But I've only been here six years."

As they stood next to each other, the tortoise and the hare, the differences between them stood out more clearly than ever. Around the hare was a radiance not only due to his shoe polish, while the tortoise was a gloomy gray in his somewhat baggy jacket.

"Vincent will emphasize that he, too, has been here for six years, and that's enough to become a partner," Goat clarified. "I can read you like an open book, Vincent."

"Maria." Vincent laughed, adjusting the deliberately loose knot of his tie. "I don't know where you got this idea that I want to promote myself."

"Probably from you," Goat answered.

"From me? No, now you have to—"

"Let me ask a straight question: Do you think you would be a good partner, Vincent?"

Vincent fell silent and stared at Maria. The stuffed animals around them held their breath.

"Yes," said Vincent at last, smiling broadly. "I would be an excellent partner, Maria. Hasn't Diego told you about our race?"

"No," she answered.

Tortoise's coffee cup was full, and he took it out of the machine.

"That," said Tortoise, snorting, "was only a whim, Vincent, wasn't it?"

Vincent did not reply, but the stuffed animals standing around the coffee machine would not forget that there was a race going on between Vincent and the tortoise, and at regular intervals they would remind Tortoise about it over the years.

Two days later Pug Jansson was named Svensson's successor and a new partner at the firm. Jansson had previously worked at Salmon & Feary, but before that had worked for five years with Daniela Fox (both at Bombardelli and at the Ministry of Finance). Everyone except Vincent Hare thought Jansson was a positive reinforcement for Bombardelli & Partners, and that his good reputation in the city would contribute to the success of the architectural firm.

"You have to admit it," said Tortoise to Vincent a week or two later, when as in old times they were having a pizza at Gino's for lunch, "Jansson is a much stronger card than you or me."

Vincent did not answer.

Vincent Hare was 33 years, 305 days, 15 hours, and about 5 minutes old, and felt Maria Goat's breath on his belly.

The room was dark. Two candles set in wine bottles stuck up from drifts of melted paraffin; the flames emitted a troubled glow over the table where he was lying. The smoke made the air heavy with cinnamon and cumin. First they drank red wine and then smoked. He had used a sheep comb on her. She had rubbed his ears with a chamois. The desire was stronger than he thought was possible. They moved slowly. Every movement a reflection. She breathed on him, and he wanted to feel her lips against his fur, but she never got that close.

"I'm not an animal who takes drugs," she whispered.

"I know that."

"I'm an animal who maintains control," she whispered.

"I know that."

"I am rational."

"I know that."

"This is not about love."

"I don't agree with that."

"I'm not searching for new experiences, Vincent. I think we've had it good the way we've had it."

"I know that. Shut up now, Maria."

"I have no desire to go further."

"Shut up."

He kissed her. On his tongue was a tablet of acid that he let her taste. It made her head sing, and slowly he drew a small but incredibly strong fan down along her back. She moaned audibly.

"I'm not a stuffed animal who moans," she said.

But when she heard herself say this she moaned even louder; she could not help it. She had never felt like this. The shame made her more aroused, his presumption made her dare, but if she let the thought reach a millimeter beyond the dining room table regret would overwhelm her. She concentrated on what she was feeling: the fan exposed fabric that had never before been exposed. It turned her coat to one side and revealed her seams. She moaned again. She let her breath make its way down his belly and against his crotch. She did not know if it was her or him making the sounds she heard. The acid on her tongue made her awareness slide sideways. When she closed her eyes she saw water, still and endless, but it didn't frighten her, it only added to the feeling of unlawful well-being. She continued down his body, he continued up her back. She had never felt this naked before. She did not know where he started and where she ended. She felt him everywhere, as an absence or a presence.

"Hold me," she whispered.

Betweenward, because there was no afterward on this night, they lay on her couch and smoked marijuana. She had not even smoked a cigarette before she met him.

"That's dangerous," he said. "Stay away from cigarettes."

"You shouldn't make me do this, should you, Vincent?" she asked.

"Of course not."

"We have to get out more. Can't we invite some friends over for dinner?"

"We don't have any friends in common. You would throw my friends out immediately. And I wouldn't protest."

"We can invite someone from the office?" she said.

"You and me and Diego Tortoise? Maybe he'd like to play, too?"

"Now you're not just disgusting, you're mean, too," she said. He laughed.

"The very idea, Vincent, of challenging Diego to a race."

"That . . . was a joke. It was about who would become a partner first."

"You wanted to become a partner instead of Jansson, didn't you?"

"I did. You have to play by the rules."

"What rules?"

"The rules of life. If you start working at an architectural firm with partners, the idea is to try to become one of them. As soon as possible."

"And if you're happy with what you have?"

"You may be happy, but you still have to believe that life can get better if you become a partner. Or if you get a higher salary. Or more power."

"Power and money are not particularly interesting," she answered.

"Only stuffed animals with power and money say that," he said. "But there are other rules for academics. There are even rules for anarchists. No one escapes."

"So life is a competition, then?"

"Yes." Vincent took a deep drag and breathed the smoke out as he slowly and jerkily gave her his view.

"We are collectors. All of Mollisan Town. We collect experiences and friends and things and wisdom, and it seems that most or biggest is best. Some compete against Magnus. Others compete for Magnus. Some who say they aren't competing are scared to death of losing. Their face or pride or integrity."

"And you, then? What do you collect?"

"Hours with you."

"That's sweet of you to say, Vincent, but that doesn't count. What do you collect?"

He became impatient.

"I don't know," he said at last. "Adult credits, I assume?"

"Adult credits? But you're over thirty, aren't you, Vincent?"

She got up and went into the kitchen.

"I collect reasons," he called after her. "You are a reason to continue playing by the rules. But you are the only reason. I need more."

Goat returned with a carafe of water. She drank right from it and again lay down on Vincent's lap.

"When you pretend you don't like life I always have a feeling you're putting on airs," she said. "I have never met anyone who lives as intensely. And I don't think you're particularly tough when you try to be disillusioned."

"I collect reasons," he repeated. "This is the best one."

And he leaned over and kissed her. The night had lacked a beginning, and she would be crushed and infinitely relieved the moment it came to an end. When an hour or two later she fell asleep on the couch, he sneaked up and sat down at the desk where he took out the gray notebook and wrote:

1. *Meaning of Life: No idea, but there are moments when it doesn't matter.*
2. *Knowledge Account: If love was the final reward, love would not be so immediately satisfying.*
3. *Bank Account: Don't know.*

Afterward, Vincent Hare tried to think that it wasn't due to the lunch. That what happened at the outdoor café at Trois Étoiles in Bois de Dalida was part of a process that had already been going on for a long time, and which was impossible to stop. He had seen the signs, and they had been insignificant or hard to interpret. He was 34 years, 63 days, 6 hours, and about 50 minutes old.

Maria Goat was not the stuffed animal he was trying to

make her into, he thought. She appreciated the details of life.
She did not stay away from work. She maintained contact with
her girlfriends. She did not deviate from routines. She loathed
an untidy home and was not ashamed to say it. Vincent understood all this, but could not dissimulate. His passion fed itself.

From never having loved, he was now filled by love in a way
he had thought impossible. He abused love the way he abused
all other drugs. Separated from Goat, he could not think of
anything but her. Whether hours or days had passed lacked
significance. He realized he overwhelmed her, frightened her,
but she let herself be carried away by his intemperance. He
could bewitch her like no one before him. He could drive her
to a level of excitement that excluded reality. He could replace
anything and everything when they were together; then she
lacked nothing because there was no time to lack.

But a part of her he never reached, and that part remained
ill at ease. It was as if she were struggling against herself. She
would be the Maria that Vincent saw only when he was near.
When he left her, if only for a while, when he shut the door
to the bathroom or went shopping, more and more often a
sense of gloom hung over her when he returned. He noticed
it but pretended not to. After their impassioned nights, after
decadent mornings or afternoons when their senses—touch,
sight, hearing, smell, and taste—were exhausted and dazed,
she withdrew. Shame took over her, and it was not always easy
to lure it out of her again.

The lunch at Trois Étoiles, he convinced himself, could have
been a dinner at home on Calle de Serrano or a breakfast at a
Springergaast somewhere in Lanceheim.

But however many times he thought that, the thought
echoed vacantly.

They had decided to have lunch in Bois de Dalida, and there
was no particular reason for that. The beautiful park in north
Tourquai was not a place they usually went to; they had only
been to Trois Étoiles separately.

Inside, every table was reserved, so they had to wait for fifteen minutes before a table was available outside. They sat down under one of the big, spanned sails that seemed to hover freely above the lunch guests, and that provided a pleasant shade. They looked out over the park with its ponds, and laughed at the fact that stuffed animals always walked so slowly there. They each ordered an asparagus salad, and while they waited, she let herself be filled up by his energy. But perhaps above all by his irresistible will to fill her up.

Vincent did not see Jack Dingo until he was standing by the table.

"We run into each other at strange places." Dingo laughed.

Vincent laughed. He knew immediately what occasion Dingo meant. They had met late one night a month ago, by chance. Vincent did not go out very often anymore, but sometimes he gave in to one of the importunate female admirers who seemed to be everywhere. There was a pink lamb he had treated badly by promising her too much. She had demanded that they meet one last time. It had nothing to do with his love for Maria Goat. Nothing had even happened: a dinner with the pink lamb, a stop by the nightclub where they ran into Jack Dingo, and then a kiss good night.

"Jack," said Vincent, expressing himself clearly. "This is Maria, the love of my life. Maria, this is an old friend, Jack Dingo."

"We've met," said Dingo, nodding at Goat.

"No, I don't believe so," Goat answered. "I'm sure I would—"

"Sure we've met, it was only a month ago. But weren't you pink then?"

Vincent Hare stayed behind in Bois de Dalida until long after darkness had fallen. He sat protected by a hawthorn bush on a stone on one of the small islands that were connected by bridges in the park across from the restaurant. He told himself it had nothing to do with Dingo, it had nothing to do with lunch, it had nothing to do with the pink lamb. It was only about him and Maria. The two of them were basically too different to be together, and sooner or later that bomb would have dropped.

But he didn't believe a thing he told himself. No explanation or excuse or even curse helped him.

When Dingo left their table, only the truth about the night with the pink lamb remained. Goat had not taken it well. She was rational by nature, but she was also principled. What he had done was a violation she could not accept. Now it was evening, many hours had passed, and Vincent did not want to think about their quarrel. He had already repressed it. There had been an explosion, and he knew it was not only due to Dingo's revelation.

How he hated that animal.

But more than that, stronger than hate he felt pain and guilt.

Vincent raised his eyes. The islands in the park rested in a mild glow from the spotlights that discreetly lit up the large trees and the arched wooden bridges. Stuffed animals walked here in the evening, but not many. Right now he saw no one.

Vincent Hare had exerted himself. He had realized that life lacked meaning, and tried to live anyway. The last few years had been different. His existential questions had paled more and more in relation to what he felt for Maria. Now he realized this was self-deception: an illusion that in the long run was impossible to maintain. Now he knew he had been blinded. It had only been a matter of time. The sand in the hourglass ran no faster and no slower.

Vincent Hare took out the matchbox he had brought with him from the restaurant. He opened it and took out a match. He drew the sulfur of the match head against the striking surface, and saw the flame light up. He leaned over and set fire to his shoelace. It took a few seconds before it started to burn.

PART TWO

When the storm tore up the sea at night, Vincent Hare asked the nurses to open the window so he could hear the sound of the foaming waves as they furiously struck the shore. He thought of them as if they were his rage. The odor of salt and seaweed filled the sterile room; he tore off the covers, and twisted his lower body so his legs tumbled out of bed. The nurses helped him the two steps over to the bamboo chair in front of the window, where he then sat until long past midnight, listening to the rumbling eternity. If the staff came back too soon and tried to put him to bed, he became agitated. They learned to let him be until he called for them himself.

During his first year at the hospital, every day he made the nurses roll him out across the large lawn and down to the stone beach, where he sat for hours, staring in fascination at the swells rolling toward land in wave after wave. He imagined he was seeing time itself taking form before him. While he was growing up he had not left the cluttered streets of Mindie for even one day, and not until his teens did he know that Hillevie and the sea existed. In the circles in which Lion Rosenlind moved, a summer place in Hillevie was of course a hygienic requirement, so in recent years Hare had been here many times. But usually in the evening, at parties and dinners, and to be honest, the view had not been what interested him the most.

He himself could not explain his enchantment. The endlessness that waited beyond the knife-sharp horizon both frightened and freed him. The intellectual existentialism, all the defenses and barricades that had been his security through the years, dissolved and disappeared as he stared out over the sea and let the damp Breeze penetrate his body and stuffing. He closed his eyes and listened to the shrieking of the gulls as they flew, high up and far out of reach of an ordinary stuffed animal. He adjusted the blanket over his legs. The insignificance of a stuffed animal's life was beyond all questioning.

In this certainty Vincent Hare could rest in his wheelchair for week upon week and month after month.

A cat who jogged in Bois de Dalida every evening discovered the fire from far off. The cat was an outdoor animal who spent every weekend in the forest, and when he saw the flames he reacted instinctively. In the midst of the rare trees and beautiful wooden bridges in the park—which was a historical monument—a forest fire would be disastrous. It was not hard to calculate how quickly it could spread.

The cat ran for all he was worth, and when he came up to the unconscious Vincent Hare both of the hare's legs were burning. A currant bush beside him had also caught fire. Using his thin jogging jacket, the cat managed to smother the flames, and the ambulance was on the scene within fifteen minutes.

The amputation occurred at the Lucretzia hospital in Tourquai. Vincent Hare was lucky. Thanks to the short distance from the park to the hospital, the legs could be amputated before the smoke damage to his stuffing was judged to be serious. He was assigned to a single room (Bombardelli quietly saw to it that Hare received the best imaginable care, which it took months for the hare to realize), and it was anxiety, not physical pains, that called for heavy medication well into the third week. The faint odor of smoke that lingered in his cotton was apparent every time he moved, so he tried to move as little as possible. With the pills he slept dreamlessly.

Hare knew a little about how long the lines for spare parts were in Mollisan Town after having worked for Jack Dingo, so it was a surprise when the doctors reported that there was a pair of new legs for him after just six weeks. These were not even used limbs; a completely new pair had been sewn up. This was very unusual and required numerous dispensations and stamps, something only granted to noted athletes or stuffed animals with great power. Hare would long believe it was Lion Rosenlind who paid for the new legs, but it was Bombardelli who was behind this, too.

Hare ought to have been relieved and happy to hear about his new legs, but he felt nothing at all, not even indifference.

The operation was performed early one morning in May. For ninety-five minutes the patient was on the operating table, and afterward the operating team agreed that the intervention had been successful. The seams were discreet and the shade of the fabric only slightly darker than the original body. In leg reconstructions there was always the risk that the stuffing in the groin was too soft, but on the fifth day—considered the most critical—the doctors' opinion was that the firmness was good and did not require risky supplementation. Hare was discharged after another week of observation, and referred to the rehabilitation center in Yok to which patients went during the day while they lived at home.

But Hare did not show up at the rehabilitation center. The day after doctors discharged him from the hospital he should have signed in, but he was not seen on the second or third day either. After two weeks, staff was sent to Hare's residence to look for him. They found him in bed, drugged and malnourished. He claimed that the new legs would not carry him. Soon it was determined that the problem was not medical. The legs were excellent and the operation had been a success. Hare still maintained he could not walk. A few days later he was sent to Lakestead House. Hare did not ask who was paying the bill now either.

Upon arrival at the turn-of-the-century Victorian mansion by the coast, where thirty-some patients were cared for, new samples were taken and a series of tests conducted. It was found that a combination of physical stagnation and mental deconstruction was behind Hare's condition. He was placed in a wheelchair, given antidepressant pills, and started on therapy. They had considerable experience with patients like Hare, and knew that the symptoms of psychosomatic illness were no different from any others.

During his first year at Lakestead House, Vincent exhibited listlessness both provocative and stubborn. It was explained to him that it was important to interact with other patients as soon as possible. When a patient was taken into Lakestead House, he or she was typically stuck in thought patterns that were hard to get out of on one's own. Along with the on-site doctors, therapists, and nurses, the other patients were decisive for recovery. Vincent showed no signs, however, of socializing. The energy that had been Vincent's fundamental characteristic before the fire had disappeared.

But he would not try again.

When he woke up at Lucretzia after the operation, that was the first thought he had. He had tried to take his life, but failed. Could you sink lower? At the same time—and this feeling was worse—he regretted it. It would take time before he dared express this bitter truth, and this did not automatically mean he felt any desire to live. But he regretted it, and he would not try again.

His room at Lakestead was small, on the bottom floor in the east wing. A bed, a white bamboo chair, two small closets for clothes, and between the closets a light blue painting so uninteresting he still couldn't say what it depicted after several months. Next to the chair was a round glass table where you could set newspapers and books from the house's beautiful library. But Vincent did not borrow any books. The only thing he liked about the room was the view of the sea.

The patients took their meals in the dining room in the main building, but for several months Vincent managed to avoid the fellowship by pointing to his limp legs and requesting food in his room. It was explained to him that mealtime was not just about eating. Still he resisted. He had always been comfortable with solitude; now it was imperative.

The therapy sessions began the same week Vincent was admitted to Lakestead, but it took time before he felt comfortable with them. Lifelong brooding had accustomed him to self-examination, but sharing this with someone else? That was a much different endeavor.

Every day right before lunch he was rolled into Dr. Seinstein's office. She was a panda in a white coat who sat at a very small desk where there was a notepad and pen and nothing else. She set one leg over the other and asked him in an annoyingly ingratiating way to get settled.

Vincent gloomily observed the narrow, oblong room. On the far wall was a window that looked out over the forest north of the house. On the wall to the left hung an impressionist painting above a worn divan on which there was a gray sheepskin. There was a faint odor of disinfectant. The nurse, still holding Vincent's wheelchair, pushed him symbolically a few more inches into the room so that the wheels were firmly on a striped rag rug, and then left him with the therapist. He heard an ominous *click* as the door was closed.

"I see," said Dr. Seinstein. "So, let's start with your personal information . . . Your name?"

"Vincent Hare."

"Fine. And, Vincent, you live on Calle de Serrano?"

"That's right."

"Fine. And what kind of work do you do?"

"I work at an architectural firm. Or . . . I assume I'm on sick leave right now . . ."

"Fine," said the therapist, her voice was affectedly gentle. "My name is Panda Seinstein, and you and I are going to see each other quite a bit to start with, Vincent."

Panda gave Vincent an opportunity to react, but he refrained.

"So, Vincent, how do you feel about all this? Lakestead House and the wheelchair and . . ."

She placed her paws in her lap. The idea was that he should finish the sentence. Dr. Seinstein had thick, white eyelashes and she strove for a neutral, cultivated exterior.

"I don't know," he said. "I don't know if I care."

The weeks in the hospital after the operation and the time that followed, in the apartment on Calle de Serrano where the telephone soon stopped ringing and his friends knew that he didn't intend to open the door however much they banged, were veiled in a haze of drugs.

"I can't cope right now," he continued, no longer looking at her. "I don't have the energy to feel anything. I can't bear to dwell on what I think about this. I'm here. That wasn't the idea."

"Fine," said the doctor. "That was a very nice beginning. Here you don't need to cope, Vincent. We can sit quietly a while, if you want."

Vincent sat quietly, certain that was not what he wanted.

"There's no point in sitting and dwelling on things," he said at last.

"What do you mean by 'dwelling'?" asked Seinstein.

The sun barely made it through the dense foliage outside the window, and the room was pleasantly cool.

"You never get anywhere," said Vincent. "It's meaningless. Nothing changes, even though we always think so."

Seinstein sat quietly and let Vincent tell her what he had figured out. Developments in technology had exploded, he said, and stuffed animals communicate in a way that had been science fiction just twenty years ago. Yet nothing had happened. You only had to go to old movies, age-old novels, or even older theater plays and take a look: the same revenge, the same love, same hatred, same happiness, and even the same humor now as hundreds and thousands of years ago. That was depressing.

"Repetition," said Vincent. "Everything is just repetition. Art, literature, and music—repetition, endless variations that don't add to or change anything. The same triads, the same dissonances, same betrayal and love, the differences are insignificant. Everything is already thought and done. It's damned meaningless."

"I don't understand," said Seinstein cautiously. "What is meaningless?"

"Trying to change anything," said Vincent. "Trying to create anything new. Trying to develop. There's no point anyway."

"And the 'variations' that you mentioned?" said Seinstein. "Can't development and change be small things? I understand you're an artist, Vincent, that you paint?"

"That was a long time ago."

"Your paintings were unique?"

"In the sense that I had made them. Otherwise, my paintings were primarily uncompleted. But whatever I decided on: motif, technique, paint, composition, concept, it had already been done. Thousands of times."

"And you can't be happy that even if you used the same colors and techniques, that your expression was still unique to you?"

"It's not about paintings, Doctor," Vincent muttered.

"What is it about?"

"It's about the fact that we stuffed animals are not developing spiritually. The years pass and we come up with amazing, strange things, but we remain just as ridiculous. It shouldn't be that way. You can devote your life to developing as an individual, but it's pointless. However many books I read. Or thoughts I have. Or hours I spend in therapy."

Hare fell silent, and remained sitting in silence a few minutes.

"It would be interesting," Dr. Seinstein continued, "to hear you tell a little about yourself, Vincent. About your cubdom. Did you grow up in Mindie?"

But Vincent had no experience of talking about his life in concrete terms, and what remained of the hour passed extremely slowly. The forest had always frightened him, and the crowns of the trees outside the window were a constant reminder of how far from the city they were.

It did not get better during the weeks that followed. Listening to his own voice as the panda dragged the words out of his mouth about Mother and Father and school and the first years of puberty, about unhappiness and happiness, about revolt and love, about all the painful attempts to find an identity to put on top of the lost teenage body, was monotonous and suffocating besides. Sometimes he thought about the gray notebook that was in a drawer at home on Calle de Serrano, and how it would have helped him remember the kind of thing Seinstein was looking for, but what he wanted least of all was to let his younger self remind him of who he had once been.

Vincent experienced the therapy sessions as a protracted complaint, and this disgraceful grumbling was exactly what Dr. Seinstein was looking for. If he tried to find distance, if he tried to see it from an adult perspective, he was corrected. It was the lament she wanted to hear. The hour of therapy in the middle of the day remained a torment, and he did not notice any of the progress Dr. Seinstein maintained they were making. His legs remained unusable.

Time, however, has a habituating effect that no one can escape, and after rolling into Seinstein's room every day for twelve months, spending an hour talking about himself, and then rolling back to the waiting lunch, the routine was a part of Vincent's new life and the therapist's honey-smooth voice stopped provoking him. She asked follow-up questions as if he were mentally disabled, but at this stage he knew it was about the answer, not the question, and he had to formulate the answers himself.

At her encouragement Vincent tried to take up painting again. He knew he had talent, but when she asked what had become of his paintings, he could not reply. Maybe the half-finished canvases were still up in the attic at Calle de Serrano, maybe he had thrown them out? Seinstein made sure resources were put at his disposal, but after a few weeks in front of the easel he gave up. He had nothing to communicate.

Panda Seinstein had worked at Lakestead House for six years when Vincent was admitted to the institution. She also had a practice in Lanceheim but was only there one or two days per week. At Lakestead there was also a sense of collegiality she lacked at her own practice, and the patient base was more challenging than the stressed-out career animals she saw in the city.

Work was Seinstein's life. She recorded all her sessions, and could spend whole nights going through transcripts from patient conversations without feeling tired. She lived alone and had given up on finding a partner. She had degrees in psychology as well as literature and philosophy, but she never referred to her extensive education, because most often it frightened the patients.

She had not made the consultation rooms at either Lakestead or Lanceheim warm and cozy. There were therapists who believed in wall-to-wall carpeting, curtain arrangements, and the aroma of fresh-baked rolls. Seinstein was their opposite, preferring bare but functional furnishings.

"You often talk about Lion Rosenlind," she observed one month in Vincent's second year at Lakestead House, when his therapy sessions had been cut back to every other day. "But I get the impression you don't know him particularly well. Why do you think he has become such an important reference point in your life?"

Vincent restrained his irritation.

"Maybe I wasn't one of Lion's closest friends," Vincent answered defensively, "but I enjoyed his company, and I think he enjoyed mine."

From the first day at Lakestead House, Vincent had talked about his life in the past tense. He experienced that he was in a place, mentally as well as physically, that was an end point. He had meant to take his own life, fate wanted something else, but that did not change the conditions. Vincent did not intend to return to what had been.

"Maybe I wasn't Lion's best friend," he said, "but I didn't need to schedule a time with his secretary."

"Do you think he was more important to you than the other way around?" Seinstein asked in a soft, gentle voice.

"Yes, but that's obvious, isn't it?" said Vincent, irritated. "Lion Rosenlind is one of this city's most influential . . . one of the richest animals alive. And I was . . . no one special. Of course I wasn't particularly important to him."

"And why was he so important to you? Aren't such things usually mutual?"

Vincent waited with his reply. He stared at the painting on the wall, an explosion of colors and forms on which the patient could project anything from wild happiness to deep desperation, and then answered.

"I was never looking for friendship. I guess I didn't care whether I was particularly important to Rosenlind. As long as he invited me to his parties and talked to me when we met at the bar."

"But you said you did business together? You have hinted that these were important matters?"

"He used me sometimes," Vincent replied, shrugging his shoulders, "when none of his regular business contacts dared. On paper I was responsible for a number of different operations. I was on a number of boards that never met. I was just a name on legal documents. I didn't ask any questions. No one knew who I was. I was perfect, don't you think?"

"So he exploited you?"

"We exploited each other."

"You exploited him by going to his parties?"

"He was a trophy, Seinstein. Don't you get it? Lion Rosenlind. All I had struggled for—"

"Struggled? I haven't had the impression that you struggled. Don't you always say that exertions aren't in your line?"

All staff members at Lakestead House wore similar slippers. They were plastic and could go in the washing machine, and over time became formless. Doctors and nurses shuffled along through the corridors in these ugly things, but no one wore them as carelessly as Dr. Seinstein. Vincent had often been on the verge of asking her to take them off during their sessions, because it irritated him that they were always about to drop off her paws.

"Revolting against life is not free," he observed, raising his eyes. "Society is based on the idea that nothing is free. Toil now so you'll be rewarded later. Be bored in this life, you'll have fun in the next one. I guess during part of my life, the idea was to prove that's not so. That it was a device to keep us in check. If we don't have anything to believe in, what's left?"

Dr. Seinstein hummed in the manner Vincent had learned

to loathe; as if she understood something he didn't understand himself.

"I thought you had decided that everything was just meaningless?" she said.

"Then you haven't been listening," he exclaimed. "It's clear as hell that everything is meaningless. But accepting it . . . goes against the grain. My whole life has been based on looking for clues. Isn't that what knowledge is about? Can anyone really be happy with how absurd this life is? What do you think about waking up every morning your whole miserable life and feeling that nothing means anything? Never feeling anything—not for real, not in your heart, because every miserable emotion is constantly being undermined by how completely idiotic life is?"

"Do you want to feel?"

"That's obvious!" he exclaimed.

"And how do you act in order to make that happen?"

He lost the thread.

"What do you mean?"

But she did not develop the question. Instead she let it grow inside the hare until there was an answer.

"I'm taking it too far. Is that what you mean?" he asked. "A few steps too far. To start with I don't feel anything, no happiness, no satisfaction, and then I think that if I take a few more steps, a few more hours, then maybe it will happen. That applies to work. It applies to relationships. It applies to Lion Rosenlind. Is that what you mean?"

"I don't know," Seinstein answered. "What do you mean?"

"I mean, this motivation we've been talking about, isn't that where it comes from presumably? The unwillingness to accept life's cursed meaninglessness? I mean, something makes me get up in the morning, right? Something has always made me want more. More of everything."

"That sounds basically healthy." Seinstein smiled.

"So I thought that if it is even more intense with Maria, if

I did things with Dingo that normal stuffed animals wouldn't even dream of, then I would feel something. And the experience would be so extreme that I couldn't dismiss it?"

"And Rosenlind?"

"Rosenlind's the same thing. That's as far as you get. And I guess I thought that if I made it all the way to him and his circle then . . . I could raise myself above all the everyday stuff."

"And did you?"

"To start with, absolutely. It was amazing. Hanging out with all those self-confident stuffed animals who were swimming in money."

"And then?"

"I don't know. When the kick of being counted one of Lion Rosenlind's friends . . . where only the cream of the crop in the city are counted . . . when the kick subsided, because it did . . . then it was more a feeling of winning."

"Winning?"

"Over everyone who wanted to take life seriously. If Rosenlind and I were buddies, without my having accomplished a thing, it was like the evidence that I had chosen the fastest way."

"The fastest way to what?"

"To the goal. Everything is a race. Life is a race."

"Do you think so?"

Vincent was silent a few moments. "I should answer no. But here I sit with you hour in and hour out, trying to understand myself better. You may wonder why, if life isn't a race."

Dr. Seinstein made a note on her pad.

"That was fine, Vincent," she said, looking up.

With that, the session was over for the day.

After the sessions with Dr. Seinstein, Vincent was often exhausted from suppressed confusion, anger, or despair, but because the rules required it, he forced down a little food before he rang for the nurse and asked to be rolled down to the sea.

PANDA SEINSTEIN'S COMMENTS 1

No, I can't say anything about that. No, I have never had reason to compare my patients with one another, and the thought is not an attractive one.

What would set them apart? Everything sets them apart. Everyone is unique. It would be unprofessional to have any other attitude. Each and every one has his oddities, and you will never get me to comment on different degrees of difficulty. It's a matter of experience. It's a matter of chemistry. The relationship between therapist and patient must take time to develop and find its contours. Individuals with deep wounds in their souls take longer time. Vincent Hare was, as you know, such an individual.

To start with? He lied. I don't think I've encountered a patient who lied the same way as Vincent Hare. Not just to me; he hardly noticed it himself. No, not in that way. It was impossible to expose him. He was a master of omission. When he retold episodes and memories, he avoided the decisive emotions, he avoided telling about viewpoints and after-thoughts, and so every story became distorted and open to interpretation. True stories were no longer true. I admit that it fascinated me. Never to be caught in a lie, even though he never gave me the truth.

Distinctive? The fear. At least the first year. He was scared to death. You don't need a degree or therapeutic experience to realize it was his father who damaged him and put that terror in him. Vincent knew that. What he possibly did not realize, and what we worked on together a great deal, was the extent of the damage, and how it influenced him in ways large and small.

What was out of the ordinary was the combination of indifference—you seldom meet stuffed animals who are so little concerned with the appreciation of others—and social competency. When he wanted to, he could charm anyone. Without needing to on a deeper level. That's very special.

Toward the end of the second year Vincent could use his legs to the extent that he no longer needed help in the room. Between the bed, the chair, and the toilet he walked by himself, clumsily and with crutches, but now he knew his legs worked. He still preferred to sit in front of his open window at night and stare out at the sea, which he could not see, but heard. Sorrow and despair might attack, as they did all the time, but he fought back with the tools Dr. Seinstein had given him. More and more often it happened, however, that Vincent sank into repose with thoughts that left him restless, and there were nights when the hours until dawn passed as if time were only a friendly blink of an eye.

During the day he sought the calm at the shore. After lunch the nurses pushed the wheelchair across the grass and over toward the rocks. He asked them to place him hidden in the shadow of a small pine from where he could observe the other patients undisturbed as in twos or more they walked by the sea in the afternoon. Vincent did not long to keep them company. In the wheelchair, often with a patterned blanket on his lap so that he did not have to see the uneven shade of his legs, he felt old and used up. It was not a wholly unpleasant sensation.

Not long after he came to Lakestead, Vincent had noticed a bear who often walked by himself. There was something sympathetic about the bear's slightly slouched figure. His clothes were old and worn, his gaze amiably absent, but he did not seem to seek solitude in the same way as Vincent; it was more that solitude had found the bear.

One day, after more than two years at Lakestead House in a self-imposed isolation that was starting to bore him (even if he did not admit it), Vincent asked his nurse who the bear was. He got the answer that this was one of the "lifers," in other words, one of the patients who would not leave the institution until the Chauffeurs came and fetched him. Vincent experienced this as good news. If the bear would never leave Lakestead, he was safe to talk with. (Later in the evening Vincent realized that very thought meant that for the first time he was thinking about his own time at the institution as limited.)

The next day he gave the nurse, who at lunchtime was rolling him as usual across the lawn, instructions to wait, and when the bear came walking they intercepted him on the way toward the shore.

"Excuse me," Vincent called out. "Excuse me, my . . . my name is Vincent Hare. We don't know each other. But I've been thinking about something, and I'd like to ask your advice."

"Yes?"

The bear had stopped, and observed the hare in a friendly way.

"I have a question about patterns," said Vincent.

If this surprised the bear, he did not show it. He extended his paw.

"Teddy," he introduced himself. "Patterns?"

Vincent thought a moment, and for once he was careful as he chose his words.

"I've been thinking a bit about patterns, and repetitions. I've been wondering a little about the lives of stuffed animals, and if we ever, collectively, have a chance of taking ourselves out of these patterns."

"Oh boy," said the bear.

"We would like to appreciate all this," said Vincent, indicating the lawn and the sea beyond the shore with his paw.

"Hmm," said the bear.

"If the nurse pushes me over there to the pine tree," said Vincent, pointing, "will you come join me? And talk a little? Or perhaps just listen a little?"

"Sure, I can do that." Teddy nodded good-naturedly, and the little troop crossed the lawn toward the tree.

In this way a conversation and a friendship began which, during Vincent's third year at Lakestead House, would grow each day. It turned out that Teddy Bear lived in the room above Vincent's, in a corridor where eleven primitive paintings with maritime motifs were hanging. Already the first day, when Teddy Bear found a knotty root to lean against and sat on a couple of stones in a makeshift chair, he dismissed Vincent's suicidal fantasies as foolishness.

"Escaping from life through death is like resisting the temptation to scratch yourself on the back by cutting off your paw," said Teddy Bear seriously. "I don't want to maintain that the thought has never attracted me. Because it has. Especially after a good day, when you sense it can only get worse. But running away can't be the idea, can it? Isn't that too easy?"

The Breeze brought with it the dampness and salt of the sea, which matted the bear's fur. Patients from the building walked meditatively along the shore, and far to the south they glimpsed the piers—Hillevie's large marina—like dark stripes out into the sea.

"This is what I think," said Vincent. "Year after year I repeat myself. And I don't notice it, at least not until much later. It's a kind of substance abuse behavior. I find something:

a stuffed animal, an interest; and then I push it too far. It starts well, healthy and considered, but soon I'm manic, exaggerated, and it always ends the same way: with a crash landing. Burned bridges. I use things up, but I don't develop anything."

"Hmm," said Bear.

The nurse who was standing behind Vincent's wheelchair stared out over the sea and did not hear a word of the conversation between the hare and Bear. It had been a long time since she was interested in the conversations of lunatics.

"But then I realized," Vincent continued, "that it wasn't just me. That it applies to all of us. We don't develop. We go in circles. We repeat ourselves endlessly. We are delivered, we grow up, we love, we grieve, and when it's time for the Chauffeurs to pick us up, we are not the least bit wiser than when we arrived. We haven't managed to teach our cubs anything. We get richer. More comfortable. More modern. But spiritually we circle around the same futility we always have."

"Hmm," said Bear.

"And that is what I wanted to ask you," said Vincent. "It seems like we are all assigned our specific fate. As a species, we have been stuck in our own limitations for decades and centuries. But even personally I'm stuck. I have to be manic in my relationships. From the time I was delivered, my fate was staked out. Every time I think I've torn myself loose, every time I think I'm doing something new and different, I realize over time that in reality I only managed to fool myself. But I'm not fooling my fate. And it's obvious that in the end it's hopeless. Everything becomes meaningless. Whatever I do, I don't control my predestined role. Is that the way it is, Teddy? Does it have to be that way? But as a stuffed animal, don't you have to try to make yourself free?"

Bear nodded. It was easy for him to understand what Vincent was talking about.

"Do you have to?" asked Bear.

"Yes, but how?" asked Vincent. "And will it work?"

The dinner bell rang. They both looked up at the sky, and realized that the Breeze had died down without them noticing it.

When the nurse rolled Vincent back across the lawn, he could smell smoke. But Bear said something about someone burning leaves at the back side of the building, and then Vincent smiled involuntarily. That smell was no longer coming from him.

"Personally I fought against evil," Bear explained as they returned to the house. "And of course there are many who do. But I have devoted my life out here to fighting for goodness, too, and no one else does that. I'm not talking about religion, but about goodness. They are different. But don't worry; I'm not the missionary type. I mean, you can do as you wish, Vincent. I have a hard enough time keeping myself in line."

Vincent laughed, and adjusted the blanket on his lap.

"Perhaps I could have dinner in the dining room today?" he said, mostly to himself.

"Do that," said Bear. "It would be nice to have someone to sit with."

Vincent Hare did not want to admit the doctors were right—it had become a matter of principle—but the counseling, physical therapy, and medication showed results shortly after Vincent met Bear. True, his legs had gradually gotten steadier and Vincent's ability to use them had increased, but it was at the start of the third year that his physical recovery picked up speed. On some subconscious level Vincent realized at last that the foreign limbs were actually his own.

Every other hour with Seinstein was exchanged for an extra hour with the physical therapist, a meddlesome heifer for whom Vincent had little use. He did not doubt her professional competency, but as a stuffed animal she was not much, he thought.

The discussions with Teddy Bear deepened with time. Vincent had consciously avoided telling Seinstein about the sand of life that he started hearing again at night as it ran through the narrow waist of the hourglass. Lakestead House existed beyond time and space; that was the feeling the institution doctors consciously tried to convey to the patients, and they were successful. For that reason Vincent panicked when the sound of the sand returned, as a reminder of the life he had lived and must continue to live, and for the longest time he refused to admit even to himself that it had happened. When he was finally forced to tell someone, he chose Bear instead of Seinstein: he needed sympathy, not analysis.

Bear proved in many ways to be a wise, thoughtful stuffed animal. His trains of thought were long, logical, and consistent, he possessed self-insight and education, and Vincent wondered why the bear had chosen to live at Lakestead House. Sometimes his twin brother came to see him, and then they gladly talked about their mother, Rhinoceros Edda, who had made a brilliant political career.

"That would suit you," said Vincent. "A life in politics!"

His brother, Eric Bear, agreed politely, but Teddy did not want to talk about it. Fantasizing about a life outside Lakestead House only made him feel anxious.

When they got to know each other even better, Vincent experienced nights when he realized how impossible the thought of an existence outside Lakestead was for Bear. Bear essentially suffered from the same lack of moderation as Vincent. He was obsessed by his theories and thoughts about evil and good, which in turn led to a long series of idées fixes that made a normal life impossible.

Teddy Bear read in the afternoons: thick tomes, accessible popular science, and a bit of poetry. Vincent Hare would stumble his way up the stairs right after the rain (something his physical therapist warmly recommended even if Vincent used canes) and knock on Bear's door about the time he was done and ready to tell about what he had read.

Poetry made him melancholy.

"Love," said Bear, one afternoon almost a year after they had met for the first time down on the lawn, "is a feeling so strong I hardly dare think about it."

"Do you miss Emma?" Vincent asked kindly.

Emma Rabbit was the love of Bear's life. She had betrayed the bear in some way Vincent did not understand. He had forgiven her, but even so she did not return.

"I miss her. Even though she's here," he said, pointing to his chest. "And here." He pointed to his head. He sighed deeply, and then looked worriedly at his friend.

"And you, Vincent, do you miss anyone? Because I think you do."

To that point during his three years at Lakestead House Vincent had refrained from mentioning Maria Goat by name. Now he said, "I miss someone, too."

The moment he admitted this, he experienced how the loss overwhelmed him. Outside the afternoon was getting late, the blue of the sky deepened, and the Breeze died down.

"I miss someone," he repeated. "More than I dare think about."

"Tell me about her," Bear suggested. "It sounds like you'd like to."

The bear's plainness was disarming.

"Sure," said Vincent. "If I only knew how."

But he didn't.

Even though three years had passed since he last saw Maria, he thought about her every day. It was easy to bring up mental images, sharp and colorful: Maria on a park bench under a willow tree, or Maria raising a glass of red wine in the glow of a candle. Vincent had hundreds of images in storage, but he could never keep them alive for more than a few seconds. Then he was overwhelmed with pain. He could not put it into words. It was loss, it was regret, and anger, of course. He wanted to forget; that had been his strategy, refusing to mention her name and letting the images die away, but it was impossible. All the hours with Seinstein were suddenly of no use, all the intellectual bullshit stood out as empty and threadbare.

"If it hurts, then say so," Bear suggested.

He was now brooding over what he would have done differently, but he knew that nothing could have been different. There was sorrow in that. He could not imagine anything more tragic than starting over with Maria, because he was certain that everything would be exactly the same again.

"I'm sorry," he said.

Shortly thereafter the dinner bell rang, but the bear and the hare stayed in the room. The hare did not notice his tears running, but the pain in his chest made him unable to stand up.

"Can you tell me about your mom?" Dr. Seinstein asked, unconsciously rocking her paw so that Vincent was certain the slipper would fall off.

But the slipper did not fall off; it never did. Outside, the treetops hid the sun that otherwise would have been shining in their eyes. The doctor had set the pad and pen on the table. It was a way of getting ready, he had learned.

"About Mom?"

"You seldom talk about your parents, Vincent. Yet when you do, I get the sense that your mom was close to you, right?"

Vincent shrugged his shoulders. That was confirmation.

"And your dad?"

"He never really knew I existed," answered Vincent. "Being a parent wasn't his thing."

"What was his thing?"

"Don't know. I really don't know what he did. I think he

drove a taxi for a while. Worked in construction a few years. But I don't know. He didn't see me. He never talked with me."

"Literally?"

"Literally. He never talked with me."

"And your mom?"

"He didn't talk with her either," said Vincent, and the bitterness came out in his voice. "But she disappeared when I was five. Then it was just him and me."

"When you were five? I got the impression that . . . you have many memories of her anyway?"

"Do I? Maybe I have. I don't know. She was strong. In her way."

"She was a camel?"

"A donkey," he said.

Silence settled over the room. Seinstein's patience was endless as she waited for his reaction. But now Vincent did not know what he was expected to say or feel.

"It seems," said the panda at last, "as if you grew up without parents. Emotionally without parents."

He thought before he answered.

"Maybe?"

"What do you think that has meant to you?"

He thought again. He had carried the memory of his mother through his entire cubdom. It was painful, a bitter memory, and in the longing from which he never could free himself, hope had finally abandoned him. He had been forced to realize that she would never come back. For that he hated her. He needed her.

Dad was no use. Vincent had learned to keep to himself. That way he came to no harm. At the age of twelve or thirteen he was big enough to disappear from home for several days at a time. When the Chauffeurs picked up Dad, life got easier, but basically nothing changed.

"I don't know," he answered honestly.

"You never felt safe, did you, Vincent?"

"No," he answered.

"Do you think anything would have been different if you had?"

He sat quietly. "I don't know," he said at last. "Probably."

That night Vincent woke up right after midnight. He was suddenly aware that he was 38 years, 9 days, 16 hours, and about 10 or 20 minutes old. In the dream he had tried to scream, but only got out a muffled sound, which woke him for real. He sat up in bed, looked around the little room, and remembered where he was. Without waiting for waking reflection, he put on his light blue bathrobe, crept into his felt slippers, and with a crutch under one arm, he limped through the corridor, up the stairs, and to Bear's door. He knocked and waited a few moments until the sleepy stuffed animal opened.

"I love her, Teddy," he said. "That's the problem. I love her, but I'm never going to be able to live with her."

Bear took a step to the side, so that Vincent could enter.

"I know how it feels," said Bear. "At least, I know how the same thing feels to me."

Before Vincent came to Lakestead House he had never cried, and afterward he would never cry again. The tears he had, he shed there. He stumbled up to Bear's bed, sat on the edge, let his head sink heavily down in his paws, and sobbed quietly. He, who had never let himself be overcome by emotions, could suddenly not think clearly. The sorrow reached a depth he was not aware of. He longed for Maria so that his body was shaking, and he fell back on Bear's bed, twisted to one side and drew his knees up toward his chin. He would never get to hold her again. When after all the years he finally dared lose himself in someone, he had lost.

Despite Bear's attempts to get Vincent to calm down, tears were all the hare was capable of.

"Come," said Bear at last. "Let's go down to Buffalo."

Bear led the weeping hare from the room, and in the darkness they slipped through the corridor, back down the stairs, and over to the west wing, where they knocked on a door that soon opened.

"Buffalo Bill," Bear introduced. "Buffalo, this is Vincent Hare. He is very sad tonight. May he stay with you?"

Bill nodded, and at the same moment Bear slipped away. In his three years at Lakestead, Vincent had never seen the buffalo who was standing in the doorway.

"You can take my chair," Bill offered the devastated hare, showing him a white bamboo chair identical to the one in Vincent's room.

Vincent sat down and his tears returned. He found himself in a state between sleep and wakefulness; he was desperate and confused. The image of Maria had been replaced by the feeling of her.

"I said I loved her," he explained to Buffalo Bill. "But I said it so many times, I didn't hear when I finally meant it."

Vincent felt ridiculous, like a lovesick little cub, but Bill did not seem uncomfortable. The buffalo wore a threadbare light blue bathrobe. He lay down on top of the made bed and stared worriedly up at the ceiling. The lamp on the nightstand was on and spread a pleasant, yellowish glow.

"You should be careful about what you say," said Buffalo. "Images of what you've said can stay hanging in the air for days and months, and you don't always want to be reminded of old things, do you?"

Vincent made an effort to pull himself together.

"Love can't be a projection, can it?" he said, trying to regain his old, intellectual self between tears. "Could Maria have been anyone at all, and when I say that we will never stay together that's just a defense? Maria can't be just anyone, can she?"

"Everything is a projection, my friend," said Bill. "That's

how you get sight of yourself. The only way. You look at the projections. Like at a movie. You don't have eyes on the inside, do you?"

Vincent stayed in Bill's room until after dawn. When the night's desperate sorrow turned into melancholy, it felt easy to share the feeling with the buffalo, who did not ask about details but nevertheless seemed to understand the whole. Vincent must have fallen asleep in the chair, because he was awakened by a nurse who came in with breakfast.

"It's time for you to go now," explained the buffalo, who took all his meals in his room and ate alone.

Vincent nodded and got up.

"But you're welcome to come back."

Vincent could not explain why, but that made him extremely happy.

Vincent Hare kept his courage up. He spent the mornings with Teddy Bear on the shore. After lunch, PT or therapy awaited, and then he went back up to Bear right before dinner. Their discussion was untiring and endless. Bear was comfortable in his intellectualization, but displays of emotion made him uncomfortable.

So when his energy ran low and hopelessness took possession of Vincent, he sought out Buffalo. Because Bill hardly ever left his room and never seemed to sleep, he was a perfect after-hours friend. The buffalo and the hare's conversations also went on for weeks and months, as neither of them exerted himself to understand exactly what the other one meant.

Buffalo Bill was one of Mollisan Town's greatest musical geniuses of all time; an unstable, willful, and sometimes violent individual who was interned at Lakestead House early on. The therapists agreed that Bill was best suited to his own company. In his younger days he had written and orchestrated symphonies without needing paper, pen, or instruments. For several decades he maintained that he could no longer hear music.

"I'm getting nowhere," Vincent admitted. "I talk and talk and think and think, but I get nowhere."

Bill was lying on his bed; it was dark outside.

"Where do you want to go?" asked Bill.

"Forward," said Vincent. "Maybe I wanted it to go faster before, but I still want to get ahead."

"Then you can rest easy," said Bill, "because you can never go in any other direction. And only as fast as it was ever intended. There is a picture that is more magnificent than any other. It is hanging at the National History Museum and depicts a meadow: thousands, perhaps hundreds of thousands of blades of grass. It explains everything. Vincent, my friend, you must study it."

Bill seldom said anything that made Vincent feel better. But the way the buffalo talked was consoling. Perhaps it was only about a tone of voice?

Three months into Hare's fourth year at Lakestead House the phone rang in his room. He had not been aware that he had a phone in the room. It took him a while to find it, hanging alongside one of the closets. Vincent moved smoothly now, and it was impossible to tell that he had been in a wheelchair eighteen months earlier.

"Mr. Hare, you have a visitor waiting in reception," stated a formal voice in the receiver.

"A visitor?"

"A Maria Goat. Will you come out here, or do you want me to bring her to your room?"

Vincent stood at a loss with the phone in his paw, aware that he was 39 years, 87 days, 10 hours, and about 40 minutes old.

"Mr. Hare?" repeated the voice, which belonged to a nurse in reception. "Which would you prefer?"

"I'm coming," Vincent said.

Like in a dream he hung the receiver back in its cradle, and his first thought was: This is reality coming to visit.

His second thought was: This is the reality I'm fleeing from, that's why I'm here.

For a moment his perspective shifted, and he sensed what Maria Goat and the rest of the city must think. The thought made him dizzy, the feeling overwhelmed him and he sat down on the bed.

I'm hiding, he thought.

He had not realized it until just now.

On his way through the corridors of the wing to the main building and reception, it struck him that presumably there were only a few who knew he was admitted here. Bombardelli, who got an invoice every month from Lakestead House, had never been in touch or visited.

Missed by no one, Vincent thought before he caught sight of Maria Goat on the couch in the lobby, where she was leafing through one of the institution brochures. He got a shock. The Maria who lived in his memory was someone else. The real version was even more beautiful, but above all looked different. There was something about her eyes as she read, the expression around her mouth, that radiated an ability to take action. He had forgotten this about her.

When she saw him, she threw down the brochure and flew up from the couch. He noted that she did not even glance at his legs, which he found strange. Perhaps she didn't know what had happened?

The Breeze was still good and the sky blue, so he suggested a walk along the shore.

Going down to the ocean, he did not know if he dared look at her, or if he would prefer to keep his memories. She talked about the trip on the train out to the coast, and he heard how nervous she was. He realized after a while that he wasn't saying anything at all. It was not like him, and she must have gotten the impression that he had changed.

He took her to a place where orange trees grew in the sand, and where two stones often served as chairs for him and Teddy Bear. The swells hissed on the edge of the shore and dry bunches of seaweed crunched beneath their shoes as they went and sat down.

"I thought you would be in touch," she said.

He shook his head. He was ashamed. He did not think he had anything to say. After years in therapy, the years in exile in this house by the sea where he didn't need to care about anyone other than himself, he had decided that her reaction had been the only sound one. She had been able to get herself out of the symbiosis he had tried to create, and his reaction— his suicide attempt—had nothing to do with sorrow, it was only an expression of defeat.

Vincent could not say any of this. It would sound pejorative and self-centered.

"I haven't been feeling all that well," he answered.

She nodded. He was aware of her scent. At least the aroma he remembered. The dammed-up loss rose up in his chest and made him fall silent, and he swallowed a few times to get rid of it.

In his silence she told about Bombardelli and the office. She talked passionately about the projects she was working on, and made him remember details about stuffed animals they had both worked with but whom he hadn't thought about for a long time. Vincent thought it was as if she was talking about scenes from a movie he knew he had seen, but no longer remembered. The more she talked, the more engaged she got, and slowly her nervousness disappeared.

When they saw the mist drawing together on the horizon, they got up and walked slowly back toward the house. He had hardly said anything at all. He wanted to, but it hadn't been possible. There was no way to tell an outsider about life at Lakestead House. But seeing her for real, hearing her talk, made the remembered Maria disappear. She was no more than a stuffed animal, just like him.

"I'm glad I came," she said when they again stood facing each other in reception.

"It wasn't your fault," he answered. "It's obvious, it doesn't need to be said, but I'll say it anyway. It wasn't your fault. It was me. I learned a lesson, I think."

The tears welled up in her eyes; he had never seen it as literally as right then, but she held them in place.

"I loved you, Vincent," she said.

Before he could answer, she turned and left.

He remained standing and watched her. A few days later Vincent realized that he, too, was forced to return to reality. Almost five years had passed, and there was no reason to stay at Lakestead House. He called Bombardelli the day before he discharged himself, but only reached the rattlesnake's answering machine. It was enough; all he wanted to say was that the invoices from Lakestead House would stop now. Then Vincent spent the evening with Bear.

"Keep in mind," said Teddy Bear before he let Vincent go, giving his friend a serious look, "it's the experience that counts, not the intention."

Vincent nodded.

PANDA SEINSTEIN'S COMMENTS 2

There is no such thing as done. And there is no point in trying to finish. That's not how therapy works. I've been in therapy as long as I've been a therapist myself, even longer, all of us have . . . and no serious therapist would use the word "complete." I see Vincent Hare as a patient, whether he comes once a year or every day.

No, I don't think so. No, I don't agree with that. But as with all of us intellectual stuffed animals, Vincent's intellectualism got in the way of his insights. Without violating a confidence, I can give an example with his relationship to his father. Vincent made no secret of the fact that he had had a tough cubdom. He realized, of course, what had happened to him, and understood that the lack of affirmation and love that marked his youth also impeded him as an adult. But like many affected cubs, he found explanations for his father's behavior, lots of excuses, which was a defense mechanism; convincing himself that his father's behavior was not because of him. In a way you might say that Vincent chose the easy way out; on unjust grounds he forgave, swallowed hard, and tried to forget. If, when I said something, he perceived a hint of criticism of his father, and it was hard to talk about him in a way that did not sound critical, he immediately went on counterattack. He had honed the arguments for defending indefensible behavior for so many years that it took a while before he himself heard how hollow they sounded. Listening with your heart is hard for most, and it is particularly ironic that it seems even harder for highly intelligent stuffed animals.

No, I don't think so. I don't know why you want to make such a drama out of this. No, I'm not diminishing Vincent's life, but it's striking how stereotypical the fates of stuffed animals are, if we dare to see the similarities. I use the word "dare" because often we feel unique, even though we aren't. Vincent himself had that idea, that most things are variations on the same basic themes. Vincent Hare may seem special, but if we look at the events that defined him, it's not hard to recognize yourself in one or more of them:

1. *An absent parent (in Vincent's case, a mother who disappears traumatically, which adds pain to the picture, but above all it is her absence that shapes him).*
2. *A dictatorial father figure (in Vincent's case this is not about one who hits or demands, but rather one who treats him like air, as if he didn't exist, which may be worse).*
3. *An uncomprehending school and/or adult world (in Vincent's case, as in so many others, a system that is not capable of taking care of individuals, and which therefore represses individual talent instead of encouraging it).*
4. *Devastating self-censorship (which is a natural consequence after the experiences of cubdom; instead of developing his artistic talent, Vincent himself became the first to diminish and criticize himself).*

5. *Bad company (the need to find a context, security, is fundamental, and we are subject to group pressure: Even if we are forced to stretch our sense of morals, we are prepared to do so to fit in).*

6. *A second chance (and that Vincent actually broke with Jack Dingo and started at the architectural firm is the only thing in Vincent's life that surprised me, and I am still not clear how he had the strength and energy to do it).*

7. *The desperate passion and the unhappy love (of which I believe we all have some experience, of one kind or another).*

8. *The bottomless sorrow (and here I have no comment, and anyone who has experienced it knows what that entails).*

We are not unique. Not you, not me, and not Vincent Hare. Sometimes the hard thing is realizing that. Other times what's difficult is accepting that insight.

’m really glad you got in touch," said Lion Rosenlind for the second time, shaking Vincent's paw. "Now that you're . . . back . . . we'll have to see about getting together more often. It's really great that you got in touch."

Vincent didn't know what to say. He was 39 years, 175 days, 7 hours, and about 30 minutes old. As of a few weeks ago he had been living on Calle de Serrano again. Every stuffed animal he met seemed to have aged or changed, both physically and mentally, and objects, streets, and buildings did not appear as he remembered them. He knew it was him and not the outside world that had changed, but it was impossible to grasp that thought when Lion Rosenlind was standing before him, acting this way.

Vincent stood up. He had on a red jacket he had made a few days after returning to Yok, and wrapped around his neck was a dark yellow silk scarf. He held the napkin in his paw. The food was still on the table, but Rosenlind was in such a hurry he couldn't even wait until the waiter had cleared it. He owned the restaurant, so there wouldn't be a bill.

"Stay where you are," said the lion. "I'm sorry I have to run, but you know how it is. Really great to see you again."

The awkwardness finally came to an end, and Vincent, exhausted, sat down when the lion had left. His idea had been to ask Rosenlind about a job. But after a gluten-free salad with scallops and carrots, it was obvious that neither a job nor invitations would be given to an animal who had spent five years at the "mental hospital," as Rosenlind put it. Lion ordered two glasses of white wine and then changed his mind.

"Oh, excuse me, maybe you shouldn't?"

Vincent observed his former friend with surprise.

"What do you mean?"

"I thought . . . wine . . . perhaps you shouldn't have alcohol?"

Vincent did not know what Rosenlind was imagining, but apparently Vincent was a pariah in these circles, suspected of everything from alcoholism to madness. That explained a few incidents that had occurred during the past week.

"I still drink wine," said Vincent. "I'm not all that different."

It was not true, but he said it anyway. Rosenlind looked at him with open skepticism, and nodded encouragingly as if it were meaningless to discuss it. When the lion disappeared, Vincent took out his gray notebook, pushed aside the plate of salad, and wrote:

1. *Meaning of Life: Can the meaning of life be to seek the meaning of life?*
2. *Knowledge Account: Nothing scares us more than what we don't understand.*
3. *Bank Account: Quickly running out.*

Returning to a normal life after the years by the sea proved to be harder than Vincent thought, and he decided not to call the rattlesnake for help. He knew he could get a job with Bombardelli, because he was a damn capable project manager and architect. He refrained anyway. He had said to Dr. Seinstein during their last session that it had to do with Maria. Nothing suggested that he would fall in love with her again, but there were other, more constructive risks to take in the new life he had to build up, Vincent reasoned, than working a few yards from Maria Goat. The argument sounded so reasonable he did not need to search for additional reasons.

What he had not told Dr. Seinstein, on the other hand (and it will remain unsaid whether she understood it anyway), was the shame he felt when he thought about all the money Bombardelli had spent during the years that passed. Despite the hours, weeks, months, and years in therapy, he had only partly managed to dismantle the pedestal on which he placed himself. And his still inflated self-esteem was hard to combine with the simple gratitude he ought to show Rattlesnake Bombardelli. For that reason the simplest thing was not to make contact at all.

After calling around to his old friends and booking a long series of dinners and lunches neither he nor his friends looked forward to (with a few exceptions), and after getting the phone, mail, electricity, and gas working again, he was sitting one evening in the apartment where he grew up and realized that he would never be satisfied with solitude as his only roommate.

He had done his best to make the time pass, but this evening it was unusually hard. He leafed through a magazine to an article on alternative energy sources, but he was bored before the introduction was over. The silence became intrusive if he turned off the TV, so he left it on even though he was not watching. On the table was a cup of cold coffee, the same cup he had used all week and that he rinsed out with hot water in the morning. There was no soul in this home, he thought. He knew he needed plants, but he was overwhelmed by the choices when he stepped into a plant store, and always left empty-handed. He got suggestions from Dr. Seinstein about books to read, meditations, and thoughts to think on those evenings when melancholy came to call, but he did not have the focus for intellectual exertions. It was Thursday, the Evening Storm had abated, and he was not tired.

Vincent threw the magazine on the table, got up, and went into the hall. He pulled on his jacket and jogged down the steps. In the solitude of a bar it was easier to lose yourself.

He ended up at Les Pommes Rouges in southeast Tourquai. It was a recently opened nightclub on Avenue Gabriel, furnished in dark blue plastic and red leather. Along with a complicated lighting system that consisted of thousands of encapsulated diodes, the decor gave both an enclosed and colorful impression. Three months had passed since Vincent left Lakestead House, and it was the first time in many years he had decided to drink until his head exploded. He had not reached any of his old associates—only a few of them still went out—but it was easy to make new friends if you paid for a few rounds.

Vincent managed to get one of the small tables to the right of the bar, from which he had a view of the dance floor and the entry. That was how he noticed Jack Dingo. It had been more than five years since he had seen his old friend. Without wanting to, Vincent felt exhilarated. The episode in Bois de Dalida that afternoon was long forgotten and forgiven. In his life after Lakestead, Vincent lacked friendship. He had made an agreement with himself never to return to the house by the sea, and for that reason he had no contact with Teddy Bear. Jack Dingo was still a stuffed animal Vincent knew well, and he got up from the table.

Dingo was on his way into the place with a beautiful cat in a long, black dress. He had on a white jacket and was moving at a calculated slow pace, his chest thrust out and head high. He laughed at something the cat said, but the laugh was a way to mark territory. When he lit his cigarette, he made sure his claws flashed a little more.

Dingo and his companion went up to the bar and ordered drinks. Vincent squeezed his way between tightly packed stuffed-animal bodies. On his way images popped up, pleasant and less pleasant memories. Together with Jack Dingo, Vincent had experienced a lot.

Finally he came up, tapped Dingo on the shoulder and smiled broadly.

"Jack! It's been a long time!"

It was obvious from the expression in Dingo's eyes that he didn't have a clue who was standing in front of him.

"It's me, Vincent," the hare said, disappointed.

Dingo nodded.

"Of course I recognized you," the dingo answered.

But it was not true, and after a few minutes Dingo turned his back to Vincent and concentrated entirely on his beautiful companion.

Vincent took a taxi home right after that. He sat staring out over the deserted streets in Tourquai which after a while turned into worn streets in Yok. Here and there was a light in a window, stuffed animals lay sleeping in doorways under thick layers of blankets and rugs, music was faintly heard from a transistor radio that was suddenly turned off, and as the taxi passed rainbow-colored Calle de Tremp he heard the engines of the Pirates' motorcycles; their headquarters was in an old bread factory farther down the street.

The memory of the life he had once lived at clubs and bars, Vincent realized, was too old. There was no way back; he no longer had the furious, blind energy needed to reestablish his place at the bars of the city. He had to find a new way forward. There was no way of turning the hourglass around.

Vincent is dreaming. The dream is familiar. He is getting on board a train. In the opening between the asphalt and the train he glimpses the rails. They glisten. In the narrow corridor of the coach there are burning-hot radiators below the windows. He opens the first door to the left. Inside waits a dark compartment where he sits down by the window. The sounds from the train station fill his empty thoughts.

Outside the window a massive emptiness is piling up. The high sheet metal roof held up by massive iron beams. The many platforms next to one another. The large monitors where departure times flip past in an endless stream, even though there are no other trains there.

Just as he sits down, the train accelerates so vehemently that he is pressed back against the seatback. A few moments later they drive into a tunnel. Through the gap in the window he can hear the chugging of the steam engine echo through the mountain. It sounds ominous and distant. He realizes that the tunnel is endless. He closes his eyes. It smells cold and damp. His heart rhythm adapts to the thumping rail joints and just as he opens his eyes, the train shoots out of the tunnel. The sunlight is blinding.

The rails turn out to be laid through Yok. At a hysterical speed the train thumps along through narrow alleys. It is a reckless ride. The wheels screech from sudden turns. Sparks hiss, stuffed animals throw themselves out of the way. Vincent takes hold of the edge of the seat. They are going faster than he can conceive. Sometimes he recognizes a street, a doorway, a stuffed animal. He glimpses Dingo on a street corner. He sees Gavin Zebra in a window. He leans forward, and catches sight of Maria. But the train has come out onto Avinguda des Pedrables and further increased its speed. Their eyes meet, but he has already left her behind. The city is reduced to colors. Streaks of blue, orange, and turquoise glide past. His heartbeats increase in frequency. His pulse tries to keep up. His body shakes, spasms that soon make him vibrate. The vibrations increase in force, and he feels how he is rising out of the seat. Hovering up in the air. The experience is marvelous, but after only a few moments it is over. The speed is too great. The vibrations too powerful. He has passed the crescendo, there is only one way to wake up. He is going to crash.

Ten days later Vincent Hare was standing at a rotating sky bar on the top floor of Plaza Costeau, looking out over Tourquai's skyline. He was 39 years, 265 days, and about 9 hours old. He was the one who asked for the meeting, but he had not chosen the place. He had on a narrow, pinstriped jacket, white shirt, and narrow black tie. In the afternoon the bar smelled of old booze and nicotine. It was furnished in shining steel and black leather, the windows were from floor to ceiling, and the bar was long enough for a couple of cricket teams to stand at. But there were only two of them, and the weather was brilliantly clear outside.

"I'll just have mineral water," said Daniela Fox. "No carbonation."

The bartender nodded, and Vincent Hare felt ashamed about his martini.

"You're sure you want to come back?" Daniela Fox asked again. "Because I've heard otherwise."

Fox was, as always, the image of success. Her manicure was perfect, her fur glistened, and her clothes were expensive in the modest way only wealthy equals could appreciate. She wore a simple chain with a single but large diamond around her neck. She had a slight lisp that did not distract, but only made her more attractive.

"Stuffed animals talk," Vincent declared, "but it's seldom worth listening to."

"And Bombardelli?"

"What do you mean?" he asked, taking the olive from the glass.

"Bombardelli called and asked if I could see you. He suggested I try to get you to come back."

"Flattering."

"Maybe. But I don't get why you're using me as a proxy. Something you want to tell me?"

Vincent sipped his martini. The bar was on a floor that slowly turned 360 degrees. It took fifteen minutes for it to rotate all the way around.

"I called Bombardelli," Vincent admitted. "But . . . I didn't want him to hire me for the wrong reasons."

"But you do need a job?" asked Fox.

Vincent shrugged his shoulders. He needed not only a job; he needed a life.

"I thought you were great," said Fox. "It's been a while, but as soon as I came in I remembered your charisma. No one at the office has the same kind of . . . energy. It's because you know you have talent, Vincent. You know it. It gives you the kind of self-confidence that . . . even when we're in this situation . . . it feels like you're interviewing me, and not the other way around."

She laughed. She had never flirted with him, and he had never asked her out. Right now that made them both content. He finished his drink.

"I'm good with customers," he admitted. "I'm good at selling things."

"You're good at selling architecture," she corrected. "Because you know it."

"I want the job. I don't intend to argue."

"You've got the job. You'll work with me. I've talked with Bombardelli. You start on Monday. Same terms as when you quit."

Vincent nodded.

"One more thing: Maria isn't working there anymore. She left a few months ago. Don't know where she went, but it was her decision."

Fox slid down from the bar stool and left him with the bill. She had not touched her glass of water.

Vincent Hare met Diego Tortoise by the coffee machine the second day back at the office. Vincent greeted him enthusiastically, as if he had a bad conscience, and noted that it did not look as if Tortoise had aged at all.

"You look like you're . . . feeling well, too, Vincent," Tortoise answered in his hesitant way.

"Noticed that you're still in your old place in Dung-Beetle's corner?"

"You got one of the offices?" said Tortoise.

"My career has advanced." Vincent laughed.

"Yes, there was that competition you were involved in," Tortoise answered, and Vincent thought he detected a sting of bitterness in the tone.

"If you mean me and my race for partnership," said Vincent with a broad smile, "you're completely right. The race continues. All races continue. We've just taken slightly different routes."

Tortoise mumbled something Vincent did not hear, and returned to the office area, where he made his way to his corner. Vincent laughed and pressed the button for espresso.

After a week at Bombardelli & Partners, Vincent found that mentally he felt better than in many years. It was a new start in more ways than one. At the architectural firm there was just the right mix of old and recently hired stuffed animals, which made the workplace familiar but new and exciting at the same time. The only thing that seemed untouched from before was the coffee machine.

The empty days at Lakestead House had been a strain on him, and now he felt stronger and stronger when he woke up in the morning. It was not so much the routine as the intellectual stimulation he needed. When he came home late in the evening, he was mentally tired, and when he went to bed it was with a feeling of satisfaction. During a normal day at Bombardelli, he was faced with a stream of challenges. Questions were asked and solutions sought, and he contributed and was important. Working with Daniela Fox was simple. She had an ability to sense when Vincent needed to shine, and when he could stay in the background.

After the first workweek was over, he wrote in his gray notebook:

1. *Meaning of Life: If life is a transition, can it be about making it as smooth as possible?*
2. *Knowledge Account: Is a self-imposed task less satisfying than performing a task someone else has formulated? Are we a race of rulers and slaves? Do I have the soul of a slave?*
3. *Bank Account: Growing.*

RATTLESNAKE BOMBARDELLI'S COMMENTS

Do you know who I am? Do you? Because you don't seem to. You seem to think I'm the head of an architectural firm. Yes, yes, but you don't seem to understand what it means that the firm bears my name. I'm not the head of an architectural firm. That's not my role. That's not my identity. Bosses are a dime a dozen. I happen to be the boss, but that's only a function of my talent. A side effect. A secondary effect, you might say. Besides, I never worked directly with Vincent. Not once. I have no idea what he was like at work. You'll have to ask someone else.

Yes, I did. I'm proud of that. I've never made a secret of it. Sure, it cost a lot of money. No, nothing. I did not demand anything. No, why should I be? He never asked for help, it was my own decision. I would have been surprised if he came running hat in hand to bow and scrape to thank me.

Yes. I can tell you that. One evening more than twenty years ago, my good friend Tony Horse called and told me to come down to the gallery. Tony had been an art dealer his whole life, he was a friend of my father, and he'd watched me grow up. He knew I understood art. He knew it required talent to discover talent. I asked what was going on, he said he wanted to show me something. He didn't want to say too much in advance and ruin the surprise. For Tony's sake I did as he asked, even though I wasn't particularly eager. There hadn't been a decent artist in this city in the past hundred years.

Tony was hanging canvases before an exhibition that would have an opening the following day, and he wanted to ask my advice about that, he said. That wasn't true. He wanted to show me what he considered to be the most talented artist he had yet run across. I walked around the gallery and looked dumbfounded at the pieces. It was unreal, how good it was. Even though it was everything I despised: paint and abstractions and pretentions, it was unreal how good it was. I asked to buy one of the paintings. To this day it's the best work I own. Of course I had never heard of the artist before, but no one else had either. I never would have guessed that Vincent Hare would remain unknown.

I can sympathize with that. As an artist I can understand it, in a way. Or at least respect it. I had nothing to do with him applying for a job, but when it was clear to me the Hare we had hired was the same Hare who had done the paintings at Tony's gallery, I was proud. It was a great joy. Being able to contribute to Hare's existence, being able to help him to an orderly life with orderly finances. I was happy to do it. More than that, I took up his cause. Without his asking me. That money I spent on his legs and the years at Lakestead House was nothing. Nothing.

I promise you, the drawings that Vincent Hare has contributed to over the years, never as lead architect because he doesn't have that expertise, but as an inspiration, as attendant, as an artist, I can pick those out anytime. Unmistakable. He has an eye that is unique. Vincent Hare is one of the most sensitive temperaments of our time, and I am one of the few who know it. Maybe the only one? That gives me a responsibility that goes far beyond a few simple invoices.

One morning, five months to the day after Hare started back at Bombardelli, when he was 40 years, 55 days, 3 hours, and about 15 minutes old, a white, handwritten envelope was sitting on his desk. He immediately slit it open, and saw that he had been invited to dinner at the home of his boss, the great architect, the following Friday. To this point Vincent had successfully avoided Rattlesnake Bombardelli, and his instinct was also to decline the invitation. Later the same afternoon it became clear to him, however, that Daniela Fox had also received an invitation, and relieved, he realized it was not a private invitation but a kind of company event.

Apart from the phone call that resulted in the meeting with Daniela Fox at Plaza Costeau, Vincent had not spoken with Bombardelli since he'd been discharged from Lakestead House. With every day that passed he found it more and more difficult to imagine this conversation. Vincent had tried to calculate how much money Bombardelli had spent on his care, but the amounts were dizzying.

When Friday arrived, Vincent was very uncomfortable, and he was careful to make sure he was accompanied by Fox.

"You're joking? You mean you've never been here before?" said Daniela on their way up the steps, and Vincent let out a hissing sound that could most easily be interpreted as disinterest.

The door was opened by a grasshopper dressed in livery whose feelers were the longest Vincent had seen, and it was obvious the servant must have had the feelers sewn on recently. With a light, almost feminine voice ill-suited to his theatrical dress, he asked them to come in.

The smell of incense was noticeable even in the hall, but it overwhelmed them as they stepped into the living room, a room that resembled the inside of a windowless silo. The walls were painted with black enamel paint, in contrast to the worn wooden floor. Bloodred leather furniture stood in three groups around a teak coffee table, Bombardelli was sitting at an elegant desk that Vincent thought he had seen before, at Lion Rosenlind's house many years ago. He wondered if it was the same piece; had Bombardelli purchased it? The rattlesnake rose as they came in.

"Daniela, Vincent! Wonderful to have you here!"

He was wearing a black silk cape with red lining over a double-breasted suit, and as he swept the cape around him, the draft produced a small cloud of incense. The aroma was sweet, almost exotic, with a hint of musk and honey. Vincent coughed, Fox lit a cigarette in an attempt at counterfire, but Bombardelli pretended not to hear. The grasshopper with the feelers served champagne in glasses so tall and narrow they were hard to drink out of, and Bombardelli proudly told about various antique finds he had decorated the room with, but did not say a word about what had been, or give Vincent a look to suggest any special mutual understanding.

Dinner was served in the dining room, which proved to be located behind the heavy draperies along one wall of the room.

The dimensions in there were different; a small room with a low ceiling and dark curtains on the windows. The dining room furniture was just as massive and terrifying as the desk. Candelabras stuck up under drifts of melted wax. Candles were the only illumination, and Vincent could not see what he was eating. On the wall above a display case hung the oil painting Bombardelli had purchased from his father's friend so many years ago, but Vincent did not see the painting and the rattlesnake did not draw his attention to it. Bombardelli experienced a subtle sensation in finally having Vincent Hare in the room, without the artist even noticing his own work.

"Excuse me," said Vincent, as the grasshopper set out plates with blintzes and caviar, "but it was dark when we arrived . . . what kind of building is this? I don't live far from here, but I don't think I've seen a tower from the outside?"

That Bombardelli also lived in Yok was a surprise. Vincent had imagined the rattlesnake in one of the prosperous suburbs of Amberville or Tourquai, and then it turned out that he lived only a couple of miles away.

Bombardelli laughed, snorting and ready to tell, and his answer lasted through the appetizer and partway through the entrée. In summary, thirty years ago he had a modernized form of treehouse built. Like many houses in Mindie, the building on rainbow-colored Calle de Tremp had been a ruin when he found it, but a ruin built of stone. Inside the stone building Bombardelli had partitioned a foundation, on which he had his home erected, coal-black so that it looked like it was burnt, and therefore fit into the environment.

"Soon it will be a ruin standing in a ruin. You don't see it, with a little paint you can cover anything, but thirty years is a long time, my friends."

While Bombardelli talked, the grasshopper served a heavy, almost undrinkable red wine.

"You're wondering, of course, why I invited you here this evening?" the rattlesnake called out a while later when the main course was finished and another couple of bottles of red wine had been emptied.

He got up from the dinner table and went toward one of the draperies flanking the serving table. Apparently, Vincent noted, Bombardelli had replaced doors with draperies throughout.

The architect led them into an office room flooded with light. They had become accustomed to the darkness in the dining room, and were blinded by the strong lamps. On a table in the middle of the room was a white model of the same kind they used at work, but this was only topography, land without buildings.

"This is my lot," Bombardelli explained. "I've bought it."

He pointed to the model with his tail in a sweeping gesture, and Fox and Vincent placed themselves alongside.

"I want you to design the house that will be on it," said Bombardelli. "The two of you are the best I have. The best this city has. I intend to retire, but not until you have designed my house for me."

"How much time do we have?" asked Fox.

"One month," Bombardelli answered. "As of today, but not a day longer. You will have to consider this your true examination."

Already that evening it was clear to Vincent what he wanted to produce, and right after the dinner with Bombardelli he took Daniela Fox with him to a bar not far from Bombardelli's house, and even closer to his own on Calle de Serrano. In Mindie there were no respectable bars, but there were a number of holes-in-the-wall where you were guaranteed not to meet anyone you knew and could therefore talk undisturbed.

Vincent ordered two glasses of red wine, and expanded on what he had in mind. Fox protested. She had a few ideas of her own about what Bombardelli might conceivably be looking for, but carefully Vincent took her out of one suggestion after another.

"Excuse me, Daniela, but Bombardelli will never be comfortable in a building that is not created out of passion," said Vincent, and when he heard his own words he believed them. "We will never be able to speculate our way into what he wants. But I have a vision, Daniela. Call me ridiculous, but . . ."

And then he spoke uninterrupted for an hour about what he was visualizing, and the monument he wanted to create for Rattlesnake Bombardelli.

Exhausted and overwhelmed, Fox staggered out of the bar long after the chill of the night had taken possession of the city. In Mindie there were no taxis, and at this time of night she could not convince anyone to come down and get her. She hadn't taken the bus since her teens, but Vincent took her to the stop and waited with her until the No. 6 arrived.

"Passion, Daniela," was the last thing he said. "Now we'll design the house we will never get to design again."

He was so full of his own ideas that sleep was impossible. After sitting at the kitchen table doing a number of sketches, he found his gray notebook and wrote as he drank strong black coffee:

1. *Meaning of Life: Work? Thoughtless, fulfilling, impassioned work? Moving society from one place to another, and giving the next generation something we didn't have? Is hard, rewarding work the meaning?*
2. *Knowledge Account: All of us need a benefactor.*
3. *Bank Account: Feels less important.*

They gathered their team and started work the following day. They had four weeks. They set up their headquarters in Daniela's office, and put cardboard over the windows of the office to isolate themselves from the others at the firm. Five of them would work full-time on the project, and put everything else aside.

If Vincent Hare before had created a professional role that charmed his colleagues with a kind of friendly nonchalance, this project—which they dubbed *Casa Magnifica*—was something quite different. After a hesitant start when Vincent found it frustrating and difficult in words as well as in sketches to express his grandiose intentions, the project took off during the second week, and by the middle of the third week Vincent brought a pillow and blanket from home to avoid leaving Fox's office at all. His enthusiasm was contagious. Another two on the team kept Vincent company on the couches and on the floor, despite Fox's mild protests. Meals were ordered in from pizzerias and bakeries in the neighborhood, and the scale model they built as they were drawing grew day by day.

"I'm going to need to disinfect this office afterward," Fox sighed.

But she, too, had been seized by the magic around Vincent, and the trance into which he put himself and the others.

He got them to build a palace. A castle taken from fairy tales not yet written. Moats, drawbridges, towers, and spires. Ballrooms, atriums, and secret passageways. Gilded cupolas, arched stairwells, and optical illusions. Vincent's ideas surpassed one another in wild excess. The contractors protested; Fox, who believed that budget limitations should be a parameter, put in her veto, but the force behind Vincent's will conquered them all. With each day he ate and slept less and less. He allowed no one to rest, he allowed no objections, and when the fourth week reached its end all of them, including Fox, were sincerely tired of him, and glad it was over.

On the morning of the first of May, the appointed day for the presentation, Vincent Hare woke up with a peculiar feeling of not wanting to finish the project. He was 40 years, 86 days, and 1 hour old. During the night the hourglass of time had again turned in his head, and the sand was running indefatigably. There were thousands and more thousands of details to refine and develop on *Casa Magnifica*, and the mood he found himself in the past ten days had been an intoxication he already missed. For that reason, to the surprise of his teammates, he let out a heavy sigh when he opened the door to Fox's office right before lunch, and together with the others carried the model out to get Bombardelli's assessment.

Even as they crossed the threshold, something happened to the office. Silence spread, concentration electrified the air, and scattered whispers soon died out. Within a minute or two all the personnel at the firm gathered around Fox and Hare's fairy-tale castle. Bombardelli did not delay. The rattlesnake came quickly slithering through the office area, and then circled mutely around the model to view it from all angles. No one said anything. The attentiveness was magical and strange all at once.

At last it was Diego Tortoise who broke the silence.

"This is unbelievable," he said. "This is the most beautiful building I've ever seen."

A hurricane of applause and cheers broke out. Bombardelli wrapped himself around Fox and Hare in turn. The great architect seemed speechless with emotion for a few moments.

"My friends!" he then exclaimed, getting everyone to fall silent. "This was better than I could dream of. I will retire to this house. Here you see Bombardelli's new boss, and her new partner!"

It was like setting off a sound curtain. The applause and cheers never seemed to end. Daniela Fox would succeed Rattlesnake Bombardelli, Vincent Hare would be the firm's new partner.

EPILOGUE

The next morning Vincent Hare woke up as the second of two partners in Bombardelli & Partners. He had been hired at the architectural office 13 years, 49 days, and about 3 hours earlier, and even before getting the job he had challenged Diego Tortoise to a race.

He pulled on his bathrobe and went into the kitchen. On the way he passed the hall, where the morning newspaper waited below the mail slot. In the kitchen he measured out water and coffee and turned on the coffeemaker. While the hot water ran through the ground coffee, he squeezed three oranges and then put two pieces of ice in the glass. As the ice melted he poured coffee into a dark green cup, and finally sat down at the kitchen table with coffee, orange juice, and the newspaper. But it took several minutes before he realized he wasn't reading; he hadn't even glanced at the headlines on the front page.

He had won.

The idea distracted him. What was surprising was that this not only pleased him; it fulfilled him. He felt a kind of satisfaction he had not felt since . . . He did not recall that he had ever felt that way. It wasn't right. Life once again showed its banal side. A partnership was worldly and worth nothing in relation to the great questions of life. He played with the idea of excusing the feeling by giving himself a different explanation. Perhaps it was passion that made him the winner? Perhaps the moral of the story was that he had abandoned himself completely, and thereby won? Something to write up on the Knowledge Account? But he was the first to dismiss that sort of stereotypical connection in every other case. It was the partnership itself, which he had jokingly talked about and pretended to strive for so many years, that made him happy.

Think if Mom had known, thought Vincent. And his next thought was spontaneously about Maria Goat. Of course she would hear about his new partnership in time, but could this perhaps be an excuse to call her even today?

Vincent Hare was musing in this way when there was an unexpected knock at the door. Because it still had not clouded over outside, Vincent knew it was early in the morning. It was with tense expectation that he went out in the hall and opened the door. The idea that someone had already sent flowers or a telegram both pleased and surprised him.

He opened the door, and stared right into a pair of yellow eyes that had seen most everything. Within the course of a second, everything changed. From the experience that the future lay open, it was all over.

Under the cowl Chauffeur Tiger's face was enormous, his fur gray and battered, his eyes hard and cold. In the background out in the stairwell Chauffeur Tiger's colleague was visible; they always came in twos.

"You don't need to bring anything with you," said Chauffeur Tiger.

His voice was deep and raspy. His large coat smelled bad.

"You don't need to lock up, just come along," he said. "You don't need any shoes, the car is right outside."

The sand running.

Vincent heard it as a rumble that drowned out the fear.

Then it became silent.

This was the moment he had waited for. Like all stuffed animals in Mollisan Town, he knew that when the Chauffeurs came in their red pickup, it was over. The upper part of the hourglass was empty. But even though he had always known this would happen, he was seized with terror and panic.

"I can't go," he protested. "I have . . . the coffeemaker is on. And I have a meeting after the Morning Rain I have to be at. If I don't go to that meeting, the project won't go ahead."

Chauffeur Tiger grimaced.

"Let's go," he said.

"But I have to get my notebook," said Vincent. "I've got to have it."

Chauffeur Tiger placed his large paw on the hare's shoulder and forced the stuffed animal across the threshold and out onto the stairs. The Chauffeur shoved Vincent ahead of him down toward the doorway, and even though he came up with a number of important, irrefutable arguments for why he could not already be fetched (one of them naturally had to do with his age), he knew that nothing he said would influence the Chauffeurs.

In the red pickup waiting down on the street, there were already three stuffed animals. Two wept quietly. The third, a wirehaired dachshund, began arguing the moment the Chauffeurs got in the truck and started the engine. Many of the dachshund's arguments Vincent himself could have used.

The pickup drove out on South Avenue, and the stuffed animals fell silent. Slowly the insight sank into all four of them. Life was over.

"We are only stuffed animals," said Vincent as the pickup drove out of the city and into the forest. "We know nothing besides this, besides Mollisan Town. Where are we going now? Where are you taking us?"

"What kind of question is that?" snarled Chauffeur Tiger, who sat behind the wheel.

"Where are we going?"

"Did you hear what the hare is asking?" Chauffeur Tiger growled to his associate. "He's wondering where we're taking him."

His associate grunted, but it was hard to interpret the meaning of the grunt.

"But what happens after life in Mollisan Town?" asked Vincent.

"What do you mean?"

"The life after this one? There must have been a reason for everything that has happened up to now? What's in the forest? Beyond the forest?"

"Nothing," Chauffeur Tiger answered. "There's nothing besides this."

He shifted down to second as the asphalt road ended and they drove onto a narrow gravel path.

"But there must be something else," said Vincent, realizing that he never had thought about that before, not like this: for real. "There must be some idea with placing all the stuffed animals in the city? The factories that manufacture us, who owns them? Who runs them?"

"What does that matter?" asked Chauffeur Tiger.

Vincent thought. He did not know whether it mattered. While the pickup drove deeper into the forest, his despair increased.

"But there must be someone behind all this. Is it Magnus? What is his plan?"

"Shut up now, Vincent Hare," said Chauffeur Tiger. "There is no plan, there is no point, it just ends. Get it? The end."